Fountain of Youth

by

Cassandra Leuthold

Fountain of Youth
Copyright © 2017 Cassandra Leuthold

Published by Green Hill Press
South Bend, IN

ISBN-10: 0991131991
ISBN-13: 978-0-9911319-9-0

Cover design by Deranged Doctor Design

for my mother

Fountain of Youth

1917

Delhi, India

Chapter One

Milton's oxfords echoed off the concrete floor. In the glow from the hall, his gloved hand reached through his office doorway. He twisted the dial on the wall, flicking the chandelier's flame to life. Six chains supported the brass holder beneath the high ceiling, one of them concealing the narrow tube carrying the gas fueling its inner fire. Light burst through the holes and swirls, dissipating the room's shadows into a general haze. Milton deposited his hat on a peg of the wooden coat rack in the nearest corner. He ambled across the colorful carpet, its thickness muffling his movements. He rotated the silver knob on the desk lamp's base. Its metal stand arced away and back towards him, suspending an amber-colored glass dome. He spun the switch until the light fanned to full brilliance.

Milton wiped his forehead and turned away from the covered window. The furniture and its domain stood the way it had for over two years. His absence during the weekend gave it a strange separateness, an unfamiliarity that would reverse itself over time. The desk, manufactured by the British in the Chinese style, boasted more detail than every one he had used before India. The dark mahogany cupboard provided two columns of storage with an open cubby between them. The wooden plank on top supported his lamp and various envelopes of correspondence. A short rail ran around the two sides and the back, carved into arches, crosshatches, and two flourishes flanking a floral basket. Smooth, honey-gold leather finished the desktop. Its base offered seven drawers supported by bamboo-shaped legs. The intricate, diamond-shaped designs on every door and drawer found balance beside the simple chair. Black leather upholstered its cherry wood back and wide seat. Milton drew his gloved fingertips along the top of one low, sturdy chair arm.

His grey eyes slid sidelong to another surface across the room. A rectangular rosewood table, inlaid with ivory leaves and bone starbursts, held more correspondence. One piece mocked him, its white page breaking up the mosaic border of ebony and brass.

Outside the window, a small motor chugged louder until Milton recognized it. The push and pull of the pistons subsided, and Milton fell into the reality of the day. The four walls around him remained. His best friend and colleague did not. Milton stepped over to the side table, lifting the offending paper.

Received at Chandni Chowk Road Post Office, Delhi, India. December 18, 1916.

The building's front door opened on the other side of the neighboring room.

Mr. Milton Longshaw
Fitzgerald and Longshaw, Meena Bazaar Plaza
Hurried footsteps shuffled closer down the hall.

I'm sorry again for the favors I asked of you. I leave Nashville today. I'll say goodbye to my father.

Bryce whisked through the doorway. Milton held up a finger to keep him quiet even before his sharp eyes glanced up at the young man. Bryce's mouth hung open, ready to speak, just as Milton had assumed. He fought a cruel smirk and returned to the message in his hand.

Then I'll meet with his closest partners at the company on Monday, the first of the year, at 10 a.m.

Clementine Fitzgerald

Milton skimmed the address at the bottom and let the fax drift onto the table.

Bryce adjusted his woolen newsboy cap and combed his fingers through the light brown hair sticking out beneath it. He jerked his chin at the fax. "Is that a new one?" He unbuttoned his double-breasted houndstooth coat and hung it on the rack.

The young man's chocolate-brown suit and two-toned leather shoes gave him a neater style than normal. He had shaved his cheeks and chin, not that Milton thought it would take long to rid them of their sophomoric attempts at beards. Milton always agreed with Mark Twain that clothes made a man, but Bryce required far more than tweed coats and fashionable shoes to mold him into anything close to Clements' partner. In fact, without his usual pretense of stubble, Bryce looked exactly the part Milton always thought of him as: a boy.

"It's an old message." Milton's answer, even in clipped, dry syllables, presented another ocean of difference between them. Bryce's accent, like him through most of his life, never left Oklahoma. To Milton, Bryce constantly sounded like a Southerner attempting to enunciate and failing. Milton resented having tempered his Philadelphia twang with the same drawl, but at least he could hear his travels in his voice. His worldliness reverberated every time he spoke.

Bryce picked up the paper. His eyes traced each line, his mouth twitching in disappointed ticks. "I guess I hoped she'd change her mind."

"No." Milton lingered on the fax. How much better the day would have gone – the last three weeks! – if these faxes from the States had been much different. "If the thought occurred to her, she lacked the good sense to send such a pardon."

"I didn't even know Clements had a daughter."

Milton's shoulders seized. *Clements.* As if they were both mature adults. Equals. He snatched the fax and tossed it on the table where it was easier to ignore. "Well…" How many times had Clements mentioned his family? His offspring? How long ago had that been? "He didn't talk about her much, even to me."

Bryce shuddered and removed his newsboy. He strung it over the top of his hanging coat. "What a miserable New Year."

Milton relaxed in shared resentment. "I know. When we could use a drink the most, a woman we've never met requests a meeting the following morning."

"While we're still getting over our colleague tripping down the stairs and breaking his neck."

Milton grunted. "One of our favorite people in the world. It's unfathomable."

"Unforgiveable."

Milton tapped his fingertips on the table. It might be bad for business to show outright disapproval for Bryce, but his true feelings for Clementine? Those were fair game. "You wanted a drink last night, did you?"

"Yes. Share some Indian rum with the locals and some imported pale ale with the Brits."

"But?" Milton raised his eyebrows.

Bryce stuffed his hands in his pockets. "Stayed home. Did nothing. Drank water."

"Fascinating, as well as my night alone." Milton gestured behind Bryce, his mouth arcing. "Close that door, would you?"

Bryce's eyes darted. He hesitated, but he guided the door closed until it latched. "Do you want the fan on?"

"No. We won't stay long enough for it to matter." Milton licked his lips. "Have you gotten any faxes you haven't told me about?"

Bryce shook his head. "Why would I get anything?"

Milton lifted his hands out from his sides. "How much do we know about Miss Fitzgerald, anyway?"

"You know more about her and Clements than I do."

Milton poked a finger at Bryce. "Precisely, and I know next to nothing about her." He grinned. "I'll tell you what I do know."

"What?" Bryce edged closer.

"She hasn't seen her father since she was a girl."

Bryce crinkled his nose up. "That's awful."

"Terrible, but not in the way you think." Milton stretched his arm out, indicating the global map decorating the wall above the inlaid table. "Clements was a man of the world. Don't you forget it. Four US states. Approximately one dozen foreign countries."

Bryce considered the map, rocking in a gentle sway between his toes and his heels. "That sounds right. He told me about his travels sometimes. I wouldn't even be in India if it wasn't for Clements."

The old sting of truth stabbed Milton. He faltered but recovered. He preferred to focus on their common enemy for now, not the only way Clements had ever slighted him. "Clements kept in touch with her over the years."

Bryce's lips curved in appreciation.

Milton shot down the boy's hope. "Postcards, mostly. I don't know if they exchanged longer letters or personal facts."

"Did she ever write to him or send him cards?"

"If she did, I never saw them." Milton paused for a beat. "Do you understand what I mean? There's an overwhelming chance this young lady has never left Tennessee." He stepped toward the map and tapped the United States. "Whoever raised her, she's grown up without her father. And he was the most intelligent, inventive man I ever met."

Solemnity leveled Bryce's mouth into a line. "You said as much in your eulogy at the funeral."

Milton raised his index finger. "One more reason to harbor disdain for Miss Fitzgerald."

"Why?"

Bitterness spiked in Milton's chest. "She was his family." He slapped his hand flat against the map. "She should've been here, and she should've made the arrangements. Instead, what do I receive? A Blickensderfer fax instructing me to put my grief aside and prepare every detail. He was my friend. He spent more time in my life than hers. And…"

Milton wagged a finger at Bryce, wandering away from the map. "For what? After I planned the whole affair, who attended? His bucktoothed housekeeper, Miss Higginbotham. You, me, and the factory workers. A few neighbors who barely knew him."

Bryce slid his hands free from his pockets. "I thought Miss Fitzgerald asked you nicely."

Milton swatted the air. "Ask. Command. When you're twelve thousand miles apart, there's no asking. Only telling."

"Maybe she didn't mean to…"

Milton glowered at Bryce until he trailed off into nothing. "Bryce, I want you to understand today's full gravity. Our friend, my partner, your boss, is gone. He's never coming back, and the project isn't finished. It's up to us and the team we've assembled. If we work hard and stay dedicated, we can have the cream bottled and ready to ship by the end of the year. Clements left us in a fairly good position. This doesn't have to slow us down completely."

Bryce concurred with serious nods.

"On the other hand..." Milton selected the white paper. "...is this death sentence. For the last two weeks, when we should've been pulling together and pushing forward, we've been distracted by this slip of processed wood. We don't know what she wants, and I can only guess at the awfulness that's about to confront us."

"What do you mean?"

Milton crumpled the typed page and tossed it at the small, round garbage can by the desk. It bounced off the rim and padded onto the rug. He frowned. "Miss Fitzgerald might be a snotty brat of a teenager. She's likely ignorant and uneducated. With Clements all but absent from helping her mature, there's no telling what sort of bipedal beast comes to badger us."

Bryce inched nearer. "You think she'll be that bad? Wasn't she smart enough to exchange postcards with Clements?"

"Perhaps she got a schoolmarm to read them to her. I don't think we can overprepare ourselves for the shock of her." Milton shuffled over to his chair and swiveled it away from the desk. He plopped into the supple leather interior. "We might not even understand her between her accent and her loose grasp of English speech."

Bryce exhaled through his nostrils.

"You don't believe me? How much do you know about Tennessee?"

Bryce cracked a grin and rubbed the back of his neck. "I heard about a railway line out there. The ETWNC. The railroad workers in the City called it Eatin' Taters and Wearin' No Clothes."

Milton tipped his head back and cackled. He liked Bryce better by the minute. "You see what we might be up against."

Bryce folded his arms. "Do you think she wants money?"

"I'm not worried about it. I'll turn her away without a cent, a farthing, or a pie. I can't imagine what else she wants. Hopefully nothing so sentimental as to meet those who worked closest with her father these last three years. Although, I'd accept an apology for all the help I gave her while she sat at home doing nothing."

"Probably rollicking barefoot through some farmers' fields."

Milton cocked his head. "Isn't that how you spent your childhood?"

Bryce held Milton's gaze with a mix of hurt and pride. "Yeah, between mending fences, milking cows, sowing seeds, harvesting crops, going to school…"

Milton waved his hand. "I see your point."

Bryce walked over to the garbage can and picked up the crumpled paper ball. He unfurled it and shook his head. "Nashville. And you think she's spent her whole life there?"

Milton rose to his feet. "It's worse. She's not from the city. She's a country bumpkin who can't tell her leg from a stick."

"You're sure?"

"Clements left her in a one-door house with a single story and three windows. It sounds more like a shack than a proper dwelling. He told me so himself."

Bryce patted the backs of his fingers against the page. "What was she doing in Nashville? There's a city address for her."

"It could belong to anybody. A friend or relative. The nearest building to a bridge she sleeps under. Of course she needed the city. Where else was she going to find a post office with a fax machine? They don't build them in cow pastures."

Bryce balled the paper between his hands and dropped it into the garbage can.

"You can see her now, can't you?" Milton baited him. "Bad teeth. Probably missing half of them. Pocked skin. Greasy, stringy hair."

"I think so."

Milton indicated his long wool coat and suit. "Rags full of holes. Skinny as a bean or helplessly engorged."

Bryce scoffed. "If she's so poor, how's she getting fat?"

Milton shrugged. "Eating the gristly scraps no one else wants. Small where it counts." He patted his chest. "Even if her schooling persevered past the fifth grade, she'll be too homely to look in the eye while she serves her dissertation."

Bryce hushed. "And her name. Is that for real?"

"Clementine. On both faxes."

"Like the song?"

"Like Clements himself. But you're right." Milton lowered his forehead into the cradling comfort of his gloved palm.

Under his breath, Bryce began to sing. "In the center of a valley dwelt a maiden so divine."

Milton chuckled.

"A pretty creature, miner's daughter, by the name of Clementine."

Laughter rippled out of the old man's body.

Bryce raised his crooning to speaking level. "Oh, my darling. Oh, my darling. Oh, my darling, Clementine."

Milton lifted his head, amusement warbling his accompaniment. "You are lost to me forever. Dreadful sorry, Clementine."

Bryce squinted at Milton. "Did you learn this as a boy during the gold rush of '49?"

Milton sneered. "It was a few years before my time. Shut up and sing the next verse."

Together, they called out the words the best they could remember them. "The foreman miner, forty-niner, in his dreams and thoughts sublime lived in comfort with his daughter, little pretty Clementine."

Milton stuck his elbow out, and Bryce looped his arm through Milton's. They swung each other around in a circle in the middle of the rug.

Louder still, they launched into a raucous version of the chorus. "Oh, my darling…"

The door handle shifted. Milton flew apart from Bryce, the song forgotten mid-word. He froze facing the door, and Bryce stumbled to right himself at Milton's side.

A black glove rested on the handle as the door swung in. Illuminated from the front and back cut the tall, thin figure of a woman.

Chapter Two

The woman reeled her hand in but otherwise remained motionless. Beneath her brown cloche hat, her expression wavered between blank and tense. Her hunter-green coat fanned out around her waist and hips, falling to her shins. Butterscotch leather boots laced up above her ankles to disappear under the midnight-blue hem of her dress.

Bryce panted from dancing, bellowing, and the fear she had heard it all. He wished he had switched on the fan when Milton brushed off the idea. Its gentle whirring would tune out his heart's thrashing and stir the weekend's stale air into something fresher.

The woman stepped into the office and removed her hat. She extended her hand toward the middle of the room. "I'm Clementine Fitzgerald. Thank you for meeting me. I know this hasn't been the best of times."

Bryce stared at her. Her accent was hardly a backwoods atrocity. It held music in it, each syllable connected to the next in stilted, lyrical harmony. And she was not some bedraggled, inexperienced teenager. Far from being a woman as Bryce used the term, she was certainly near his own age.

Milton shook Clementine's hand. "Milton Longshaw. Welcome to India."

Clementine attempted a smile that emerged as a polite grimace.

She turned to Bryce, the bronze lantern above them casting a discerning glow over her features. His lungs held onto his breath and refused to let go. Where was the dry, scarred skin Milton led him to picture? Clementine's tanned face held glittering green eyes buffered by high cheekbones. Her glossy, honey-colored hair hid her ears as it gathered behind her head in a modest style. Her full lips presented glimpses of what resembled a full set of maintained teeth.

His introduction blurted out of him. "Bryce Bloom." He took his first breath in half a minute and shook the hand she reached out to him. "It's nice to finally meet you in person."

Milton cleared his throat, focused on Clementine. "I'm immensely sorry about your father. As you may know, he and I were close friends."

Clementine slid her gloves off and tucked them in her coat pockets. "For many years, I believe."

"Fifteen. He and I were scheduled to eat dinner the day he passed away."

Clementine nodded, bouncing her silver-and-aquamarine earrings. "Miss Higginbotham told me. How upsetting that must've been for you."

"It was."

"Both of you." Her eyes landed on Bryce.

Milton flung a hand out. "Oh, no. Bryce knew nothing about our plans. Your father and I often enjoyed meals together."

Bryce stood up taller, harnessing all of his willpower to keep from scowling at Milton. "Clements and I had dinner, too. Sometimes at his house."

Milton puffed up his chest. "We'd talk about business and the direction of the company. I'm afraid your father and I were a pair of serious, aging men. Quite boring and set in our ways. But I did have the fortunate opportunity to see some of the postcards he bought for you in South America and Africa."

Clementine dipped her head in acknowledgement. "He'll be missed." Her lips pressed together, and she squeezed her eyes shut.

Milton waved Bryce away from the desk and pulled the chair further out into the room. "Why don't you sit, Miss Fitzgerald?"

She sniffed. "I'm fine." Her eyes popped open, shining with renewed purpose. "Y'all–"

The word hung in the air like a missed note sung too high or low. The corner of Milton's mouth ticked, but Bryce waited for her to continue.

"You," Clementine corrected herself, "are my father's only partners at the company? The decision makers?"

Milton laid a hand on the chest of his coat. "I'm Clements' sole partner. We formed Fitzgerald and Longshaw shortly after we met. There have been no others considered or actualized."

Clementine bit at her lip. "Mr. Bloom…"

Milton chuckled. "He was close to your father, yes, but Bryce served as his assistant. He performed errands and helped Clements manage his extensive research."

Bryce opened his mouth to protest.

"I see." Clementine's long fingers unfastened the line of buttons cascading down the front of her coat.

Bryce inched forward, intent on absolving his name. Here was the Milton he had suffered for the last three years, disappearing for mere minutes of camaraderie like a wolf lurking among the sheep.

Clementine slipped her coat off. "It's a comfort you knew him, at least, Mr. Bloom. Even if what I have to say is aimed at Mr. Longshaw."

Bryce lunged to take her coat, but Milton plucked it away. The older man secured the coat on a wooden peg. He flipped a switch beside the door that gave the ceiling fan permission to circulate a much-needed breeze.

Bryce glared at Milton before returning more civilized attentions to Clementine. The small bustline Milton had guessed at graced her slender figure along with narrow hips, but Bryce forgave her these slights of nature at once. A black netted fabric left her dress sleeves sheer, and he tried not to peer through them at her arms. "I'm sure we could both benefit from what you have to say."

Clementine smoothed the dress' satin skirt, which hung in three scalloped tiers almost to her ankles. "I'm going through my father's papers to put his estate in order. It'll take time, but it will be done."

Milton bypassed Clementine and Bryce, helping himself to the armchair. "I have faith. Mr. Morris and Mr. Callaghan are professionals. I recommended them to your father when we were in Oklahoma City. I would've entrusted them with my affairs if I weren't so entrenched with my own lawyer and account manager. I hope they treat you well."

Clementine nodded.

Bryce's mind wandered. "Did you float here on an airship?"

Milton's eyes shrank into disapproving slits.

"I'm sorry," Bryce added. "I don't understand lawyers and accounts. After traveling halfway around the world, transportation is one thing I do understand."

Clementine maintained her solemn composure. "I sailed in the old kind of ship."

"That's too bad." Bryce kicked at the rug. "I wanted to fly here, but Clements said we couldn't. Our books and equipment wouldn't fit. There's not enough storage, not to mention the weight."

"I'm sure it was a smart decision."

"Sure, but not as exciting. Did you hear the president's having a special airship built just for him? For any president to use who gets elected to the White House."

"I recall hearing it."

"It might be the smallest one they've built yet."

Milton sounded a low, flat hum. "Miss Fitzgerald, was there anything specific you wanted to tell me about your father's personal business?"

"Personal, no." Clementine swallowed hard. "I want to take his place at the company."

Milton pushed himself out of his seat. "Is this a joke?"

"No, sir. I have the same training my father did before he left Tennessee. I know herbs and plants like the back of my hand. I heal wounds. I identify sicknesses and strengthen people to fight them off."

"Clements educated himself every day of his life." Milton descended into the chair.

"So do I. Maybe you have a problem with my age." She glanced at Bryce. "But I see I'm not the only young person here."

"That was your father's decision. Entirely. How old are you, if it's a fair question."

Clementine braced her shoulders. "Twenty-three."

Bryce lit up. "Me, too."

Clementine's jaw tensed. "I've taught myself everything there is to know about plants. I know what my father and others taught me from around where I grew up. I've learned from books and my own trying."

Milton curved one hand around the scroll carved into the end of the chair's arm. "Even if you're half as familiar with plants as Clements was, do you know anything about the product we're developing now?"

She answered with a sharp bob of her head. "I've been reading the notes he had at the house. You're making a beauty serum. Correct?"

"A treatment," Milton allowed. "Based on the exotic plants and blossoms of India, which you likely haven't encountered before."

"I'm a quick learner. I left school early, and I've dedicated myself to plants ever since."

Milton considered her for a long moment. "Let's suppose what you're saying is true. I accompanied your father for a decade and a half from country to country. Continent to continent. I trusted him, and he never failed to accomplish what he promised to."

Bryce relaxed into a small smile.

Milton drew in a bitter breath. "Before today, I only knew you by two faxes I received from you. Now you're in India, where I've known you in person for a total of..." Milton consulted a wall clock above the desk, an oval ringed in metal flowers and scrollwork. "...five minutes. And you propose to elevate yourself to the level your father reached as a much older, more experienced man."

Clementine shook her head. "I don't want to elevate myself."

Milton raised an eyebrow. "No?"

"I only want to help with the project, and I know you need me."

Milton held up an upraised palm. "Explain."

Bryce leaned against Milton's desk.

Clementine's fingers fidgeted at her sides, then fell calm. "Mr. Bloom, Mr. Longshaw, I'm already here. I'm ready to start. Right now, if it comes to that. By the state of my father's records, you have a lot more work on your hands, and you don't have him anymore. Who else could possibly replace him? Tell me. What botanists are you interviewing? What herbalists? What healers? I can top them all."

Milton rested his arm across the chair's wooden support. "We've interviewed no one. I have no plans to."

"And here I am, offering my services in my father's place. I know what he knew when he left Tennessee. I've asked him questions, and I've gotten *his* answers. *His* knowledge." Clementine tapped her chest. "They live on in me."

Milton replied with croaking ambivalence. "Perhaps."

She swept a step towards him. "I'm not slinking off. If you send me away, I'll stay right here in Delhi. Miss Higginbotham told me the English live in one area, and the few of us Americans are thrown into that lot. You're bound to see me over and over, so you might as well hear me out before you dismiss me. The factory's only a few miles from there, and I'm well used to walking. I'd come here every day if I thought it'd do any good."

"As you said, your father's left many notes. No offense, but why do we need you?"

Clementine straightened up, standing an inch or two taller than Bryce in her heeled boots. "No offense to you, sir, but you must be even older than my father. How freely do you spring out of bed in the morning? How do you walk these cold halls in the winter? I hear India scorches with heat in the summer. That, combined with this workload, must tax you a lot."

Milton ground his teeth together. "Point taken."

Clementine stepped forward almost to the rounded tips of Milton's oxfords. "A close friend of my father's would also know I haven't seen him for seventeen years."

Milton's casual pose stiffened. "I'm aware you were estranged."

"Estranged." Clementine swayed back but stayed where she was. "You two weren't. Why haven't you interviewed to replace my father's worth?"

"Giving myself a new partner isn't important at this juncture."

"Why is the factory empty?"

Milton met her eyes as if clenched in a match of wills. "We offer the workers a day off following the New Year celebrations."

"It's not true that after fifteen years of friendship, you feel my father's simply irreplaceable?"

Milton's jaw trembled, and he pulled his arm down into his lap.

"You're not thankful for a day off to rest after his funeral?"

"It was a blow," Milton admitted, his voice uncertain but well founded.

"How many more decisions will you base on your grief? Either of you?" She scanned Bryce with humble but determined eyes. "I've had distance from him. I might think more clearly than you for a while."

Milton stood up, sliding his chair back to give more space between Clementine and himself. "Even if I allowed you to take Clements' place, why would I let you make decisions at the company we built?"

Clementine folded her hands. "I'd prove my worth, and you'd change your mind. I'm willing to say the rest of the people who work here miss my father as well."

"Very much. We've lost a few workers who would rather leave than continue in his absence."

Clementine almost smiled. "Don't you understand how perfect this is? You see, my father and I might've been estranged, but I'm still his closest family. Who better than me to take his place and continue his legacy? If you want to stop losing your workers and give your company its best chance to succeed, put me in my father's shoes. Make me your partner, and I won't seem like a brand-new choice. I'll represent to them and you the one person you can't get back. My father."

Bryce consulted Milton with intensity burning in his chest and his moss-green eyes. "She's right. The investors. The workers. Everybody knew and loved Clements. We could go ahead on schedule without missing anything."

Milton eyed Clementine, his eyebrows askance. "You're ready to begin as soon as possible?"

"Absolutely."

"There will be paperwork to draw up to make you an official partner."

"I'd read and sign it carefully. You have my word."

Milton adjusted the fit of his gloves. "You're a hard worker, Miss Fitzgerald?"

"The hardest. I didn't have to come to India. I could've stayed in my native state in my own country and let my father's body be shipped to me. I chose to come here, to pay my respects to him in the city where he died and make my case to you."

Bryce studied Milton for any sign he was for or against Clementine. The young man propped his hand over the edge of the desk and drummed his fingertips against the top drawers. "She came all the way by boat, Milton."

Clementine pressed her lips together. "By the fanciness in this building and my father's house, I traveled a cheaper class than you did."

"We rode in first," Bryce admitted. "The way that's most comfortable. Although, Clements and I agreed an airship would've been the height of–"

Milton coughed. "Enough. I reserve the right to contest this partnership at any point. I won't have fifteen years of ideas and enterprises be demolished, no matter how far you sailed."

Bryce stood up from the desk, his heart fluttering near the top of his ribcage. "It's not just sailing. It's a train to the coast, a steamship to Bombay, and another train to Delhi. All by herself."

Milton cast a steady eye down at Bryce until the young man set his lips together and exhaled in silence. Milton lifted his brows at Clementine. "It's been a long time since I signed or read such papers. I'll need to contact the company lawyers here in Delhi and have them draw them up."

"Equal to my father's existing wording should be fine."

Milton pulled his gloves on tighter. "Indeed. I'll transmit a fax from the nearest post office immediately."

Milton took two steps toward the door, and Clementine laid her hand on his arm.

He pursed his lips. "What is it?"

Clementine clasped her hands in front of her. "I want to change the course of the research."

Milton rolled his eyes. His hands flexed into claws, and he forced them to loosen. "You're not even a partner yet, Miss Fitzgerald."

The lecturing bite Milton imbued into her name made Bryce's mouth spring open to insist she was not a child to be scolded.

Clementine cut him off without looking at him. "I know. That's why I'm speaking now, to keep things honest. Before you get the papers and think I hid this from you."

Milton folded his arms against his stomach. "Why isn't the vanity cream good enough?"

"It's a fine ambition. One I know you and my father have succeeded with in other countries."

"This treatment promises to be our best quality yet."

Clementine wet her lips with the tip of her tongue. "I think a nobler, wiser aim would be a serum that could really help people."

"Like a tonic? That's not what we do."

"I know. I was thinking of something much bigger."

Bryce moved closer, waiting.

Clementine met him with her eyes. "A product that reverses the effects of aging."

The huge scope of such a project expanded in Bryce's mind. The fact finding. The interviews. The pivot from every direction in which Clements had ever led one of his teams.

The fortune and the awe of everyone alive if they succeeded.

Milton collapsed into the wood-and-leather chair. "That's what we're promising. Filling out wrinkles. Fading out sunspots, scars, and redness. Moisturizing flaky skin into dewy radiance."

Clementine shook her head. "A real cure that gives people back what they used to have."

"What was that?"

"More energy. Sharper thinking. Better appetite. You must remember–"

Milton raised his hand. "Be careful not to use me as your only example."

She took a breath. "Less pain in their joints and muscles. Happier moods. Clearer eyesight."

"You want to offer all this in one little bottle?"

She dipped her head in one big nod. "A whole lot of little bottles. You have containers, don't you?"

"Yes. For a simple beauty treatment called the Fountain of Youth."

"That's perfect. We can keep the name."

"It still requires a new logo and labels. We'll have to scrap the written advertising and commission more. The analysis and experiments – three years' worth – might have to be redone."

Bryce tapped the backs of his fingers against Milton's shoulder. "I already thought of it."

Milton's upper lip curled. "Anticipating it demands much less than executing it."

Clementine wrung her hands together. "Is it money? I don't know how much you'll pay me or how much my father earned."

Milton lowered his forehead. "It was substantial."

"I won't need all of it. What will it take to alter the project? Cut my earnings in half if you like and split it between you."

Bryce blinked in slow motion, then twice in quick succession.

Clementine gestured to him. "How much did you make as my father's assistant? I can double it, I'm sure."

Milton rose to his full height above the younger duo. "You forget I make the decisions, not him."

"What amount would make this trouble worth your time and effort, Mr. Longshaw? I'm prepared to make my case as strong as you need it to change your mind."

Milton waved her off. He produced a pad of paper and a pen from the cupboard on the desk. "I'll subtract ten percent of your salary for Bryce and ten percent for me. That's more than fair if you put in your share of the work." He wrote a short note and folded it.

Clementine's shoulders slumped in gratitude. "Thank you." She reached out and shook both his hands.

"Now." Milton strode to the door. "I wouldn't have given up my chair for the dozenth time this morning if I didn't intend to move this agreement forward. It'll take me fifteen minutes to reach the post office if I don't encounter one of their errand boys along the way. For a rupee, they'll take any message just about anywhere. You're free to stay or go as you wish."

"How long will the papers take to write up?"

"Considering we're in a hurry, I can offer an incentive to speed the process if they have other obligations. It might take a day or two, so let's say three to play it safe. If you'll meet here at the factory Thursday morning, we'll sign the papers and induct you into Fitzgerald and Longshaw."

Clementine pressed her palms against her chest. "Thank you, sir."

Milton reclaimed his hat from the coat rack and fit it on his head. He widened the door's opening and gazed over his shoulder at Bryce. "If you leave, switch the lights and fan off."

Bryce smoldered with contempt.

Without waiting for an answer, Milton strode out the door and hooked left in the hallway.

Clementine inflated herself with a deep breath and let it seep out through parted lips. "It was a pleasure to meet you, Mr. Bloom." She walked away from him toward the coat rack.

Bryce broke away from Milton's desk. "Miss Fitzgerald, I want you to know I was more than just your father's assistant. When he picked me for his apprentice, that was three full years ago in Oklahoma. Your father saw potential in me. An eagerness to learn the business, to travel and see the world. He could've chosen someone else, but he asked me to come along with him and learn what he knows. Kind of like how he shared his knowledge with you."

Clementine nodded.

"He believed in me." Bryce spread a hand across his chest. "It's Milton who doesn't. Clements never talked down to me the way Milton does."

"I'm sure I'll realize everyone's roles and skills the longer I work with you."

"Milton understands people, but he doesn't know plants." Bryce shadowed her partway across the rug. "I worked with your father very closely. I remember the books we referenced and the people we chatted with." He advanced another step. "I know all the ideas we threw out that didn't work for a beauty product. The native Indians believe there's something sacred and special about the Ganges River. They say it has cleansing properties. It heals and kills disease."

Clementine lingered by the coat rack. "We can use that in the formula. We should find out everything we can about the water. Is it close?"

"Less than a hundred miles east. We can make the trek ourselves or send someone to collect samples."

"That sounds promising. I'll go myself if I can get away." Clementine swung the door out of her way and put on her cloche.

"I've got many more leads for us just off the top of my head. I'm a lot like you. I'm young, but I know what I know. I might not have a degree in chemistry or biology, but I'm a valuable member of this team whether the man who invited me onto it is alive or not."

Clementine gave absent nods while she pulled on her coat and fastened its buttons. She was here, in India, in Delhi, in her father's factory. She was part of it now.

She turned to Bryce and caught him smiling.

"Did you find the key to your father's autocarriage? Have you taken a spin in it yet? Is that how you got to the factory?"

Clementine shuddered. "No, I took the trolley."

Bryce bunched up the smooth plane between his eyebrows. "The tram, as the English call it."

"Yes. I hear that word a lot."

"You'll get used to it."

"What?" Clementine adjusted the fit of her hat over her hair.

"The languages. Even the English isn't English, if you know what I mean. It isn't American like we're used to. It's all trams and lorries and biscuits and lifts. Have you heard them pronounce *airship* as *aeroship*? It's practically a different language."

She tugged her dress sleeves further down her wrists beneath her coat cuffs. "I'm sure I will. I'm not convinced I'll ever use my father's autocarriage. I prefer horses to engines. I'm more comfortable with animals."

Bryce clapped his hands low while his brows rose into the sky. "You've never driven something with an engine? It's terribly fun. You might've seen my steambike out in the parking lot before you walked in. Your father bought it for me."

Clementine sidled into the doorway.

"It seats two people." Bryce patted his palms together with nervous energy. "It's comfortable. The engine, the water, the fuel, and the fire all fit in the sidecar, so even in the summer, it's tolerable to drive it."

Clementine plucked her gloves from her pockets. She took a breath to say goodbye when at the far end of the hall, Milton rounded the corner. Three closed doors on her left punctuated the shrinking space between them.

Milton tipped his hat. "You're still here."

She angled her thumb at the lobby twenty feet on her right. "I was just on my way out."

Bryce stepped closer, and the three of them formed a neat triangle between the office and the hall.

Milton removed his hat. "I've passed our message along to the lawyers to draw up new papers to the old agreements. We can change them as we see fit, but this will move the process along."

Clementine took in the beige walls and the occasional lights suspended from the ceiling like her buttons dotted her coat. "I look forward to working with you and seeing more of the factory."

"Of course. I'll arrange a tour for you on Thursday."

"Three days," Clementine reassured herself under her breath.

Bryce knocked on the wooden doorframe. "I've got an idea. It's almost lunch time. Why don't we find a restaurant where we can eat and get to know each other better?"

Milton put his hat on. "This is my day off, and I'd like to keep it that way as much as possible. We've had a little too much business for a holiday, don't you think?"

Clementine fiddled with her gloves. "I agree. I'm still settling into my father's house, and I'd like to rest as much as possible."

Milton laid a hand on her wrist. "Getting accustomed to India and Delhi as well, aren't you?"

"Yes."

"It must be quite different from Tennessee."

"If I can make it in Nashville, I can make it anywhere."

Nash-*vul.*

Her pronunciation, casual and heartfelt, echoed in Bryce's mind. More natural and exotic than Milton's and his insistence on Nash-*ville*, so academic and precise. His heart sped through its next two beats. "Some other time, then. For eating and getting to know each other."

"Yes." Clementine walked away, passing a door marked *Meeting Room*.

Bryce called out to her. "Don't let them give you too much trouble on the trolley to Civil Lines."

Clementine answered over her shoulder. "I won't. I'll see you both soon." She crossed the lobby's rug-strewn floor and pulled the front door open.

Summers and heat, indeed.

The still air chilled her nose and ears. She had already found during her brief stint in Delhi that as long as she maintained her hat, coat, and gloves, she could brave the winter temperatures just fine.

Stranger than the cold hovering a full twenty degrees warmer than the snow-kissed air back home, an uncanny white fog draped over the entire city. She followed the curve in the front walk to the parking lot. She considered herself lucky to be able to see the road up ahead leading out of the lot.

Two engine-powered vehicles waited by the building where she had seen them on arrival. The nearer one shared the shape of a horse carriage with a roof and glass windows. Beside it, Bryce's steambike barely resembled a bicycle at all. Its frame was bulkier and more complex, like merging the silhouettes of a horse and a bicycle. The sidecar, as he called it, was shaped like an egg on one wheel. Two metal rods attached it to the bike itself, and Clementine could not decide whether they were sturdy enough to hold the components together.

She let the steambike slip from her mind. She reached the end of the parking lot and set off down the road toward the street. She kicked at the packed dirt beneath her.

Y'all?

She swung a furious kick, sending a cloud of dust flying. No wonder Milton struggled to take her seriously. She would not make that mistake a second time if she could help it.

At the end of the road, she turned right, already picking up the haggling and chattering of the Meena Bazaar up ahead.

The trolley stop she had walked in from not long ago stood behind her now, and she was glad to leave it. The trolley had merely allowed her to arrive to her appointment on time without sore feet. Strolling through countryside and city streets alike suited her better than riding in any contraption, horse drawn or motor forced.

But she had done it. She had convinced them, and she was only three days away from embarking on the project of her life.

Clementine tucked her hands in her pockets as she approached the packed bustle of bodies and outdoor stalls. Everything in India seemed somehow *more* than anything she had experienced before. Metal and paper clamored. People crowded together in endless numbers. The brightest colors exuded from every place. Back home, people ranged from pale peach to dark walnut. Their buildings were maroon brick, tree brown, or vanilla white. Here, faces filled in shades Clementine had never known. Earth, sienna, flax, and sand. Jewelry flashed from ears and nostrils in glinting metals and jewel hues. Yellows, greens, and blues blared from shops and houses. Their languages flowed like rivulets into a sea of beautiful intonations Clementine could not decipher.

She navigated the crowd as well as she could, finally squeezing between two groups of shoppers to arrive at covered halls. Flanking her and the road, two long, white buildings gaped open in peaked, three-story arches. Shops and their customers stretched the full length of each interior.

Clementine reached the main thoroughfare and slowed her steps. Across the street, red-grey blocks paved a generous walkway to one of the most ornate properties she had ever seen. The surrounding wall was not quite a barricade as much as a series of arches. In the center of the front wall stood a three-story building replete with a high, peaked doorway and towering minarets. Beyond this, across a sandstone courtyard, the white-and-red beauty of a wondrous building rose into the mist. Its wide, round columns and flared domes intermingled with the straight lines and sharp corners Clementine found more recognizable.

With only the barest of her journey completed, she veered right and resolved herself to the long trek north to Civil Lines. She skirted around men in turbans with flowing, black beards. Jovial men chewing paan spat far-reaching streams of garnet saliva into the street. Dogs barked and chased each other past Clementine's sides, rippling the wool of her coat. When a cow stopped to eye her with a languid gaze from the middle of the street, it blocked the varied traffic of horse-drawn carriages, steam-driven machines, and human-drawn rickshaws.

Clementine peered into the cow's dark, dismissive eyes and continued on her way.

At a busier intersection, Clementine chose another right. On the verge of more familiar territory, she eagerly selected the next left. She followed the thoroughfare through its curves and bendbacks. Despite the heavy lagging in her feet, she walked on.

At last, the shops and crowds fell away, depositing Clementine in an even stranger section of the city. Moss crumbled centuries-old monuments alongside British-built houses a fraction of their age. The streets, though some of them wound like brooks, formed straighter lanes. The neighborhoods forged space and order in a city of alleyways and cramped quarters. The garbage littering the urban streets did not appear amidst these lawns and gardens.

After a few more blocks, Clementine made her final turn. Several houses later, she arrived at her father's burgundy door.

No. Her door.

She could not keep torturing herself with muddling that distinction. Clements Fitzgerald would never lumber through that doorway again. Never set foot in India once more or set one foot anywhere, for that matter.

Clementine sucked in a labored inhale and pulled the key from her pocket. India's summer heat, according to Miss Edith Higginbotham, drained the energy, will, and breath out of anyone who dared to move. Without it, Clementine still felt exhausted. Her father's unexpected passing, followed by the complex journey overseas, had worn her to weariness. Three miles of barely familiar streets, picking her way through the thickets of people, had sapped the rest of her strength. She unlocked the door and let herself in.

Closing the portal, she propped herself against it, her vision roaming over the surroundings that greeted her.

To her left, a rectangular alcove stretched out between the front wall of the house and the staircase rising to the landing near the second floor. Four carved leaves, exquisite details swelling their midribs and shaping their outlines, covered the finial atop the post at the stairway's bottom. Expanding in front of her and to her right, the gigantic great room stood as the heart of the house.

Dark wooden beams offset milk-colored walls. Dark woods and cane formed couches, chairs, and tables of varying sizes. A fireplace emerged from the far, right-hand wall, diagonal to a set of double doors leading out to the courtyard. Each piece stamped another weighted shadow in the light and airy space. Golden candelabras branched out on the mantelpiece. Rugs wove maroon blooms and jade-green leaves against cream backgrounds. Every choice mounted contrast upon drama. Obvious, striking, and opulent.

Clementine moved forward and rested her hand on the stair post's leaf canopy.

No, she could never mistake this place for home. Home was a tiny wooden house, practically a cabin, north of Livingston, where she had spent most of her life. A homestead that could fit inside this enormous room. Home was the current apartment near her small office in Nashville. The places she had lived were modest. They harbored wooden walls, plain wallpaper, and few amenities.

Back home, salvaged nails kept worn furniture together. Someone had shoved each piece where it would fit and serve the inhabitants best, not where it pleased some grand design.

A tear streaked down Clementine's cheek, accompanied by another and one more. She brushed them away with the back of her glove.

She stood alone in the house, but its true emptiness came from the absolute absence of her father. His possessions remained. She owned too many of them now. To replace the inanimate forms and baubles with her father would have been a natural trade. But no such possibility existed.

Clementine wandered away from the finial. A song bubbled up in her memory and her chest until she murmured it. Even under her breath, it filled and warmed the great room.

"Was in the merry month of May when flowers were a-blooming." She pulled her gloves off and used them to swipe a fresh tear off her cheek. She barely registered the sound of her own voice. From the wisps of her oldest memories, her father serenaded her with his Virginia-tinged, Scotch-Irish brogue. "Sweet William on his deathbed lay for the love of Barbara Allen."

Clementine draped her gloves over the arm of a cane chair and swept her fingers over the couch's embroidered cushions. "As she was walking through the fields, she heard the death bells knelling. With every toll, they seemed to say, 'Hardhearted Barbara Allen.'"

Her throat trembled, and she balled up in an armchair near the double doors. She covered her face with her hands. "Oh, Mother, Mother, make my bed. Oh, make it long and narrow." The darkness made the room easier to bear, but the aching of her heart spread through her shaking muscles. "Sweet William died for me today."

She paused, not sure if she was prophesying or finishing the verse. "I'll die for him tomorrow."

Chapter Three

Clementine held her head high, topped by a brimmed, black-feathered hat. She strode up the front path of Fitzgerald and Longshaw as it curved to the door. With a hand still gloved in solemn black, she pushed the door open and stepped into the lobby.

Unlike her previous visit, the ceiling fan swirled a refreshing breeze through the room. Across from her, a short Indian man sat at the tall desk. His raven hair glistened in a neat, parted style as precise as his thick moustache. Wide shoulders topped his muscular arms, perceptible despite the loose fit of his emerald-green kurta. Baritone timbres fell in other rooms like murmurs.

The man at the desk stood up and met her with a short bow. "Good morning." His native language tempered his precise pronunciation. "I am Aatmaj Kakkar. You must be Miss Fitzgerald?" His head bobbed, his dark-copper eyes shining.

"Yes." Clementine was not sure what else to say. The factory thrummed, and she had only been exposed to a miniscule part of its operations.

Movement out of the corner of her eye alerted her to a second presence on her left.

Bryce stood up from the settee, splaying one hand over his vest. "I'm glad you're back. Normally, Mr. Kakkar would've messaged us through the tube system that you'd arrived. But you're not just any guest, are you?"

Bryce offered his arm, and Clementine took it to gain any measure of stability.

He guided her toward the hallway to the left of the desk. "I waited in the lobby so I could escort you."

"Thank you."

Bryce offered a salute to Aatmaj. "Thank you, Mr. Kakkar."

The Indian answered with his rounded, sculpted English. "You are very welcome, sir."

Clementine almost whispered. "Things are much different today. I guessed they would be, but I didn't imagine…"

"All this?" Bryce gestured to the stimulated hallway air and the several competing languages mumbling out of sight. "Don't worry. I'm not sure what you're used to. But we've made a comfortable place here. As tidy and friendly as a factory can be."

They reached the closed door for Milton's office, and Clementine stopped walking.

Bryce motioned up ahead. "One more room. I think you'll like the surprise."

Clementine's belly plummeted. "I've had nothing but surprises since I got to India. More like shocks, to be honest."

"Did you ever leave the States before?"

She shook her head and took her hat off.

Bryce confided in her. "I hadn't, either, before I met Clements and sailed here. They say India isn't like other places. It's more like its own continent than a simple country."

Clementine stammered. "I see why."

Bryce's mouth ticked in sympathy. "You'll like this surprise. Milton and I will be with you for the tour. We can answer any questions you have and be your most familiar faces."

"Thank you."

Bryce stopped at the next door and presented it to her with a flourish.

Clementine read over the engraved metal plaque several times. *Miss Clementine Fitzgerald, Copartner, Research and Development.*

Bryce pulled his arm against hers. "Exciting, isn't it?"

She felt dizzy but forced herself to keep upright and still. "Very."

Bryce opened the door. "It's a little premature, but…"

Clementine swept her eyes over the office. Its similarity to Milton's struck her at once. The form and function were the same, but not the style.

A fan with broad blades spun overhead, dangling three gas-burning lanterns beneath it. A walnut, roll-top desk stood against the right-hand wall, replete with drawers and pigeonholes. Milton rose from the chair that accompanied it, exposing a plain oak seat. Pale leather upholstered the low, curved back and tops of the long arms.

Bryce's tone stiffened as Milton approached them. "Here's Milton with the papers."

Milton directed a genteel grin to Clementine. "Making our agreements official is the first order of the day."

Clementine nodded.

"I hope the office suits you. Your father had incredible taste."

"I'm sure it's fine."

"You can always refurnish it if you wish." Milton guided Clementine to the desk and stood over her as she took the chair. He slid the pages on the desk closer to her. "Read them at your leisure. I'm sure you'll notice the wording on your door complements this document."

Clementine set her hat on the desk. She picked up the pages and scanned them for the only information that interested her. *A full partner in the company... Continuing her father's duties of research, managing product development, and associated work... To be paid the same salary as her father, minus twenty percent.*

She laid the agreement on the desk.

Milton passed her a black fountain pen. "I've already filled it with ink. All you have to do is sign if the conditions satisfy you."

Clementine wrote her name in haste and scooted the chair back. She jumped to her feet while Milton added his signature.

Bryce offered his hand to her. "Congratulations. I look forward to working with you."

Clementine met his grip with hers and shook hands with Milton as well.

The old man pulled two keys from a desk cubby and handed them to her. "These unlock your office and the front entrance you've been using."

Clementine buried them in her pocket.

Milton scribbled a note on a piece of paper at the desk. He secured it in a small glass tube strengthened with gradiated metal caps at either end. "This is just one of the modern advances we employ here." In the wall beside the desk, Milton inserted the tube into a horizontal opening. Above the enclosure, a switch shaped like a clock hand pointed upwards beneath the fanned-out numbers one through seven. He swiveled it to the gleaming metal five. With the push of a button, the suctioning of air whisked the tube away.

Clementine started but kept herself from lifting fully off the carpet.

Milton wagged a finger at the apparatus. "The Blickensderfer fax machine may send messages around the world, but we have our own way of sharing information at a moment's notice. We'll teach you how to use it as you spend more time in the building."

"What do I do now?"

"Meet the rest of the employees. I'll deliver the partnership agreement to the lawyers later."

Clementine slipped off her gloves as her hands sweated. "How many people would you say there are?"

"Several dozen. We'll need to hire more when we complete the formula. We have to bottle it, label it, pack it, and box it. Plus more men to store it in the warehouse and load the boxes on the trucks for shipment."

The word tumbled from Clementine's lips. "Shipment." She stuffed her gloves in her coat pockets and unfastened its buttons. "I'm sorry. I never had to worry about production before. Back home, I…" *Pick the herbs I need from my garden or nature, mix them up in the form that works best, and administer it to the patient.* No matter how many lives she had bettered and saved, her process would sound simplistic and uneducated. "I tend directly to the sick. No packaging involved."

"The manufacturing process itself falls under my purview. Experiment and create the new formula. I'll make sure it's ready for the customer." As an afterthought, Milton added, "Bryce will help you."

Bryce shot him a stare.

Clementine wandered away to find a mahogany coat rack behind the door. She hung up her coat. "You're both so kind."

Milton's smile spread across his thin lips. "Thank you for stepping in during our time of need and alerting us to your expertise. If you'll come with me, I have someone special I'd like to introduce you to first."

"I met Mr. Kakkar, was it? On the way in."

Milton reached the doorway. "Yes. Good. He's been with us almost since we set up in Delhi. He makes a great first impression for our guests and employees. His strength gives him the added role of providing security. You were able to understand him?"

Clementine stepped past Milton into the hall. "Perfectly."

"You'll find that not every person in India speaks English, and if they do, it might not be much. It may be hard to understand them. Mr. Kakkar knows a lot of daily phrases, but he lacks some of the technical and botany terms you might need to converse with." Milton joined Clementine in the corridor. "This way."

Clementine kept in step at Milton's side, Bryce lagging a few paces behind them. Clementine peeked around Milton in his grey suit at the plaques marking each door they passed. *Accounting and Accounts. Restrooms.* They rounded the corner near a small, square alcove providing a door emblazoned *Employee Lounge.*

Outside the next door close on the right waited a man. One end of his olivine turban trailed down his back. Black eyebrows shaded his glowing rich-amber eyes. A one-inch fringe of beard cradled the strong lines of his long, pointed nose and low, round cheeks.

As the trio slowed to a halt, he greeted them with a deep bow. *"Assalamu alaikum."* As he straightened, he kept his eyes from meeting Clementine's. He placed his right hand over his heart. "Welcome to India." His accent was softer and narrower than Aatmaj's, intriguing Clementine as much as it surprised her.

Milton and Bryce returned the gesture, and Clementine hurried to mimic them.

Milton, still the tallest figure in the hall, gripped the man's arm. "This is Mustafa Shah Ali. He's our principal translator. He's worked with every department and every employee, including your father."

The man patted his heart.

"Now, I'd like for him to work with you, Miss Fitzgerald. Many of our workers on the factory floor grasp little English. Mr. Mustafa, as he prefers to be called, can be a great asset to you. We trust him very much."

Mr. Mustafa clapped Milton on the shoulder. "Thank you, Mr. Milton." His eyes trailed in a loose focus to one side of Clementine. "I'm sorry for the loss of your father. He was a great man. He's already missed."

Clementine bowed her head. "Thank you."

Milton broke his one-armed embrace with the translator. "I believe we're ready for the factory."

Mr. Mustafa slid the door panel aside into a recess in the wall.

Milton patted the opposite jamb. "We avoided swinging doors in the factory itself. It reduces accidents and wastes of space."

Mr. Mustafa stepped aside, and Milton strode through the doorway. Bryce motioned to Clementine, and she followed Milton into the largest room she had seen in the building. She glanced behind her, where Mr. Mustafa hovered near her left shoulder and Bryce on her right. Eighteen rectangular machines loomed in three perfect rows across the room's depth. Each stood six feet tall, not counting five metal rods ascending into the ceiling. The top third of each contraption consisted of a clear glass enclosure. Inside each case hung a three-inch-thick slab of horizontal metal. Glinting aluminum formed the machines' bases.

Standing between Clementine and the machines lingered roughly thirty men. Almost all of them wore matching kurtas and pants in natural hues. Beads formed patterns of jade leaves and silver tubes around the necklines and hems. Flashing embroidery wove chain motifs down the outsides of the pant legs. The workers welcomed her with bows, palms touched together, and hands held over their hearts. These signals had surrounded Clementine in the streets and bazaars, but she had yet to fully embrace them. She rested her hand over her heart.

Milton arced his outstretched hand toward the workers. "These uniforms were your father's idea. They blend our cultures, respect the local styles, and show them as employees of Fitzgerald and Longshaw."

Clementine absorbed this without comment, uncertain what else to do.

Milton's fingertips alighted on her upper back, and he raised his volume. "Gentlemen, I'm honored to introduce my new business partner, Miss Fitzgerald. She's excited to join us and continue her father's work."

Mr. Mustafa moved away from Clementine where the workers could see him. He repeated Milton's message in unfaltering syllables that mystified and eluded her the second they had passed. The workers applauded, and two men advanced from the front of the crowd.

One of them smiled at her from a rectangular face with kind, hooded eyes. Faint creases spread out from the outer corners, marking the tops of his shallow cheeks. Grey lightened his dark hair and beard.

Milton spoke up. "This is Govinda Magar. He's in charge of our payroll and accounts. If you have questions about money, you can direct them to him. Like you, he's not a native

Indian. He moved here with his wife and children from Nepal some years ago."

Clementine liked him already. "It's nice to meet you."

Mr. Mustafa translated on cue.

With a pleasant but grim countenance, Govinda held up a finger to ask for patience. "I am sorry for losing your father."

Salt water tickled Clementine's eyes, and she blinked it away.

Milton turned to her. "He learned that especially for you, to say to you in your own language."

"Thank you, Mr. Magar."

Like Aatmaj in the lobby, the second worker parted his straight, black hair into two kempt sections. His brown eyes twinkled above an aquiline nose, and his moustache warmed his thick lips. He placed his palms together in front of his chest. *"Namaskar."*

Milton and Mr. Mustafa interjected at the same time.

The grey-haired man acquiesced with a bow. "As you can see, Mr. Mustafa performs his job very well. Please continue, Mr. Mustafa."

The translator drew himself up. *"Namaskar* is an Indian greeting. You'll hear it a lot while you're here."

Clementine's elbows twitched to bend. "Do I do it back to him?"

"You may, as a sign of respect. It has a spiritual meaning less obvious in the day-to-day."

Clementine touched her palms against each other. *"Namaskar,"* she pronounced in slow vowels.

The room erupted in applause and slaps of the thighs.

Clementine released an exhale of relief, lifting her spirits.

Milton shook the man's hand. "This is our foreman, Nithya Menon. I'll be in more communication with him than you will. He's a bridge between those of us in the offices and the workers on the floor."

Clementine looked over the workmen in the room. "It's an honor to meet all of you. Thank you for helping make my father's and Mr. Longshaw's plans come true."

Mr. Mustafa expressed this in such different sounds, Clementine could hardly believe they imparted the same meaning. She marveled at how much trust she already placed in him to convey her messages on her behalf. He could mistranslate her or completely discredit her, and she would never know.

Milton extended his elbow to Clementine, and she hooked her arm around his. "Those are the people who make this factory operate. I can show you the unpacking rooms where we rinse and store the plants another time." He gestured to a set of plain, bulky desks against the right-hand wall. "We have some work stations for quality control and other tasks. What I'm most proud of are the machines you see for extraction."

Clementine's chest sank a little. What herbs, roots, flowers, and spices did the team receive here? She knew so few of India's indigenous species. The only ones she could remember were the ones she had recognized in her father's notes. Ginger, basil, marigolds, roses.

Milton's voice purred. "They're also the most dangerous."

Clementine eyed the machines with suspicion as Milton led her closer to them. "Why are you proudest of what can hurt you?"

"In the process of what we accomplish here, the extractors are the first vital step toward creating a product from the raw materials we ship in. Without these temperamental beasts, we'd simply rinse dirt off various plants and mix them together. We'd make salads instead of potions."

Mr. Mustafa spoke at length. He set the tips of his fingers under his chin and flung them toward the crowd. He chuckled, and the rest of the room laughed with him.

Milton tapped a gloved finger against a machine's glass enclosure. "Are you interested in mechanical contraptions?"

"I believe I should get to know the process as much as I can. It's only fair and can only help our cause."

"Well said."

Clementine checked over her shoulder. Bryce hung back a few feet, his hands clutched behind him. He rocked in slow swings from his toes to his heels. He widened his big grey-green eyes in exaggerated boredom. Amusement toyed with the corners of Clementine's mouth. She fought it as she reset her attention on Milton and the machine before them.

"Extractors run on motors concealed inside their housings." Milton touched the aluminum base rising to the bottom of his chest.

"Where's the problem?"

Milton opened a panel in the base and flicked a switch upward. A motor chugged to life, and the cement floor vibrated beneath Clementine's boots. Milton activated a second switch, and the glass housing rose up on the track set into the four outermost rods attached to the ceiling. The bottom of the glass case cleared the height where its top once rested, and the mechanism stopped. "Impressed? These are specialty machines, designed and built for our purposes."

"Very much so."

"This is the stage at which one of our operators can use the machine. The plants to be extracted from are brought in from across the hall. The operator places them on this mesh bed." Milton patted the interlaced wires leaving tiny holes in the base's surface, held in place by a metal frame. He reverted the last switch to the downward position, and the four rods lowered the glass walls around the mesh. "From here, the operator opens the steam valve."

Milton rotated a dial, and pure, white mist wafted up through the screen. "This loosens the fibers, rendering them malleable."

Clementine tipped her head aside. "The steam cooks the plants like boiling them in water."

"Correct. It's a gentler way of breaking them down."

Clementine sensed movement on her vacant side. Bryce stepped up next to her and folded his arms in a loose knot over his stomach.

She pointed to the steam gathering inside the case. "This must be the problem. Steam causes terrible burns."

"That's true," Milton allowed. "We release it from the box through the ventilating shaft in the central column." With the flip of a mechanism, the steam rose toward a newly opened hole in the cage, disappearing into the wide metal rod connected to the ceiling. "The real danger is this." Milton pushed a button, and the thick metal slab sank from its moorings at the top of the cage, clinking and grinding as it neared the mesh. Their meeting rung through the air, and the noise stopped. "One miscalibration. One missed measurement or slipped chain. And we could have a real disaster on our hands. Quite literally."

Clementine slipped her hands into the pockets of her peach-colored dress. "What does the machine do for the elixir?"

"This steel block condenses the material. Its liquid, its essence, its microscopic components are collected from underneath the mesh. We then pack the ingredients in cold storage."

Milton turned to Nithya, who inspected the proceedings with proud, shining eyes. "Would you power down the extractor, please?" Nithya hurried to its control panel as Milton walked Clementine away between the machines. He guided her to the left, where a door stood in the center of the long wall. Bryce and Mr. Mustafa followed them.

Milton unlocked the door and slid it open into the wall. "I wouldn't recommend browsing for very long without your hat and coat, but you're welcome to take a peek."

Clementine's heart thumped at the chance to see the extractors' products. The coolness rushed to surround her as she stepped down into the room. She pulled her hands free of her pockets and massaged her arms to warm them. Countless shelves in the rectangular space stretched twelve feet into the air. Ladders inclined at either end of the room. On every shelf sat hundreds of jars, bottles, vials, and pots. She leaned closer to read their hand-printed labels. *Aloe vera juice. Saffron oil. Sandalwood oil. Pomegranate juice.*

Clementine called out. "These were for the beauty treatment?"

Milton stuck his head in the doorway. "Yes."

Carrot seed powder. Turmeric oil.

Clementine tore herself away from the mysterious contents. "Mr. Bloom."

Milton retreated as Bryce's eager expression popped into the doorway.

Clementine's arms hummed with the promise of opportunity. "This is where we begin. Some of these plants might be useful for our new purpose."

"I agree."

A shiver rippled through Clementine's spine. She rubbed her arms with vigor and took her final glimpses at the loaded shelves.

Milton reappeared and lifted a hand toward the back wall of the storage space. An identical door stood across from him. "That leads to the factory's mixing room. It's more easily – and comfortably – accessed from the door directly between them." He indicated the front of the extraction room.

Clementine slid the door ajar and peered into the mixing room. The same size and shape as the extraction area, the only difference was the kind of equipment occupying it. The mixing machines squatted shorter and wider without steam vents extending to the ceiling. She secured the door and stepped out through the open exit. Milton slid the panel closed and locked it.

Clementine could barely see past the curious workmen to the extraction room entrance to reorient herself. "How will I memorize all these doors and halls?"

Milton offered a one-sided smile. "You will. Be glad Clements and I envisioned it with a single story instead of two." He engaged the crowd. "Gentlemen, may your patience be rewarded for waiting."

Mr. Mustafa rattled off the words in at least one other language. Clementine could not discern for sure.

Milton clasped his hands in front of him. "The announcement I wanted to make is of a change in plans at the company."

Mr. Mustafa translated while knots wound themselves in Clementine's stomach. In the cavernous, expansive room, she could swear the air had thinned to nothing.

Milton wrapped a long arm around her shoulders. "With Miss Fitzgerald's and my bold leadership, we're changing the course of the product. We'll keep the factory running as it is and output the same high quality."

Clementine struggled to hold onto Mr. Mustafa's reassuring confidence as he orated. Her knees buckled, and she braced them beneath her.

"What we're making is no mere tonic for the complexion. Miss Fitzgerald, like her father before her, possesses great vision. She aims for more worthwhile heights, and I share her sentiments. Beginning today, our project elevates into a health-conscious and ambitious pursuit. We're engaging the reversal of time itself, a concoction to not only relieve the suffering of our fellow people. But to revive their younger, more vibrant selves." Milton studied Clementine. "Have I done it justice?"

She swallowed, her mouth remaining dry and puckered. "That's exactly what I had in mind."

Milton nodded to Mr. Mustafa. The turbaned man spoke to the crowd, every expressive gesture of his hands eliciting stroked chins and wide eyes.

Milton removed his arm from Clementine's shoulders.

She addressed him sidelong. "I didn't know you hadn't told them."

He murmured back. "I thought it best to reveal the alterations with both of us here. You've earned their trust by now."

"How do you know?"

"It's the way of the East. They decide right away whether they like you or not. If any of them disagree with the new direction, they'll give me a polite excuse to resign."

A few men applauded, and others joined them. Clementine beamed in gratitude. Others bowed over pressed palms or observed her with grim-set lips. Her ribs squeezed her lungs to think of any of them forfeiting a job over her ideas.

She stood up taller. "Mr. Mustafa, will you tell them we'll look out for them as surely as our serum will aid people in need?"

Mr. Mustafa clamped his hands together. He reiterated her statement with solemnity and a touch of what Clementine registered as hope.

The men clapped with percussive enthusiasm. Clementine blew out a breath, slackening some of the tension stretched across her ribcage.

Milton encouraged her forward with a hand on the back of her arm. "We should reconvene in the offices. I have a few more things to review with you."

Clementine floated high on the workmen's acceptance of her. They parted for her with little bows and words that missed her understanding.

Mr. Mustafa followed a step behind her. "They pass on their condolences about your father, Miss Fitzgerald."

"Please give them my thanks."

Mr. Mustafa trailed Clementine beyond the crowd of workers before he bowed to them with utmost sincerity. *"Dhanyavaad. Shukriya."*

Milton and Bryce caught up to them. The older man led the way out, and Clementine shadowed him up the hallway.

Mr. Mustafa stepped up to her side as they turned the corner.

She glanced at him, but he did not meet her gaze. "That was a very polite *thank you*."

"In India, we verbalize our gratitude rarely, mostly to strangers. As I've known most of them for years and you'll acquaint yourself with them soon, I wanted to properly convey your earnestness."

Clementine blinked, trying to fathom it. "You don't say *thank you* here?"

"It'd insult your friends and family. Anyone you know well."

"My kin live thousands of miles away."

"You'll make new friends. You've already started with the other workers and me. We want to be kind. We want to serve you and do what's right. There's no need to thank us. Simply offer to repay the favor and do so when you can. If you must say *thank you*, do it honestly."

"I'll try to remember that." Clementine bit her lip. "Where I come from in my country is called the South, Mr. Mustafa. Have you heard of it?"

"Not in particular."

"We're known for our manners and hospitality. Being kind, like you said about the people here. Except there, we show kindness by letting people know we appreciate them."

"It's the same in spirit. Instead of words, we prefer to act."

Clementine's heart stung. She had been so sure all her life that manners were built on sharing your appreciation with a simple phrase. Were these teachings wrong or merely different?

Milton stopped the group in front of Clementine's office. "Mr. Mustafa, superbly done. Let Nithya and the workers know I'll go over the production schedule with them shortly. Then I'll meet with Govinda about the budget for sourcing additional materials." He ducked his head in the room to consult the clock above the desk. "If you wait in the lobby when you're done, Miss Fitzgerald will be along soon."

Mr. Mustafa bowed and walked away.

Clementine examined Milton as fear crept over her, seizing her lungs. "What do you need to talk to me about? What business do I have with Mr. Mustafa?"

Milton strolled into the office and waved her in. "I'll explain everything. Is it such a surprise that you and I have matters to discuss?"

"I'm only taken off guard about what they might be."

Milton nodded.

Bryce stood in the doorway. "Do you have instructions for me? This is technically where I'd be working if Clements were here. I assume since Miss Fitzgerald is filling in for her father, I'll assist her in the same way."

Milton tapped his fingertip on the air. "Not quite, at least, not yet. There are other urgent issues. You said yourself lawyers and banking aren't your strong suits. As I'll be going over related subjects, I'd hate to bore you with such complex details."

Bryce scrunched up his freckled cheeks, peering into Milton's eyes like shotguns aimed at prey. "What would you like me to do, then?"

"You can dredge up the information Miss Fitzgerald needs to catch up on the properties of the plants we've been working with."

Bryce pointed between Milton and Clementine to the desk. "Can you meet in your office? You're blocking the files."

"We're almost done."

Bryce huffed and skirted around Clementine to the desk. He crouched down in front of the left-hand drawers. He slid open the bottom one and pulled out several notebooks. He set them on the rug.

Milton cleared his throat, regaining Clementine's attention. "I'm sorry if I startled you with my vague directions. The truth is this. I presume I may discuss it plainly?"

Clementine's fingertips played with the point of her dress' large, grey collar. "Of course."

"To make a product, we need labor and materials. Nothing worth using is free. Your father and I did business together for fifteen years. In the beginning, we had little money of our own. We sought out investors, completed our inventions, and used the sales to earn everybody a nice, tidy profit."

Clementine's head swam. She fought to recover her clarity and dropped her anxious hand to her side. "It's like renting my office in Nashville. I have to make enough money tending to people to pay for what's due there and at my apartment."

Milton flashed her a genuine smile. "Exactly. As the years wore on, we needed fewer investors each time. But there are benefits to gaining investors even now. They're precisely that – invested – in our product. In our success. They have a tangible need to see it explode on the market and shower us all with more money than we put into it. These people become allies. They recognize potential in our goals and back it up with funding."

"They don't want to lose it."

"They want to expand it. They become some of our best marketers and supporters."

Clementine swallowed. "That sounds good. What's the problem?"

"The investors we have in India signed on because they believe in the probability of a beauty treatment to produce a fortune."

"And I changed it. Oh, dear."

Milton lowered his head to catch her eyes. "Not to worry. All we have to do is be forthcoming. We let them know how and why the project has transformed. We illustrate how it's a better, nobler product. Then we ask them to reaffirm their faith in our ability to complete the work."

"We could lose investors."

"It's possible, but I doubt it."

"You have a plan?"

Milton straightened up, tilting his narrow chin back. "Who could say no to Clements Fitzgerald's only daughter, come all the way overseas to reenergize his company with fresh proposals?"

Clementine's mouth plunged open. "You're sending me to meet with them? I don't know them. I don't understand their customs or their languages. Do I?" She pressed her lips together. Perhaps their investors all spoke English. Bryce could escort her through the city as he had guided her from the lobby to her office earlier that morning. Had it been that same morning? She rubbed her slick palms against each other.

"They're harmless, I assure you. You'll be fine. Mr. Mustafa will serve as your interpreter and guide."

"You already told him I'd do this?" Clementine could not discern whether she sounded certain or was asking a question.

"I consider it fair. I made the business contacts, presented prospective investors with our proposition, and clinched their support. I admire your courage to travel halfway around the world to alter that course, but you did alter it. Who better than you to explain it to the investors for all the reasons you gave me you should become my business partner?"

Clementine hung her head. "It's fair."

"I'm glad to hear it. I've already set up a few appointments for you today." Milton moved over to the desk and plucked a folded piece of paper from a cubbyhole.

Bryce, still crouched near the other half of the desk, scowled up at him.

Milton held the paper out to Clementine. "There are three of them. They're all early, one after the other. Once you've concluded, you're free to do as you wish. Take the afternoon off and rest if it appeals to you."

"I came to work, not to lounge about in my father's house." Clementine selected the piece of paper and opened it. *Nivriti Singh. Udit Varma. Lowell Dodd.* Only the last name looked recognizable – British? American? – and imbued Clementine with hope.

"Until we know for sure our principal investors won't request refunds, you wouldn't accomplish much sitting around here. It's just as important as developing the new formula. For the moment, it supersedes it."

"Very well." Clementine closed the paper and pinched it along its creases. "I suppose I'll see you tomorrow."

"An oral report in the morning will suffice. There's no need for grand presentations. Let me know what they say."

"I will."

"Good luck. Stay relaxed, and you'll do fine." Milton walked out of the office.

Clementine ran the pads of her index finger and thumb over the page.

Bryce stood up and dropped his stack of notebooks on the desk. His efforts stained his cheeks ruddy. "Didn't you notice how you were honest and told him everything before you signed the papers?"

"Are you saying I shouldn't trust Mr. Longshaw?"

Bryce kept his voice down. "My advice is to do your best and watch your back. On his good days, your best is fantastic. On his bad days – which are many, especially if you're me – your best might be enough to save you."

Clementine strained to inhale, and the breath escaped her as soon as it could. She swung the door aside to retrieve her winter gear from the coat rack. She buttoned up her coat and nestled her hat over her hair.

Bryce wiped his hands on his pants. "Good luck."

"Thank you." Clementine winced. It was such an automatic saying. She met Bryce's fiery, sympathetic eyes. "I wish you were going with me."

"Me, too." Bryce offered a tight-lipped wobble of a smile and turned to the notebooks.

Clementine took her gloves out of her pockets. "Do I leave either of my keys with you for locking up when you go?"

"No, I have my own set." He paused. "Does it bother you that I have a key to your office? I worked so closely with your father, it was never an issue."

Clementine moved into the doorway and sized Bryce up. His hair had a thick, unruly lie to it. His big eyes seemed a scant quarter inch too far apart, barely noticeable without inspecting him. The freckles scattered over his cheeks and nose retained a boyish air. His plain lips sat above his small chin. His navy-blue suit, the same good quality as Milton's, harbored wrinkles in more places than his recently bent knees. His black leather shoes shone, and he waited in silence for her answer.

"It won't be a problem, Mr. Bloom. I wish you luck as well."

Clementine whisked into the hallway, curving to her right. She strode twenty feet to the lobby, where Mr. Mustafa stood up from the settee beside her. She pulled her gloves on and set her resoluteness in stone.

Mr. Mustafa gazed at her coat's lapel. "Are you ready?"

With one final tug, her second glove fit as intended. "Yes. Lead on."

Chapter Four

Mr. Mustafa walked around one of the autocarriages in the parking lot to its left-hand door. "I hear you don't appreciate certain steam-powered vehicles. I hope you won't protest too strongly about taking advantage of this one."

Clementine's pulse picked up. "Where did you hear that?" Could Bryce indeed be trusted, or would he repeat everything she said to the others at the company?

"Mr. Milton told me."

She gestured to the autocarriage. "Why do you talk like you don't own it?"

"It's Mr. Milton's. I'll return it to the factory when we finish our day's meetings. I've driven it before. All you have to do at the end of our schedule is let me know where to leave you."

"You don't own one yourself?"

"I live close by." Mr. Mustafa unlocked the door and opened it. "If you'll kindly step inside, I'll drive us to our first destination."

Clementine tried not to think about what she was doing. She gripped the handle on the outside of the autocarriage and used the step plate to boost herself into its interior. She settled in on the leather seat, and Mr. Mustafa closed the door. A smaller handle bolted to the silver metal wall curved toward her, and Clementine resolved only to grab it in case of emergency.

Mr. Mustafa disappeared and arrived outside the autocarriage's other door. He lifted a brown, oval case from the pocket of his loose-fitting pants and opened the hinged lid. Pulling out a pair of sterling silver pince-nez glasses, he clamped them to the bridge of his nose. He tucked the case away and climbed behind the wheel. He inserted the key into a slit in the dashboard, and the motor whirred into action. A vibration like the one from the extractor or the trolley hummed through Clementine.

The turbaned man checked the mirror affixed to the front of the ceiling. He adjusted a lever on the dash, his foot weighed down a floor pedal, and the vehicle rolled backward.

Clementine's hand jerked toward the wall bar, but she stopped herself. Reversing was hardly an emergency. She would have to get used to riding in steam-driven vehicles, that was all – backwards and forwards.

Mr. Mustafa aimed the autocarriage at the white mist surrounding the parking lot's exit. He repositioned the lever, applied pressure with his boot, and steered them straight ahead.

Clementine peeked at him, anxious to keep her own eyes locked on their path as well. "Mr. Mustafa, I don't mean to be rude, but I'm curious. Why are you the only person who calls other men by mister and their first name?"

"India's my country. This is true. But it's not where I was born."

"Like me and Mr. Magar?"

"Yes. I was born in Afghanistan. My father moved our family when I was a boy." Mr. Mustafa brought the autocarriage to a brief stop at the intersection and turned right onto the street. "We didn't even have a last name there. My father was asked to choose one for record keeping and so forth. He chose Ali, and I've kept it myself for over twenty years. I could change it anytime I wish. It's a custom to call each other like this. Perhaps one day, if it's appropriate, I'll call you the same way."

Clementine knew better than to pry into his differing rules. Americans employed him and insisted on additional formalities between the two sexes. He merely followed suit. Or was it a clause from his country of origin? "Do you have a family of your own now?"

Mr. Mustafa's shoulders bunched beneath his knee-length, cotton shirt. "In the country I come from, such inquiries are not so welcome."

Clementine buttressed her elbow against the autocarriage's wall and cradled her head in her hand. "Where I'm from, it's rude *not* to ask about somebody's kin. How am I ever going to make it here when everything's the opposite of what I know?"

"Not everything." Mr. Mustafa grinned. "I only said it was true of people from Afghanistan. You'll find many Indian people are very different."

Clementine eyed him, not sure what pleasures or horrors awaited her in her meetings.

"I suppose, being where we are, I can give an answer to your question. Perhaps I'm discourteous in refusing to respond."

"No. You're not obligated to answer my questions here or anywhere."

Mr. Mustafa's foot retracted from the pedal, coasting the autocarriage between the crowds shopping in the Meena Bazaar. "I have a wife and three children."

"Is your wife..." Clementine hesitated. Here she was asking intrusive questions again. She pushed out the rest of her inquiry. "...also from Afghanistan?"

"Yes."

Clementine relegated herself to silence and small talk for the rest of their errands.

The vehicle halted across from the mesmerizing, red-stone complex Clementine had studied several times. Mr. Mustafa directed the autocarriage to the left, speeding into the curve. He slowed to avoid striking the cart in front of them. "Do you know this building? What it is?"

Clementine removed her elbow from its prop and sat up straight. "No."

"It's the Jama Masjid, the largest mosque in all of India."

"A mosque." Clementine tried the foreign word to suss out its meaning.

"It's holy ground. Sacred space."

"Like a church or a consecrated place."

"For Muslims like me." At a T in the road, Mr. Mustafa chose the right-hand fork at the back corner of the mosque.

Clementine cradled her palms in her lap. "When we met, I thought I'd offended you. You never look me in the eye. Then you break the traditions you're comfortable with to tell me about your family and educate me about your places of worship."

Mr. Mustafa steered the autocarriage down the next left-hand avenue. The cart continued along their former path, and now they drove behind a fellow steam-run vehicle. "India is a place of many people. In number. In traditions. In histories and futures. I must sometimes put aside my discomforts to try to keep everyone together."

"Is there a danger of so many different people pulling apart?" Back home, she had seen this, too, between groups. Would India suffer the same fate? Had it already? Or did it hold a solution that could be used to benefit the world?

"Always this problem exists. How do we cohabitate in peace? What does one person do that brings people together? What do you or I do that break us apart? These are questions we must ask, or everything will crumble."

"Mr. Longshaw said in the East, people know how they feel about you right away."

"This is true. Are you my friend or my enemy? Do you wish to harm me or help me?"

"But with questions like that, doesn't it push people away and separate them?"

"This is why we inquire, to get closer to the unreachable bottom of everything. I may mean well to every person I meet, but do they respect me?"

"At home, we call that hoping for the best and planning for the worst."

"Yes, that's it. Your country interests me."

Guilt snaked through Clementine's chest. She avoided mentioning how Mr. Mustafa would likely be treated in America. "We have our problems, too. With different peoples."

"When you meet these different peoples, do you wish them good things?"

"I do."

"Then you are part of the solution. You act from here." Mr. Mustafa took one hand off the wheel and patted his heart.

"Do you think that's the problem? Not enough people listen to their hearts?"

"Feelings are how we know friend from foe. I didn't judge you based on your appearance but on how you presented yourself. How you treated me and others. The British who rule this country act from here." Mr. Mustafa tapped his temple. "To be smart is good. It can save you when your emotions are confused or misguided. But they behave as if logic as cold as snow will save us. Whether they believe this or not, it's in every move they make."

"So I should follow my heart unless I know otherwise."

"Are you comfortable with that?"

"I think so."

The autocarriage in front of them came to rest, and Mr. Mustafa stopped their vehicle as well. He glanced toward Clementine. "The reason I don't meet your eyes is also a difference in custom. In Afghanistan, it would dishonor you. I only talk to you because we were introduced by men and we work together. Even in this country, you have to understand. The women are still coming out of hiding, from behind curtains, veils, and closed doors. They're not as free as you, but they're finding an independence they haven't known before."

The vehicle ahead bounced forward, and Mr. Mustafa lent the autocarriage gradual speed. As they crawled along, they passed a cow munching on grass at roadside, its eyes lost on some distant point.

Clementine unfolded Milton's note. "What can you tell me about Nivriti Singh? Have you met this person?"

"Yes. I accompanied Mr. Milton when he first presented the idea for the beauty treatment to potential investors."

"That was several years ago."

"I have a good memory."

"You must. How many languages do you know?" Clementine tapped one boot against the other. She must remember not to pry into Mr. Mustafa's life so much.

"I'm fluent in Pashto and Dari from Afghanistan. When I came to India, my teachers taught me Hindi, Urdu, and English."

Clementine diverted the conversation away from divulging her answer to the same question. "What do you think of changing the course of the company's research? Do you think we'll succeed?"

Mr. Mustafa responded slowly. "To reverse the relentless flow of time would seem a miracle. The world is short on these right now."

He turned the autocarriage into a long, paved driveway and continued through an open iron gate. Trees and flowers in full bloom decorated the front lawn. Bold, scarlet poinsettias clustered together. Pastel-pink rhododendrons loaded down thick, expansive bushes. Chrysanthemums flourished in white, dusky rose, and tangerine orange. Clementine marveled at them. She had left Nashville with a light dusting of snow covering every barren tree. Mr. Mustafa parked in front of the carriage house.

Out the window rose a peach-colored, two-story house. In Clementine's estimation, it stretched half the size of a mansion. Panic sparked through her. "We're here?"

"This is where Mrs. Singh lives."

"Is there anything I need to know about her?"

"Greet her as she greets you. Her husband died five years ago, and she remains here with some of her family. Let me translate for you. She speaks not a word of English, although I'm sure she understands more than she admits."

"Try not to say *thank you*," Clementine coached herself.

Mr. Mustafa climbed out and took a brisk walk around the vehicle. He opened Clementine's door, and she used the inner grab bar to steady herself on the way down.

She nodded to Mr. Mustafa, keeping the unneeded phrase of gratitude from bursting out of her mouth. "I hope to repay your hospitality."

He offered a short bow. For the first time, humor and approval twinkled in his amber eyes. "Come. I'll introduce you to Mrs. Singh."

"Do you think she'll like what I have to say?" Clementine tucked the list of names into her coat pocket.

Mr. Mustafa took the path through the garden. "I don't know." He put his pince-nez glasses in their case and tucked it in his pocket. "She has an agreeable personality, and she's fond of visitors."

Clementine looked ahead to the entrance. Several stairs led up to a shallow alcove, flanked by columns topped with a scalloped arch. Painted purple lotuses, ruby roses, and pink lilies graced the façade alongside the columns and followed the arch's ascent to its peak. "This is a far cry from visiting neighbors back home and sitting on their shady porches."

Mr. Mustafa patted the left side of his chest, and Clementine nodded. *Follow my heart.* He knocked on the door.

Clementine fired hushed questions at him. "Do I take my shoes off? What about my hat and coat? What if she offers me something to drink?"

Mr. Mustafa peered at her, bridging the handful of inches between their heights. His mouth bent in slight amusement. "Breathe. That's all you need to do."

The door opened. A man regarded them dressed in white from his neat turban to his kurta and pants. His bare feet widened Clementine's eyes. She had not expected it in such a fancy house, seeming at odds with the exotic, patterned wooden floor beneath his toes.

Mr. Mustafa bowed his head over pressed palms. *"Namaskar."* It was the first and only word he spoke that Clementine recognized.

The man in the house mimicked the gesture, and Clementine gave it back.

The barefooted man responded as he backed up from the doorway.

Mr. Mustafa explained in low, respectful tones. "This man is one of their servants. He'll take us to the room where we'll converse with Mrs. Singh."

He stepped into the foyer, and Clementine followed him. Dark wooden columns served as doorjambs to adjoining rooms. They softened the corners of the golden walls where the foyer expanded into a sitting area on the left. A stone fountain stood in the middle of the room, bathed in filtered sunlight. Clementine followed it upward past two stories of balconies. In the ceiling high above them, a large, square hole opened the house to the sky, barred only by angled slats of wood. Clementine imagined, with the gadgetry she had already seen in India, the servants being able to adjust the slats to keep out rain or errant breezes.

The servant closed the door and led them into the room on their right. A lavish couch and several chairs added pops of purple against walls the color of robins' eggs. A rug woven in many hues covered the center of the floor, the visible tiles around it just as engaging in their simpler pattern. The servant spoke to Mr. Mustafa and whisked out of sight across the foyer.

Mr. Mustafa waved a hand at the couch and chairs. "Take a seat wherever you like."

Clementine claimed the armchair closest to her, and Mr. Mustafa accepted the next chair. Clementine hesitated to move but unbuttoned her coat. Letting herself become overheated in the house's comfortable air would not do.

A second servant in the same outfit, younger with a thin moustache, emerged from the foyer. He balanced a tray replete with a silver tea set. The nearer he carried it, the more detail Clementine could discern in its design. Dozens of leaves sprouted from long, curving stems to cover the pot, the sugar bowl, the creamer, the cups, and their saucers. She had never seen anything like it except the one Edith Higginbotham had pointed out in her father's house.

Her house.

The servant deposited the tray on the wooden coffee table in the center of the rug. He lifted the teapot. *"Chai?"*

Mr. Mustafa leaned forward in his chair. *"Haan.* He offers us tea."

Clementine slid off her gloves and held them in her lap. "Yes, please."

Mr. Mustafa wobbled his head.

The servant poured a sienna-brown liquid into two silver cups. *"Cheeni? Doodh?"*

"Ji. Would you like sugar or milk, Miss Fitzgerald?"

"However you prefer it. I'm sure I've never had this kind before."

"Haan."

With small tongs, the servant deposited a sugar cube in each cup and poured in a splash of milk. He handed the cups on saucers to Clementine and Mr. Mustafa. The tea's steam was lucky to rise, as ladened down as it was with spices and sweetness. Clementine blew ripples across the tea to cool it down.

Footsteps snapped her attention to the doorway. A woman glided in, a scarf covering her head. Deep wrinkles etched her face like the branches of a tree forming shapes against the sky. A topaz jewel sparkled from one nostril. Her sari folded around her in magenta and midnight blue, the length of it edged in swirling gold. The short sleeves of her white blouse bared her arms, where bangles glittered from her wrists.

Mr. Mustafa stood up. *"Namaskar."*

Clementine mirrored his greeting.

Youth glittered in the old woman's dark eyes. She rested herself in the middle of the couch across from her visitors, who settled back into their chairs. The servant performed a quick job of filling the third cup with tea. He added sugar and a dollop of milk. The old woman accepted it, and the servant dismissed himself. He closed the double doors as he reached the foyer, shutting in the trio without him.

The old woman delivered a short monologue, a grin wavering on her lips.

Mr. Mustafa addressed Clementine. "This is Mrs. Singh. She sent out all of her relatives and bribed the servants not to tell so she could wear one of her old saris for us. It's Hindu custom for widows to wear white and keep to themselves. She knew she was meeting someone new and didn't want to scare you. She wanted to be her radiant self again."

Clementine darkened. For Mrs. Singh to plan for her, Milton must have plotted to send Clementine on these errands when he made the appointments. Nivriti's wish reminded Clementine of her intentions for the anti-aging formula, however, an encouraging opportunity. She licked her lips and balanced her cup on its saucer to keep from spilling.

"I'm going to introduce you to her now." Mr. Mustafa switched languages, and the only words Clementine understood were her own name and her father's.

Nivriti beamed, her interest roaming over Clementine from her hat to her shoes. She replied, and Clementine waited for Mr. Mustafa to translate.

"Mrs. Singh is honored to meet you. You resemble your father very much, and she's sorry for his passing. She had a lot of respect for him because he always respected the Indian people. She's pleased to serve you in her home."

Clementine scooted forward in her seat. "Tell Mrs. Singh I'm excited to taste her delicious-smelling tea. I'm taking over for my father at the company, and I have many of his same qualifications. I've worked with herbal cures since I was small."

Mr. Mustafa's translation made her message sound lyrical and smooth. He gave Mrs. Singh the chance to answer and changed to English for Clementine. "She wants to know if you've been in India long."

Clementine blinked at the departure from her business subject. "Less than two weeks."

"When was the last time you saw your father? Mrs. Singh remembers he'd been in the country for a few years."

Clementine stammered. "Not in a long while."

"And she wants to know how your father died."

Clementine sipped her tea for lack of a better option. Full, creamy liquid swirled biting spices and depth of flavor around her tongue. She swallowed and took another drink before she found the stamina to respond. "It was an accident. At the house. He fell. Didn't you know?"

"I did, but Mrs. Singh directed her inquiry to you." Mr. Mustafa reverted to Nivriti's native language.

The old woman shook her head and replied.

Mr. Mustafa sipped his tea. "She wants to know if you've also made your living by plants as your father did."

"Yes, I practiced herbal medicine in my home country. Why does she want to know so much about me?"

"Indians are eager to learn about everybody." Mr. Mustafa translated Clementine's answer for Mrs. Singh and vice versa. "Did you make much money? Were you successful?"

Clementine bristled but remembered her task in Nivriti's house. To gain the woman's cooperation in keeping her investment for a different reason than originally intended. "I made enough to live on. I eventually saved enough money to move us from the country to the city."

Mr. Mustafa rattled off Clementine's message in foreign words.

Nivriti took a prolonged sip of tea. She perched the cup and saucer on the coffee table. She spoke briefly in the same language.

"Mrs. Singh is ready to discuss business. What has brought us here about her investment?"

Clementine relegated her cup and saucer to the table as well, her strained nerves clinking the pieces together. "Mrs. Singh. My father, Mr. Longshaw, and I recognize your faith in our company's goals. We're giving our best efforts to earn you the biggest profit we can. But we've decided to make a different Fountain of Youth." She crossed one ankle over the other and swung it back again. "It's no longer a beauty treatment. It's a serum for good health. It'll reverse aging, if you will. I want to know if you're all right supporting this change at Fitzgerald and Longshaw. The company my father built with his friend."

Mr. Mustafa spoke at length.

Nivriti's pleasant countenance drew down into a thoughtful frown. She murmured a response, peeling the headscarf off. Only the barest stubble of grey hairs covered her head.

"Mrs. Singh asks why she, an ostracized widow forced to shave off her hair, would seek to extend her life."

Clementine closed her eyes. "I don't know. Maybe to spend more time with her children or enjoy better health."

Mustafa passed on Clementine's message and translated Nivriti's retort. "Her children rebuke her. Only through the insistence of her widowed sister and herself has she retained any quality of life."

Clementine slumped. Dressing well and adorning oneself was not an invitation to extend one's life. She should have asked more questions and discovered Nivriti's deeper needs.

Mr. Mustafa continued. "But she can see why many other people would prefer a cure instead of a lotion for bad skin."

Clementine met Nivriti's glowing gaze. "She'll keep her funding with the company?"

"Her late husband served as a soldier, and after that, a spice merchant. He spared no effort in his business, and as you've witnessed, he became quite successful. Mrs. Singh understands the value of plants. She trusts in the holistic powers of Ayurveda and the healing herbs it suggests. She wants to know if you believe you can invent such a remedy."

Clementine clasped her hands over her knees. "I know we can." The small, nagging creep of doubt tugged at the back of her mind, but she ignored it.

An animated exchange with Nivriti left Mr. Mustafa smiling. "Mrs. Singh will leave her money with the company. She considers it well invested. She prays to the goddess Lakshmi to bless your undertakings and shower you with abundance."

The word blurted out before Clementine could stop it. "Thank–" She reoriented herself. "Tell Mrs. Singh I pray the same for her."

Mr. Mustafa articulated this, and Nivriti stood up. Clementine gathered her gloves from her lap before she rose to her feet. Mr. Mustafa rested his cup and saucer on the coffee table as he reached his full height.

Nivriti placed her palms together and shook them with excitement. *"Namaste."*

Mr. Mustafa echoed her farewell. "It means the same as *namaskar*. You can use either word you wish."

Clementine pushed her palms together in front of her. *"Namaskar."* Best to learn one word at a time and perfect it.

Nivriti pulled on a cord by the wall, and within seconds, the original servant parted the room's double doors. He led Clementine and Mr. Mustafa through the shifting patches of sunlight in the foyer. He opened the front door, and Clementine trailed Mr. Mustafa into the garden.

She blew out a breath, relieved and exhilarated. "We did it. Two appointments to go."

They traversed between the sweet, fragrant blossoms and climbed into the autocarriage. Mr. Mustafa arranged his pince-nez glasses on his nose before he powered up the engine.

Clementine pulled her gloves on. "This is why I'll never get used to this side of the world. It's intrusive for me to ask about your family, and it's rude where I come from to ask a stranger about their finances."

"In this country, so is rushing into talk of business." Mr. Mustafa's lips perked up. "Such is India."

Chapter Five

Clementine pulled out the paper with her appointment names on it, slightly wrinkled from its captivity in her pocket. *Udit Varma.* "What can you tell me about our next investor?"

"Mr. Udit often travels for work and will likely be elsewhere. If that's the case, we're to meet with his wife. She administers their household with his wishes in mind and should be able to impart a decision to us."

Mr. Mustafa turned the vehicle around in the driveway and drove out through the gate. At the street, he chose the way from which they had approached. After several minutes, he curved left past the street leading to the Jama Masjid. He directed them between animals, people on foot, and other vehicles competing for road space.

When Mr. Mustafa pulled into another fenced compound, Clementine could not discern which force was winning her inner battle. Part of her wanted the day hurried through and over. The other half hoped to prolong it until its duties fell to someone else. Milton had made these contacts. Surely, meeting with an already trusted businessman appealed more to investors than expressing condolences to his late partner's daughter.

The house greeted her in rich, rustic brown. Mr. Mustafa let Clementine down from the autocarriage, and she followed him to the grand entrance. Pillars and high arches formed the alcove shielding the passageway from the elements. Mr. Mustafa rapped on the door.

Nervous jitters spurred Clementine to tap her foot. "Do the Varmas have servants, too?"

"They did before."

The door swung open, and astonishment widened Clementine's eyes. This man wore the same white attire as the servants at Nivriti's house.

A man called out from inside where Clementine could not see him.

Mr. Mustafa's jaw twitched. "He wants to know who's at the door." He explained in the same sounds Clementine had heard at Nivriti's, gesturing with his hands.

A man in a turquoise kurta and pants shouldered his way into the doorway. He knocked the servant aside and locked eyes with Mr. Mustafa. They exchanged sentences, the stranger waving a hand at Clementine.

She clutched her coat. "Is something wrong?"

Mr. Mustafa paused his persistence in the foreign language. "It's a small problem. Mr. Udit's son, Nishil, refuses to deal with the British. I'm in the process of explaining you're American."

Clementine breathed out desperation and stress. "I'm as American as Mr. Longshaw, and he found his way in."

The man raised his nose at her. *"Safed."*

Mr. Mustafa snorted. "He's being stubborn because British or American, you're white."

"Not completely." Clementine patted her chest. "My country has Indians, too. Natives of our land mistreated by others. Some of these Indians were my ancestors."

Mr. Mustafa translated until soprano chatter from inside flew out the gaping doorway. Two women squeezed into the passage at Nishil's sides, and Clementine's shoulders fell limp.

Mr. Mustafa presented the prayer pose of his hands. *"Namaste."* To Clementine, he added, "The woman on the right is Mr. Udit's wife, Padma."

The woman was nothing if not statuesque, a lime-green sari wrapped around the curves of her body. A matching scarf covered her raven locks, silver hairs decorating them like the veins of feathers. She wore twice as much jewelry as Nivriti, her earrings and nose decoration shimmering. Bangles clanked from her wrists and ankles.

Padma raised her eyebrows at Mr. Mustafa, and he repeated his explanation.

She clapped her hands together, staring at him with wide, brown eyes. *"Bhartiya?"*

Mr. Mustafa shook his head. *"Amriki nivasi."*

"Kaafi hai." Padma bowed to her son, murmuring to him. Despite her patient eyes, her jaw tensed.

Nishil threw his hands up and stalked into the house. The woman on his other side, a few years younger than him and outfitted in a blush-pink sari, scurried after him.

Clementine remained awed and humbled in Padma's presence. "I didn't mean to cause a fight."

Mr. Mustafa deliberated with Padma and turned toward Clementine. "All is well with Mrs. Varma. She settled things with her son. She's arguing in your favor because in her eyes, Native American and native Indian are close enough."

Padma formed the prayer pose, her eyes shining at Clementine. *"Namaste."*

Clementine repeated the motion. *"Namaskar."*

Mr. Mustafa stepped forward. "Let's go in."

Padma retreated into the foyer, and Clementine tailed Mr. Mustafa into the long room. Padma led them the full length of it. The front door closed behind them, and Clementine peered over her shoulder. The servant who had answered Mr. Mustafa's knocks secured the door and went on his way. Padma took a large wool shawl from a wall hook and spread it around her body. She opened the door at the back end of the foyer, and the trio filed out into a courtyard.

Windowed walls rose up on all sides to two or sometimes three stories. The air hung calm and still, even as Padma closed the door. She folded her arms under her amethyst-colored shawl, pulling it in around her. She spoke, and Mr. Mustafa translated.

"She apologizes for the cold. She doesn't know what else to do. Any room in the house might make her family suspect she's hiding her dealings with us from them. Her husband, as I suspected, is tending to his business. She only wishes to honor her husband and family as well as Mr. Udit's investment with the company."

"That's very kind." Clementine scrambled for another topic with which to break the ice. "She must be thankful for a son who cares about his family's wellbeing as much as he does. Will you tell her for me?"

Mr. Mustafa bobbed his head at Padma, the foreign words tumbling from his lips.

Padma ducked her head and shifted the shawl's fabric around her elegant neck. Her words eluded Clementine's grasp.

"She hopes she can repay your understanding. Mr. Nishil is very protective, indeed. She asks if you have any children, if you're married."

Clementine cleared her throat. "I'm not married. No children."

Mr. Mustafa conveyed this to Padma and iterated her response. "She wishes you much happiness and success in seeking a husband. She prays you'll have only contented, loyal children. She wants to know if women in your country often put off marriage as you have."

Clementine blinked. The day's questions certainly granted Mr. Mustafa an education in her personal life. "Some of my friends married before they were twenty." Ginger-haired May Johnson had wed her cousin at sixteen. Sly, silver-tongued Judson Lloyd had lived up to his impulsive reputation – or cemented it – by marrying an eighteen-year-old blonde three weeks after she arrived in Livingston. They fought as strongly as they loved, and within as many months, she packed up for Memphis.

Mr. Mustafa exchanged a few lines with Padma. "How much do you know about your Indian family?"

Clementine felt right back in the small cabin sandwiched between woods and farmers' fields. She could almost reach through time and touch the thick, cotton quilt on her mother's bed. "My great-great-grandmother on my mother's side was full-blooded Shawnee."

Mr. Mustafa relayed this to Padma and shared her reply. "Mrs. Varma wants to express how truly sorry she is you've lost your father. The passing of her own father was particularly painful as she adored him very much. It would've devastated her mother had she not passed away several years before."

Clementine lowered her head. "I'm sorry for her losses as well."

"She wishes to know if your mother's still alive."

Clementine's answer came out hoarse with worry. "Yes, she is."

"How is she bearing the news of your father's death?"

Clementine's eyes roamed the stone paths under their feet. A fountain stood behind Padma, its white paint chipping along the lip. Decorated ceramic pots held miniature trees in various corners of the courtyard. Benches offered cobalt-blue, cardinal-red, and grass-green resting places. Clementine arrived where she had started, at Mr. Mustafa's inquiry. She folded her hands behind her back. "My mother's strong. She'll handle it with sadness and eventually acceptance, as we all have."

Mr. Mustafa translated this for Padma. "You may approach your business now, Miss Fitzgerald. We know it's hard for you to ruminate on such things."

Clementine nodded. "Mrs. Varma, I'd like to inform you in all honesty that we're changing the product we make at the company. I know your husband agreed to fund a beauty cream, but we're pursuing a more complicated elixir. One that can truly reverse the effects of aging from the inside rather than outside."

Mr. Mustafa explained this, and Clementine tried to draw each breath as normal. Sometimes she forgot to take one or let one sit in her lungs for too long.

The skin wrinkled between Padma's arched, well-defined brows. Her frantic eyes examined Clementine as she took a step back. She fired off several questions.

Mr. Mustafa retained his professional, even cadence. "Mrs. Varma's concerned because she was eager for the skin treatment. How exactly would the serum work?"

Clementine pinched at her coat's loose fabric. "It'd help the body be more efficient. By strengthening one's health and providing a barrier against disease, I'm confident the outcome will restore vitality and youthfulness to those who drink it."

"Without your father here to conduct the research, she's sure her husband will inquire about your credentials."

"I've learned from my father all my life. I've dedicated myself to the best uses of medicinal plants. I helped many families where I lived in Tennessee."

Mr. Mustafa spoke to Padma. Her eyes popped in interest, and she rubbed her lips together. She responded quickly, and Mr. Mustafa clarified it for Clementine. "She wonders if you could recommend herbs for some particular ailments."

"Of course. I only know ones that grow in the United States, but I'm sure the British brought many of them here."

"She asks about pain, muscle weakness, numbness, sinus problems, and skin sores."

Chickweed. Nettle. Dandelion. Spearmint. "I can help those conditions." Clementine gave Padma a light assessment, but the woman seemed to stand in comfort. She did not sniffle or sound congested. Before she had snuggled up in her shawl, Clementine had not noticed any ulcers on her hands or throat. Perhaps the illnesses spread across the range of family members who lived with her.

Mr. Mustafa reassured Padma, eliciting a gasp of relief.

Clementine acknowledged her responsibility to gather further details. "Can she tell me more about who the herbs are for? Their ages or added problems that afflict them."

Mr. Mustafa entered another exchange with Padma. "She doesn't think it's necessary. It's for someone she knows. There are no other problems she's aware of."

Padma nibbled the inside of her lip.

Clementine melted. "It's obviously important. I brought some herbs with me in case I needed them. If Mrs. Varma trusts me and is willing to put her faith in plants that might be unfamiliar, I'll personally bring her the herbs I recommend."

Mr. Mustafa rattled the suggestion off to Padma.

She clasped her hands in front of her shawl, brown eyes glittering anew. *"Bahut dhanyavaad."*

Mr. Mustafa watched Clementine, waiting.

A spark of understanding flared in Clementine's head. "She's thanking me."

His voice warmed ever so slightly. "Yes."

Padma continued, and Mr. Mustafa translated. "She'll tell her husband of the change and recommend he keep his money invested. She hopes she can repay you for your generosity with the herbs."

"Mrs. Varma owes me nothing. I appreciate her support of the Fountain of Youth, no matter which product it describes."

Mr. Mustafa repeated this to Padma, and she led them into the house. They traversed the long foyer, and a servant appeared on hurried feet to open the front door.

Clementine searched his complexion, hands, and feet. All smooth and unmarked. His movements fast, effortless, and precise. "Please tell Mrs. Varma I'll be back as soon as I can. No one should suffer longer than they have to."

Mr. Mustafa imparted this to Padma, and Clementine followed him out into the alcove.

When the servant had closed the door, Clementine consulted Mr. Mustafa. "How did I do?"

He held back from letting his gaze glint too brightly. "You're a quick study. I see how you know so much at such a young age."

"You left your home country earlier than I did. And you know more languages at a younger age than my father. You must be the same way."

Chapter Six

Mr. Mustafa directed the autocarriage into familiar territory. The Jama Masjid's grand architecture felt less imposing each time Clementine passed it, but it impressed her all the same. She recognized the extensive thoroughfare she had walked to get home three days before, and they rode in the same direction. North.

Clementine recovered her list of names, earning new creases each time she stored it in her pocket. "Does Lowell Dodd live in Civil Lines?"

"Along with the other Englishmen, their wives, daughters, and you few Americans."

"Do any white or mostly white people live outside that part of the city?"

"Tourists, maybe. For a week or two."

Nishil's outrage at finding a seemingly white woman outside his house echoed in Clementine's ears. "I understand. Serious tensions furrow at home, too."

Clementine scanned the list even though she did not need to. Mr. Mustafa, Nivriti, and Padma had all been perfectly pleasant and welcoming. They had taught her things about their cultures and their needs. Clementine wished she could show them more gratefulness than she was able, but Lowell's name pulled at her. Not a fellow countryman but a native English speaker nonetheless. Her first one since saying goodbye to Bryce an hour before. Had it only been an hour? Guilt prodded Clementine for being so relieved to meet with someone closer to her own culture, but she tried to comfort herself. It was natural to cling to what she knew, to want to return to a more similar culture than the unknown complexities of the East, and talk without the necessity of an interpreter for almost every word.

This realization emerged with awkward disappointment when Clementine mentioned it. "I won't need you to translate for me."

Mr. Mustafa glanced over from his vigilance through the windshield. "Will you miss me?"

Clementine wondered at him. Was that humor? "I think I will. I'm used to hearing everything said twice now and waiting for you to tell me the other person's answer."

Solemnity darkened him. "I'll be close by."

"Do you think I'll be in danger?"

"It's not likely. But for a woman to be alone with a man who's not her husband…"

Clementine guessed at his meaning. "It's improper. In Afghanistan?"

"Yes."

Clementine folded up her page of names and tucked it away for the final time. She snuck a small smile at Mr. Mustafa. "People disapprove of it where I come from, too." A new thought made her frown. "Will they mistreat you in Civil Lines the way Nishil Varma wanted to bar me from his house?"

"No. They'll tolerate me because I'm with you."

Clementine tried not to stare at Mr. Mustafa, although she could hardly feel surprised. She had just expected more from her fellow citizens of the world. "I can walk the rest of the way if it's a problem. I won't have them be rude to you."

"Not to worry." Mr. Mustafa flexed his fingers away from the top of the wheel, stretching and resetting them around the leather grip. "Once they realize I'm a temporary fixture, they'll serve me manners and tea the same as you."

Clementine hoped for his sake he was exaggerating, even to the smallest degree. She watched out the window as the boxy, European houses surrounded them. An occasional rounded corner or elongated balcony was scarcely enough to make them represent India. The white walls, burgundy bricks, and other neutral colors loomed a far cry from the bold blues, reds, and purples Clementine had drunk in earlier that morning.

Mr. Mustafa drove past the turnoff for Clementine's house and veered right. With one more left-hand curve, he slowed the autocarriage. He parked in the driveway of a clean, white two-story house in crisp, straight lines. Several balconies appeared around the upper floor. Below them, the garden flourished in crimsons and golds.

Clementine allowed Mr. Mustafa to walk around the vehicle and open her door. Used to riding alone during her rare travels in personal carriages, she remained unaccustomed to the tradition.

For once, Mr. Mustafa stayed at her side on the path to the sheltered porch. Clementine could only assume he judged it the best position in which to accompany her. In front, he was out of place in this neighborhood. Behind her, he failed her as a capable escort. Beside her suited Clementine fine, but she gathered she should neglect to acknowledge it.

She spoke in a hush as they reached the steps to the broad wooden porch. "If anyone shows you discourtesy, let me know. I can't abide it. You're my guide and my colleague."

Mr. Mustafa made use of the polished metal knocker. Acceptance mixed with disapproval in his eyes.

She whispered even more quietly. "I'm sorry. I'm sure you can fight your own battles. I just…"

The door latch clicked. Clementine swallowed the rest of her words along with her fears. Her misgivings and her hopes had no place here. She came on business, and she would conduct it to the best of her ability.

She opened her mouth to greet whoever answered the door. A flash of brilliant white clothing rendered her mute. A short, young Indian man bowed to the visitors. Clementine sought out his feet, which once again proved uncovered.

Mr. Mustafa greeted the servant, and Clementine mirrored him.

The servant ushered them inside, uttering words Clementine could not understand.

Mr. Mustafa stepped in ahead of her. "Mr. Dodd will be along soon."

"He's not here?" Numerous concerns flew through Clementine's head. Would they have to sit and wait? Would the servant dismiss them to visit another day? What if Lowell Dodd's late arrival led to a brusque, inefficient meeting that ended in him pulling his funding from the Fountain of Youth?

"His servant assures me he'll arrive."

Clementine moved into the foyer. "How does he know?"

A woman's silken British accent sailed in from the next room. "My husband always does as he says he will. He's anticipated this appointment all week."

Clementine's cheeks caught fire. Of course in this house her English words were no longer secrets. Clementine worked to hold her head upright. The foyer wrapped around her in four white walls striped with cornflower blue. A living room opened on Clementine's right, where the woman approached. Her stiff dress' cerulean fabric and alabaster apron made her the foyer's living counterpart. Bright azure eyes twinkled with curiosity.

Clementine let herself relax, acting as if she were right back in Tennessee. "Forgive me. I'm sure he'll be here any minute."

The woman flicked her eyes to the servant. "Close the door and bring the tea, Sandeep."

He secured the portal closed and scurried off into a room on the left.

The woman elevated her thin, black eyebrows at Clementine. "You like tea, don't you?"

Clementine inched toward the living room. "Yes, thank you."

"I'm Daisy, by the way. Such a shame about your father. Lowell got on with him all right."

Clementine bit back a heated comment. "I'm glad to hear it. I hope Mr. Dodd accepts what I have to say with the same respect."

Daisy raised her palms in defeat. "Best to save it for Lowell. I don't have a head for this business of business. If you'll come with me, I can show you to Lowell's study. I know he wants to talk to you in private."

Clementine sought out Mr. Mustafa, who remained behind her. "I won't be long."

Mr. Mustafa bowed his head. "I won't be far."

Clementine hesitated as she joined Daisy. "Mr. Mustafa's my interpreter. He's been very helpful with my appointments so far."

Daisy's wide lips teetered in a wobbly line. "How nice. We'll ensure he's comfortable."

Clementine followed Daisy through the living room, its white cushions on dark furniture reminding her of her father's décor. They entered a narrow passageway, where Daisy led Clementine into a room on the right.

Clementine found it larger than expected. A massive desk occupied the middle, set over a rug woven with bamboo and elephants. Two rattan chairs pointed at each other across the long edges of the desk. Shelves spanned the left-hand wall, exhibiting all manner of collectibles and photographs. Silver flasks, ivory tusks, one-handled pitchers, colored bottles, carved animal figurines, small plants, assorted books, a white-and-orange conch shell about five inches long, and a box of cigars. Straight across the room, an arched window framed a lovely view of the flowering garden backed by hazy mist. Over her shoulder, Clementine found a shallow case mounted to the wall. Pins tacked three dozen taxidermied butterflies to the backboard, their hued wings ranging from goldenrod to earth brown to azure sky. Beneath it, a tray supported various glass and crystal liquor bottles on a small cabinet.

Daisy gestured to the seat across the desk. "Make yourself at home. I'll have Lowell come right in when he arrives."

"Thank you."

Daisy whirled out of the office, and Clementine sank into the chair. She perused the photographs on the shelves now that she sat closer to them. Most of them showed Daisy along with a fair-haired man, his large ears protruding from the sides of his head. Many of their pictures included up to four children. The remaining photographs captured the man by himself or with other men in suits. One of these pictures placed him in front of a tavern, beaming beside seven or eight others. All of them thrust hearty pints of dark liquid into the air.

A door closed across the house, and Clementine shot her gaze to the doorway. Bassy murmurs made her sit up straighter. If Lowell Dodd had gone out of his way to keep this appointment, she was prepared to present her best.

The throaty timbre laughed like the muted resoundings of a piano key in its lower register. The servant who had opened the door rushed into the office, setting a tray on the desk. The man from the photographs walked in, short like Daisy and wide with muscles under his sand-colored suit. The servant lifted the teapot, but the man brushed him away.

The servant retreated with a bow, and the remaining man closed the door. His presence intimidated Clementine, a worldly man like her father's travels had made him. She stood up to be courteous, but he spoke before she could.

"Lowell Dodd." His voice rumbled like a jungle cat's gradual growl. He had the same musical accent as his wife. "It's lovely to meet you. Please, sit."

Clementine made herself comfortable in the chair. "Mr. Longshaw must've told you about me."

"He did." Lowell wandered to the wooden cabinet beneath the butterfly case and selected a crystal decanter filled with glowing, ruby contents. "Would you like a glass of port? I brought it back with me from England the last time I was there."

"No, thank you."

Lowell opened the cabinet and fetched a short-stemmed glass. "I didn't think so. It's not quite noon. Perhaps your job isn't quite as demanding as mine or you put up with the tension better."

Ask for more information or flatter him? Clementine felt the direction of the meeting slipping from her control, but it seemed more important to reassure him than herself. He had the decision to make. She only needed to steer him toward the path she wanted him to take. She squared her shoulders to loosen them. "No matter what you do, Mr. Dodd, you have a lovely home. I'm sure your wife appreciates your labors."

Lowell set the glass on the desk. "More so than the children, I'm afraid."

Clementine motioned to the photographs she had been admiring or trying to learn from. "Are these your children? Do you have any others?"

"Four are quite enough." Lowell poured half a glass of port, then added another two splashes. "Tea for you?"

"Yes, please."

"You can tell me about your voyage, your indoctrination into your father's company, or simply launch into business." Lowell fit the stopper into the decanter's mouth, its multi-faceted ball flashing with opalescence. "I know I'm not your first appointment, and I also know the natives are keen on discussing other matters before facts and figures."

"However you prefer it. You're my last appointment of the day. I have nowhere else to be if you'd like to hear about my adventures."

Lowell set the decanter on the cabinet. He sat down across the desk from Clementine and picked up the creamer. "Milk?"

"Sure."

Lowell poured it into two of the teacups. "Your schedule appeals to me more than mine does."

Clementine scrambled to her defense lest he assume her lazy or negligent. "It's the timeline Mr. Longshaw worked out for me. I'll be putting in much fuller days from now on. We have a lot of work to do."

"And something important to tell me about it." Lowell traded the creamer for a long-handled metal strainer. He held its small mesh basket over one of the cups and dispensed tea from the pot through it. His dark blue eyes darted to Clementine. "Your father conducted himself the same way. Very professional. Jovial but serious. Practical. He always dealt with the big issues himself, never relegated them to a lesser employee."

Her stomach soured, but Clementine pushed on. "It's my goal to earn your trust as well as my father did."

"I always thought Americans were charming. You're like us but not like us." Lowell strained a helping of tea into the second cup. "When you go in, you go all in. You're almost inherently compelled to design creative solutions to every problem. And you mix cultures with the best of us."

"I certainly hope we'll find all the solutions we need at Fitzgerald and Longshaw."

"You're keeping the name? That's understandable. People know it, it works for you, and it saves you money. All very important." Lowell passed a cup on a saucer to Clementine.

She sipped at the caramel-colored liquid, bitter entwined with sweet. Simpler than the flavor at Nivriti's but just as effective. "I have a little English on my mother's side."

"Do you?" Lowell slid the tea tray to the side. "How nice."

Clementine wet her parched mouth with a generous drink of tea. "I'd like to talk to you about the project."

"Yes, from the day Milton mentioned it to me, my wife was intrigued. We were sitting right in this office. The woman's borne me four children. The least I can do is invest in a product she'd eagerly use. She's still beautiful, isn't she? But if she chooses to pamper herself with creams and potions, well..." Lowell tasted his port. "Who am I to stand in her way? Just because I have no need of such things is no indication of their worth. Am I right?"

Clementine reeled. Was his heart set on the beauty product? Was Daisy's? She avoided the photographs of their children and shifted in her seat. "I agree. That's the exact purpose of my visit. Mr. Longshaw and I agreed to change what the Fountain of Youth does."

"Oh?" His pale brows lifted into his wide forehead. "What to?"

Clementine made herself say it. "A medical serum that reverses the effects of aging."

Lowell sipped his tea and shook off the effects of it mingling with the port. "From beauty to science."

"Yes, sir."

"A bold move. Especially since your father championed a complexion enhancer. I would've guessed it the other way around. And after years of work on the former idea."

"The team worked hard on the beauty cream, but we're confident we can build on the research we have to churn out the new product without much delay. The factory's facilities seem capable of the change."

Lowell enjoyed more of his port, lowering the line of its garnet color in the glass. "Do you know Edwin Lutyens?"

"I don't recognize the name. Is he another patron?"

Lowell grinned, summing her up. "He's a patron of sorts, although not of Fitzgerald and Longshaw. Maybe India is a patron for him. Anyway, Milton didn't tell you what I do for a living?"

"No."

"You see, Delhi is a small and desolate place. But five years ago – six now, with the new year – the British Crown proclaimed brilliant plans for it. It'll be expanded and built up heavily to the south. It won't be a city anymore. It'll be its country's capital. The jewel in the crown of the British empire. Some call it the future Rome of Asia. Edwin and his friend of many years, Herbert Baker, head the team of architects responsible for this. My job is to manage and oversee the execution of this transformation."

Lowell rested his port glass on the desk, twirling it between large fingers. "Men are measuring, excavating, and building as we converse. I left the site to meet with you here."

At a loss for what to say, Clementine hazarded a guess. "It sounds as if your project will take longer than mine."

Lowell tossed the rest of the port down his throat and pushed the empty glass across the desk. "Even longer than you think. Strong in friendship, weak in business. Their disagreements and pivots of vision continually delay the entire undertaking. Other commissions draw them out of the country over and over. They leave India more than I do, and they have ten times the responsibility."

He swept a heavy hand down one side of his face. It plunged in a loose fist onto the desktop. "Why am I telling you this? Because the size of Delhi will more than triple in the next ten to twenty years. I know because I plan to see it through. That means hundreds of thousands more citizens. The interests of the British empire, the nation, and the world will focus here when they christen it New Delhi."

"That's a lot more customers right where we're developing the mixture."

"Exactly." Lowell jerked his head to one side. "I'm surprised you picked up on that. I didn't think you had much experience in business."

"Not with this big of a company." Clementine debated telling him nothing personal about herself, but she was still asking for a leap of faith. Offering her trust could help build the strong bridge their professional relationship needed to survive. She rubbed her fingers in a ring around her opposite wrist. "I used to live and work outside a small town. When I moved to Nashville, much larger, finding customers became easier."

"Same principal, yes. Excellent. I think you're missing the even bigger opportunity." Lowell slid his port glass next to his teacup saucer. "Your beauty treatment, if I may, is like a vintage port. A brilliant idea. Many people latch onto it. They'll yearn for it, devour it, pay through the nose for it, and swear they couldn't live without it."

Lowell pointed to Clementine's teacup. "But only I accepted the port, and you opted to go without." He slid the glass aside. "Just as Milton and Clements intended to market the beauty treatment to women alone. Some women would've shunned it, and some men might've tried it. That's neither here nor there. The point is, taking care of one's complexion doesn't appeal to everybody."

Clementine interjected for a reprieve from Lowell's unrelenting speech. "You think a medical antidote is more like tea."

He raised his hands in the air, palms up. "Ubiquitous. Universal. We can't escape it. It's practically in our blood, almost what makes us human. Did you already drink tea this morning?"

"Yes. Twice, actually. Once before I left the house and another cup at my first meeting."

Lowell beamed. "What other substance or activity can we engage in three times a day without being accused of insanity?"

"You think an anti-aging liquid will have a wider market?"

"Yes, especially if you keep words like *medical* off the label. People want what they want, and the more they crave it, the more they'll pay. What are most people afraid of more than anything? Death. What leads to death but aging?" He gestured to Clementine. "Stave it off, give them more years, or at least make them think it works, and your tonic will make all of us more money than we can dream of."

Clementine set her cup and saucer on the desk, mostly untouched. The elixir *would* work. It was not a get-rich scheme, and she would *not* label it to mislead anybody. She took a steadying breath and let it out. If she sounded angry, Lowell could take offense and demand his money back. She folded her hands over her knees. "Thank you for your considerations. I'm afraid I'm taking up your entire break from work. My only question left is whether you'd like to keep your investment or have it refunded."

"I'll leave it. The new mixture's a risky change but genius. I await updates of your success, and I'll contact Milton if I wish to invest more."

Clementine popped up from her seat. "Thank you for your time."

Lowell rose to his feet. "It was a nice break from construction to meet you. I'm glad the company's projects are developing so well."

Clementine moved to the door. "Why do the British maintain control here? Why go through so much trouble to move the capital when it's not really theirs to begin with?"

"Such an American inquiry. I'm sure you'll find the answers the longer you're in India."

"I'd appreciate it if you enlightened me now."

"Haven't you noticed a certain lack in deliberateness?" Lowell propped the fingertips of one hand on the desktop. "Bobbing their heads and using their hands when they speak. Animals roaming the streets. I tell you, it's a good thing the British empire gained control. I shudder to think where the country'd be without us."

For how little breath seeped in and out of her lungs, Clementine could have sworn her throat had closed.

He advanced toward her a step. "Tell me. Was Sandeep or any other servant disrespectful when you arrived?"

She tried to keep her contempt from showing in her sidelong meeting of his eyes. "No. Everyone was polite and accommodating."

"Good. I'm relieved you came when you did. If the children were out of school, they might've climbed all over you like monkeys in the street. I'm not sure they've ever met an American. Sometimes their manners are worse than the natives'."

"Good day, Mr. Dodd." Clementine wrenched the door open. She sped down the hallway into the living room. She peeked around for Mr. Mustafa, hoping her desperation did not show. Finding the room's seats empty, she burst into the foyer about to call his name like a frenzied child.

Mr. Mustafa stood on her right, holding a cup of tea.

She forced her words out through clenched teeth. "We should go."

Mr. Mustafa peeled his back off the wall. "Sandeep."

The servant appeared from the next room on the left. He accepted the cup and saucer from Mr. Mustafa, sweeping ahead to the door. He opened it for them, and Clementine stormed out onto the porch.

Mr. Mustafa joined her, and as soon as the door closed, Clementine emitted a fierce groan. She descended the stairs, kicking at the grass growing beside the lane. She wheeled toward Mr. Mustafa, walking without seeing where she was going.

"I've met some racists in my day, but never one I had to shut up around because of money." She grunted. "Did they treat you all right?"

Mr. Mustafa reached his arm out and kept Clementine from striding into a flower patch. "I'm fine."

"Why didn't they let you sit down to wait for me?"

"I chose to stand."

"Why?"

"It's quicker to leave that way, and I didn't want to be accused of eavesdropping by sitting in the next room."

"So it's about appearances." Clementine swung her gaze ahead of her. The autocarriage leapt out of nowhere, and she set her hands on its hood to keep from slamming into it. "Escape and wrongful accusations."

Mr. Mustafa opened the door for her, wryness curving one side of his lips. "I assume you didn't tell him you're an *Amriki nivasi*."

"No. Is there no way out from all this?" She climbed up into the seat and arranged the skirt of her dress out of the door's path.

He secured her inside and walked around to his seat. He settled in beside her, attaching his glasses and starting the engine. "No way I've found with people like him."

"Is that why you like working for Fitzgerald and Longshaw? We show you respect?"

"You treat me as a human being. That's already better than most of the English." Mr. Mustafa pulled out of the Dodds' driveway, retracing the route they took to the house. "I hold no illusions. I fear the day will come your courtesy was merely a ruse to control us and gain cooperation."

Clementine's stomach churned, and she rested her hand over it. "Has it happened before at the company?"

"No. This is India. The East. The British can march in with their order, plans, practicality, and stability all they like. This land has seen one wave after another of religions and invasions. The Mughals who built the Jama Masjid. The East Empire Company who lost control of India to the British Crown. There's always one more presence, a change, an inclusion. Everything always adds on to what was here. Nothing is truly lost."

"I hope that's true in a positive way."

Mr. Mustafa stopped the autocarriage at the junction with the main road through Civil Lines. "Where should I take you, Miss Fitzgerald? We're done for today."

"Home. To my father's house. Make a right and take the next left."

Mr. Mustafa obeyed her.

Clementine squinted at the houses rolling by outside the window. "I wish I'd never met Mr. Dodd. How could Mr. Longshaw and my father take money from him?"

Mr. Mustafa's answer treaded low and respectful. "For the same reason you keep his money."

"Well, I hate it." Clementine swept at her coat covering her legs. "If I didn't need it to fund the project, I'd give it back. We just need to find more investors, that's all."

"Many people are invested in themselves with no extra currency to impart to others." Mr. Mustafa parked in front of Clementine's house.

She sounded distracted. "Another wave is coming, isn't it? Soon? It has to be. No country can go on divided forever."

"Was your country ever divided?"

"Yes. We fought a civil war over it, and my state was one of the most divided there was."

"Did it solve anything?"

"A little, but we're still split apart. Some people aren't free the way they're meant to be. There's nothing civil about a war, and there's not much civil about Civil Lines." Clementine stepped down from the autocarriage, holding the door open. "I never want to insult you, Mr. Mustafa. I don't mean to. I'd really like for us to be friends."

"We shall try." Even though his eyes did not quite meet hers, Mr. Mustafa spread a genuine smile between his ears. "I'll see you soon."

Chapter Seven

Clementine arrived at Fitzgerald and Longshaw with a single purpose. She let herself in the front door, gave a polite greeting to Aatmaj behind the desk, and swept around the corner to Milton's office. The door gaped ajar, and Milton stood across the room beside his desk with his back to her. He grumbled under his breath, fiddling with one of the hollow glass tubes and its recess in the wall.

Clementine knocked on the doorjamb. "Good morning. Might I speak with you?"

"It'd accomplish a lot more than struggling with this malfunctioning junk." Milton relegated the glass tube to his desk and wandered over to Clementine.

She peeked past him at the wall's aperture, her brows knit in concern. "Does it break often?"

"Rarely, but mine gives us the most trouble. I overuse it since I manage most of the building's departments. The holiday's creating a delay in having it repaired."

Knowing next to nothing about the communication tubes snaking their way through the walls, Clementine returned to her original concern. "My appointments ended well yesterday. All three investors are keeping their funding with us."

Milton grinned. "Marvelous. Fantastic work. Who was the hardest to convince?"

"Mrs. Singh, I believe."

"Interesting, but I might've guessed it. Her family already considers her a drain on their finances despite her husband having earned most of it before he died. She's shrewd, but I admire that. The Varmas have their entire family to think about, but they're progressive when it comes to calculated risks. Lowell will jump on any opportunity that appeals to him."

"That's what I wanted to talk to you about." Clementine shifted her shoulders inside her coat. "I don't think I should do any more investor interviews."

Milton raised a greying eyebrow. "Shouldn't or don't want to?"

Clementine planted her feet. "It's not my area of expertise. I work with sick people who need my help. Securing investments and explaining changes in research in a country I'm not used to…"

"All right." Milton signaled for her to stop. "I agree. Your father, Bryce, and I had months of experience in India before we settled in Delhi. We held mostly casual and intellectual conversations until then. I rushed you into dealing with the locals in a more in-depth capacity, and I'm sorry."

"It made sense, but the investors know you better. I think meetings with you will go much smoother."

"It's time to let you get on with the analysis you're familiar with. You've proved your willingness to work and throw yourself into foreign territory. I'll reclaim my part and meet with the remaining investors."

"Thank you."

"Bryce is probably in your office going over the information he and Clements collected. He can show you their notes and point you in the right direction."

"Is Mr. Mustafa here? I want to let him know I won't be traveling with him for any more meetings."

Milton tugged at the fingertips of his gloved hands. "You wouldn't have gone on any interviews today. It's Friday, Mr. Mustafa's day off for religious observance."

Clementine's focus ran over the furrows in Milton's forehead, the creases fanning toward his temples, and the fine lines accenting his lips. He had let her play all her cards before admitting she would have spent the day well within her comfort zone. A smug light hung in his eyes, relishing everything he knew that she did not. He watched for her reaction, and she wanted to disappoint him as much as possible.

In a cheery, cheeky display, Clementine plucked off her gloves and shoved them in her pockets. "Good for Mr.

Mustafa. I'll spend the day with Mr. Bloom, then. Can I count on you for answers if I have other questions?"

His tone drooped. "Of course."

"I hope you get your tubes fixed." Clementine motioned to the wall and ducked out of Milton's office.

She stalked into her own next door, unbuttoning her coat with inner mumblings about self-centered old men. She had encountered such types in Nashville. Although she could only benefit from remaining professional with her current business partner, it would not stop her from despising ageist superiority.

Bryce sat at the desk, flipping through a large notebook. A stack of thinner ones towered over him, and a second stack rested on the floor. He checked over his shoulder twice in quick succession. "I didn't hear you come in." He got up in a rush, taking just enough care to step around the notebooks piled at his feet. He combed a hand through his hair. "Is there anything I can help you find?"

"We're working together for now." Clementine removed her hat and coat, relegating them to the wooden rack behind the door. "Mr. Longshaw's letting me quit the appointments and get on with what I know. He seems to think you know my father's research, and it looks like you've already gathered a lot of it."

"Yes." Bryce smoothed a hand over his charcoal-grey vest. "I pulled out all the records we kept in the office."

Clementine frowned and grabbed her coat. "There are books at the house. I've read through some of them, but there might be a dozen or more. We'll have to make a trip to get them."

Bryce reached out to her. "You just got in. We can concentrate on these notes first and retrieve the others when we need them."

"I'd prefer to have everything in one place when we begin. No interruptions." Clementine propped her hat on her head and wriggled into her coat. "What can you tell me about the meeting room at the end of the hall?"

Bryce hustled across the rug to snatch his hat and coat from the rack. "It's rarely used for its intended purpose. Clements and I often holed up in it, poring over our notes."

"Good. We'll bring the other books here and set up in the meeting room. Are there blank books for making new observations in?"

"Plenty. We bought so many supplies when we stocked the factory, we thought we'd never use them all. But it's all proved necessary." Bryce set his newsboy over his hair and threw his coat on.

"Do you have an autocarriage, Mr. Bloom?"

"Are you still walking and taking the trolley?"

Clementine nodded. "They haven't let me down."

"It's true the steambike doesn't offer much luggage space." Bryce slipped past her into the hall. He called out. "Milton, can we borrow your autocarriage? We don't have a practical vehicle between us for toting materials."

Clementine hung back in the hall while Bryce stepped into Milton's office.

The old man's reply reached her anyway. "What about Clements' vehicle? He splurged on that upgraded engine. Isn't she driving it?"

"Not yet. Give her time."

Keys clinked and chimed in the air. "How much time? The world wasn't meant to rely on horses forever."

"It's done pretty well so far."

"Sure, until equine influenza shuts down entire cities."

"Did you ever see it happen?"

"When I was a teenager. It broke out in Canada and ravaged one state after another. The newspapers reported on it every day."

"Did it hit Oklahoma?"

"I don't remember. Not like there were any reporters out there to let us know. It wasn't even a state for a few more decades."

"Before my time," Bryce quipped, backing up into the doorway.

"Take good care of my autocarriage, or it'll be past your time."

Bryce saluted. "Yes, sir." He joined Clementine in the hall, holding up the key. "Let's go. I'll drive."

Clementine strolled with him to the lobby and out into the parking lot. She peered at the thin fog looming at a distance. "The sky seems clearer today."

"For now." Bryce tossed the key in the air and caught it.

"Does everybody borrow Mr. Longshaw's autocarriage when they need to go somewhere?"

"Just the people he's closest to." Bryce bounced up to the side of Milton's vehicle. He unlocked the door and held it open.

Clementine hesitated. When Mr. Mustafa had shown her the same kindness, it seemed only proper. He was older than she was and therefore protective. Bryce, on the other hand, shared her youth. His gentility reminded her of being back home, helped into the back of a wagon for a dusk-time hayride.

She ascended into the passenger seat. She had already asked for one favor this morning, and Milton had awarded her the opportunity to prove herself as an herbalist. What more could she ask of her new coworkers? That Bryce stop showing her common courtesy because it seemed more personal than professional? Clementine had proven the company's investors supported their change in product. She had no clue how to back up her excuse for feeling uncomfortable when Bryce accommodated her into a vehicle.

He jogged around to the driver's seat and hoisted himself inside.

Clementine's heart leapt at one small victory. "You already know the way, don't you?"

"Yes, ma'am." Bryce swiveled the key in the dashboard, and the vehicle rumbled beneath them.

Clementine relaxed. Without needing to provide directions, she might be able to ride out the trip in silence.

"How did your meetings go yesterday? Your first day at the company."

Clementine dropped her chin almost to her chest. "I got through it. It wasn't that bad. It's hard to learn so many customs."

Bryce backed the autocarriage up and chartered it toward the road. "I don't really know when my first day was. I guess when your father hired me back in Oklahoma." He turned right to head through Meena Bazaar. "Did you get along with Mr. Mustafa?"

"Yes. He's very nice. He knows a lot."

"Yeah. Do you think we'll be able to stay on time with redirecting the project and everything? Milton aimed to finish the old one by the end of the year. Having it ready to stock the shelves in Delhi and ship out to America."

"I won't know for sure until I see how much work we have to do. But if the plant species in India are anything like the ones in Tennessee, they're all good for more than one thing. The odds of my father's legwork paying off are pretty high."

"Milton will be happy to hear that. He's worried we'll have to throw away plants we already processed. Plus, we have to buy new plants and put them through the extractors."

Clementine eyed the toes of her shoes peeking out from the hem of her dress. They remained smooth with no scuffs, and she aimed to keep them that way. "He'll have to learn to have more faith in me."

"I trust you. I know I'm not an official partner, but I sometimes have some sway over Milton." Bryce steered the autocarriage onto the next, busier road in front of the Jama Masjid. "I secured this for us, didn't I?"

"You did." Clementine gave up on finding peace in the small space with Bryce. "Do you know why my father kept some of his notes at the house? Didn't he have a hand in designing the factory? He could've given himself a bigger office and stored all his books in one place."

Bryce shrugged. "I think with a building full of shelves, Clements would've taken notebooks home. He liked reading them in the evenings to see if he'd missed or forgotten anything. He mostly took home the volumes we weren't relying on every day. The older interviews. The plants we experimented with and decided not to include."

"It sounds like information we can use. That saves us time."

"Clements liked to be thorough. He'd examine every plant from every angle. The formula we were working on was brilliant. As you said, each herb, spice, and flower has several qualities. We packed as much as we could into that lotion."

Clementine's idea might render those countless hours of labor wasted, and it crushed her a little. "I'm sorry."

Bryce scratched his head, nudging his newsboy out of place. "It's okay. We didn't perfect it, so it's as good a place to branch out from as any." He slowed the autocarriage to comply with traffic.

Clementine stretched her neck to try to see around the carriages in front of them. "Is it a cow?"

"Maybe. Or a food seller or some dogs or a wagon with a broken wheel."

Traffic lurched forward, and Bryce lit up. He sped up the autocarriage, and Clementine mirrored him in peering out the window to see the culprit. The cow adjusted its hooves on the side of the road, its eyes glassy and dismissive.

Bryce shook one hand in the air. "Just as you thought!"

"I'm not used to this," Clementine confided. "Dogs I understand. But cows? Where's their pasture? Where's their gate?"

"They're sacred here. They can wander wherever they like."

"They do, indeed."

"What was it like proposing the altered project to the investors? It's been years since I went with Clements to interview anybody."

"Did you go along for the original investment meetings?"

"No, I stayed in my apartment and went over our notes on plants. The factory wasn't built yet. It was just a vacant lot we were eyeing. We wanted investor money before we took that leap. Delhi's the most industrial city in a country of farmland, so that's why we set up here."

"Smart." How many years had Clementine practiced rural medicine among the farmers, basket weavers, and moonshiners before she saved up enough for the move to Nashville? But, as Bryce had asked her, what of her first day in the field in India? "It was mostly all right. I think I overreacted because I didn't know what to expect. I was still getting to know Mr. Mustafa, and suddenly, I had an Indian widow asking me about back home."

Clementine paused, almost content to leave her experiences at Nivriti. Almost. "The Varmas were a completely different experience. Chaos erupted when we got there, and not dealing with Mr. Varma directly wracked my nerves. I had to win over his wife to put in a good word for us. Mr. Dodd…" She shook her head, rubbing her gloved palms against each other. "I thought he'd be the highlight of my day. He's so dratted arrogant. He'd invest in anything we produced if he thought it'd make him money."

Bryce crumpled his eyebrows. "Probably best to let Milton deal with him."

"What progress did you make yesterday?"

Bryce drove across the wide intersecting street, heading into Civil Lines. "I listed which plants might survive the crossover into an anti-aging serum. Indian gooseberries, turmeric, holy basil. We already have those on hand."

"Good."

"There's a lot I don't think we can use. Indian women use sandalwood and rose oils on their complexions all the time, from what we learned. I'm not sure we'll be able to convince Englishwomen that drinking tree and flower oils will make them younger."

"I see." Lowell's deep-throated lilt thrummed in her head. *Especially if you keep words like "medical" off the label.* She huffed. "It really is all about the words we use to sell this to people."

"You mean misleading them to sell more bottles?" Bryce rolled the autocarriage onto Clementine's street. "I didn't think so. Who said it was?"

"Mr. Dodd. You made it sound like that, too."

Bryce parked in Clementine's driveway. "I guess it was easier with the lotion. Everything we planned to say in the ads was true. It smoothed out wrinkles. It made your skin glow. Do you think people will be harder to convince about the real deal refreshing their entire body?"

"Mr. Dodd believed it'd be simpler."

Bryce adjusted his newsboy and silenced the engine. "We'll make sure the tonic works as well as the old treatment. We'll stay honest the whole way through."

"Mr. Longshaw will agree with this?"

"We'll force him. It's two against one."

Bryce hopped out of the autocarriage, and Clementine let herself down to keep him from opening her door. She led him along the front walk to the wooden porch.

Bryce hung back a few steps, rocking forward and back on his soles. "The last time I was here, your father was laid out in the living room."

"I'm sorry you had to deal with my father's death." Clementine unlocked the door and opened it. "I'm sure he would've been glad to know you cared, and I assure you he's not in here now."

She stepped inside, and the faint stench of paint tickled her nose.

Bryce followed her and gasped. "Everything's different."

He walked ahead of her into the great room. Clementine closed the door, trying to avoid seeing the new furnishings. The acrid fumes irritating her nostrils reminded her she had paid to have the walls refinished a clean, pure white. A crew of muscled men had carried out the brown-black furniture, expensive knickknacks, and brightly colored rugs. The replacements they positioned for her around the room were sparse but cozy. Rocking chairs and armchairs in honey-toned woods. The cushions relaxed in cool sage green, and the rug centering the large room held similar outdoor hues. The fireplace mantel lay bare, waiting for trinkets and statuettes Clementine did not own. In India, anyway.

Clementine left her hat and gloves on. She wanted to grab the errant books and get back to the factory. She strode past Bryce but stopped when he did not follow.

He coursed his hand over the couch's straight, grey back. "Did you change everything in the house?"

Clementine drew her spine up into a resolute line. "It was hard being here with my father's things. They made me think of him constantly. Since I'm staying here for the time being and he's not, I sold his furniture and bought my own."

"It looks so…" Bryce patted the rounded scroll top of the couch. "Like back home."

"Yes."

"Do you miss Tennessee?"

"My friends and family are there." Clementine continued through the second half of the room.

"This couch is like velvet."

"Dralon, the man said. Fancier than I'm used to, but it's comfortable."

Clementine led Bryce past the wide opening to the dining room on her left. At the end of the great room, a hallway ran to either side of them. To the right, a door to the garden stood in a small alcove, hidden from the living space. Clementine veered left, headed to the nearby double doors. Farther down the hall stood a door to a small water closet and an open door at the end intersecting with a servants' corridor.

Bryce spoke up behind her. "What did you do in the study?"

She parted the doors. Subdued sunbeams glowed in through the eastern windows on their right. A settee cushioned in hunter green sat against the nearest wall. A globe set in a rosewood stand occupied the corner. Bookshelves covered half the wall across from them. Papers almost buried a large, rectangular desk off to the left.

Bryce moseyed over to the globe, palming its blue-and-tan surface. "This is still here."

"There was no reason to get rid of it." Clementine went over to the shelves. "All of these books and notebooks are my father's. Mine are upstairs."

Bryce walked up to her side, perusing the maroon fabric spines. "Are you sure you want to take everything?"

"If only we had a wheelbarrow." Clementine stacked a few volumes against her forearm, bearing their weight against her ribs.

Bryce followed suit. "Good thing there are two of us, eh?"

Clementine gave a cursory lift of her chin.

"Did Miss Higginbotham help you with the furniture and everything? Getting it bought and sold, I mean."

"Yes. She was quite helpful. She seemed to know Delhi very well."

"She's lived here most of her life, I think."

"I felt bad letting her go. I know my father died, but I got the impression she wanted to stay on. Keep living in the servants' quarters and be a housekeeper for me. But I couldn't spare the money." Clementine skirted around Bryce to the desk to retrieve a book she had consulted the night before.

Bryce turned away from the shelves. "You don't think that's creepy or maudlin? She worked for Clements over two and a half years. To keep living in the house where he died?" Bryce shivered. His expression lengthened in remorse. "I'm sorry."

"It's all right." Clementine raked her sharpened concentration over the desk's papers, so many hills and valleys, they completely submerged anything else.

"If you don't like staying here – and it's understandable if you don't – I'm sure we can help you find a suitable hotel."

Clementine murmured, distracted. "I'm fine." She stacked the books on one side of the desk and sorted through some of her notes and lists.

"Are these Clements' papers?"

"Some. Most of them are mine." She dug deeper, peeking under sheaves and single sheets. "I've left it such a mess already, I can't find anything."

"I used to work in a hotel, you know. It's how Clements and I met." Bryce reached his free hand into the fray, shifting an assortment of written ideas and questions.

A worn, crimson corner peeked out from the sea of white and ink. Clementine sighed and lifted it free. "Thank you, Mr. Bloom. No, I didn't know that."

"Milton was there, too, but he's not the one who wanted to hire me."

"I guessed as much from the way he treats you."

Bryce rested his pile of books on the desk. "I want you to realize how much your father trusted me. I worked more closely with him during the last few years than Milton did. Milton beguiled the investors and keeps the workers on schedule. But Clements and I were a team. We talked to countless women, herbalists, doctors, botanists, and explorers." He tapped the volumes on the desk. "To get this information."

"I understand you assisted my father–"

Bryce exhaled through his nose and hung his head for a moment. "Milton's ruined the way you think about me. I might not have been Clements' equal in title or salary, but he acted like I was."

Clementine added the found book to her pile and picked up the stack of them. "I'll try to consider you the same way, but I'm still getting to know you and Mr. Longshaw. I'm sure if I relegate you to an offensive rank, you'll let me know."

Bryce showed her his palms. "It's not my intent to badger you into treating me the way your father did."

"He left all of us in a bind. We're doing the best we can."

Clementine left the room. Bryce scrambled to gather up the rest of the books and hurry after her. She pried the front door open. His arms supported a tower of volumes tucked under his chin as he stepped out onto the porch. Clementine locked up and accompanied him down the steps to the path.

Bryce adjusted his fingers around the books. "I'm just saying you can rely on me. You don't have to go to Milton about everything. I know the data. He doesn't."

A hazy shadow leapt off the roof in Clementine's periphery and landed on Bryce's shoulder.

He yelped, gripping the bound notes tightly. "What is it?"

The grey rhesus macaque, about the size of a cat, perched beside Bryce's head. It flipped his hat off and rummaged through his hair in quick, neat rows.

Clementine could hardly believe her eyes or her ears as she heard her breathless answer. "It's a monkey."

Under Bryce's calm volume, tension squeezed his enunciation. "Get your books to the car. He can stop grooming me any minute and scamper off with our research."

Clementine fought the urges to sprint and to stay, caught in the middle of the impossible. "I can't leave you here."

"There's nothing else you can do. Save those books and come back for these."

Clementine rushed a few steps toward the autocarriage, then slowed down in case she upset the macaque. She opened the vehicle's back door and dumped her books in an avalanche across the seat.

Bryce stood a few feet from the porch, mumbling in a soothing, fearful tone. "Nice monkey. Good monkey."

Clementine approached him in careful, measured stretches of each foot in front of the other. She kept her eyes on the monkey. Watching Bryce only spiked her nerves. The macaque licked Bryce's hair, leaving patches of it awry. The small, golden-copper eyes flicked to Clementine, and she leaned away. The monkey continued its inspection of Bryce's head, and Clementine reached for the books. The macaque swung a paw at them, and Clementine darted back. Bryce tilted his head toward the monkey, and it rifled in deft motions through his hair. Clementine inched forward, and Bryce let the books go. They landed against her chest with a thump, a few volumes flopping into the grass.

"Sorry," Bryce whispered.

"We can save apologies for later." Clementine trekked to the autocarriage and deposited the load of hardcovers inside it.

She debated the books held captive at Bryce's feet and dried sweat off her forehead with her coat sleeve. A cobalt-and-red tin poked out from under the front passenger seat. She pulled out a box of salted soda crackers from the National Biscuit Company. She rubbed her thumb over the words *made in USA*, but this was no time to entertain nostalgia. Clementine popped the lid off and fished a square cracker out of the protective wax paper lining.

Clementine issued a shrill whistle through her teeth, arresting the macaque's curiosity. She held up the cracker. "You want a snack?" She reeled her arm back and pitched the baked morsel up onto the roof sloping over the porch.

With a squeal, the macaque launched off Bryce's shoulder, eliciting another shout from the hapless young man. The monkey galloped over the shingles, snatched the cracker in one paw, and raced around the corner of the house on its remaining limbs.

Bryce brushed off his coat and collected his newsboy from the lawn.

Laughter cracked through Clementine's astonishment. She bubbled with it, replacing the lid on the tin and stowing it under the seat. The unbelievable surrealism broke out of her in loud, unladylike bursts. She attempted to hold them back with her gloved hands, but she could only succeed in muffling her wicked enjoyment of Bryce's predicament.

He collected the fallen books and sidled up to her, his grim mouth twitching with humor. "I'm glad I could relieve your stress with an impromptu monkey attack."

Clementine waved fresh air into her heated cheeks. "I'm sorry."

He added the stray books to the lot of them. "I guess it's time for apologies now, like you said."

"It was scary at the moment."

"What did you throw for it?"

"Milton had a box of crackers in the autocarriage."

Bryce pulled his hat back and forth on his head. "Lucky for us the old man needs a snack now and then."

"So did the monkey."

Clementine leaned her arm against the vehicle's frame. Another barrage of amusement shook her body. "I'm sorry. Really, this is awful of me. Has anything like this happened to you before?"

"No, but I've heard stories of it from just about everybody I've talked to."

"It's the first monkey I've noticed in Civil Lines."

"They usually stick to the heart of the city. The police shoo them away from these neighborhoods, but they're clever things. They can climb anything, and they do."

Clementine doubled over with fresh giggles. "That one was willing to make his perch anywhere."

"You're no longer sorry for benefiting at my expense, are you?" Bryce swept at his coat sleeves. "There are snake charmers and dancing bears. Do you want them to harass me the next time you feel blue?"

"No, I wouldn't impose on you like that." Clementine straightened up and swallowed the rest of her tear-jerking guffaws. She kept a smile on for Bryce, to smooth over any animosity she might have caused.

Bryce's eyes, the color of algae water floating over river rocks, sparkled at her. The curve of his lips matched hers except for a hint of triumph.

Clementine's mood faltered. Bryce's smile was not for the moment. It was for her because he liked her. A lot. Had he not rushed to accommodate her since her arrival Monday morning?

Clementine covered up the gloom taking her over from the inside. She closed the autocarriage's back door and opened the one in front. "We should drive back to the factory. I want to make headway before we stop for lunch."

"Of course." Bryce hurried to the driver's seat.

As Clementine closed herself in with him, she dwelled on the one fact she did not yet know. He had a crush on her, but was it a good thing?

Chapter Eight

Milton dug through his coat pocket where the garment hung on the rack in his office. He pulled out his keys and handed one to Clementine.

She held it up to indicate it. "I appreciate the favor."

He nodded with absent attention. "I have to go over my schedule for tomorrow, anyway."

"Have we lost investors?"

His small grey eyes met hers, and a broad grin spread across his long face. "Not one, thanks to us."

"Good. I'll be sure to congratulate Mr. Mustafa, too, when I see him. Do you know where I might find him?"

"Try the employee room at the end of the hall."

Clementine wrapped her fingers around the key and exited Milton's office. She passed her own vacant room and Govinda's accounting office, silent behind its closed door. She reached the alcove at the end of the hall and pushed the door open.

Mr. Mustafa knelt on a woven rug near the opposite end of the room facing the wall. Behind him, tables and chairs filled most of the space. Over Clementine's shoulder, she found a small kitchen for storing and preparing food.

Mr. Mustafa's hands rested on his legs just shy of his knees, index fingers raised. He spoke in clear, gentle intonations. *"Rabbana atina fid-dunya hasanatan wa fil akhirati hasanatan waqina adhaban-nar."* He turned his head to his right, noting Clementine but continuing his practice. *"Assalamu alaikum."* He looked to his left. *"Assalamu alaikum."*

Clementine averted her gaze as Mr. Mustafa stood up. He rolled up his rug and approached her.

Her most genuine apology fell from her lips. "I'm sorry. Mr. Longshaw told me where you were, but he didn't mention you were praying."

Tranquil confidence shone in his eyes. "How did you know what I was doing?"

"I've seen people from different backgrounds commune with their gods. Am I wrong?"

"No."

Clementine admired the rug's periwinkle, gold, and soaked-earth threads forming pictures she could only see fragments of. Claret flowers branched off from an undulating vine framing its center. Wreathed in small, pointed leaves, a star and crescent moon hovered against a scarlet background. "You used the same words you said to me when we met."

"Yes, a wish for peace for my fellow people. I also prayed for good things and protection from hellfire. These are what all Muslims ask for."

"Everyone seeks out help and safety."

Mr. Mustafa carried his prayer rug across the room and stowed it in a wooden cabinet. "You were searching for me?"

"To ask for your help. I promised Mrs. Varma I'd bring her some herbs to help the ailments we discussed. I wondered if you'd be so kind as to drive me to her house."

"It's the end of the day. Doesn't Mr. Milton need his autocarriage to go home?"

Clementine dangled the key from her fingers. "Not yet. He already gave me permission to use it."

"Then I'll drive you. This is why I say my daily prayers as early as I can. I never know what might disrupt them."

"You pray every day?"

"Five times each day." Mr. Mustafa accepted the key. "It reminds me Allah is with me and to be a good person. Whom do you pray to?"

"Whoever's listening."

Clementine backtracked out of the room. Mr. Mustafa walked with her to her office. Numerous vermilion books occupied the desk in two groups. A small handful sat on the left, the few she and Bryce had read through that day. The other piles, including those on the floor, added up to dozens left to sift through. Weariness threatened to topple Clementine and confine her to the desk chair, but she pushed past it.

On her other side, a wide-mouthed rattan basket sat on the side table. It held several envelopes marked in Clementine's small, straight handwriting. *Bergamot. Goldenseal. Blue vervain.*

Mr. Mustafa laid a hand on the basket. "Are these for Mrs. Varma?"

"Yes. I also have a surprise to show you." Clementine went to the desk and opened a drawer. She pulled out a wad of fabric and unwound it into a long, fuchsia scarf. She spread its width over her head and wrapped the ends around her neck, letting them drape. "Last week, when we worked together, you embraced cultures that aren't your own. I want you to know I'm willing to do the same."

Mr. Mustafa regained his professional solemnity. "It isn't necessary."

In the relaxed muscles of his countenance, Clementine swore she saw pleasure and approval. "Do you think the Varmas will like it, or will it offend them?"

"They already call you *Bhartiya.* Perhaps nothing you do will astonish them."

"It'll warm my head in any case."

Mr. Mustafa picked up the basket of herbs, and Clementine threw her coat on. They stepped out into the hall, and she locked up her office. She passed Milton's open door, leaving him to study at his desk. Mr. Mustafa let them out into the parking lot and stored the basket in the back of the autocarriage. He helped Clementine into the passenger seat and climbed up behind the wheel. He put on his pince-nez glasses and drove them onto the road cutting through Meena Bazaar.

For once, the sounds of the city dominated the air inside the vehicle. Engines whirring and chugging. Animal hooves striking the road. Adults' mature utterances and children's high squeals. Temple bells pealing.

Mr. Mustafa directed the autocarriage around the Jama Masjid and away from it. Within ten minutes, he stopped in the Varmas' driveway. Clementine clambered down from her seat while he collected the basket.

She walked with him to the door. "Do you think the younger Mr. Varma will be home?"

Mr. Mustafa allowed her the honesty of a slight smirk. "Perhaps he's toiling late like Mr. Milton."

Clementine knocked.

The same servant answered in his white clothes and turban.

Mr. Mustafa conferred with him, and the servant beckoned them inside. He motioned up the long hall to the courtyard, but Padma's voice floated down, echoing from several different places. She entered from the stairwell ahead on the left. Her eyes lit up as they met Clementine's. She bowed over pressed palms and chatted in energized syllables.

Mr. Mustafa glanced in Clementine's direction. "Mrs. Varma says she knew it would be you. She prayed for your return."

Clementine squirmed, not used to being the answer to someone's prayers. She only acted as was right and necessary. "Ask her what she'd like me to do."

Mr. Mustafa relayed Clementine's request and followed up with Padma's answer. "If you have time, she'd appreciate your help in preparing the herbs for their intended patient. She also wants to learn what each of them is for. Over time."

Clementine grinned. The allusion to repeated visits was as good as a warm invitation. "I'll gladly make the tea and poultice. Where should I start?"

Mr. Mustafa translated, and Padma waved for them to follow her. The clinks of utensils against bowls and taps of glasses on wood resounded from the floor above them.

Clementine looked to Mr. Mustafa. "Did I interrupt their supper?"

"Would you like me to inquire?"

Padma led them with light, quick feet into the kitchen on their right. She flung excited hands at a length of open countertop.

Clementine shook her head. "She wouldn't be here with us if she wanted to eat. We'll just be as brief as we can."

Mr. Mustafa set the basket on the opposite counter near the stove.

Clementine relied on him to repeat all of her questions and explanations to Padma as she opened the envelopes. "Some of these will go in the tea. Some will make the poultice. A few of them will go in both."

Padma filled a kettle with water and set it on the stove to boil. She fetched a bowl, and Clementine took it to mix the poultice in.

She shook ground blossoms, roots, leaves, and stems out of the envelopes into the container. "We'll need to cover the mixture after we apply it to the person's skin. Gauze or cloth will work."

Padma strode out of the kitchen.

Mr. Mustafa removed his glasses and stored them in the case in his pocket. "May I be of any more service to you, Miss Fitzgerald?"

Clementine took the lid off the brass teapot and sprinkled pinches of herbs into its simmering contents. "I could use a little cool water in the bowl. Just enough to moisten the herbs."

Mr. Mustafa carried the container to the sink and rotated the knob on one of the metal spigots. He let it flow for a second before he arrested it.

Padma appeared in the doorway, holding up rolls of white bandages.

"Perfect." The water popped and bubbled in the kettle, and Clementine switched off the gas to the stove burner. "Please ask Mrs. Varma to strain the herbs out of the tea and put the liquid in a cup."

Clementine tuned out Mr. Mustafa's murmurs, focused on bringing their efforts to a successful close. She stirred the poultice with her fingers, testing its consistency. Adding an extra burst of water made it easier to spread into a paste. Padma passed her a towel, and she wiped off her hand.

Clementine laid the towel aside and was about to give her final instructions to Mr. Mustafa to pass on. Padma gave her the rolls of bandages and produced a wooden tray from a cabinet. She arranged the cup of tea and the bowl of wet herbs on it.

Mr. Mustafa translated her words for Clementine. "Mrs. Varma requests you take the tray upstairs to the first closed door you see. Enter that room. I'm to remain here."

Clementine's eyebrows bent askance. "Am I to leave the tray there?"

"Those are the instructions as Mrs. Varma wishes me to provide them."

Padma rocked her head from one side to the other.

Clementine took a breath to still her tensing nerves. She deposited the bandages on the tray and picked it up. "I don't need a translator? What about her family?"

"I've heard it said that danger should be feared when distant and braved when present."

"Courageous I shall be, then."

Clementine left the kitchen and crossed the foyer to the stairwell. An alternative entrance called to her with promises of a quick escape, but Clementine ignored it. She ascended the stairs to a lavender room housing a desk and framed religious pictures decorating the walls.

The closed door aroused her heartbeat and her dread. Why had Padma sent her up here? Alone? With little direction?

Clementine shrugged off the other questions that tried to follow. She tiptoed forward, conversation sparking from another part of the floor. The higher pitches fell away, leaving only the timbre Clementine recognized as Nishil Varma's. Closed, canary-yellow panels like window shutters completed the wall on her left. A pair of them swung partway open. Through the crack, Clementine spied across the empty space of the inner courtyard. Nishil sat at a large table, suspending a piece of flatbread in his hand while he orated. The young woman who had come to the door the day Clementine first arrived listened from the chair next to him. Another woman sat at the far end, a lock of her greying black hair fallen free from her pink headscarf.

The appointed door whispered to Clementine, and she crept over to it. She pushed it open into a dark, silent room. Draperies drawn across the two windows on her right filtered minimal light into the gloom. A round table gleamed a short distance ahead of her, and Clementine advanced enough to lay the tray on its surface.

"Close the door, please."

For a moment, the delicate request perplexed Clementine. It murmured English from the shadows, but the accent was not hers. She squinted into the abyss.

"You do speak English, don't you?"

Clementine blinked herself into action. She revisited the room's entrance and closed the door.

The curtain shifted near the farthest window. "Mother told me you would come."

Clementine tried to avoid wasting time figuring out exactly who addressed her. "Yes. I've brought some tea made from skullcap, sage, and rosemary, among other things." She paused, but no response came from the room. "And a poultice of agrimony, perilla, and thyme."

"Won't you sit down?"

Clementine warred with herself. Neither she nor Mr. Mustafa had traveled home yet for dinner. They were currently keeping Padma from savoring hers. Clementine edged forward, but the rest of the room remained shrouded in mystery. "I can't see a chair."

Fingers wrapped around the drapery and pulled it a few inches from the window. In the sparse stream of light, a chair appeared beside the round table. A woven design patterned the rich wood around its full-back rattan cushion and down its curved legs. The arms broadened into detailed leaves that scrolled down to meet with the front of the seat.

Clementine perched on it, unnerved by her unseen greeter. "May I ask your name?"

The voice quickened. "Samvidha."

"Nice to meet you. I'm Clementine. And your mother is…?"

"Padma. She said you have herbal medicine from the other side of the world."

"I do." Why had Padma not mentioned these cures were for her daughter? "You know English well. Did someone teach you?"

The curtain moved, illuminating books and newspapers on shelves and other tables in the room. Reading English on them shocked Clementine. *The Heart of Rachael. Diane of the Green Van. Snakes, tigers, and other wild beasts killed thousands in British India in the past year. The British government continues to monitor fuel consumption due to the rising number of steam-powered vehicles. Mr. HH Manghirmalani of Hyderabad drafted a pamphlet outlining steps to Indian self-government based on Australia's success gained through federation.*

Samvidha swayed side to side. "I rarely leave my room, so I've been learning English as a way to entertain myself." In the dim haze, her palms rubbed one another. "Sometimes, my hands give me trouble, and I can't hold onto the books. I have problems flipping the pages. The servants teach me words they hear. My brother, too."

"Your brother doesn't seem fond of the English or Americans."

"He has different hurts than I do."

Samvidha crept forward into the light. Her hair hung loose and wavy past her shoulders. Large dark eyes observed Clementine from above a broad, pointed nose. Her wide cheekbones offset a narrow chin. Gold polka dots decorated her orange sari, cloaking her in the brilliance of the sun.

Blood dribbled from her nose, and Clementine jumped up from her chair. She grabbed a roll of bandages and dipped the end of the cloth into the tea to moisten it. "You're bleeding. Let me help you."

Samvidha swiped at the crimson, smearing it across her cheek. Her eyes closed in defeat. "Forgive me. I'll call for my mother."

Clementine approached her and dotted the wet bandage above Samvidha's mouth. "She must've wanted me to meet you."

Samvidha's lips trembled. "It's dangerous. For you and for me."

"Why?" Clementine washed the blood away and took Samvidha's wrist. She slid off Samvidha's white glove and stopped.

Dry, blanched skin spread a crust over parts of Samvidha's hand. Pink blisters and open sores dotted her fingers and wrist.

Samvidha drew in a shaky breath. "No one can know this happened to me, and you might catch it."

Clementine strengthened her resolve. She pulled the round table across the vibrant rug toward the window. She set the bloodied bandage roll on the tray and dipped her first two fingers into the poultice. She held Samvidha's hand steady while she applied the mixture. "I have herbs that can keep me healthy. I've touched rashes and illnesses before."

"No one else in the house has caught it. The leprosy."

"I'm sorry you did." Clementine reached for Samvidha's other hand and slathered her wounds with a layer of green-brown paste.

"It's been years since I saw anyone with the disease. But it was..." Samvidha shuddered and examined Clementine's movements. "All of my old friends have gotten married or engaged. My cousins, too. Mother told me."

"Do they think you're somewhere else?"

"Up north, where my mother's family came from years ago."

Clementine wrapped her fingers around Samvidha's hand and held it. The rough patches of her skin frightened

Clementine, but she knew loneliness. And how much the power of touch could heal both illness and a despondent heart.

"Are you married, Clementine?"

Nivriti had asked her the same question. Clementine found it easier to answer coming from the desperate young sufferer. "No."

"You must be older than I am."

"Probably." Clementine retrieved a clean bandage roll. Her fingers pinned one end of the cloth to Samvidha's wrist while she wrapped two revolutions around it to hold the bandage in place.

"Most Hindu women are engaged very young. It's all I planned for, and no one can even know I'm in the city. What am I to do?" Her speech wavered. "How am I supposed to spend the rest of my life?"

Clementine looped the bandage around Samvidha's hand, bringing it back around to include her thumb. "You can't sit in the dark every day. You have to see the sun and let it see you, too."

"Have you been sick for a long time like I have?"

Clementine circled the fabric around again, spreading it around each of Samvidha's fingers. "Someone close to me has."

"Is this person with you in Delhi?"

"No, she's back in the States." Clementine noticed a small pair of scissors on the tray and snatched them up. She cut off the excess cloth and secured the end of the bandage against Samvidha's palm. She took the young woman's other hand – woman or teenager? – and began the process anew.

"Do you miss her?"

"More than anything."

"Do you wrap my hands because they could be hers?"

Clementine sniffled and blinked tears out of her eyes. "I tend to you because I can't stand to let people stay sick, no matter who they are."

Samvidha settled into silence, and Clementine finished tending her hand.

Clementine left the supplies on the tray. "Fresh poultice and bandages should be applied at least every day."

"What are they supposed to do?"

"Keep dirt out of your wounds and help them heal. The tea will minimize the symptoms your mother mentioned. Pain. Numbness. Your sinus and muscle problems."

Samvidha wrapped her arms around Clementine. "I shall repay you twentyfold when I can find a way."

Clementine patted her bandaged hand. "I'll come back when I can and take care of you myself."

"And visit with me?"

"We'll talk." Clementine lifted the cup and saucer off the tray. "Drink your tea before it gets cold."

"Bless you." Samvidha accepted it, her face hovering above the cup. "Parvati, Lakshmi, Vishnu, and Tara give you what you need as you have helped me."

"I'll see you in a week or two."

Clementine walked across the room and let herself out. The dinner gathering across the inner courtyard exploded with laughter and singing. She descended the stairs to the foyer, where Mr. Mustafa talked with Padma. Clementine rubbed any remains of the poultice off her fingers onto her coat.

Mr. Mustafa stepped towards her. "Ready to leave?"

Clementine nodded.

Mr. Mustafa exchanged a few words with Padma. The servant rushed from the kitchen and opened the front door. Clementine preceded Mr. Mustafa to the autocarriage in the driveway.

"In a hurry?" Mr. Mustafa aided her into the vehicle and put himself in beside her.

"I have a lot to think about."

"Will you need me to bring you back here in the future?"

"Yes. We've done enough for one day, though."

"Would you like me to drive you home before I restore the autocarriage to the factory?"

"If it wouldn't be more imposing than I've already done."

Mr. Mustafa circled the vehicle around and directed it into the street. "My wife will keep my food hot until I arrive."

Clementine leaned against the interior of the autocarriage's metal frame. Caring for Samvidha did not remind her of her mother. It was another day entirely playing out in her mind.

The urgency felt palpable that warm afternoon. Clementine borrowed a horse and cart from the neighbors, shooting through the grassy fields to Ledford Farm. As soon as she stopped the cart and jumped out, men pointed her to a small house apart from the main homestead.

Clementine grabbed her bag of herbs and tattered cloths. Running into the house, labored exhales guided her to a sparsely decorated bedroom. A man with cropped, curly black hair lay in the bed. One leg stuck out of the covers, the pant fabric ripped and soaked with blood.

Another man sat in a wooden chair a few feet away, bending toward the injured man. He looked up as Clementine swept in. "Are you the doctor?"

"I'm who the Ledfords sent for. I patched up Mr. Coleman himself at his farm last year." Clementine set her bag on the dresser and opened it. "Did Mrs. Ledford make a pot of water for me?"

"I think so." The man stood up and patted the shoulder of the man in the bed. "I'll leave you in good hands, then. We still have to fix that tractor."

The reclined man nodded. "Give it my best."

The response grumbled. "I'll put it to rest like they do the sick horses." He ambled out of the room.

Clementine approached the bed. "Mr. Chester Alred? I'm Clementine Heidel. I'm going to wash and bandage your leg."

"That'll be fine."

She pulled the covers free of the mattress and bunched them up under Chester's calf. "You'll want to keep your leg propped up so less blood flows into it."

Chester clucked his tongue. "For the time being, it seems my blood wants to flow out of my leg."

"We'll see what we can do about that." Clementine strode to the head of the bed and set the back of her hand against Chester's forehead. "You're not feverish. Let's keep you that way."

"You can really do all that?"

"Sure, and I aim to prove it." Clementine whisked out of the room, following the bubbling of water until she reached the kitchen. She blew out the stove's flame and used a pot holder to move the vessel to the counter. She found a bowl in one of the cabinets and poured a small amount of hot water into it. Carrying it back to Chester's room, she singled out the pitcher on the low shelf of the wash basin stand. Clementine mixed cool water into the hot until the temperature reached a comfortable warmth.

Chester's question rumbled low in his chest. "How'd you learn to do all this?"

Clementine retrieved a handful of cloths from her bag and set them on the foot of the bed. She moved the bowl of water to the floor and knelt beside it. "My daddy taught me some. I learned the rest as I went."

"My daddy taught me how to handle tools and work the land."

"Wasn't it working with tools that got you cut?"

"Yeah. He was a good teacher, though. I can tell you how it happened if you're not too squeamish."

"How squeamish are you, Mr. Alred? I've gotta pull your clothing back now and see this wound for myself."

"Go ahead."

Clementine braced herself and rolled his tan pant leg back from his shin. His skin parted in a four-inch-long pointed oval, raw and red. Blood flowed from it to his ankle and the sheets beneath it.

"Well, doc? What's your professional proclamation?"

"I can treat it. I'm glad it's not any worse."

Chester chuckled. "Me, too."

"I'm gonna wipe the extra blood away first." Clementine dipped a clean rag in the warm water. "Now's a good time for you to tell your story."

Chester interlaced his fingers on his chest. "It's one of them newfangled tractors, you understand. With the steam engine and everything."

Clementine washed the vermillion away, making her swipes and presses gentler the closer she got to the wound.

Chester winced and sucked in a breath. "Anyway, it quit running yesterday night, and we couldn't fix it. So we put it up on a couple of concrete blocks to see it better. We had about six or seven of us tinkering with it, and that's when the blocks shifted. The tractor came at me, and I almost got away in time. It caught my leg there."

"I'm sure it hurts like the dickens, but you got pretty lucky. I've seen far worse from farm equipment. Mr. Coleman's father lost his leg before he died. That was several years ago." Clementine spread a dry rag on the floor and set the bloodied ones on top.

"I've seen a man's thumb just about torn off." Chester traced the tip of one thumb along the other's base where it met the back of his hand.

"Did they patch it or take it?"

"It was a good deal of both in the end."

Clementine stood up and pulled her bag of herbs down to the floor with her.

"What's next?" Chester prompted.

"I'll cover your wound with plants that make it heal faster."

"And without that fever you mentioned."

"Right." Clementine retrieved jars and sacks in various sizes, shapes, and colors from her bag. She shook St. John's wort, valerian, and goldenseal into the water. She snatched up a new cloth and used her fingers to scoop the herbs onto it. They came out wet and stuck together as she had hoped. "I apologize for any pain this causes you."

"I blame the tractor for all of it."

Clementine patted the cloth of smashed leaves and broken roots to Chester's open wound. He emitted only a croak of protest. Clementine rested her palm flat over the herbs and his shin, her tan looking pale against his dark brown skin.

He forced words through clenched teeth. "Then you wrap it up, right? That's what the doctor did for me when I cut my forearm open in the spring."

Clementine laid a second cloth over the wound and pulled a longer ribbon of cotton from her bag. "They should've called for me. But yes, I'll wrap it up to protect it from any more harm." She spiraled the bandage around Chester's shin from his ankle to his knee. "Can you wiggle your toes?"

Chester flexed his foot. "Yes, ma'am."

"That means it's loose enough." Clementine put away the cloths and closed up her bag.

Chester pushed his upper body up on his elbows. "Do I get a crutch or anything?"

"No." Clementine walked over and set her hand on Chester's chest. "You need to rest and stay off that leg."

"I gotta help them get that tractor moving."

"What about the rest of the six or seven people you said were working on it? You don't think they're out there figuring it out?"

"They need me." Chester raised himself up on his hands.

Clementine pushed against his chest, strong in her mission. "Although I have no doubts about your great abilities with tools and machinery, which one of us is the healer? Who's the patient in the bed?"

"You're the doctor, ma'am." Chester unfurled onto his back.

"That's right." Clementine fluffed the pillow around his head, finding it thinner than she would have liked. "I'll bring you a better pillow when I come back, too."

"How long do I have to wait?"

"I'll be here tomorrow to change your dressing."

"I'm sure someone on the farm could do it if you wanted to save yourself the trip."

"I need to check for infection and see how well the wound reacts to the treatment. I'm betting this gash is worse than the one you suffered to your arm."

"It is."

Clementine hoisted her bag off the floor and walked to the doorway. "I'm gonna make sure it heals up as well as your arm did. Is there anything else I can get for you before I leave? A companion to keep you from getting bored?"

Chester shook his head. "No, thank you. I'll just be here resting like you told me to."

"I know it feels like it's taking forever already, but you'll heal up faster than you ever have. I guarantee it."

The autocarriage came to a stop, swaying Clementine out of her reverie. Mr. Mustafa sat beside her half a world away from Chester.

"May I one day repay the favors you do for me." She popped the door open and stepped down onto the driveway.

Mr. Mustafa peered at her through his pince-nez frames. "May you find the peace you search for."

Chapter Nine

Clementine reached across the mahogany meeting room table and grabbed another scarlet notebook. "If turmeric root powder is so orange, how did you mix it into a cream?"

Bryce weighed his book open with his hands. "There was a lot of trial and error. Mostly error until we got the amount small enough to work without staining the user like a pumpkin."

"What do you know about the rest of the plant?" Clementine flipped through the handwritten notes.

"The leaves are useful. For the skin and the body."

Clementine found the page she half-remembered from the day before. "Indians use them in cooking to improve digestion. They're also a part of Ayurveda and may help fight the effects of aging." She added turmeric leaves to her list of the serum's potential ingredients.

"Another one we should strongly consider is gotu kola." Bryce pointed to Clementine's paper. "It has several properties we'll lose by making an internal formula, but we can't deny its other benefits."

"Fights aging, speeds wound healing, improves brain function, and relieves stress. Good catch." Clementine jotted it down.

A knock on the door disrupted her train of thought. Bryce frowned, sulking as he sat up straight in his chair.

Clementine called out a short, "Yes?"

The door opened, and Milton stepped in. "I apologize for interrupting."

Bryce narrowed his eyes.

Clementine broke away from her facts and observations. "What's so important, Mr. Longshaw?"

"An additional facet to finalize." Milton set his fingertips on the edge of the table. "Your father and I spent weeks scrutinizing every angle of it."

"Can we keep the decision as it is and move forward from there?"

"We could, but I want your opinion. Changing the Fountain of Youth might create complex circumstances for our product testers."

One more side of running a business Clementine had neglected to think of. She sat back in her chair. "I see. Who makes up our testers now?"

"An assemblage of women eager to improve their skin and receive free cream with which to do so. This includes Daisy Dodd, her eldest daughter, Udit Varma's daughter-in-law, and every woman in Nivriti Singh's family over the age of twelve. Those are just the participants with whom you're familiar. We have dozens more who sampled early versions of the project and are waiting to hear from us about the next trial."

Clementine tucked her folded arms against her belly. "How do you suggest we proceed?"

"I can approach them the same way we've met with investors. The product has altered, but the goal is similar. Appear younger, feel better, and become more attractive. It's just from the inside instead of the outside."

"And we can open the trials to men. Mr. Dodd pointed out the wider appeal of our new mission."

"Correct. I'll have to take some time to word the explanation properly. I don't want anyone to think I'm calling them *old*."

Bryce opened his mouth.

"Diplomacy," Milton purred with a hint of aggression. "That's the key."

Clementine picked up the book in front of her. "It seems so." She raked her attention over her father's handwriting, as familiar as her own by now. Milton remained at the head of the table. She gave up and closed the book. "Was there something else?"

"A small matter that pertains less to the project at large and more to me." Milton lifted his hands into tented fingers in front of him. "I'm concluding my meetings with investors and still have production to oversee. I have multiple presentations to make in the future regarding the trials. You employ Bryce as your helper, and in the light of my increased duties, I require my own assistant."

"Do you need my advice or my agreement?"

"I'd welcome it since this person would work with us all. His or her salary would be added to the expenses in Govinda's budget."

Clementine nodded. "If you need an aide, hire one. I trust your judgment."

Bryce sucked in a breath to speak.

Milton slapped his hands flat on the table, interrupting him. "If there's nothing you need from me, Miss Fitzgerald, I'll retire to my office for the afternoon. I want to compose the ad for the position."

Bryce propped his elbow on the table and settled his cheek against his fist. "An ad? In the newspaper? What good did that ever do anybody?"

Milton warned Bryce with sharp eyes. "A lot, young man. You'd know that if you ever spent more than a couple of years in cities with a population larger than two."

"I got this job without one. Miss Fitzgerald, did you ever use a newspaper for anything?"

Clementine hid a sly smile behind her hand to save Milton's pride. "To wrap herbs in."

Milton planted his palms on the table. "You don't read about what's going on around us? The struggles for power, for reform, for basic, common understanding?" He slicked a gloved hand over his hair. "Only the young would be so brash and bold as to ignore the events shaping the world you'll one day inherit. All you care about is the president's obsession with airships. That's exciting to you, I suppose."

Bryce grinned. "What do you think they'll name it?"

Milton fought a sneer. "That's the problem. You've got more years left than I do. You're the very people who should care but don't. You should keep up with news and world events, Bryce. It could only benefit you."

"Like what?"

"The election in the States last fall. Do you know who won?"

Bryce shrugged.

"Theodore Roosevelt. Of which party?"

Bryce pointed at Milton. "The New Year's Eve party."

Clementine stifled a giggle.

Milton covered his eyes for a moment. "In 1904, William McKinley tried for office a third time and succeeded. This is important because?"

Bryce turned his hand in ambivalent circles in the air.

Milton huffed. "It ended the three-term series of Democrats. President McKinley was good to have in office for what reason?"

"Otherwise, we'd have had nobody running the country?"

Milton flexed his fingers in aggravation at his sides. "He was pro-business, and we control a company, in case you haven't noticed. He supported tariffs on foreign goods to strengthen American independence. He served a second term and passed the baton to Theodore Roosevelt in 1912."

Bryce laid his arm on the table and rested his head on it. He inhaled in snoring ripples that made Clementine laugh under her breath. Bryce smiled.

Milton continued through tense jaws. "President Roosevelt has been celebrated for creating national parks. He's ensured better health for his citizens by regulating food and drug processing. Despite a history of crippling asthma, he engages in the most vivacious lifestyle of any man alive."

Bryce whined and opened his eyes. "This is so boring. What does any of this have to do with us? My original question."

Milton reached across the table and swooped his hand through Bryce's hair. "Since we're stationed in India, any product we ship to the US may be subject to McKinley's tariffs. We have to consider our pricing and our customers back home. President Roosevelt being a fellow naturalist and explorer should be of some interest to you. Did you ever think a man who's battled incurable illness all his life might be intrigued to try a refreshing bottle or two of the Fountain of Youth?" Milton swatted at Bryce's ruffled mop.

Bryce ducked. "All right. I get the point."

"Politics are anything but a time to go to sleep. If they were, why did Roosevelt explain his second campaign for office by saying life would be too boring otherwise?"

"He's a glutton for work?"

Milton raised his hand, and Bryce shied farther from him. "Do you realize the biggest war we've ever known could've unfolded right around us?"

Bryce scrunched his face up. "Now you're taking it too far."

"Am I? Check this morning's paper. The king and queen of England, the emperor and empress of India, have invited Prince Franz von Harrach to visit them. It's been two and a half years since he saved the lives of the Austrian archduke Franz Ferdinand and his wife. Obviously, the British royalty know something you don't."

"Which is?"

"If the gunmen hit their mark, the political machinations behind the assassination could've surged through country after country. Unprecedented chaos would've erupted across Europe. War doesn't respect borders and boundaries. It obliterates and redefines them. I know action and reaction on a greater scale than you do. It could've included the Middle East, the Far East, or even America."

Bryce swung a dismissive hand at Milton. "You're joking. Why would all those countries want to be pulled into a war over two men with the same name?"

"Because everybody wants something, and they all think it's worth fighting for. Money. Resources. Land. Power. Prince von Harrach was a count before he tackled that gunman and protected the archduke. He jumped off the running board of their car with no regard for his own safety and might've rescued half the world in the process."

"I'll give him my thanks and congratulations when I see him next at high tea."

Clementine sputtered and held the book up to cover her smile from Milton. "Thank you for the impromptu lesson, Mr. Longshaw. You're well informed."

"I should hope so." Milton turned to go.

Bryce pulled a stack of three volumes across the table to him. "Speaking of tea, Miss Fitzgerald, would you like to do something fun with me when we finish for the day? Not that it has to be anything as stuffy as sipping hot beverages with our pinkies in the air."

"What do you find enjoyable?"

"I catch movies at the cinema. There are excellent restaurants around if you don't mind ordering your food by pointing at what other people are eating. There's always the thrill of the roads through the countryside around the city."

Clementine intended to decline Bryce's invitation in the most polite way possible when movement distracted her from the doorway. Milton's small grey eyes rested on her, disapproval firming his brow. He set his narrow jaw in a sternness she barely understood and hardly welcomed.

Her voice hardened. "Perhaps Mr. Longshaw would join us."

Milton gripped the door handle. "I have neither the time nor the inclination."

Clementine softened her tone. "Maybe another day, Mr. Bloom."

Milton exited and closed the door. Clementine preferred to spend her evenings alone and thought it best to remain as professional with Bryce as she could. She imagined Milton agreed with that. Although, unlike the changing of presidents and near-assassinations printed in the papers, her schedule was scarcely his business.

Chapter Ten

Clementine borrowed the neighbor's dappled horse and simple cart again. She arrived on the Ledford farm in a blast of afternoon sunlight, a constant breeze cooling her warm skin. She recognized Chester's laugh right away, the pain and deprecation in it lessening with each passing week.

His vibrancy lifted pounds of concern off her shoulders. He sounded so well, she left her bag of supplies in the cart. Walking toward Chester's silky cadence, she found him with two other men in the shade of a giant oak.

Chester took a swig from a thin bottle of sassafras tea. His teeth gleamed in the sun, his brimmed hat lending him additional refuge from the striking rays. He reset his feet in a casual, cocky stance. "I've got one. It comes in dry. It goes out wet. It tickles your stomach. It makes you sweat. What is it?"

The other men stroked their chins and drank from their bottles. They shook their heads.

"You never heard that one?" Chester spread his arms out from his sides. "A washboard. It's how you use it. In dry. Out wet."

The men groaned.

One of them set his hand against the other's arm. "I got something that'll trip you up. What has eyes but can't see, a tongue but can't talk, and no legs but can walk?"

The other man lifted his boot off the ground and pointed to it. "Shoes. I know one that goes kinda similar like that. What has a tongue and can't talk, can run but can't walk?"

Chester smiled. "I know that. That's a wagon."

Clementine walked up to them, measuring the straightness of Chester's posture with her eyes. "Good afternoon. How's the day treating y'all?"

The men nodded and murmured, "Fine."

Chester indicated his friends with a sweep of his bottle. "We were just watering ourselves and finding entertainment in some old riddles we used to hear."

Clementine stayed under the tree instead of rushing Chester off to inspect his wound. "I knew the one about the washboard."

"You like riddles, Miss Heidel? What's another one you remember?"

Clementine took a moment to conjure one that would truly stump them, something passed down through her family. "What's at the end of everything?"

One of the other men hollered. "That's a deep one, now."

"Not really." Clementine's eyes shimmered with mischief.

Chester held her gaze, thoughts shifting in his eyes. "The letter G."

Clementine took a humored breath. "That's right."

"My turn." Chester's finger stroked the curve of his bottle. "Here's a good one for you. It's crooked as a rainbow with teeth like a cat. Guess all your life. You won't guess that."

"Mr. Alred, that was handpicked for me. You don't think I've tended to the scratches a prickly briar patch delivers to unsuspecting folk?"

He beamed. "Briar it is."

"Let's see about that leg."

"My break's over, boys." Chester upended his bottle over his mouth to finish it.

The two men remained under the tree while Clementine and Chester headed away toward the small house. The instant they passed out of the shade, the heat struck their skin and their spirits. Chester jogged the last twenty feet to the door and held it open for Clementine.

"I see you're doing much better. You're happy to be out of bed."

"Ma'am, I'm mighty relieved and grateful to you. Wait 'til you see what you done for me."

Clementine hurried into the house, and Chester sat down in a nearby chair in the living room. She crouched at his feet and rolled up his pant leg. What had once been gaping and red had knitted down into a smooth purple scar. "Much better."

"Thanks to you. I'm glad they sent for you." Chester left his bottle on the wooden floor beside him. "You're the best doctor I ever had."

"Are you in the habit of injuring yourself?" Clementine unfurled his pant leg and stood up.

"I've been farming all my life." Chester got to his feet and spread his hands out. "I got scars, nicks, and scratches. Sometimes my fingers go a bit numb from using them so much."

"I can bring you herbs for that."

"You do that."

"Make sure if a tractor lunges at you again, the Ledfords come for me straight away."

Chester bobbed his head. "Of course I will. I'm much obliged to you."

Milton's office door slammed. Clementine jumped out of her reverie, her hands rustling the pages spread across her desk.

All day, his door had squeaked and banged. Every hour she and Bryce had dug through research in the meeting room, the hum of chatter bubbled from the packed lobby outside.

Despite Bryce's arguing against the efficacy of placing an ad for the job, a hundred people responded to it. As the day wore on, so did an irritating rhythm. The door latch clicked, Milton dismissed the last applicant, Aatmaj introduced the next person, and the door would thump.

To Clementine's greater aggravation, she discerned an unwavering pattern. When a man's baritone accompanied Aatmaj's, Milton's interview lasted a few brief minutes. If higher, more delicate pitches sounded, a longer time passed before Milton reopened his door. Like several other things around the factory, Clementine did not know what it meant. She only knew its implications bothered her.

Clementine shook off her preoccupation with Milton's shady dealings. She finished writing herself a note for where to resume her analyses on Monday. She slipped the paper into an open book on the desk. Closing it felt like a pardon. She had served her first full week at the company. Now she could spend the weekend reading at her leisure and preparing for next week.

She put on her coat and hat. She snatched up another book she and Bryce had not yet gotten to. It would make for engaging browsing on the front porch, in the great room, or in the courtyard. She locked her office as she left. Murmuring filled the lobby, snippets of foreign languages tumbling down the hallway. The twisting of Milton's doorknob as Clementine passed his office plummeted her heart into the pit of her stomach. She hurried toward the lobby.

Milton's oration resonated, smooth and cheerful. "Your English is very good. We barely needed Mr. Mustafa to translate. I think you're perfect for the position."

The response dug into Clementine, youthful, gushing, and feminine. "I do want the job."

"I offered it to you, and you accepted. There's nothing left to talk about." Milton called out. "Miss Fitzgerald."

Clementine's shoulders hunched. A few more steps, and she would have escaped his sight. She stood in the midst of the dozen or so people crowding the lobby. Five women squeezed together on the sofa. Men stood along the opposite wall, half topped with turbans and the others gripping hats in their hands.

In a slow rotation, Clementine faced Milton and the young woman beside him. A goldenrod headscarf crowned her parted, black hair. Her dark eyes sparkled like Clementine had never seen. The large, round apples of her cheeks flanked a pointed nose. She wore a blue long-sleeved blouse under her navy sari. The swaths of fabric could hardly disguise the full curves of her figure.

Mr. Mustafa arrived in the doorway next to Milton. He bowed to the room. "Mr. Milton respects your time for coming. He was glad to have you all here. He filled the position, so you're free to return home in time for dinner." Mr. Mustafa added other languages, and the waiting crowd trickled out.

Clementine's muscles tightened across her ribs. Although Mr. Mustafa had agreed to work on his usual Friday off, Milton's decision to request his services angered her.

Milton gestured from the woman to Clementine. "I'd like you to meet Miss Indira Datta, my new assistant. I think she'll fit in very well."

The women bowed to each other.

"This is Miss Clementine Fitzgerald, my business partner."

Indira observed Clementine with shining eyes. "You're so young and beautiful."

Clementine managed a shaky smile. "As are you." She meant to ask about her qualifications when Indira interjected.

"I'm happy to meet you. I never thought I would have this chance." Indira clasped her hands together. "Now I am here. And you are here. We are changing India, you and me."

Clementine slipped her question in while she could. "Have you worked in an office or a factory before?"

"No. I told this to Mr. Longshaw."

"And he gave you the job anyway." Clementine glanced at Milton to gauge his reaction.

One eyelid twitched, and his jaws clenched.

Indira beamed. "Yes. I am very excited to start here on Monday."

Her enthusiasm assuaged some of Clementine's chagrin. "It'll be nice to have another woman around. I suspect you're even younger than I am."

"Yes, but look how much you have done. This place." Indira motioned to the lobby around them. "Beautiful. Together, we will make medicine. I want to do big things. I wish to be like you."

Clementine studied Indira more closely. "You want to work?"

"Yes. To make things with my hands. To learn and to grow."

Clementine struggled to keep herself from seeking out Milton's response to this. "We can teach you many things,

Miss Datta. I think Mr. Longshaw was right to hire you. You'll be an asset to the team."

Indira tensed her brows and sought out Mr. Mustafa. He translated, and she laughed. "Asset. Yes. Already you teach me a new English word. I will be an asset for you. I show you."

"You already have. Welcome to the company. It'll be lovely working with you."

Chapter Eleven

Clementine closed her last book for the day. "Do we need more strawberries? When would we be able to order more if we did?"

Bryce clapped another volume shut at her side. He grabbed a spare piece of paper and scribbled a note. "I don't know what's in storage. We can check on it tomorrow. They're in season through March, so if we want them, we've got less than two months to buy them."

They stood up from the table. Bryce hurried over to the door in time to pry it open for Clementine.

She stepped out into the hall. "We'll have to make sure Mr. Mustafa can translate for us when we go into storage. I don't know how else we can explain to Mr. Menon or the others what we're investigating."

Bryce reached Clementine's side. "Dry storage is across the hall from the extractors, if you remember. It should be quiet there. We haven't arranged for a shipment in about a month. It'll be more involved getting into cold storage."

During Clementine's short time inside the chilled environment, the shelves full of bottles and jars had towered over her like mountain cliffs. Its fond memories warmed her. All the same, tracking down which herbs they possessed and their amounts seemed taxing. "There's not an inventory we can read instead?"

"I'm afraid not. We instituted one, but maintaining it while developing the lotion proved too difficult. One missed record at a time, the reporting fell behind. We tried to catch up between batches, but then…"

Clementine filled in the missing piece. Her father died.

"It just never happened."

Clementine opened her office door. "Maybe once we finish the bulk of the new research, we can look into starting–"

A sharp bang sounded from the lobby. Clementine jumped, her heart racing but gaining no ground inside her chest.

Shouting in a foreign language ripped through the building.

Bryce stepped between her and the lobby. "Maybe you should go in your office."

Clementine grabbed Bryce's sleeve. "Are you moving closer?"

"It's the only way to find out what's going on." Bryce craned his neck toward the lobby.

"Do you see anybody?" Clementine whispered, wringing her hands.

"Not from here."

Bryce slipped away toward the front door, and Clementine only waited half a second before she followed him. A short, young Indian man raged at Aatmaj, who left his post behind the desk. Aatmaj set his mouth in a firm line and shooed the visitor toward the door.

Clementine looked to Bryce. "Do you understand anything he's saying?"

"No."

Clementine caught one word of the man's rampage, and it chilled her blood. *Datta*. She shook Bryce's arm. "Get Mr. Mustafa. We have to find out what he wants."

Bryce ran off into the factory.

Clementine backed up as Aatmaj attempted to steer the visitor outside. If the irate man threw a punch at Aatmaj, she did not want to stand too close to them. The visitor zeroed in on her and stormed toward her, yelling words she did not understand.

From behind her, responses fired down the hall. Only when Clementine peeked over her shoulder did she realize the terse replies came from Mr. Mustafa. She had never heard him speak like this. He strode past her, joining the argument with Aatmaj and the raving visitor.

Bryce stopped next to Clementine.

His presence emboldened her. "Mr. Mustafa, what's going on? Why's he here?"

Mr. Mustafa stepped closer to her. "This is Mr. Ravi Lal. He demands to see his fiancée, Indira Datta."

A heavy breath sank out of Clementine. "Why? What has she done?"

Indira's answer resounded from ten feet behind Clementine. "I take the job."

Ravi exploded, his eyes bulging at Indira.

"He does not like me to work." Indira walked past Clementine toward Ravi. "Only for him to work. He tells me not to speak English. But I like to learn it. I want you to know what I say."

Ravi ranted in response.

Clementine dodged spittle flying from his mouth. "What's he saying?"

"I hurt my father's house. He works for my father to be able to marry me. It is bad already. I make it worse because I work here."

"Because he can't provide for you."

Mr. Mustafa nodded.

Clementine stood up straighter, reassured with so many other people circling Ravi. "Mr. Mustafa, would you ask Mr. Lal–"

Indira flew at Ravi, shouting in his same language. Clementine's mouth fell open.

Indira rocked her head from side to side. "I want to work here. You cannot tell me *no*. I work, and you work. It is okay."

Ravi wiped perspiration off his forehead with the end of his sleeve. He made a command through gritted teeth.

Indira shook her head. "I work here. I go home when it is done. Soon." She spoke to him in the other language.

Clementine wanted to jump in, but to do what? To support Indira? To insert herself into their private quarrel? Bring an outsider's view to Indian culture? "Mr. Mustafa, assure Mr. Lal…" Indira had only worked one day at the company. Clementine was not positive what she could claim quite yet. "…we care about her deeply. His wish to take care of her is admirable."

Ravi threw his hands up before Mr. Mustafa had the chance to translate. Spitting angry words, Ravi stomped out the door.

Indira trembled. "It is done. I am sorry."

Clementine softened. "It's okay."

"No. I am treated like a bad woman because I work. Many women want to work. The men do not like it."

Clementine grunted. She understood this too well.

The heckling from two years before still echoed in her brain. She had locked up her office for the night, a bag of herbs hefted in one arm. Two men crossed the street toward her, adorned in fancy suits, top hats, and canes.

One of them jeered at her. "Aren't you the girl who was just at Dr. Robbins' asking all kinds of questions?"

Every muscle in her body threatened to freeze rigid, but she squared her shoulders. "Yes. What of it?"

The man scratched the side of his head. He shrank his pale blue eyes to exaggerated slits at the building behind her. He slipped into a thick, rural accent. "Lemme see now."

The other man laughed.

"My vision ain't what it used to be, but if I'm not mistaken, your place of business says *herbal medicine*. What would you need with Dr. Robbins, then, unless what you do in there doesn't work?"

Clementine squeezed her jaws so hard, they ached. "If you want to talk business, that's none of yours."

The man held his hand out, covered in a pristine white glove. "There's no need for disrespect. After all, it was a visit about your mother. What's more precious in the whole, wide world than one's mother?"

"I have nothing to say to you. I have an appointment."

The man rapped the tip of his cane on the sidewalk. "Could it be true this so-called healer can't cure her own mother?" He *tched* his tongue in a series behind his teeth. "If you can't even help the woman who birthed you, what on earth will enable you to erase anyone else's afflictions? Pardon me. I should've used smaller words you might understand."

Clementine glared at him. "My mother's no concern of yours."

The other man piped up, angling his top hat off his high, wrinkled forehead. "What exactly is your schooling, Miss Heidel? Did you study for a medical degree, or did you stop off somewhere in the neighborhood of second grade?"

"I don't mislead anybody. All my patients know my qualifications."

"Like being able to tell a leaf from a hole in the ground?"

Clementine swung her bag of herbs at them. "You're mad they came to me because you failed them."

They flinched, but their grimaces widened.

The first man trained his eyes on her bag. "You could've gone to medical school, you know. They do allow women, but for the life of me, I can't grasp why. Observe the difference in manners."

Clementine snapped at them. "Wearing top hats doesn't make you gentlemen. You have nothing better to do than harass me? Leave me and my mother alone. Go back to your patients. Your poor wives. The brats you call children. Go on!" She shoved the bag at them until they stumbled off the curb.

The first man barked at her. "Don't cry to us if you break your arm or catch a cold."

"I won't. Stay off this street, and you'll never see me again."

Clementine took a deep, shaky inhale. She blinked herself into the present. Over ten thousand miles away, surrounded by people who revered her knowledge, the insolence still fired indignation through her veins.

Aatmaj sank into his seat behind the desk.

Indira patted her headscarf over her hair. "I go back to work now."

Mr. Mustafa escorted her up the hall.

At the far end of the corridor, Milton waited with folded hands. Clementine could not tell how much of his seeming patience was real.

The trio disappeared around the corner. This might not be Ravi's only entrance to the factory, and Milton's fascination with Indira might not have died out yet, either. Clementine touched light fingertips to her temple. She drifted into her office with Bryce behind her.

He snapped his fingers. "One final note for tomorrow before I forget." He went to the desk and scrounged up what he needed. He bent over, writing.

Clementine tugged at her dress sleeves' cuffs, accomplishing nothing. "Do you think Mr. Lal will come in again?"

"It's hard to tell. He might, but I hope not." Bryce set the pen down and crossed the room to pick up his hat from the wooden rack. "You and I are done for the day, right?"

Clementine nodded.

A high-pitched scream shot through the air. Terror seized Clementine as she realized only one person on the grounds could have issued it.

Bryce threw his hat on the side table.

Clementine tore off down the hall with him on her heels. "Miss Datta! Are you okay?" Responsibility for the young woman's welfare dragged her down. She could have confronted Milton about his hiring choice instead of encouraging it. She should have asked if all possible precautions would be taken. Clementine rounded the corner, where Indira's voice floated out the open door of the extraction room.

"It is nothing. Very little pain. I was…" She added another language.

Mr. Mustafa's deeper timbre took over. "She was more surprised than injured."

Clementine and Bryce strode into the extraction area. Workmen stood in different places and positions around the room. Some carried brooms in mid-sweep. Others held wet rags against the metal machines. Milton, Mr. Mustafa, and Indira huddled by the nearest machine on the right.

Clementine made a beeline for them. "Is everything all right?"

Indira held out her hand. "Small pain. Big surprise."

Clementine accepted Indira's hand and examined it. The outer edge of her index finger blazed in a ruby line. "What happened?"

Indira widened imploring eyes at Milton and Mr. Mustafa.

The older man stepped forward. "This accursed machine malfunctioned. I was finishing my explanation of its operation, and Miss Datta set her hand on the rim of its block. The glass case slammed down and pinched her finger."

Indira's face drew in toward the middle. "I am blessed it is not worse."

Clementine let Indira take her hand back. "It needs ice. No matter how much or how little it stings."

Indira cradled her injured hand in her other one. She nibbled her lip, squeezing her eyes shut for long moments at a time.

Clementine sought out the factory supervisor. "Mr. Mustafa, would you ask Mr. Menon to contact someone about recalibrating this machine?"

Mr. Mustafa whisked away.

Milton rested his hand on Indira's arm. "I'm sorry. I shouldn't have let it maim you like this. It's my fault."

Indira pulled her hands against her stomach. "The problem is mine. I put my hand there. Can I still work for you? Do not send me away. I learn. I do better."

Milton's thumb stroked her arm. "You can work for me. It's a simple mistake."

Clementine labored to keep a sneer at bay. "Mr. Longshaw, the best remedy for a pinch is ice. Do we have any?"

Bryce held a finger up. "I'll get some from cold storage."

Milton lurched forward. "I'll go." He jogged across the room, dodging the workers easing into slow-motion duties.

Clementine focused on Indira. "I'm sorry, too. Tell me if the throbbing gets worse."

Indira peeked at her bruising finger, seething through her teeth. "Stupid accident."

"Your job is safe. We care more about you than the machine."

Bryce chirped up. "You can always join us in the offices if you can't work on the floor."

Indira grinned. "You are kind, Mr. Bloom. Everyone here finds a place for me."

Milton reappeared, holding chunks of ice wrapped in a handkerchief. "Hold this to your finger." He took Indira's hand, setting the bundle against the crimson line.

"So good, all of you."

"I'll drive you home." Milton adjusted the ice's position. "You can't walk the streets or ride the trolley like this. Someone could take advantage of you."

Clementine glowered a hole through him. *And beat you to it?*

Indira took over using the icepack. "I can go myself. I do not wish to make a bad thing. I want to be here tomorrow. Work with machines. Do you understand me?"

Milton's frown mellowed. "Yes. It's no problem."

Clementine guided Indira toward the door. "Why don't you take a few minutes in the restroom to relax? Someone will check on you soon."

Indira walked out of the room.

Bryce shook his arms out. "That was close. She could've broken her hand."

Milton waved it off. "We'll get the machine fixed. It won't happen again."

Bryce blew out a sigh at Clementine. "No better evening to catch a movie and forget our troubles, is there?"

Clementine wiped sweat off her palms onto the skirt of her dress. "I appreciate the suggestion, but I must decline. Today had enough excitement for me. My heart couldn't take any more."

"Well said. I'll see you both tomorrow." Bryce strolled away, turning into the hallway in the same direction Indira had gone.

Clementine locked eyes with Milton, and the words came out of their mouths at the same time. "Can I talk to you... alone?"

Milton barreled out of the room, and Clementine stayed in step with him, letting him choose the location. He crossed the hallway and unlocked the door with *Dry Storage* embossed on its plaque. Clementine joined him in the silent room. Wooden shelves lined the walls with several more units filling the middle of the area. Boxes and jars took up half the space.

Milton closed the door behind them. "You're my business partner."

Clementine knotted her arms. "Your equal."

"And we employ Bryce. I take issue with you socializing with him in this manner."

Clementine's mouth gaped open. "I've been nothing but professional with Mr. Bloom."

"You're vague and indirect. That's why you got another invitation. You haven't made it clear it would be inappropriate to fraternize outside this building."

"You give me no credit for being polite while I reject him?" Clementine jabbed a pointed finger toward the floor. "Mr. Bloom works for us. I have every reason to treat him with as much respect as I do you."

"Bryce doesn't respond to nice brush-offs and subtle hints. He doesn't think you're saying *no* forever. He thinks you only mean it for the day."

Clementine held her tongue, and Milton reached for the door handle. Her disapproval rushed out of her. "What about Miss Datta? Did you hire her for her loveliness or her mind?"

Milton aimed a gloved finger at her. "Beware what you accuse me of, Miss Fitzgerald."

"I didn't have to see you conduct those interviews because my ears witnessed enough. You skipped over those men. Mr. Mustafa introduced them to you. Educated. Experienced.

Desperate for work. Yet you had all the time in the world for the women who came in. Very few of them literate. Almost none of them knew English. And at quitting time, you announced your choice. So tell me, because I'm making my question as direct and expressive as I can. Did you hire Miss Datta because of her beauty or her eager, intelligent mind?"

Milton stared. He stood perfectly still except for blinking and breathing in and out of his thin chest. "Perhaps I underestimated you."

"It seems you did."

"You agreed with my choice to make Miss Datta my assistant, so my exact process is of no interest to you."

Clementine retied her arms across her stomach. "You're wrong. It intrigues me a great deal."

"It appears we've reached our first impasse. How about we agree to disagree? I won't interfere in your personal life, and you can stop scrutinizing mine."

"That's fine, but I won't let Miss Datta get hurt. By those machines or by you."

"I won't let your indecision about Bryce's fanciful inclinations demolish this company."

They watched each other, waiting, although Clementine did not know what either of them waited for. At last, Milton opened the door, and they spilled out into the hall. She walked away, the click of his key in the lock at odds with her boot heels striking the floor.

Indira came out of the water closet up ahead, pressing the wrapped ice to her finger.

Knowing Milton remained behind her, Clementine addressed Indira full on. "Don't worry, Miss Datta. You can work here as long as you like."

Despite her discomfort, Indira's grimace spread into a smile.

Chapter Twelve

Clementine swept into her office with Bryce close on her heels. "We'll place our new orders by Monday's end," she agreed. "How soon do you think we'll receive the shipments?"

He scratched his head, his hair mussed from a day of research and rushing around the factory. "That depends on how far the plants need to travel. Most of them grow within a few hundred miles of here."

"And the herbs we haven't ordered before?"

"We'll have to source them. We can contact the farms and companies we already have relationships with. We'll find others if we need to. But we should act quickly while some of these herbs are in season."

Bryce grabbed his newsboy cap and coat off the wooden rack. He put them on in his quick, haphazard way. Clementine squeezed past him and retrieved her own winter wear. She stepped into the center of the rug to button her coat up over her cream-and-butter-yellow dress.

Milton walked by in the corridor with Indira, aimed toward the lobby. "You did a good job this week."

Her gentle, accented voice dragged with insistence. "I wounded my hand. I broke the machine."

"Nonsense. It'll be fixed soon, anyway. Let me see your finger where it pinched you."

Clementine fired ember hot but said nothing.

Milton hummed to himself. "It's better already. I think you'll have a full recovery. You'll be well soon."

Clementine fumed under her breath. "So you're a healer now?"

Bryce snapped out of a trance, his finger tracing the inlaid details in the side table. "What?"

"Let's go home. We've done all we can for today."

Bryce ambled into the hallway, and Clementine secured her office door. Milton waved to Indira from the entrance to the lobby at the end of the hall.

Clementine glanced at Bryce. She spoke as clearly as she could, a little louder than necessary. "Mr. Bloom, if you have no plans and our work hasn't worn you out, would it be forward of me to accept your suggestions of a trip to the cinema?"

Milton turned, scowling.

Bryce's big, grey-green eyes grew an extra size. "Well, no. I couldn't think of a nicer way to spend a few hours. I'd be honored to share one of my favorite pastimes with you."

Milton skulked toward them, trudging into his office next door.

Clementine called out to him, lilting. "How about you, Mr. Longshaw? Do you wish to join us?"

Milton confined his answer to a low, even, "No."

Bryce's grin spread. "Who needs him, anyway? You know the best way to get to the cinema, don't you?"

They traipsed up the hall in energetic strides.

Clementine pulled her gloves on. "How?"

"On my steambike, of course."

Clementine paused at the lobby's threshold, and Bryce passed her by several paces. She struck up again, catching up to him. "In the end-of-the-day traffic? Is it safe?"

"We'll avoid it. I know the best roads. Trust me."

Bryce swung the door open to the still, warm evening. Clementine walked out into the brightest weather she had seen in Delhi so far, its veil of mist almost sheer. She determined to enjoy herself on this outing, not just go through with it to anger Milton. She had traversed all the way from Nashville to India. What part of riding a steambike loomed more dangerous or a bigger adventure than traveling halfway around the world?

Bryce led the way to the contraption a few spaces away.

Clementine inspected the vehicle anew as if she were one of its inventors, deciding whether it was safe enough for the masses or better to scrap for junk. "There's only one seat."

"Technically." Bryce crouched down at the back of the egg-shaped sidecar. He opened a metal panel and peered inside. "It holds two people."

"Have you ever tried it?"

"Yeah. Some of the locals begged me to take them one at a time around the block when we first moved here." Bryce closed the panel. "Plenty of water and fuel."

"You're sure?" Clementine whirled her finger in circles at the vehicle. "It won't go too slow? Or too fast?" She was not sure which prospect worried her more, blocking other drivers or slamming into something. She squeaked. Now she knew which terrified her the most.

"I've had no accidents in the years I've owned it. Mr. Longshaw assured me I should take comfort in the fact it's a Studebaker instead of a Ford. Something about quality and Mr. Ford's ideas not working out."

"What did you say to that?"

"I sure had a close call." Bryce slung imaginary sweat off his forehead. "Either way, I wouldn't let anything happen to you." He lifted the steambike's seat, exposing a storage bin. He pulled out a white helmet padded with brown leather. "I only have one of these. You should wear it."

"What about my hat?"

Bryce lifted it in a delicate motion off her head. "If I may." He set it inside the storage space and added his newsboy. He closed the seat over them.

"How do I...?"

Bryce took the helmet and fit it onto Clementine's head. He tucked the flaps on either side down to cover her ears and fastened the strap under her chin. The helmet muffled him to a hollow whisper. "Can you hear me?"

She nodded. "A little. I can barely hear myself."

Bryce straddled the bike, meeting Clementine's gaze over his shoulder. "Now you get on."

Clementine was glad her mother could not see her – or anyone else she knew from home. She gathered up the lengths of her coat and dress to her knees. With all the grace of a baby deer taking its initial steps, Clementine lurched one foot over the steambike. She half fell into place behind Bryce.

"Hold on. I'm starting it up. And don't forget to enjoy the ride."

The motor rumbled, vibrating Clementine's whole body. She looked for handles, but all that presented themselves as stabilizing devices were the bike and Bryce himself. She hovered her hands near Bryce's sides.

The vehicle backed up, and Clementine jumped. She rested her hands on Bryce to give her some grip. He adjusted a switch in front of him and grabbed the handles.

The bike gained speed across the parking lot. Bryce barely slowed to bear left onto Meena Bazaar. Clementine had never taken it in this direction. She sought out the tents, crowds, and merchants behind her, already feeling lost and backwards. But perhaps a bit exhilarated.

Bryce selected a right onto the next road, which cut diagonally through the neighborhood. Other autocarriages and wagons made him decelerate the bike. He tapped his fingers on the handlebar until he accelerated again. After a few turns, the steambike shot out through a red-and-brown-brick gate, exiting the walled city.

The wind whipped in Clementine's face where it could reach her behind Bryce. They followed the curving road to the left, but Clementine no longer cared which direction they headed. She felt as light and free as a bird. As long as she held onto Bryce, she might never learn what it meant to fall from the nest.

Close by on her right, a lazy river stretched out along the city. Faded blue ripples fluttered across it to the other side. Every tree on the opposite shore lacked detail, like the green strokes of an artist's brush.

The steambike chugged as Bryce increased its speed. They coasted along the shore, past small boats and wild vegetation. Birds chirped and trilled, lulling Clementine into forgetting she was halfway around the world from the species she knew. Only when she spotted them on a branch or in flight did they convince her they were not chickadees, cardinals, or sparrows. She did not see long scarlet beaks at home. Brilliant teal, orange, and chartreuse feathers were too exotic in their shades and orientations for the woods of Tennessee.

Bryce steered them the entire length of Delhi's wall, ducking back into the city. To her surprise, Clementine recognized one of the neighborhoods she passed through on her way in and out of Civil Lines. Bryce directed them away from it, slowing the steambike as the crowds thickened. He pulled over into a short space between two autocarriages parked at the roadside.

Clementine unfastened the chin strap under her jaw and pulled off the helmet. Bryce stopped the engine and climbed off the bike. He took the helmet, steadying Clementine's descent from the vehicle with his other hand. He retrieved their hats while Clementine patted in vain at her hair. Strands looped away from her head, and stray locks drooped around her ears. She put her hat on, begrudging it would have to be good enough.

Bryce crowned himself with his newsboy and stowed the helmet under the seat. "Are you hungry? They serve food nearby."

"American?" Clementine frowned at the way she sounded. "I didn't ask Edith much about the food here. I've been using whatever ingredients I find to make the foods I'm used to. I've been too busy to ask anyone about local dishes."

"I'll pick out something you'll like."

"Something simple."

"All right, but you can't live and work here without real, honest-to-goodness Indian food."

"Maybe one day."

Clementine was not sure if a second half of her sentence hung in the air. *Maybe one day... you can show me.* She wondered about the implications of it but let it be. When she had put off Bryce's invitations to spend time together, he respected her wishes. If she needed more time to herself, she assumed he would give it to her.

She linked her arm around his to keep track of him in the sea of people making their way up and down the street. Men called out in front of several shop entrances around them, each bellow louder than the last. Bryce led her to a short line of people in turbans and saris. Bells and a tambourine rattled somewhere, lost in the crowd's thickness.

Within minutes, they advanced to the front of the line. The operation Bryce had chosen was shockingly sparse, a collection of tables at the side of the road. Large platters showed off mountains of beans and chopped potatoes. Halved and hollowed-out fruits and vegetables lay ready for some preparation Clementine could not guess. A bowl of dough sat mostly covered with a cloth.

Bryce pointed to the dough and a few smaller bowls of glistening sauces. *"Do."*

The bearded man seated behind the front table tore two balls of dough from the mass of it. He flattened them on the table, topping one of them with a mound of vegetables. He slapped the other disc on top, pinching the two together around the edge. He laid the arrangement on an iron griddle beside him, where the dough popped and sizzled. The earthy aromas of frying bread and oil spiked Clementine's curiosity.

She spoke up in Bryce's ear. "What is it?"

"Stuffed paratha. It's a flatbread. It's delicious."

The man flipped the dough, its partially cooked side showing brown, crispy spots. He spread white butter over it before he turned it again. He made a second pairing of flattened dough circles and a scoop of vegetables. As soon as he laid the cooked paratha on a swath of crinkling newspaper, he added the new one to the griddle.

Bryce paid him and handed the first paratha to Clementine. He waited for the second to cook and accepted it. He led Clementine aside to a pocket in the crowd where they pulled apart.

Clementine wondered at him. "I didn't know you spoke any of the languages here. When did you learn?"

"I picked up a little Hindi as I went along. All those interviews. The Brits who've been here a long time like Miss Higginbotham. The men in the factory." He pinched off a wedge of stuffed paratha, gold with blackened bits. Carrot slivers, green peas, and other vegetables poked out of the flatbread. "Don't be too impressed with me. I only know the numbers through ten."

"After three years?"

"I've been busy learning plants and navigating the customs here."

Clementine understood his point. "Like Mr. Mustafa."

"Exactly. Only give things to other people with your right hand. Don't confuse any of the dozen religions with each other. Be kind to the animals walking the streets. You can visit a mosque, but you must remove your shoes."

"It sounds so difficult when you say them one after the other." Clementine ripped a mouthful of food free from the paratha nestled in the newspaper. "But it's beautiful, isn't it?" Clementine yearned for home, the sweet simplicity of sitting in her porch's shade in the summer. Trekking through knee-deep maroon and yellow leaves during the fall to get from one house to another. Trading snowballs with the Lloyd boys, ducking behind trees for cover. Spying the first crocuses of the year poke up through the wilted grass to spread violet petals in anticipation of spring. "I've been here a few weeks now, and it doesn't seem quite as strange to me."

Bryce choked on his food. "I'm sorry. I didn't realize monkey attacks were a common occurrence in Tennessee."

"Hardly. Elephants come through in the circuses, but I don't have time for those." Clementine tasted her first bite of paratha, crunchy on the outside and soft in the middle. Spices lit up her tongue, vegetables taking her home just to sweep her away on the next unexpected flavor. "I wish I would've known about these when I first came here."

Bryce's eyes sparkled. "I told you I was good for information. The vendor's got kulle and other delicacies if you want to try more."

"One a day will be fine."

Bryce shook his head. "You haven't even tried a paratha with pickled vegetables or chutney yet. Let alone the sweet paratha."

Clementine sighed and chewed another bite. "I'm behind, aren't I?"

"Terribly so." Bryce hesitated to jump into the rest of his food. "If you were too busy for the circus, what were you doing?"

Clementine coughed on a mouthful of hot, buttery flatbread.

"You perfected the usage of plants. That takes dedication. But you act like you don't know what fun is. Were things tough for you?"

Clementine nodded but stuffed more paratha into her mouth. Chewing and swallowing bought her time to decide how to answer. "My mother was sick. I had to take care of her."

Bryce scrunched his face up. "That's awful. I don't know where I would've been without my mother. There were five of us kids, and Dad needed all our help running the farm. Ma could milk a cow in five minutes flat while keeping us from killing each other. She's quite the woman."

Clementine chowed down the rest of her paratha, realizing how hungry she had been.

"But your mother. That's hard. Was it just the two of you?"

"In the family. But in our little part of the world, we had ways of making our own family. Neighbors and other people we met in Nashville after we moved."

Bryce's gaze graced her face.

Clementine balled up the empty paper, seeking out a proper receptacle. Flat, crumpled, and smashed newspapers littered the street. With passing regret, she released her own among them.

Bryce finished his paratha and left its wrapping behind. "I guess when I said newspapers weren't good for much, I forgot about street food."

"I can't imagine Mr. Longshaw visiting a man with a griddle and eating with his hands in the street."

"He's been uptight the whole time I've known him."

Bryce took Clementine's arm and led her a few doors down to a white building with a grand claret façade. Gold letters spelled out the name in winding script followed by the English word *Hall*. Steam escaped into the air from a pipe in the roof.

A potbellied man pushed a billboard on wheels toward them, submerged in the crowd. He shouted, too, but all Clementine could do was survey the pictures painted on his sign. The top half championed a man with long hair, thick eyebrows, and a wide moustache in white, traditional Indian dress. Words underscored it proclaiming *Raja Harishchandra.*

Clementine defaulted to Bryce. "What's this?"

"It's the first movie ever made by an Indian. They still show it. I've seen it at least three times."

A golden town filled the bottom half of the billboard, its minarets ablaze, the orange flames billowing into the sky. A partially-clothed monkey flew over them, accompanied by the words *Lanka Dahan.*

Clementine pointed to it. "Are we seeing this one, then? Do you think we should after our own adventure with our furry friend?"

"That's not just any monkey. It's one of their gods, I think. They base a lot of their movies on stories about their heroes and gods. As long as the only monkey in the theater is on the screen, we'll be okay."

The man rolled his billboard up the street, and Bryce guided Clementine through the front doors of the establishment. He approached the nearest ticket seller. *"Do."*

The young man behind the counter laid out two tickets and spoke back to Bryce. The American pulled a few coins from his pocket and traded them for the tickets.

"We have cinemas in Nashville," Clementine admitted. "I haven't made time for them. Only once. Then I felt guilty."

"You shouldn't feel bad about it now. How's your mother doing?"

"She gets by."

"You left her in good hands with your friends?"

"I did." Clementine's tension barely waned, her fingers clutching Bryce's arm. "It's not so strange, you know. Having animals as gods."

Bryce blinked at her. "You surprise me all the time."

He passed their tickets to the next employee, who guided them further into the building.

Clementine marveled at the golden columns and vermillion walls. "What else can you tell me about the hall?"

Bryce licked his lips. "This particular place keeps being converted. There weren't any theaters before the British came. Until *Raja Harishchandra* found success in Bombay, they had no reason to show films here. Now India makes movies with the best of them, and this new art form is gaining some ground."

"Where did you learn all this?"

"Miss Higginbotham and Mr. Mustafa." He paused. "And an old newspaper we wrapped some of our equipment in as we traveled."

"So you do read it sometimes," Clementine teased.

"Not about war, only fun and games, so it wouldn't make Milton happy. It'd just earn me another lecture."

"At least you'd get another nap."

The usher stopped and ripped the tickets in half. He passed two halves back and gestured up ahead.

Clementine and Bryce passed through a pair of parted doors into a large auditorium arched into a twenty-foot ceiling. Chairs sat in rows in the middle of the room. Bryce selected a pair of open seats in the back corner, and Clementine settled in next to him. Laughter and numerous languages volleyed through the chamber.

Clementine slid her fingertips along her dress' angled neckline.

"Are you all right?" Bryce asked.

"I keep thinking about all those books at the office. Normally, I'd have taken one home and read through it over the weekend. Instead, I'm at the movies."

"I know you're not used to it, but you've got to relax."

"There are so many people counting on me." Clementine's fidgeting fell to the sash around her waist, twisting its peach-colored tie. "On *us* as a company. They're in pain, Mr. Bloom, and…"

Bryce hesitated but placed a light hand over Clementine's. "You have to trust the team. It's more than just you on the project, but you act like you're the only one who can make it succeed. Milton's been at this for over a decade. I've put three years in working for him and Clements. All of the men are trained."

"There are setbacks. Miss Datta got injured."

Bryce raised his eyebrows, concern pulling at his mouth. "It's Friday night. It's after six o'clock. We've got hot, crispy parathas in our bellies, and we're about to struggle our way through a movie about a monkey in a burning city."

"But…"

"You're worried about your mother?"

"She was very ill."

"She got better, right? I'm sure your friends are taking great care of her."

Clementine's throat threatened to close up and keep any more words from coming out. "I'm halfway around the world. In a theater. In Delhi. If anything happened, it'd take more than a week for me to get home."

Bryce shook his head. "On your new salary, I'd take an airship. But I see your point. I used to feel weird being thirty miles away from my family. They stayed in Guthrie on the farm, and I moved to the City – Oklahoma City – to get other work. Being thousands of miles away is hard at first. I know."

"I haven't…" Clementine studied Bryce's earnest eyes. "I don't have people I can talk to here. Not since Miss Higginbotham moved back into her parents' house. I get letters from home, but it's not the same. I've never felt this alone."

"And your father's gone, too." Bryce held her hand. "You must be going through the toughest time of your life. I'm here if you want to talk. It's been difficult for me without Clements to rely on. It's got to be harder for you."

"I've learned what you meant about Mr. Longshaw. I'm sorry he's rude to you. He doesn't always treat me much better."

Bryce looked down at their hands, cheering up as he lifted his head. "Do you want to hear how I got this job?"

"Please. Anything to take my mind off things."

The lights dimmed in the large hall except for a beam of concentrated light extending from high up the back wall. It spread out to illuminate a tall set of garnet curtains at the front of the room. Two men pulled the curtains aside to reveal a plain black screen. Half the room applauded. With a muffled, rhythmic chugging like the engine of an autocarriage, the light transformed to play out the credits of the film.

Clementine could barely see Bryce in the faint dimness of the audience.

He leaned closer, his breath warm on her ear. "I worked in the Lee-Huckins Hotel. Did you ever hear of it?"

"No."

"Rich and famous people come through there. It has the first steam-engine elevator. That's what I ran. The *lift*, as the British call it."

Clementine grinned but wondered at Bryce's history. "You didn't work with plants or medicine?"

The crowd whooped. Clementine glanced at the scene projected on the wall, but she could not tell who the people were being portrayed there.

Bryce answered her. "No. I'm familiar with plants in general from growing up on the farm."

"What made my father hire you?"

"That's what makes it a fantastic story. I didn't know who they were at first. Milton apologized that Clements had to stay in the hotel at all. Your father didn't mind. We did everything we could to make the guests happy, and he liked staying there.

It was only two dollars a night for a private room with its own bath. He wasn't complaining about any of it. Milton criticized everything."

Clementine bucked her eyebrows up. "I wish it surprised me."

"They planned to leave for India soon, and Milton was bitter about their lack of assistants. They needed people to help them carry equipment and organize their research. Your father claimed he could make a great assistant out of anyone. They stepped onto the elevator at that point."

Clementine tried to keep herself from guessing the rest of the story. "What did you say to him?"

"I asked what floor they wanted. It was Clements who asked me who I was and if I was happy tending the elevator. It suited me all right, but when he asked if I wanted to go to India, I couldn't say no. How many times in a farmer boy's life does he get an opportunity like that? It didn't cost me anything. It's earned me money." Bryce clasped his hands together. "My parents always said I took after my ma's dad. A bit of a dreamer. Not as practical as the rest of them. When my choices were to work the farm, direct an elevator, or gather information in India, I chose what appealed to me the most."

"Has it disappointed you in any way?"

The crowd jeered and shook their fists in the air. On the screen, a man made off with a woman in a white sari.

Bryce tapped his foot. "I've gotten more than Clements promised me."

"Did you know how long you'd be here?"

"Not really. They said it could be several months but probably years. That's the way things played out in the other countries they worked in."

Clementine toyed with one earring, humored by Bryce's tale. "Do you ever pay attention to the movies when you come here?"

"Sometimes. The dialog they show you isn't always in English. I don't know the original stories. I usually watch the action and make up my own."

The audience erupted in cheers, and Clementine rejoined their interest in the movie. A person playing the half-clothed monkey from the billboard filled the screen. "Why is the monkey there?"

"To stop that man from completing his important research, obviously."

Clementine laughed.

As the film went on, Bryce filled her in on his theories. When the monkey god, Hanuman, reached the kidnapped Sita, Bryce whispered, "The animal's helping to free the man's research partner." While the monkey's burning tail spread fire throughout the island city, Bryce exclaimed, "What did they expect?" In the end, Hanuman extinguished himself in the ocean, and Bryce collapsed back in his chair. "One more monkey attack finally over."

Clementine walked out of the hall with Bryce, a weak smirk on her lips. "The movie titles said Ravana, the demon king, angered Hanuman by refusing to return Sita to her husband."

Bryce swatted his hand through the air despite the cramped space of the exiting crowd. "Sometimes they use the wrong words. She was pulled away from her work by her opinionated, boorish business partner. The monkey attack only made matters worse."

Clementine chuckled. They walked along the street until they reached Bryce's steambike. She traded her elegant hat for his helmet, and he drove them into Civil Lines. She held onto him in the dark, streetlamps and stars dotting the world. He parked in her driveway. Climbing off the dangerous but exhilarating contraption left her sighing with relief. As she realized she would say goodbye to the closest person she had to a friend on that continent, loneliness crept in. But Monday would come with its duties and their analyses. Soon enough.

Bryce held onto the helmet. "Let me guide you all the way to the door. My mother would send me to the dickens if I rode away without making sure you're in safely."

Clementine took a slow stroll at his side up the path. "We didn't have this many machines where I lived growing up. It seems like they're everywhere now."

"I know what you mean. Engines are replacing foot pedals and horses and manual labor. We wouldn't have movie theaters without them."

"I guess I should be glad for them, then."

Bryce paused at the foot of the porch steps. "The cameras can be cranked by hand. They don't need a motor. But who wants to sit by the projector and move every frame through it by hand? They use a steam engine for it and focus the light of the fire down a chute at the screen. That's really all I can tell you. I don't know how the rest of it works."

"You understand more about movies and theaters than anyone else I know."

"It's an old habit. I had to understand the equipment at the farm and the hotel, so when that newspaper explained it, I read the whole article. I've since avoided the newspaper and devoted my time to the cinema. And the serum, of course."

Clementine trekked up the steps with him and took out her key. "Thank you for inviting me. It was nice getting to know more about you."

"The same goes for me."

"You'll be careful riding home on your bike?"

"Yes, ma'am. It's not far."

Around them, the cool evening invited the mist back into Clementine's periphery. With the pale, squared houses, they could have been standing in England. Or Nashville. Perhaps Oklahoma City. She owed Bryce so much to be able to talk to him freely in person. "I should stick up for you at the factory. It's not fair the way Mr. Longshaw picks on you."

Bryce's fingertips traced the helmet's front curve. "It's not your job. You've barely gotten used to him yourself. You should save the arguing for things that really matter."

Milton had ushered them into the dry storage room just to accuse Clementine of getting too personal with Bryce. She had volleyed with her disdain for Milton's questionable practices, but Bryce did not need to know that. "That's good advice."

"I'm sorry for the tragedy that brought you here. But I'm glad to know you. I'm happy you made the journey. I wouldn't have had the guts to make it on my own."

"Didn't you move to Oklahoma City by yourself?"

"That was thirty miles. I had the support of my whole family behind me. They know what it is to move to get work."

"Did your mother cry when you left?"

Bryce deflated. "Like a baby. Yours, too?"

Clementine touched her fingertips down one of her cheeks. "Tears falling down her face."

"Well, with your determination and my knowledge and Milton's talking and everybody else's skills, we'll have this formula done by the end of the year. You'll see your mother in no time."

Clementine could have squeezed him for giving her hope. She restrained herself and used the key in the door lock. "I'm sure you're right. Will you go back to Oklahoma City?"

"I was planning on it."

"You'll have a lot of experience when you get home. You'll probably be able to get any job you want. Good night. Thank you for a lovely evening."

"Anytime." Bryce put on the helmet and fastened it under his round, narrow chin. "The steambike can go much faster. I have so much left to show you if you'll let me."

Clementine shied away from thoughts of speeding along the riverside on the open vehicle. It felt sturdy, but it was no reason to test its limits. She opened the door. "Prove you're right about the spicy, unfamiliar foods I've been too afraid to try. Then I'll think about letting you drive faster when I ride with you."

"How fast does Clements' autocarriage go? Have you tried it?"

"Some of us are less adventurous than you. I came to do a job. Not to race around in strange vehicles."

"Good night, Miss Fitzgerald." With a twinkle in his eyes, Bryce jogged away down the steps toward his bike.

Clementine went into the house and closed the door. Things would be different on Monday. More shared jokes. Deeper confidences traded. She removed her hat and coat, relegating them to the hooks beside the door. Would work become more tolerable? Pleasant? Making jabs about Milton under their breaths. Blaming his pointed notions and commands on his aging mind. He came from a former generation impossible to understand in their youth.

Clementine wandered into the large expanse of the great room. Maybe she could make it here. Without Edith Higginbotham. Without her father. Maybe Bryce's same age was not the annoyance she had found it to be. It could be a gift, a way to stave off the pains of being far from home. It would not prevent her from devoting herself to the project's completion, so there could be no harm in making a friend. Especially if they worked together.

Chapter Thirteen

Knocks on the meeting room door left Clementine with only one guess as to who wanted in. She cracked a red book open on the table's edge and called out with faint interest. "Come in."

Bryce muttered next to her. "Try not to break a hip."

Clementine stifled a chuckle.

Milton opened the door and stepped in. "The workman left. He recalibrated all the extractors."

Clementine balked at the change in plans. "Won't we have to make up for that extra expense?"

"It's worth it to be safe. It won't smash Miss Datta anymore, which saves us from finding a new assistant to replace her." Milton tugged at the hems of his gloves.

Bryce leaned over the book spread open in front of him. "Isn't it warm in here for gloves today?"

Milton perused Bryce's hair and brown suit. "I don't tell you how to dress. Obviously." He backed out of the room and shut the door.

Bryce puffed up his chest and summoned a deep baritone. "I don't dress you, do I, sonny boy?"

Clementine let her laughter out. "You've imitated Mr. Longshaw for years, haven't you?"

"Yes, but I have to be careful. Clements thought it was funny, but I can't have word of it getting back to Milton."

"Of course. You can't lose your job because he's stodgy."

"We can't blame it on his wife, either. Mrs. Longshaw's—"

The door squealed open, clamming Bryce up into tight-lipped humility.

Milton intoned. "Your delivery's arrived, by the way."

He ambled off, and Clementine stood up from her chair. "I'm anxious to see it."

Bryce got up and walked with her. In the delivery room, workmen parted the large doors to rays of misty sunlight. A truck backed up toward the bay. The elongated pipe on top emitted breaths of white cloud. Two men climbed down from the cab. They lifted the back panel of the truck, exposing stacks of boxes. Workmen outfitted in thick gloves moved forward, hauling the cargo inside.

Clementine and Bryce remained by the side wall with Mr. Mustafa and Nithya Menon. The foreman directed the organization of the boxes across the cement floor. Mr. Mustafa facilitated the conversation. When a workman collected the last box, Nithya walked the room. His brown eyes honed in on every package, his moustache twitching. He checked off places on the page on his clipboard and shared his conclusions.

Mr. Mustafa uttered them in English. "The full delivery has been received."

Most of the workers took small knives out of their pockets and sliced the boxes open. Clementine wandered closer. Despite the cool air wafting in from outside, sweat tickled her forehead. If anything had damaged the plants, it could mean the kind of setback she and Bryce hoped to avoid.

A workman pried the top of a box ajar. Clementine bent over to see inside. Plump, vermilion strawberries filled the container. Another box unpacked nearby housed a thick collection of bright green leaves Clementine recognized as holy basil.

She bowed over her pressed palms to the delivery men and Nithya. "*Namaste*. Mr. Mustafa, tell them I'm happy with the shipment."

The turbaned man dipped his head. "I will."

Clementine and Bryce walked into the hallway, where the warmer air comforted her. She relaxed into easy strides. "First one done."

"With several more on the way. It's good they're coming on different days. It'll give the men time to process each shipment."

"How long until we can start mixing?"

"As soon as we have recipes and the plants we want to use in them."

"I think strawberries and holy basil could make a good foundation. Their anti-aging properties complement each other."

"If all the ingredients are that tasty, we'll have no problems selling this elixir. We'll only have to worry about keeping up with the demand."

Clementine bounced the next few steps. Bryce's dogged optimism validated her arduous efforts.

Milton's echoing voice cut her off from saying so. "We make sure the machines are sanitized and ready. You and I don't do it, no."

Clementine tensed before she even saw him. Milton and Indira rounded the corner up ahead. Covered in a periwinkle headscarf and pink sari, Indira provided a bright burst of color in the beige corridor. She lit up like the sun when her eyes met Clementine's.

Milton droned on. "Do you remember where the machines are?"

"I do." Indira sped up, meeting Clementine and Bryce in the middle of the hallway. "I hoped to see you today."

Indira's energy renewed Clementine's good mood. "Can I do something for you?"

"I want to talk. Is that okay?"

"Of course." Clementine guided Indira to the door for dry storage. The workmen would be occupied unboxing the shipment for a while. They still had to wash and dry the plants before they would need to access the storage room. "Excuse me, Mr. Bloom. I'll only be a minute." She glanced at Milton. "I'm sure you hold no objections to me having a private conversation in the storage area?"

His tone fell flat and serious. "No."

Bryce flashed a hand at her. "I'll wait here."

Milton cast a curious, furrowed glance over him.

Clementine let Indira and herself into the storage room. She gladly closed the door on Milton's sour expression. "Do we need Mr. Mustafa's help?"

Indira beamed with slight uncertainty. "No. I will try."

"Is something wrong? Bad?"

"Me. Or Ravi." Indira rotated one of her circular bracelets around her wrist. "I'm sorry. He is very angry. I told to him never do it again."

"It's not a problem. For the company. Did Mr. Lal see your injury?"

"No. Mr. Mustafa told me the word for me. Embarrassed."

"Don't. It was his decision..." Clementine phrased it in simpler terms. "Mr. Lal did it, not you. He was mad. You're a happy person."

Indira played with the fabric of her headscarf where it hung past her neck. "I am happy to you and Mr. Longshaw. You give me this job."

"We want you to work here. Let Mr. Lal come. Let your father and your family break down the doors. You will work here as long as you want to."

Indira's eyes twinkled above her upturned lips. "Ravi makes me angry, too."

"I know. We're like each other, you and me."

"That is why you keep my job?"

"*You* keep your job. You're smart." Clementine tapped her temple. "You have a good heart." She patted the left side of her chest.

"You help my hand." Indira showed Clementine her index finger, barely a bruise discoloring its side.

"I hope to help many people with what we make."

"You help me. Many times."

Clementine kept herself from expressing her gratitude for Indira's sentiments. "Let's go back to work."

"Yes. Our work is very important." Indira approached the door but hung back from opening it. "It's different for you and me. You help all people of the world. I want to help the women of my country."

Clementine remembered how little she truly knew about India and its people. Mr. Mustafa's lesson reverberated in her ears. *The women are still coming out of hiding, from behind curtains, veils, and closed doors.* "I think you are."

"I help Ravi, too. He does not believe it."

Raps on the door made Clementine spring it open.

Milton peered down at her from his superior height. "I need my assistant back if we're going to get the extractors examined on schedule."

Clementine forced the cheeriest smile she could muster. "Your assistant is fully ready for her duties."

The two women slipped out into the hall. Indira walked away with Milton into the extraction room. Clementine resumed her stroll with Bryce into her office.

"What was that about?" he asked.

"She's terrified she'll lose her job." Clementine went over to the desk. "She's genuinely grateful for her position."

"And for you."

Clementine met Bryce's eyes, solemn and admiring. Like Indira, she was determined not to stray too far off track from her career. Clementine crouched down and pulled a fresh notebook out of a desk drawer. "As for us, we have more recipes to write out."

Bryce tucked his hands into his pockets. "We should put some basics into every formula in this batch. We agreed on strawberries and holy basil. I'd suggest gotu kola. Turmeric. Aloe vera."

"Yes. Let's write those down right now." Clementine grabbed a pen off the desk and sat down on the rug. "You don't object to working comfortably, do you, city boy?"

Bryce cracked a grin. "I have about as much of the city in me as you do."

Clementine opened the notebook to its first blank page. "I have two years of Nashville and about a month in Delhi. Considering you've been here for almost three years plus your time in Oklahoma City–"

"About a year."

"–I need not say anything more."

Bryce lowered himself next to Clementine and stretched his legs out in front of him.

Clementine wrote out the ingredients. "What else belongs on this list?"

"It'd be easier to add them with the books in front of us."

Clementine gave him a wry, sidelong look. "If I have to spend another day cooped up in that meeting room…"

He swiveled his feet from side to side. "I understand. I think Indian gooseberries have a strong case for them."

Clementine jotted them down. "Ginger? Ginseng? Clove?"

"Those carry some very powerful flavors. People have to drink this stuff, remember."

"And they'll thank us when they're done."

Bryce scanned the list before she could add any more. "We've got too many basics. We're not making a launch point. We're creating a catch-all for every plant we've inquired about. Not to mention the Ganges River samples we'll bottle up."

"What would you take off?"

Bryce grasped the notebook. He squinted at the ingredients, tapping the pen against the page. He chuckled. "Nothing. I can't remove a single one. You know what?"

Clementine grabbed the notebook.

Bryce held onto it. "It's okay. It gives us a sturdy foundation to work from. There are plenty of other plants to play with that can provide variations of this."

"How? We've already accounted for half the species in India." She tugged on the notebook.

"Hardly."

"Name another ingredient for each one on this list."

Bryce pointed to every plant. "Pomegranate. Neem. Grapes. Do you really want me to keep going?"

Clementine's eyes glimmered with provocation. "Go ahead. You're off to such a great start."

Bryce bumped his shoulder against hers and consulted the list. "Licorice. Rosemary." He struggled with his final suggestion and blurted it out. "Ashwaganda."

Clementine laughed. "Very good."

Bryce gave up the notebook. "If you hadn't distracted that monkey from taking our records, I might not have gotten all those."

Clementine scribbled her additional possibilities on a second page. "If the Fountain of Youth doesn't pay off, you can host a circus act naming plants from the mysterious East."

"Doesn't pay off?" Bryce patted the notebook. "We're most of the way to something special. I'm not naming plants from memory for nothing."

"It did save us from going back to those over-civilized chairs in the meeting room."

Bryce's pond-water eyes shone in the half-light. "Over-civilized, indeed." He crossed the inches between them and met Clementine with a kiss.

Warmed by his contact, she searched his face. Her skin tingled. She nudged toward him, risking a second kiss that made her heart flutter.

A shriek pierced her eardrums. Clementine leaped away from Bryce and scrambled to her feet.

He stood up and hurried to the doorway. "Miss Datta again?"

"I'm afraid so." Clementine tossed the notebook and pen on the floor. She darted after Bryce into the corridor.

Indira's screaming formed words. "Help! Miss Fitzgerald." She raced around the corner from the factory rooms.

Clementine ran toward her, scrutinizing Indira. She held her hands apart, not cradling one with the other. She took even strides with no signs of limping. Clementine zeroed in on a crimson spot on Indira's pink sari. "Is that blood?"

"Mr. Longshaw needs you."

Clementine and Bryce followed Indira around the corner. Workmen crept forward from the unpacking room, lingering in the far half of the hallway. Concern bunched their brows.

Clementine picked Mr. Mustafa out of the crowd. "Tell them to stay back. We've got this under control." She hoped to prove that statement true.

Indira rushed Clementine and Bryce into the extraction room. A handful of workers milled about between the machines, gesturing and uttering in foreign languages. Milton hunched over near the flat bed of the first machine on the right, plunging Clementine into flashbacks. Her spine shivered, and she hurried towards him.

Milton grunted and shook out his right hand.

Clementine stared at its bareness. The pale skin split from his pinky to the base of his thumb. She swallowed her nausea. "What happened?"

Milton shot his hand down, keeping it close to him. "That damn mechanic." He sounded breathless and scattered. "He said it was fixed. I paid him."

Clementine reached out. "Let me see it. What happened?"

Milton jerked his hand away. "Nothing that can be solved with fruits and flowers, no matter what combination they're in." He snatched his glove off the floor and tried to fit his injured hand inside it.

Indira scrunched her face in horror and spun away from him.

Clementine seethed. "Leave the glove off. You're going to harm it more."

Milton's wild eyes flicked to her. "That's the problem. Half my hand throbs, and the other half is numb."

Bryce waved Milton toward him. "We should get you to a hospital."

Clementine tossed her hands up. "Why? Is he actually going to let a doctor take care of him?"

Milton glared at her.

Indira spoke up from behind Clementine. "I know the hospital."

Bryce raised a hand. "I'll drive."

Milton hissed through clenched teeth. "In my autocarriage, thank you very much."

Clementine turned to Indira. "Will you go with them? Take them there?"

Indira's head wobbled. "Yes. Anything I can do."

Milton took a few unsteady steps toward the door. "My keys are in the coat in my office."

Bryce lent him an arm, but Milton lurched past him. Clementine and Indira rushed after the men to Milton's office. Bryce ducked inside long enough to grab Milton's winter gear. He plopped Milton's hat on the old man's head and fished the autocarriage key out of a pocket.

The party scurried into the lobby. Aatmaj jumped up behind the desk. "Is everything all right?"

Clementine nodded and motioned for him to sit. "It will be."

The foursome filed out into the thin white mist. Milton led the others to his vehicle and climbed up into the passenger seat. Bryce assisted Indira into the backseat and took the wheel.

Fear crashed over Clementine, vibrating her limbs. She dove at the passenger door and wrenched it open. Milton gazed down at her, pale and grim. "Mr. Longshaw, what do I do?"

His small, grey eyes hardened. "What on earth do you mean?"

"I've never headed a company this big by myself. What should I do?"

Milton pondered the back of his hand. "I don't know how long I'll be out of commission. I need to heal, and who knows what the pain killers will do to me. I'm certainly going to need them."

"I don't know if I can lead the factory without you."

The steam engine wound up to a consistent purr.

Milton positioned his hand in his lap, where his coat stretched over his legs like a blanket. "Miss Fitzgerald, you came into my office and gave me multiple reasons you should take your father's place. You pushed me to accept you as my business partner."

Her pulse raced. "I know. But I haven't learned everything. We're waiting on several shipments from all over the country. I can't do half your job."

"You're co-owner, so make your decision. What are you going to do in my absence?"

Clementine took a much-needed breath and let it out. "I'm closing the factory."

Milton grunted. "The shipments? The workers? The blasted broken machines?"

"I'll rearrange the shipments if I can or have someone here to receive them."

The door thumped behind her, and Clementine took grave relief in Mr. Mustafa arriving at her side. "Mr. Mustafa will help me tell the workers we're taking an unplanned vacation."

Milton grimaced. "They might not bear it well."

"I wouldn't. I'll talk with Mr. Magar about room in the budget to pay the workers for their trouble if we can."

Milton's jaw firmed.

"We'll get someone else to check that machine."

"I took my glove off to work the knobs and make sure the bed was properly sanitized." His voice broke. "The glass case came down. I wasn't as fast or lucky as Miss Datta."

"Good luck," Clementine wished him earnestly.

Bryce leaned forward where she could see him past Milton. "We should get to the hospital. His hand is swelling up."

Clementine clapped the door shut and stepped back. Bryce drove away with Milton and Indira, leaving the parking lot still and quiet.

Mr. Mustafa kept his volume low. "Another unfortunate accident?"

"It appears so." Clementine faced him no matter how hard it was to own her responsibilities. "I'm glad you came. Otherwise, I'd be alone. I'm already alone in making decisions."

"You came to India alone."

"I did." Clementine closed her eyes. The train across six states to San Francisco. A week on the Pacific Ocean. Another train from Bombay to Delhi. Standing alone by her father's casket saying goodbye while Edith Higginbotham busied herself in the kitchen, giving Clementine the privacy she had asked for.

Clementine opened her eyes, finding Mr. Mustafa as patient and composed as usual. "We should go in. The workers will want to know what's happened, and we shouldn't keep them waiting."

A sparkle of pride glinted across his eyes. "I agree."

Chapter Fourteen

Clementine laid her hands on the desk and dropped her forehead into her palms. The silence of the factory crawled under her skin and haunted her.

Bryce touched her arm. "You can't be upset."

Clementine groaned. "What am I supposed to be? Mr. Longshaw broke his hand. He needs weeks or months to recover. The workers were too kind to show their disappointment and concern when we announced we were closing the factory. Except for Mr. Mustafa, Miss Datta, and a handful of others, we've been working alone for a full week."

"But we accepted the deliveries. The other plants will get here, too."

Clementine sat up and struck her fist on the desk. "That's unacceptable. With a one-to-two-month delay, we'll miss the growing seasons on some ingredients." Her eyes blazed up at Bryce standing over her. "Miss Datta counted on me. This factory. How many times did she look me in the eye and tell me how grateful she was for the chance to work here?"

She popped out of her chair. "We have to fix this."

Bryce splayed his fingers in defeat. "Fix what? A doctor put Milton's hand back together. It's going to take time for the fractures to fuse."

"We have to find someone who knows enough to repair the extractors for good or at least someone willing to learn. We could call in Mr. Menon to teach them the mechanisms." Clementine strode toward the other side of the room.

Bryce caught her arm. "We sent faxes to every mechanic in Milton's files. There's only one thing left for us to do."

Clementine stiffened. "I'm not giving up, and I'm keeping us on track. We're releasing the Fountain of Youth this year. I'll do anything I have to do to make that happen."

"It will. I'd never suggest otherwise. But I think we've put in a busy week. It's Friday night. We've given everyone else a break whether they wanted it or not. It's time to go home for a couple of days. Or weeks."

A sob welled up in Clementine's throat. "What if I walk out the front door and never come back in?"

Bryce stepped toward the coat rack but stopped. "That's not going to happen. In what world do you, Clementine Fitzgerald, let a door stand between you and what you want?"

She considered her black shoes. "No world I know of."

"Exactly. Come on. We can skip the cinema tonight if you don't feel like it."

"We've had our share of monkeys and legends for now." Clementine gave in. She put on her hat and coat. "What else do you have in mind?"

"Something interesting I found on my rides around the city without you."

She paused for half a second. "It involves your bike."

Bryce gave her a crooked grin. "Was that fear, exasperation, or a hint of adventurousness?"

"Maybe all of them, in that order." Clementine winced. "That wasn't fair. I liked the steambike once I got used to it."

"Fresh air. Total freedom. What's not to like?"

"The possibility – or inevitability – of crashing. The faster speeds. Nothing wrapped around me to save me from birds or monkeys or other vehicles."

"It's perfectly safe. And I let you wear the only helmet."

Clementine adored Bryce's freckled cheeks and ornery hair. She had grown fond of him, and thoughts of him smashing the bike made her clutch at her chest. "That's not much consolation, you know."

"I'll buy a second helmet. If you come with me to see the surprise." Bryce plopped his hands on his hips.

"You're pretty proud of yourself, aren't you? You found the perfect way to get us both what we want."

"I'm learning to negotiate, I guess. I never had to do it before."

"Like I had to talk Mr. Longshaw into letting me work here?"

Bryce shuffled out of the office, and Clementine shut off the overhead gaslight. She stopped the fan's rotations swirling the air around the room. She skimmed its furniture and shapes in the dark, already pulled back toward it. The flip of a switch and roll of a knob were all she needed to plunge the office back into its daily operations. Books and pens and herbs and spices.

Bryce murmured. "Come on."

Clementine scrunched her eyes shut against an uninvited tear. She joined Bryce in the hall and locked the door.

He fastened his coat. "By the way, watching you negotiate with Milton was an honor. You told him exactly why he should do it, and you didn't let up until he agreed. It was the best show ever. If anyone taught me how to negotiate, it was you."

"I only have myself to blame." Clementine smiled at Bryce.

They walked the rest of the hall and passed through the empty lobby. Three weeks before, Milton's job applicants had packed the couch and the space along the opposite wall. Clementine almost longed for the chatter and activity of that day.

Bryce opened the front door, and Clementine forced herself forward through every single step. She strode outside and secured the lock. She tested the handle, and the door remained sturdy, unmoving.

She spun on her heel and accompanied Bryce to his steambike. "What did you want to show me, Mr. Bloom?"

He blanched. "It's a surprise."

"I'm not very good with surprises." She faltered but tested out his first name. "Bryce. We've become friends, haven't we?"

"I hope so."

She nodded, and he produced the helmet from the storage space under the seat. Soon they sped away from the factory, accelerating away from the Meena Bazaar and the Jama Masjid. Bryce whisked them down the wide boulevard and out the ancient gate guarding the city. Instead of curving with the road leading along the river, Bryce steered them farther from Delhi. They thudded over a set of train tracks, and Bryce steered right.

He pointed off to the left. For three full miles, a network of paved roads met and diverged across the landscape. They followed a large half circle in the road, seven streets intersecting with its circumference. Clementine marveled at its complexity. The bike shot off again, continuing in their original direction. Bryce increased their speed until Clementine clung to him, giggling even as her limbs tensed in fear.

The steambike slowed. To their left, several other roads angled towards their destination. They converged into a bull's-eye of three concentric circles. At the end of the road where it met the innermost ring, Bryce parked the bike.

Clementine scrambled off the seat and removed the helmet. She surveyed the scope and magnitude of the spider's web of vacant streets around them. "What is this place?"

Bryce stepped off the bike and settled his hands into his pockets. "We're in New Delhi. Before it's officially, you know, finished and named that."

"This is the project." Clementine stopped short of mentioning Lowell Dodd's name. "I've heard of this."

"Remarkable, isn't it?"

Clementine searched the grounds again. Arid land stretched out around them, flat in some places and disturbed in others.

"I mean, it will be when it's done. Didn't you see it when you rode in on the train from Bombay?"

"I fell asleep before we got here. I woke up at the station."

Bryce pointed toward the network of grey strips at its thickest. "The last time I was here, they were working around the hill. They talked about all the important buildings they have to put in. That's where they moved their equipment, I think."

Clementine strained to see in the fading light. Beyond the lip of the broad plain, trucks and machines loomed in the distance.

"Let's go see it before the sun goes down completely." Bryce reclaimed the front of the bike's seat.

Shadowed shapes marked the top of the hill, and Lowell's comments hummed in Clementine's head. *I always thought Americans were charming. You're like us but not like us.*

"Do you want to see it?" Bryce asked.

Delhi is a small and desolate place. It'll be expanded and built up heavily. It won't be a city anymore. It'll be its country's capital.

Clementine fastened the helmet on her head. She climbed on the bike and held onto Bryce as he powered it up. He followed the inner circle to the left, directing them down the second road branching out like the spoke of a wheel. Bryce pushed the bike for speed, and within minutes, they stopped at the top of the rise. They left the bike behind, Clementine holding onto the helmet.

Clangs and motors echoed up from below. Walking closer, Clementine made out their structures in the near-darkness. Towering cranes puffed white clouds into the sky. Wooden beams and cement blocks ladened trucks and packed-dirt plots. A massive machine supported a large funnel on top, and a long chute protruded from the bottom. Steam shot free in whistling bursts. Men called orders back and forth, both amiable and heated.

Clementine sucked in a breath to suggest she and Bryce leave.

A familiar timbre rumbled like a lion's purr. "It appears we attracted an audience."

Lowell Dodd. Clementine tapped Bryce's arm. "Isn't there something else we can do? It's almost dark."

The voice focused up the hillside. "Good evening."

Bryce looked Clementine over. "Do you think we're in trouble? They're barely working now. I'm sure it's fine."

Lowell crested the hill and broke into glowing satisfaction. "Miss Fitzgerald. I hardly suspected I'd find you here. Especially at this hour." He glanced at Bryce followed by the helmet in her hand.

Clementine ducked the helmet behind her back. "Mr. Lowell Dodd, I'd like to introduce one of our workers at the company, Mr. Bryce Bloom. He researched with my father."

Lowell clenched Bryce's hand in a firm shake. "Clements was a good man. It's a pleasure to meet you."

Bryce tucked his hands in his pockets. "I've heard your name mentioned amongst the investors."

Clementine stopped herself from rushing the conversation along. She wished she had impressed more of Lowell's arrogance and superiority on Bryce. She might have avoided this awkward reunion. "That's correct. Mr. Dodd's one of the investors I met with last month."

Lowell's smile held as much slyness as it did mirth. "You seem to be settling in nicely."

Clementine waved her free hand at the elongated streets around them. "Your project has a lot of roads."

Lowell clasped his hands together. "It's a beginning. You should've seen what we started with. A lot of effort and planning has gone into what little you see today."

Steam engines whirred and wound down into silence. The clanking of tools subsided. A loud harrumph burst out at the bottom of the hill.

A man chased a retreating figure with full strides, jabbing an erratic finger at him. "I take it back! I'll build the viceroy's house at the top of the hill as I planned."

The fleeing man wheeled around to confront him. "For such a talented architect, you make a terrible friend. You've always considered this entire project through the wrong lens." He bolted again before his pursuant could reach him.

Lowell held his arms out from his sides. "Now we've treated you to the full New Delhi experience. Mr. Lutyens and Mr. Baker never disappoint. I lost track of their arguments ages ago."

Bryce jutted his chin down the hill at the conflicting men. "This is why you've mainly got roads after all these years."

Lowell hid most of his offense behind a wall of wry humor. "Rather. How go operations at the factory?"

Clementine squeaked out a response. "Fine." She faked confidence as best she could. "Mr. Bloom and I are closing in on a formula. Fresh ingredients are rolling in on the trucks."

"Splendid." Lowell consulted the navy-charcoal sky. "I'd better close the site for the night. Nothing else is getting done in this darkness. Someone has to spur the project forward." He tipped his hat and headed off down the hill.

The new mixture's a risky change but genius. I await updates of your success.

Clementine was glad to be rid of Lowell's company. She fit the helmet on her head and walked back to the bike. Bryce accompanied her and drove them back along the deserted roads toward the city.

Haven't you noticed a certain lack in deliberateness?

Clementine pressed her cheek against Bryce's back as they rode.

Animals roaming the streets.

They passed under the gate's brick arch and slowed to meet the city's crawl of traffic.

It's a good thing the British empire gained control. I shudder to think where the country'd be without us.

Bryce followed the curving, snakelike boulevard all the way to Civil Lines.

Was Sandeep or any other servant disrespectful when you arrived?

The steambike made the final turns into Clementine's driveway and came to rest. She flung herself off the bike and ripped off the helmet. She handed it to Bryce and growled as she wandered up the front path toward the porch.

"Wait. Your hat." Bryce hastened off the seat and recovered her cloche from the hidden hollow. He hurried after her, holding it out.

"Thank you." Clementine nestled it on her head to cover up any messiness the helmet had caused her hair.

"I'm sorry if there was something about Mr. Dodd's company you didn't want."

Clementine blew out a breath and continued her ascent to the door with more controlled steps. "I dislike Mr. Dodd. He's worse than I led you to believe." She unlocked the door and popped it open. "He's greedy and obsessed with what the British are doing in India."

Bryce stood in the middle of the porch, his hair akimbo from the wind of their ride.

Clementine admonished herself. "It's not your problem."

"I can help you solve it. What do you want to do about him?"

"Tell him to keep his dirty money. We don't want it, and we don't need it. But we do need it. Mr. Longshaw's in charge of dealing with the investors, anyway. I'm not sure Mr. Dodd is my own problem these days."

"Do you think it's bad for the company to accept his money?"

"It's bad because I don't want to encourage him. I don't want him to gain from our labor. If he thinks the people of India are so disorganized and beneath him, why should he profit from our employees?"

"There must be someone else who can invest in us instead."

"But Mr. Longshaw's hurt and recuperating at home." Clementine rubbed her forehead. Permanent ridges furrowed there no matter how young she was. "You and I have enough work to do. We can't even move forward without overseeing the whole factory ourselves."

With gentle fingers, Bryce took Clementine's hand from her face. He held onto it. "Maybe it's time we rested, too. You took care of your mother. You jumped right into work here after your father died. I've been collecting data for three years. It's only for a little while."

Clementine sputtered, distraught at the idea.

"A tiny break. I promise." Bryce raised her hand to his lips and kissed it. "Milton's as old as some of the ruins around here, but he's tough. He's mean and nasty, and people like that always recover from their injuries to live another day. Don't they?"

The ghost of a smile cracked through Clementine's melancholy. Old man Coleman had been crueler than a taunted dog or territorial rooster. When a plowing accident took his leg, he hollered threats every day he would jump out of bed on his good leg and hop out to the fields. He cussed and threw chamber pots at those who tried to keep him confined. He garnered more than his full strength for several years until pneumonia and a swift horse kick to the head brought him down.

"Milton's going to be fine," Bryce assured her. "So are we."

"At any cost," Clementine repeated.

Bryce squeezed her hand. "I'll let you have the weekend to yourself if you want. Next week, instead of holing up in offices, we're going to revel in what there is to discover here. Food. People. Music."

Clementine inched closer to Bryce. "It's always food with you."

He cringed. "I shudder imagining what you're doing to these people's ingredients."

"Baked potatoes with that special butter they make. All the rice and beans and strawberries I can eat."

"We can get those in the States. Who knows how much longer we'll be in India?"

Clementine kissed him and stayed close to him. "Then show me what there is to see here."

"I'll spend my weekend planning it out."

"I'm not sure about your negotiation skills." Clementine touched his arm. "You told me what we're going to do. You didn't make sure I knew what was in it for me."

Bryce pecked her on the cheek. "We've come a long way to this colorful, mysterious world. You're worried about not passing back through the factory door a few miles away, but once we succeed with the Fountain of Youth, we might return to the States and never come back."

He swung their clasped hands back and forth. "We have the chance of a lifetime to immerse ourselves in this country.

Their elephants aren't in circuses, Clementine. Princesses ride them through the streets. Hunters ride them out to find their prey. They drag massive tree trunks for the logging industry like our country uses horses and donkeys. It'd be a shame to sail all this way for a factory and baked potatoes."

His conviction took root in Clementine, opening her up to opportunities she had never considered. "You're right." She rewarded him with a kiss. Her stomach gurgled, and she set a hand over it. "Good night, Bryce. I'll go cook one of my last American meals, and I'll see you Monday."

Chapter Fifteen

The turbaned man with the short, white beard kept up an impossible pace on the two-headed drum in his lap. He sat at the side of the dusty road, each hand patting a different rhythm. The tinny taps of his fingertips played in perfect harmony with the drum strikes of the younger man beside him. Also in a neatly tucked turban with a close-cropped moustache and beard, his hands flew over the pair of drums on the ground. His right hand splayed to percuss the animal skin with uncanny precision. His left hand bounced over the wider drumhead, producing bassier sounds to ground the eclectic melody.

To the side of the men danced three teenaged girls, their smiles as big as their movements. Headscarves protected them from the cool but tolerable afternoon. Instead of saris, they wore long-sleeved, collarless blouses buttoned up the front. Their necklaces jumped and twisted as they twirled and shimmied. Aprons covered their dark, ankle-length skirts. They lifted extra fabric into their sure but delicate hands, their arms undulating while their bare feet kicked in time to the music.

With dramatic bangs, all five performers ended on the same beat. The crowd, including Clementine and Bryce, cheered. Most of the onlookers handed coins to the girls and the musicians. Bryce tipped them as well.

Clementine wrapped her arm around Bryce's. "I never get tired of this."

He led them away along the street. "Tennessee doesn't have street performers?"

"There's a big difference between a guitar, a harmonica, a jug, and a music box and what these men do."

"A music box?"

"Not the kind that winds up. It's something they make back home. You never saw one?"

"I don't think so."

"It's a rectangular box that fits in your lap." Clementine held her hands up with two feet in between them. "Not too high. With strings going across the top and holes in the box where the sound comes out when you play it."

"Did you ever play?"

"No. Ollie Ledford tried to teach me at the farm. Lucinda Harris tried at her house. Judson Lloyd offered, but I told him there was no point. I couldn't learn it, and I had other things to do."

"Were they your friends?"

She nodded. "The Ledfords have owned that farm for generations. The Harrises moved from Twinton maybe ten years ago. I was helping Mr. Harris through black lung."

"What's that?"

"This problem coal miners get when they've worked in the mines too long. His sons hadn't gotten it yet, so they moved to get work at something else."

"Making music boxes?"

Clementine grinned. "Only as a hobby. Sometimes he couldn't breathe. He'd cough up blood and black dust."

Bryce winced. "We didn't have mines around where I lived. What about the other family?"

"The Lloyds made moonshine out of just about anything. They sold it up and down Overton County. The strongest stuff around."

Bryce gawked at her. "How do you know so many adventurous and nefarious people?"

"That's all we had. The Johnsons wove baskets. The Colemans had their farm. Sometimes there were dog or chicken fights, but I didn't care for them. Tending to animals is different from giving herbs to people. I hated seeing them in pain when I couldn't do anything."

Something bumped the hem of Clementine's dress against her ankle. A steel-grey hooded cobra wove from side to side. She darted away from it although its owner, a man in a red turban, sat one foot in front of it. He played a long, nasally flute, rocking in the snake's same fluid patterns.

Clementine tried to catch her breath and laughed at herself. She stumbled, leaning on Bryce to regain her balance.

He chuckled. "We haven't talked about snakes yet."

"I don't mind them usually. But they don't often try to dance with me."

They rounded a corner away from the mass of shoppers and onlookers.

Bryce wrapped his hand around Clementine's where it rested on his arm. "I've never heard you talk about home so much before."

She laid her other hand over her satisfied stomach. "With a belly full of korma and curried rice, I guess I'm more talkative than usual."

They ducked into a shallow alcove created by one building's façade looming farther from the road than the one beside it. In the shadowed corner, all but invisible to the thick sprawl of passersby, they snuck a kiss. Clementine glowed, for once feeling that being lost and untethered was a good thing. He kissed her again, and they blushed. A cerulean headscarf caught Clementine's eye amidst the colors in the crowd.

"I think I saw Miss Datta." Delighting in Bryce's company, the idea of getting Indira to join them lifted Clementine's spirits even higher.

Bryce searched the scene. "Where? Is she gone?"

"Do you think we can find her?"

"If it *was* Miss Datta."

"There aren't that many women on the street. I'm sure I've seen that scarf before."

Clementine led Bryce in the direction she had seen the brilliant blue. The current of people washed them along like driftwood toward the sea. Several people filed into an open doorway. Clementine hesitated, not knowing what the building was. A flash of sky blue at the front of the line encouraged her to follow it.

Bryce whispered to her. "What is this place?"

A shop unfolded around them packed with statues, incense, and beaded jewelry. Flowers filled vases on countertops. So many framed pictures hung, Clementine could barely see the turquoise walls. Most of the artwork held a single figure, varying between men and women. Animals accompanied some while others wore an animal head on a human body. A few employed multiple arms, and some had baby-blue skin. Clementine recognized such images from Nivriti Singh's and the Varmas' houses.

The flow of people continued through the shop into a large back room. Shelving units loaded with merchandise had been pushed against the walls, sometimes two or three deep. The middle of the room remained empty except for oversized, colorful pillows. Clementine scanned the people gathered there, both sitting and standing, but could only spot the barest glimpses of aquamarine on the other side of the room.

She answered Bryce's question. "I'm not sure. I'm not even positive Miss Datta's in here." She checked the door, where several men lingered. "We might not get out very easily."

Bryce and Clementine inched toward the exit. Barred by the men, they lacked the words with which to excuse themselves from the room.

A few cheers resounded from the shop's main area, and the two Americans hung back. The men parted from the doorway, and a man outfitted in a green kurta strode in. Behind him, a meeker, younger man shuffled in wearing a bright white turban.

Clementine blinked at him. "Sandeep?"

His eyebrows shot up. "You were visitor at Mr. Dodd's house."

She nodded. The man who had arrived with purpose reached the front of the room. He spoke with those around him, and Clementine was not convinced she should converse at the same time. Bryce looked between her and Sandeep. She accepted her duties. "Sandeep, this is Bryce Bloom. He works with me. Sandeep works for Mr. Dodd."

The Indian, slightly shorter than the Americans, bobbed his head. "What are you doing here?"

Clementine scratched her head. "We don't know. We were following a friend."

A thump of metal and wood distracted Clementine. Behind Sandeep, the door stood closed.

Her throat parched. "What's going on here? We don't want to make trouble."

The man in green addressed the room, quieting the conversation. He raised his hands to gain everyone's attention.

Sandeep murmured. "It is meeting."

"Should we leave?"

The man lowered his arms and delivered his ideas to the group in a halting, passionate speech. The others observed him, rapt.

Sandeep whispered to Clementine and Bryce. "If you are friends to the British and not to us, we ask that you go."

Clementine took in the man in green. He browsed the room from person to person, gesturing with his hands as he spoke. "What is he saying?"

Sandeep paused. "He says India should be free to rule itself."

"Is that why you're here? You want the British to leave?"

"We want to rule ourselves. We want to be ourselves. Not for Britain to change everything we have."

Clementine had sat across from Lowell while he described the city's expansion. She had ridden its roads and stood at the peak of its hill. Would the native Indians have built Civil Lines with straight edges, white walls, and luxurious verandas? Would they have named the king and queen of England their emperor and empress of their own free wills?

Clementine squinted at the man in green. "What's he saying now?"

Sandeep licked his lips. "He reminds us the British do not care for us. They want to use Indians who know English to spread their power. They moved people off their land south of the city – men, women, children, families – for their projects. These people had to find new places to live, and many of them are now paid to work on the project. They are builders. Some work with leather."

A familiar anger heated up in Clementine. "The British kicked them off their property to build on it and employ them for the same reason?"

Sandeep's brown eyes crinkled with worry. "You will not tell Mr. Dodd I am here?"

"Never. What else is this man saying?"

Sandeep took time to listen. "There is a man. Mohandas Gandhi. He brings people together – farmers, workers – to be peaceful but…" Sandeep's brows wrinkled. "To stand up? For themselves."

"Why? What are the British doing?"

Sandeep raised his hand about shoulder height and marked it off with a flat palm. "They want high money for land. We are treat a different way – a bad way – to the British people."

Clementine sighed with frustration and hunted for a silver lining. "Is it working?"

"Yes. They gave Mr. Gandhi the title of Mahatma for his good works. He wrote a book about his ideas. The British do not like him."

Clementine folded her arms. "I suppose they wouldn't."

The speaker increased his emphatic movements, his intense gaze shining. From the right side of Clementine's field of view, azure cloth peeked out from behind the men occupying the room between them. Clementine could not mistake Indira's profile, her large cheeks and strong nose. Indira fixated on the man in green, rarely blinking. Clementine believed the young woman barely breathed, unmoving as she listed toward him.

Others in the room rocked their heads, clasped their hands in conviction, and chewed on their lips.

Clementine left with Bryce without speaking to Indira. She bid farewell to Sandeep outside the shop and drifted away with Bryce toward their next adventure. Her thoughts lingered with Indira in the storeroom. Was it the speaker himself who lured Indira there, or was it his message of a free, ethical India?

Chapter Sixteen

Clementine let Bryce and herself into her house, their raucous laughter echoing through the great room.

"No," she insisted, "I really think I have a handle on the monkey's role in all this."

"Impossible." Bryce raised a pointed finger into the air. He closed the door behind them. "I don't think you can understand any Indian film until you've seen it for the fifth time."

Clementine carried her handbag to a table in the great room. "Seriously. He's doing the people a favor in finding the man's missing wife. Then he wreaks havoc all over the town where they're keeping her."

"Because the kidnapper refuses to cooperate?"

"It's what I'd do." Clementine pulled a ball of newspaper out of her handbag and unwrapped a brass statuette. With a monkey's head atop an athletic human body, Hanuman exuded grace, strength, and royalty.

"Right." Bryce walked over, rubbing his palm against the back of his neck. "I forgot instead of convincing Milton to make you his partner with words, you set fire to his office."

Clementine tittered. "All we need to do is call in the movie makers and stage it as a production." She lifted the figurine. "Where should I put this?"

Bryce shrugged. "It's your house. I don't even understand why you want it."

"Like you said, one day we'll be back in the States. Maybe I'll never get a chance to come back. I should have something solid to remember India by." Clementine moved over to the fireplace and set the statuette on the mantel. She wrinkled her nose up and took Hanuman down.

"Aren't memories enough?"

Clementine's mood sobered. "Sometimes, it's nice to have a token to jog those memories." She whisked away to the back of the room.

Bryce followed her into the study. He signaled at the windows to their right. "You should open these when summer comes. We need all the breezes we can get."

"It's February. Not that I haven't noticed how much warmer it is here. I left an inch of snow on the ground when I rode out of Nashville." Clementine rested Hanuman on a bookshelf where the weightless afternoon light illuminated his details.

"Come next month, we won't need coats." Bryce rippled his fingertips across the spines of a bookshelf's tomes. "We didn't leave anything here the last time I was in this room."

"I separated my father's books from his notebooks. We took out his reports, so I put his casual reading here."

The colors and subjects differed from the feminine fare in Samvidha's darkened room. A scarlet tome with gold letters spelled out *Howards End* and *E.M. Forster*. A thinner, lime-green volume boasted *The 20th Century Book of Toasts*. A dark teal copy of *The Amateur Gentleman* rivaled them for interest.

Bryce kissed Clementine's cheek. She smiled, her fingers lingering on the bookshelf. Her eyes roamed the volumes, what little she had read of them floating through her head.

Bryce remained fixated on her. "You want to remember India?"

Her arms tensed, but Bryce had never pushed too far. She knew she could trust him. "Very much."

Bryce guided her to face him. "I want to remember it, too. Because India will always be where I met you."

Butterflies swarmed in Clementine's stomach. "I didn't know what to expect when I arrived."

Bryce chuckled in scattered, uptight sounds. "I didn't know what to expect from your faxes." His thumbs stroked her arms through her sleeves. "Then you walked in. You were so pretty, so smart, and you gave me the chance to prove I'm more than Milton thinks I am. You never treated me like an assistant or an errand boy, and I'm thankful for that. You saved me from a monkey–"

Clementine could still feel the fast swing of her arm pitching the cracker onto the roof. She giggled.

Bryce rubbed her arms. "You saved me from boredom and homesickness and everything else."

Clementine smiled as she regarded his sweet, innocent face. "I only did my job. You told me not to let the monkey get away with our records, and what good would I be to the company if I let the monkey snatch you, too?"

"Was it, though?" Bryce edged closer to her. "Was it only a job and nothing more?"

Clementine's breath escaped her, but she owed Bryce a direct, honest answer. "It became something more."

"The cinema, the religious artifact shop, the kiss in your office... all the ones since..." Bryce adjusted his loose grip on her arms. "I'm not the strongest or the smartest, but my days are a lot brighter when you're in them."

Clementine's voice shrank, not sure whether Bryce's admiration pleased or frightened her. "I know you like me."

Bryce gazed at his shoes. "I've never been one to hide my feelings."

"It's good to let people know where they stand."

"When I'm with you..." Bryce nudged even closer, the tips of their shoes bumping against each other. "I want to hold you and never let go."

"We don't have to let go, Bryce." Clementine balanced just on the side of remaining instead of fleeing.

He rushed to kiss her, his fingers cradling her face. She let her reservations slip from her mind, joining Bryce in the scrambling embrace. He brushed her coat off her shoulders and her arms. It landed with a *whump* on the floor, and they parted by a narrow inch.

Their breathing rose and retreated as the only sounds in the house. Meeting Bryce's expectant eyes, Clementine considered what she was getting herself into. A love affair never crossed her plans when she sailed to India, but she liked Bryce. He told her jokes. He made her time in the country more jovial and comfortable than it would have been without his kindness.

Clementine kissed him, and they reached for each other's remaining clothes. They disposed of their hats in an instant. Bryce's coat joined hers on the rug, and he helped her out of her indigo dress. He tossed it over the back of the chair, stopping when he saw her. Coral lace decorated her cream-colored corset, a long, boned construction covering her from beneath her breasts to the bottoms of her hips. Four garters hung from it, their metal clamps holding up white cotton stockings. He kissed her with reverence giving in to hungry passion.

His fingers fumbled with the corset clasps, and Clementine unfastened two of them herself. Their hands stumbled over each other trying to unbutton his suit jacket and vest. They chuckled in nerves and amusement that further unsettled them.

They pushed forward, removing Bryce's collared shirt. His buttoned, sleeveless undershirt revealed the muscles of his arms. Years without farm work might have dulled their definition, but each flex of his biceps showed more strength in him than Clementine had anticipated. He opened the hooks lining the front of her corset, freeing her body to its natural shape beneath her thin, flimsy chemise. They perched on the green settee's edge and pulled their shoes off.

Bryce stood up, and when Clementine moved to rise to her feet, Bryce motioned for her to stay. Sunlight glowed in through the nearby windows. Bryce slid Clementine's stockings off her long, lean legs. She unfastened his pants, and he took them off. He wriggled out of his undershirt and pried off his socks, leaving only his knee-length cotton shorts.

Clementine looked up at him, feeling they were more equal now than they had ever been. His feelings for her were no longer one-sided. With work postponed, they became less and less co-owner and employee. They were friends if not something richer.

She lifted the chemise over her head and let it pool on the rug. She bared her body in the sun, unlike anything she had ever done with anyone. Bryce slipped off his undershorts and lowered himself onto one knee on the settee. He wrapped his arm around her and kissed her.

He ducked his lips to the side of her neck and sank his hips against hers. She angled herself against a pillow, and Bryce entered her with a moment's hesitation. Clementine folded her leg around Bryce's where it supported him against the floor. He pressed deeper, and Clementine hugged Bryce against her, chest to chest. They kissed in a mounting panic. She circled her arms around his neck, a hot flush spreading through her body. Bryce undulated with her until he slowed in shivering exhales. He kissed her cheek and slid his hand over her breast. A small but sure shudder trickled through Clementine. She pecked her lips against the scattered freckles dotting the tops of his cheeks and the bridge of his nose.

A hint of sheepishness belied Bryce's grin. "I didn't plan for this to happen today."

"You hoped it would happen sometime," Clementine teased him.

Bryce dipped his head. "Yes, I'll be honest."

Clementine kissed his forehead. "I've always appreciated your honesty."

Chapter Seventeen

Clementine reclined in the bed, dusk's dim haze coasting in through the northern windows. Bryce got up and recovered his undershorts from the floor. He put them on and wandered farther into the large room. A wooden screen separated the sleeping quarters from a small sitting area. It blocked her view of the single eastern window, inviting in the barest glow from the retreating sun.

Bryce picked up his undershirt from beside the screen but released it. "What should we do with the rest of our day?"

Clementine combed her fingers through her hair. Her vision roamed the ceiling, its fan whirling to cool the stuffy air. "We've been out of work for weeks. There's nothing left to do we haven't done a dozen times."

"Except watch the construction. Mr. Dodd and the displacing of the Indians ruined that for us." Bryce moseyed on, sweeping his fingertips along one panel of the wooden screen.

"I feel bad for Sandeep that he has to work for Mr. Dodd." Clementine pushed herself up and swung her legs over the edge of the bed.

Bryce paused in front of the bedroom's double doors, swung open from the hallway. "We could make food, depending on what you have in the kitchen."

"You know what I miss?" Clementine slipped her bare feet onto the rug's soft fibers and snatched her chemise from the floor. She shimmied it on over her boyish figure. "Cornbread. Baked beans. Fried chicken. Fried edamame. Any kind of pie."

Bryce rubbed his growling stomach. "Why'd you say that? Now I want a meal I can't find within thousands of miles."

"The Brits don't cook like that?"

"No. I'm hopeful to be back in Guthrie in time for next summer. The farm next door grew the sweetest watermelons I ever tasted. The wind knocked a tree over in a storm one year. We left it where it was, and my siblings and me would grab big, thick slices of watermelon. We'd sit in a row on the fallen tree and see who could spit the seeds the farthest."

The loneliness of her childhood tugged at Clementine, but she lived those happy family gatherings through Bryce's eyes. "Did you ever win?"

"Sometimes. My brothers had strong lungs from calling hogs and shouting to each other all over the farm. My sisters were good, though. I don't know what it was from. Maybe they just didn't want to be outdone, I guess."

"How many brothers and sisters do you have?"

"Two of each. I was the youngest, so by the time I grew up, they didn't need my help as much. I did what I could, but they understood when I wanted to move to the city. I'm not the stocky, farm-boy type."

Clementine managed a smile. "Your family sounds like fun."

"They are. We labored hard, don't get me wrong. But nothing beats juicy, fresh watermelon on a hot, sweaty day."

Clementine wagged a finger at Bryce. "I'm afraid you're mistaken. The best antidote for a sticky summer afternoon is a big, ripe peach."

Bryce shook his head. "No way. The heat makes them too warm. The fruit's too dense to be refreshing."

"That's where you're wrong." Clementine meandered over to Bryce. "You have to wait until it's almost too ripe. It breaks the flesh down and makes it extra light. It tastes almost like a handful of sugar. The juice flows over your chin because your mouth can't keep it all in." She gestured down from the corners of her lips.

Bryce cracked a grin. "Then what?"

"You're a tacky mess for sure, and you have to race to the creek to wash up."

They laughed.

"We had a water pump for rinsing off. We'd always fight over who got to use it first before Ma got a hold of us." A shadow fluttered into Bryce's eyes. "You had to do all that by yourself, though?"

"Mostly." Clementine swished her hands through the skirt of her chemise. "I didn't have a lot of time to think about it. I was mostly helping my mother or aiding our neighbors."

"Did they like cornbread and peaches, too?"

A gleam filled Clementine's face. "Those were the best times, when the neighbors came together. That was my family. The Lloyds would do the barbecue."

Bryce pointed at her. "They were the basket weavers, right?"

"Moonshiners. They'd slow cook ribs until the meat fell off the bones. Sally and Agnes would bake cornbread. The Johnsons brought pies. Apple, cherry, strawberry, blackberry. The Colemans and the Ledfords would join us sometimes."

"Farmers, right?"

Clementine hummed in confirmation, and her eyes sparkled. "They'd make wheat rolls and potato bread. We needed something to soak up all that barbecue sauce. And green salads full of the biggest tomato slices you ever saw."

"That all sounds delicious, but for the record, Oklahoma has the best barbecue there is anywhere."

Clementine set her hands on her narrow hips. "How do you figure?"

"My parents came from Missouri, and they brought recipes with them. Other folks settled from Kansas and Arkansas and further east. Everybody brought their own recipes, and a lot of us in Oklahoma don't like to wait to get what we want. So we didn't waste any time sorting out what the best tastes are."

Clementine smirked, retaining her good mood. "If you're ever in my neck of the woods, I'll sneak you some of the Lloyds' best barbecue. As smoky as any fire. As blackened as the logs burning in the pit. A thick sauce with enough black pepper to bite you back. And the tenderest hog meat you ever had. Your granny could chew it with her fake teeth out."

Bryce exploded in guffaws. "Where exactly is your neck of the woods? How far is it from the City?" He glanced around the room. "Where's a map?"

"I tucked my father's maps in the study."

Clementine led Bryce through the upstairs hallway to the stairs. They descended with quick footsteps to the first floor. They jogged between the great room and the dining room to the study at the back of the house. Clementine crouched by the bookshelves and procured several long, rolled pages.

Bryce rubbed the back of his head. "Where can we spread these out?"

Clementine measured the desk with her eyes. Even if she removed its papers and correspondence, the maps would barely fit. She led Bryce into the great room and set the maps on the coffee table. They moved books, notebooks, and statuettes off onto the floor. Clementine slid the rubber band off each map, unfurling South America, Africa, Australia, and India. The last page showed her the United States, and she flattened it across the table. Bryce helped her pin the corners in place with books and knickknacks.

Clementine sought out Tennessee by instinct. She pinned her finger to one of the few cities marked by name. "Here's Nashville."

Bryce kissed her on the cheek.

"Livingston must be too small to print here. It's a bit east and slightly north, but not far enough to be in the mountains."

Bryce tapped the map two states to the left. "Oklahoma City's about in the middle. It's not too far. Considering the size of the country, it's funny we travelled halfway around the world to meet each other. We have your father to thank for that."

Clementine cleared her throat. "It's not that close."

Bryce used his thumb and forefinger to gauge the distance between the two cities. He slid his calculation to the map's scale, where the lines and numbers fell short of his measured width. He groaned through a self-conscious grimace.

Clementine tapped the space between the cities. "I told you it's farther than five hundred miles."

Bryce shortened the distance between his thumb and index finger to the length of the scale. He measured west from Nashville, then pivoted his thumb around past Oklahoma City.

"Okay, so it's nine hundred miles or something. Let's see how much I remember about the railroads."

"What about them?"

Bryce's fingertip drew connections between the map's destinations. "I didn't know what I wanted to do when I got to the City. I thought about working for the railroads, so I memorized as much about the companies and their routes as I could."

He traced a diagonal line through Oklahoma City. "The St. Louis-San Francisco Railway ran here." His eyes lost their focus in deep thought. "It was probably the Southern Railway connecting Arkansas with Tennessee."

Bryce's cheeks sprang into elation. "If you rode out from Nashville – sorry, Nash-*vul* – down to Stevenson, Alabama..." He outlined the route with his fingers. "It'd take you west to Memphis and Little Rock. With a change of trains, you could get north to Oklahoma City."

Clementine flipped a stray lock of hair off her neck. "That's fine, but why would I have to travel to you? Don't your trains go both ways?"

Bryce chuckled. "I like my home state."

"You can't have a problem with traveling that distance. You're all the way in India."

He baited her with a sing-song lilt. "True."

"So what have you got against middle Tennessee?"

"How many Tennessees are there?"

"Three. Mine's the best." She angled her head to one side. "Are you afraid we'd spoil Oklahoma cooking for you?"

Bryce whooped. "I know you didn't challenge my ma's kitchen skills. Mine, well, aren't as sharp."

"Then you won't mind our backwards, uneducated ways. Isn't that what you think of us?"

Bryce squirmed. "Would you want me to visit you in Nashville or Livingston?"

A tinge of regret dampened Clementine's assertiveness. "Nashville's my home now." She nodded. "You'd probably feel more comfortable in the city, anyway."

"You said you made new friends when you moved there."

"Yeah. Mrs. Briley and Miss Sands have been good to my mother and me." Clementine removed the books and trinkets pinning down the corners of the map. It curled up partway, and she rolled it into a respectable tube. She snapped a rubber band around it to hold its shape. "Without them, I couldn't have made it here. I wouldn't have left." Clementine scrambled to her feet.

Bryce gathered up the other maps and stood up with her. "I guess I imagined you being at ease in Oklahoma. You're practical, headstrong, and capable of doing most things by yourself. You'd fit in well in the Wild West."

Clementine laughed. "Doing what? Working in a hotel or helping on a farm?"

"Why not?" Bryce tossed his chin up. "No, I see. You're too contained, too constrained laboring in a factory. You want to rope cattle and ride untamable stallions and shoot up ghost towns from petered-out gold rushes."

She threw her head back and cackled. "I suppose I would. But I can live free like that in Tennessee."

Bryce rubbed the toe of his shoe in a restless pivot on the rug. "It'd just be nice to be near you in the States like we are here."

"Oh." Heat rose in Clementine's face, but not the burning of embarrassment or anger. More like a flush of realization and surprise agreement. "I see what you're saying." She started for the study.

Bryce followed with the rest of the maps in his arms.

Clementine counted his growing silence as one of the longest she had heard from him since they met. And Milton was not there to cause it. She laid the map of the United States on the desk against the back wall. "I'll leave this here in case we want to use it some more. The rest of them can go on the shelves."

Bryce stacked them as well as he could, the traction of the rubber bands keeping them in place. He stood up and gazed out the windows across the room. "It's a lovely day, despite the fog."

"It's weird running fans to cool the rooms so early in the year. They're still huddling around the cook stoves back home."

Bryce stepped over to the desk and surveyed the mounds of notebooks and papers. He picked up a collection of pages folded in thirds together. He spread them open, his eyes roaming the first sheet. "It's a letter from Gertie Sands. You probably got it last week."

"Yes." Clementine slipped the pages out of Bryce's hands. "There's a lot to take care of for me in Nashville. My office. My apartment. My mother. Miss Sands and Mrs. Briley have been kind enough to keep me posted."

Bryce gestured to the opened envelopes and used stationery on the desk. "You've gotten all kinds of letters."

Clementine set Gertie's sheaf off to the side. "Some of them are from before I came to India. Important things I wanted to remember and keep with me."

"Like these?" Bryce picked up a few feathers all but lost among the papers.

She took in the glistening black and vermillion souvenirs. "Crow and cardinal."

"Curious keepsakes." His arranged them with gentle adjustments on the desk. His pitch peaked. "There they are."

Clementine's heart almost stopped. Bryce dove across the desk. Brushing aside several white sheets, he unearthed numerous postcards. Bright sea blues and jungle greens covered some of them. Others pictured entire cities in sepia taupes.

Bryce flipped one over. "Clements' famous postcards."

Clementine's hands fidgeted. "I kept them all."

"Of course. I only heard about Clements and Milton's adventures in these places." Bryce shifted through the lot of them. "Panama. Mexico. Memphis, Tennessee. I bet you think Nashville's better."

Clementine wetted her parched lips. "It is."

"Here's Texas. Ghana." Bryce turned the card over. "Your father wrote the staple of the diet in Ghana was the root of the cassava plant. It's starchy like a potato but doesn't taste as earthy. Africans who'd served as slaves in Brazil brought cassava farming with them when they returned. The root's poisonous unless prepared correctly in the making of gari." Bryce marveled at the postcard. "This is fascinating stuff Clements sent you."

"Yes." Clementine chewed the inside of her lip. She gave Bryce a few more seconds before she took the postcards from him.

"I'm sorry. With all our talk of food, you must be starving."

Clementine tossed the postcards on the desk. "I could use a bite."

Bryce sobered. "It's strange seeing Clements' handwriting again outside of the work we did. Milton knew he wrote to you. I guess he didn't realize how much Clements taught you over the years."

Clementine regarded Bryce with guarded interest. "What do you mean?"

"I meant it when I said I didn't know what to expect before you showed up. Even Milton didn't have a clue. Tall or short. Wide or thin. Smart or simple." Bryce rubbed Clementine's bare arm. "You gave us our answers quickly, though. Honest. You set us straight on who you are."

"Well…" Clementine sucked in a breath and huffed it out. "You would've had no way of knowing. I couldn't afford to send my father a picture of me, and you can't see smarts in a photograph. I can't hold it against you."

Bryce hung his head. "I'm embarrassed to say your name surprised us, too. Clementine. It reminded me of the song. You know. Milton figured you were named after your father."

Clementine stared at him, her mind reeling and racing. "I was."

Bryce patted her arm. "Let's see what you've got in the icebox."

Clementine barely heard the sound of her own reply. "Chicken, I think."

"If we can find tomatoes and the right spices, I can try to approximate my mother's barbecue."

Clementine shadowed him through the doorway and down the hall. They passed the small, tidy water closet and accessed the servants' perpendicular passageway. Clementine ambled across the open courtyard in a daze, Bryce's confided details of crispy chicken skin and secret herbs floating right past her. She let them into the kitchen at the back of the property, and Bryce made a beeline for the icebox. Of all the memories and thoughts screaming in her head, Clementine only said, "That sounds delicious."

Chapter Eighteen

The leaves across the landscape had brightened carrot orange, lemon yellow, and apple red. Clementine strode across the Ledfords' farm at a good clip. The sun's distant circle hovered near the horizon. If she hurried, she could ride home before the night pitched her route into darkness.

A screen door screeched open, and laughter percussed into the evening. A familiar tenor called out softly before Clementine could glance at who stood behind her.

"Is that you, Miss Heidel?"

Clementine stopped in the tall grass, clutching her bag of herbs. Chester walked toward her. The glowing sunset, the same colors as the trees, silhouetted his wide-brimmed hat. "It's me, Mr. Alred. How are you and your leg doing?"

"We're getting along just fine, ma'am. I hope all's well with you and yours."

Clementine's spine straightened with worry. "We're doing what we can."

Chester caught up to her. "Are you going home? I heard Ollie fell off a ladder today."

"He's lucky he didn't fall off the roof." Clementine picked up a slow but steady pace toward her far-off horse and cart. Chester stayed at her side. "He's bruised. His head aches. I think he popped a few ribs out of place."

"Did you put them back in?"

"No. The herbs are mostly what I do."

Chester smiled. "Lucky for me, then, that's all I needed when the tractor got me."

Clementine observed Chester's gait, satisfied she had helped him heal his wound with no visible limp. A bit of white linen wrapped around the base of one hand made her frown. "Did you hurt yourself?"

"A chicken pecked me."

"When?"

"Yesterday morning. I guess she wasn't ready to part with that egg yet."

"Let me see. Mr. Ledford didn't send anybody to get me."

Chester halted his stride. "It's a little thing. Probably heal over in no time." He unwrapped the linen strip.

Clementine dropped her bag of supplies in the grass. She took Chester's wide, grooved hand. On the back of it, a few divots ate into the flesh. She squinted in the dim light. "I wish I could see better."

"Thank you, ma'am, but it's nothing to worry about."

"You haven't caught a fever?" Clementine held one hand against his forehead, warm with summer heat instead of hot with infection. "It doesn't feel like it. That's good. If I really can't help you, just keep it clean with soap and water."

"I will." Chester tried to rewrap his hand. The fabric slipped away from him several times, and he tucked it into his pocket.

Clementine hauled her bag up and strolled along again.

Chester stayed beside her. "I thought of a new riddle for you. Based on what you do."

"Let's hear it."

"Where is there the most time?"

Clementine groaned. "It's not in my days, that's for sure."

Chester chuckled with sympathy. "In the kitchen and the garden. Get it? Thyme, like you washed my wound with."

Clementine laughed, enjoying the humor over and over. "You thought of that all by yourself? It's clever. I like it."

"Yes, ma'am. It's my own creation."

"It won't be long before everybody's telling it up and down the county."

"I don't know 'bout that. But I'm glad it pleases you."

Clementine and Chester passed the thick trunk and wide boughs of an oak tree.

She came to a stop in what remained of the dying daylight. "Let me wrap your hand. It's good to give it air now and then, but I don't want bugs and dirt to irritate it."

"If you insist." Chester retrieved the length of white linen.

Clementine took it and investigated Chester's hand. "You might be very fortunate, indeed, Mr. Alred. You might escape infection in all your wounds this year."

"I'm fortunate I spotted you."

Clementine laid her bag on the ground and stretched the cloth along the underside of Chester's hand.

He murmured on. "You're taking care of me. I got to tell you my riddle. And I got to hear you laugh. I didn't get to hear too much of that when you cared for me before."

Clementine faltered to tie a simple knot in the cloth. Her breath came in shallow, but she kept her tone casual. "It's not your job to make sure I have joy in my life."

"Life's always better with joy. Forgive me for pointing this out, but it's not your job to patch my hand tonight, either."

Chester's eyes glowed into Clementine's, but a common fear shadowed them. She cradled his hand, the fabric loose and unbidden. "I told you to send for me if you got injured."

Chester swallowed audibly. "My apologies, ma'am, but I believe you said I was to call for you if a tractor harmed me again. If this was a tractor what done this to my hand, it was the most chickenest equipment I ever seen."

Clementine tittered and clamped her hands over her mouth to keep the whole farm from hearing her. Chester beamed. She rolled up on her tiptoes and greeted him with a quick kiss.

For several moments, they breathed, staring at nothing but each other. If someone spied them, it could mean Chester's life. Tennessee was divided in the ways it thought about blacks and whites, but horrible crimes crossed the newspapers from time to time. Clementine knew they would never have shared riddles or more than passing small talk if she had not tended to his serious gash.

She slung her arms around Chester's neck and kissed him longer. His hands alighted on her back.

Guilt rushed into her chest. "Your hand."

"It's not the palm that bothers me."

Chester kissed her and stroked her hair where the work and heat of the day had loosened it from its bun. They moved under the spreading oak, its generous trunk concealing them from the houses and other people on the farm. They lay down in the shaded grass. Chester unbuttoned the front of her dress and slid his hand in around her waist.

Clementine kissed him and invited him into her while the fireflies blinked around them and cicadas buzzed in far-off trees.

By the time they rested still and complacent in the grass, the moon and stars had taken over the sky. Clementine adjusted her clothes and collected her bag of herbs.

Chester stood close by her, trailing his fingers down her arm. He whispered the most treasonous words of the evening. "Can I see you again?"

Clementine gazed into his eyes the way she had less than an hour before. Fear trembled alongside her exhilaration. "Nightfall's best."

Chester hesitated. "Leave me a note if I'm to meet you here. A riddle or something."

Clementine nodded. She shivered for his safety, but determination drew her towards him without wavering. "I'll come late tomorrow to check on Ollie. I'll see you."

Clementine hurried away, sprinting at the shape of the horse and cart. She peeked over her shoulder. Chester waved before he walked off toward his house. The white linen strip hovered over the tops of the grass blades like a ghost, abandoned and forgotten.

In the stuffy sitting area off the master bedroom in India, Clementine tied her shoelaces. Each sharp tug tightened the leather around her feet, crushing the flesh and pinching her circulation.

Bryce carried on around the other side of the wooden screen, barely muffled by its privacy. "I think a mix of American and Indian food is the best way to go. I don't know if it'll surprise anyone back home or not. Or if they're prepared to cook me parathas, naan, and kulfi."

Clementine's chest clenched, and she popped up off the couch. She brushed wrinkles, real and imaginary, out of her skirt. For the first time in weeks, she wore a professional outfit instead of a casual dress or a flimsy chemise.

Bryce walked around the screen where she could see him. "I guess it's time to ask the same question we get around to every day. What should we do with the hours we have left in it?"

Clementine picked a miniscule piece of lint off her sleeve and discharged it over the rug. Her jaws strained with so much tension, her voice emerged like ice-cold steel. "We're going back to work."

Bryce's mouth slacked open. "Is Milton healed up? Did you get a fax or something?"

Clementine peered at him with serious, dissecting eyes. "I'm co-owner of the company. It was my decision to close it down, and I choose to reopen it."

"But..." Bryce moved his mouth with uncertainty, producing no sound at all. He raked his hand through his disheveled hair. "I thought you didn't want to manage the factory alone. That's where we left everything, wasn't it? The next step involves the machines."

"The extractors, to be exact." Clementine strode toward the open double doors.

Bryce grasped her wrist. "Wait. Where are you going?"

Clementine jerked her arm free, shooting him a fierce furrow. "I need to find Mr. Mustafa. I need his help in reaching the other employees. It's Thursday, isn't it?"

Bryce stammered. "Yes."

"Good. He'll be available to work." Clementine darted into the hall. She passed a second bedroom and paused at the top of the staircase. "Are you coming or taking a longer vacation?"

Bryce blinked hard and shook his head as if to clear it. "I'll put on a suit and be right there."

"We can't afford to wait for Mr. Longshaw. As long as we have Mr. Mustafa to translate, we can trust Mr. Menon to do his job as foreman. We already know what plants to process for the first serum trials."

She barely heard Bryce's reply. "That's true."

Clementine capped her hand over the finial topping the balustrade's corner column. Her fingers squeezed the carved wooden leaves. "I'd appreciate it if you'd drive me to the office. That's where the addresses are."

"Of course."

Clementine patted the patterned wood and jogged down the stairs. She shuddered as she rounded the landing and descended the rest of the way to the bottom. Countless forces pulled at her ribs, her lungs, her heart. She would not slow down now. She could not afford to.

Chapter Nineteen

As Milton had once lectured to the workers in the extraction room's empty spaces, Clementine assembled them Monday morning. She wore a navy dress with swirls and flowers embroidered on the long sleeves and economical skirt. Her jaw firmed, but the eager workmen in front of her filled her with purpose. With Mr. Mustafa on her right and Bryce stationed on her left, she felt as certain in her position as Milton must have every day he worked there. Indira's pink-and-yellow sari brightened the edge of Clementine's vision on Mr. Mustafa's other side.

Clementine leapt into her speech without delay. "It's been a month since Mr. Longshaw's accident and our closing. I'm indebted to all of you for coming back for the reopening."

She paused to let Mr. Mustafa repeat her message. The workers smiled and bobbed their heads.

"I want to recognize Mr. Menon, Mr. Magar, Mr. Mustafa, and Mr. Kakkar for staying with us as well. Until Mr. Longshaw rejoins us, I couldn't lead the factory without them."

Mr. Mustafa relayed her appreciation. The foreman, the accountant, and the front desk security man beamed at her.

Bryce's silence clawed at Clementine, but she pushed past it. She squared her shoulders, considering the crowd. "As you may know, not everyone has stayed with Fitzgerald and Longshaw. I don't blame them. A month is a long time to wait for work, even with a partial salary."

Mr. Mustafa translated, and the men wobbled their heads in grim agreement.

"I'm glad to announce we'll never close the factory again. No matter what happens, I hold myself responsible for keeping it in useable order." Clementine clasped her hands together in front of her. "We're going to make serious strides moving forward. I plan for a saleable product by January. This means steady work, pay, and progress toward achieving the goal we set when the year began. The legendary Fountain of Youth, bottled, labeled, and sold."

Mr. Mustafa communicated this with great sweeps of his hands, and the room erupted. Indira applauded in double speed, but her eyes seemed transfixed by thoughts beyond the scope of the extraction room. The workers bowed to Clementine over hands pressed in prayer. Their excited words tumbled over each other.

Mr. Mustafa turned to Clementine. "They're happy to be back, Miss Fitzgerald. They have high hopes for the year. Some of them would like to ask a few questions."

She inclined her head. "Certainly."

"When will Mr. Milton resume here?"

"Soon." Relief boosted Clementine's confidence. "We've traded several faxes over the last few days. His broken hand is on the mend. It might take another month or two before he's fully recovered, but Mr. Longshaw is eager to join us."

Mr. Mustafa shared this with the workers and translated their replies. "Are new workers going to be hired? They're concerned about taking on too much extra work."

"We'll replace everyone who left the company. Mr. Longshaw will see to that when he gets back."

"Will you decrease their salaries? They're still worried about the time the factory was closed."

Clementine shook her head. "I'd cut my own salary first or find more investors. The workers shouldn't have to suffer for my closing the building."

Mr. Mustafa announced this, and the workmen bowed even lower, gratitude shining in their faces.

Clementine wiped her palms against each other. "Is that all?"

"I believe it is." Mr. Mustafa's grin, despite its understated brightness, displayed his true opinion. "Well done. I'm glad our paths could cross once more."

"I am, too."

"What would you like me to do next?"

"If you could wait here until I bring the processing notes for Mr. Menon, I'd be much obliged."

Mr. Mustafa gave a shallow bow.

Clementine stepped around him to Indira. "I'm happy you're working with us again, Miss Datta."

Indira's automatic smile took a moment to reach her eyes. "Yes."

"I'd like you to help anywhere you feel comfortable until Mr. Longshaw gets back."

Mr. Mustafa translated for Indira.

Her refreshed smile dazzled. "I will."

Clementine wanted to question Indira more. Did Indira really feel safe at the factory after pinching her hand in the machine's glass cage? Was she comfortable being in charge of herself there, especially without Milton even being on the property? But Indira had given her approval, and Clementine had other tasks to attend to.

Clementine swept out of the room, and Bryce followed her. They turned the corner together, approaching the offices.

Bryce tucked his hands in the pockets of his steel-grey suit. "Mr. Mustafa was right. It was a good speech."

"Thank you. I need the workers to be on our side. They deserve to know what's going on, and we can't keep wasting time with every problem that comes up."

Bryce flinched. "What do you mean?"

"Hiring new workers. Injuries that aren't crippling or fatal." Clementine rushed into her office.

Bryce kept close on her heels. "Clementine, I don't like Milton that much, but I've worked with him for years. He let you on as his partner. He didn't have to. He deserves a little respect."

Clementine threw a hasty glance at him from where she stood over the desk. "I respect Mr. Longshaw. According to you a few weeks ago, he would've been a complete idiot to ignore the excellent reasons I gave him for partnering with me."

She snatched up a barely used notebook from the desk. Opening it to the first few pages, she confirmed it held the information she had jotted down for Nithya Menon. A list of plants greeted her, further broken down into the part of the plant she wanted processed and what final form the material should take. Bryce had helped her add the Hindi name for each species beside the English terms. She closed the notebook to avoid dwelling on his contributions.

Bryce inched toward her. "Milton was smart to bring you on, but you have to remember you're still new here. Milton and your father spent fifteen years on this company all over the world."

Footsteps in the hallway made Bryce stop. Aatmaj Kakkar walked by the open door without a word.

Bryce moved over to Clementine and tempered his voice. "I know barely anyone in this building speaks much English, but it doesn't do either of us any good to throw around words like *idiot* in relation to Milton. They're probably more loyal to him than to you."

Clementine drew herself up in defiance and wounded pride. "Oh."

Bryce cringed. "That came out wrong."

Clementine strode past him to the doorway. "I'm sure it's true. Why should they listen to me or like me? I shut down the factory when it didn't need to be. I was weak and fled to Civil Lines instead of trying my wings. Maybe I could've succeeded. You're always reminding me I came all the way from Tennessee by myself."

Bryce's lips parted in regret. "I didn't mean to put it that way. We're all glad to have you here."

Clementine summed him up, boyish charm and sincerity written all over him. The fancy, well-fitting suit did little to mature him. "I'll be right back. I want to run these notes to Mr. Menon."

Bryce gestured to the rooms next door. "I'll wait for you in the meeting room if that's all right."

Clementine heaved a tense sigh. "That's not necessary. I have a new assignment for you."

Bryce's smooth brows crinkled. He could hardly force out words. "New... assignment...?"

"I'd like you to check on the design for the labels and the rewritten advertising campaign."

"Those are Milton's duties. Won't he do that when he gets back? You said it'd be soon."

"It will be, but we don't need two people doing research. We have all the information we need. We don't have Milton back yet, and I'd like to keep moving with the redesigns as soon as possible."

"Of course," Bryce grumbled. "We can't waste any more time."

"Mr. Longshaw sent over his office key. It's on the desk behind you. He said the addresses for the design and advertising companies are in a ledger on his desk."

Bryce lifted the key from Clementine's desk. "You consulted Milton about this?"

"As I said, we shared faxes over the weekend."

"I mean about the change in my assignment."

Clementine shifted her hold on the notebook in her hands. "I didn't need to discuss it with Mr. Longshaw. I made the decision. I'm sure he'll agree with it."

She stepped into the hall but ducked back into her office. "One more thing. The notebooks haven't been carried out of the meeting room. You should take care of your duties elsewhere."

Each fevered sound fell like dead weight from Bryce's lips. "You're getting rid of me." He strengthened himself. "I can move the books. It's no trouble."

"I'd prefer to move them myself. I want to make sure they're marked appropriately so I can find what I need in the future."

Clementine strode out into the hall. She did not double back with any more points, and Bryce did not chase her.

He called out to her from her office. "Should I report to you when I'm done?"

Clementine passed Govinda's office at a furious pace. Over her shoulder, she shot Bryce an answer. "That's fine."

Chapter Twenty

Within two days, applause and cheerful whoops rang out in the extraction room. Milton received them with a self-conscious but courteous grin. His hands covered once more with his genteel gloves, he waved to the animated workers.

Clementine stood at his side, generating the loudest clapping of all. His participation could only mean the unobstructed continuation of their efforts. They would make do no longer. The expert and leader had returned.

Bryce lingered a foot behind her trying to muster a solid show of support. Mr. Mustafa and Indira clustered on Milton's opposite side.

Milton pushed down on the air until the crowd quieted. "I appreciate the warm welcome. The cast came off yesterday, and I'm ready to resume my work. I'm told Miss Fitzgerald did a fine job reopening the company, and each of you has risen to the challenge of moving forward. Now, let's create that potion and finally get around to this business of making money."

Mr. Mustafa translated with sweeps and arcs of his hands. The workmen applauded. Nithya Menon shook Milton's healthy hand before rounding up his employees.

Mr. Mustafa greeted Milton, resting his hand over his heart. "It's good to have you back."

"Thank you. I'm glad I only have to catch up for the last two days."

Clementine brushed at her skirt. "I wrote out all the notes on our activities for you."

Milton gave a decisive rise of his chin. "Excellent. We'll discuss them in my office."

Clementine turned to Bryce. "Find Mr. Menon and ask how far they've come with the extractions."

Bryce slunk away. Mr. Mustafa accompanied him.

Milton sought out Indira hovering nearby. "You may come with us."

The trio walked into the hall and trekked to Milton's office.

Indira chattered. "You are both from the same country, yes?"

They nodded.

"I am learning new things about the United States. The British ruled you, too."

Milton snorted. "Over a hundred years ago."

"How did you do it? Make free."

"Break free from the British?" Milton led the two women into his office. "We stood up for ourselves and said we weren't going to take it anymore."

Clementine watched Indira for signs she did not understand Milton's terms.

Indira's eyebrows twitched with uncertainty, but her lips curved. "Take what?"

"They taxed us but didn't let us have any say in our own lives."

"Yes!" Indira's eyes widened. "It is the same thing. Taxes. No say."

Clementine almost admitted she had seen Indira at the political meeting in the Hindu shop's back room. In case this was not her secret to reveal, Clementine held her tongue.

Milton angled his back to the women, sorting through papers on his desk. "We had to fight for our independence, but I don't know of any country that wants to be ruled by another."

Indira took a step towards him. "Is this what you would tell India to do? Fight?"

"Sure, unless you want to deal with the British like this forever." Milton tossed a glance over his shoulder at Indira. "Your English has gotten better while I've been away."

"I learned from Mr. Mustafa."

Clementine eased forward, eager to move the day's duties ahead. "Without you here, Mr. Longshaw, I let Miss Datta roam where she wanted. She stuck by Mr. Mustafa, and he taught her new words."

"Wonderful." Milton tidied a stack of pages. "Miss Datta, would you follow Mr. Mustafa some more today? I have items to review with Miss Fitzgerald."

Indira gave emphatic nods. "Yes. If that is what you need." She took his forearm in her hands. "You know so much about America and the British. I am happy you teach me these things."

Milton calmed, basking in Indira's glowing admiration. He swept his gaze over her fingers on the sleeve of his suit jacket. "You're very welcome."

Indira strolled out of the room.

With a loose gesture, Milton indicated the open door. "Close that, please."

Clementine clasped the portal shut. "Miss Datta might understand even more English and more about the company if we talked matters over in front of her."

"I have something important I need to inform you of." Milton scooted the chair away from his desk and propped himself in it. "I'm not sure I want to continue with the project."

Clementine's heart plummeted. "We agreed. We just spent two days extracting ingredients for the new serum. The Fountain of Youth…"

Milton waved for her to stop. "You may persist with it all you like. I think it's time I bowed out."

"Of our partnership?"

"Of the daily operations, at least. Let's be blunt. I was old when you arrived, and I've only gotten older." Milton supported his right hand on the chair's arm rest. "Crushing my hand in the extractor cage made me think very hard about my participation in this venture. I've had a month to consider it."

Clementine forced her lungs to work. "There are other ways of handling this. You don't have to go into the extraction room anymore. You don't have to use the machines yourself. We can hire new people to finish the work that needs to be done. Mr. Menon could oversee all of that."

Milton drummed the fingertips of his left hand on the desktop. "You're not listening. I feel exhausted and useless. Now you suggest I hide in my office like a cockroach skulking in the shadows?"

Clementine almost retaliated with a sharp remark. She steadied herself. "What would you rather do?"

"Retire and go home."

"I can't manage the factory by myself."

"Yes, you can. Don't underestimate your abilities. You've been here two days without me. The floors are swept. The workers are content and on time."

Clementine trembled. "What if more of them leave because they'd rather work for you?"

Milton retained his flat, serious air. "Hire more."

"We'll have the project done by January. I promised the workers. Can't you stay on a few more months?"

"It's the end of February. There's more than a few months until December." Milton raised his head, considering a new point. "Did you ever hear how your father and I went into business together?"

"No." Clementine backed up and supported herself against the wall.

Milton's aimless fingers tapped the desktop. "I was on vacation with my wife in Caracas near the coast of Venezuela. Did you know I had a wife?"

Clementine responded in a daze. "Bryce–Mr. Bloom mentioned it."

Milton barely paused. "I believe your father might've sent you a postcard from that sprawling valley city."

Her arms stiffened. "He did."

"In Oklahoma, I owned a staffing business. When Clements and I hit it off, I agreed to partner with him. It meant traveling the world with him as he was already doing by himself." Milton leaned forward. "I built that staffing company – and I mean *built it* – with my own two hands. No one gave me anything. The idea was mine. The labor was mine. I managed it myself every day."

"What did you do?"

Milton reclined against the back of the chair. "I'll be honest. When I moved to the City, it was hard to find a decent job. I did whatever was available. Driving wagons full of merchandise. Delivering packages. Stocking store shelves.

"The idea for my company came while I was stocking goods. The job seems simple, but there are people who do it well and people who fumble. There are speed and efficiency. Then there are slowness and misunderstandings." Milton jabbed a finger at Clementine. "When an accident kept one of my fellow employees from showing up to work, my boss grabbed the first free man he could find to fill the vacancy. What a mistake it was.

"Several broken bottles and dented cans later, I realized what Oklahoma City needed. Someone with a keen eye for talent and the directness of speech to organize it. In my business, anyone without a job could come and give me their specific capabilities. Any business owner seeking skilled labor could rely on me to supply the best workers in their field."

Clementine relaxed enough to appreciate Milton's creativity. "It's brilliant."

Milton tented his fingers in front of him. "I clawed my way up from someone who transported other people's products to someone who arranged for others to do it." His tone sharpened. "I changed my accent for that place because they treated me like an outsider when I got there. I renounced Philadelphia to appease the City, and I became one of its most successful business owners."

Clementine spoke up with a soft question. "What does all of this have to do with me?"

"It's what I gave up to work with your father. I saw an opportunity to make more money and see the world while I was at it. I seized that chance. I'd put a trustworthy manager in charge of the business before I left on vacation, and I sent orders to let him keep supervising it for me." Milton stood up. "You don't need me. All you need is a good manager to aid you in my place."

"You're sure retirement is your best option?"

"I've barely been home in the last fifteen years. You have your motives for pushing forward with this commendable Fountain of Youth, but I had no grand aspirations for joining forces with Clements. All I wanted was to make money. That's still what I want."

Clementine's heart raced. She gravitated toward Milton. "Maybe you're not as old as you think you are."

Milton balked. "Numbers don't lie. I'm several times your age, young lady."

"Isn't the point of the Fountain of Youth to laugh at the nature of aging?"

"We're not there yet. I'm aging organically and progressively, I assure you."

Clementine's throat parched as she reached out and held onto Milton's forearm where Indira had touched him. "I think you're mistaking experience for maturity. No manager, no matter how well I chose him, would have your knowledge and expertise."

Milton flushed. "Kind words and possibly true."

Clementine inched closer to him. "Please stay on the project a little longer. I won't keep you past the end of December."

Milton said nothing.

Clementine breathed in his cologne, a complex aroma that revealed itself in layers. First, a feather-light brightness, like eating fresh fruit in a rose garden. Then an arrangement of headier flowers and herbs. At the base of it all waited the heavy scents, reminiscent of sitting in a leather chair surrounded by exotic treasures and conquered animals. Clementine redoubled her efforts. "If it's money you want, we'll make much more with your involvement. Then you can retire to the States, and the time in between will be over faster than you think. Stores will sell the elixir everywhere. You can feel good you stayed to help me and didn't leave until it was finished."

Milton slowly moved his other hand and brushed the end of Clementine's butter-yellow sleeve.

"I can give you more of the profits."

"No." Milton patted her hand. "I'll manage with what I'm getting already."

"But you'll stay? It would mean so much to me if you didn't leave me. The whole team needs you."

Milton laid his hand over hers. "I'll see the project all the way through with you."

"Thank you, Mr. Longshaw."

As the door swung open, they pulled apart. Clementine took an extra half step away from Milton.

Bryce came in, his eyebrows flicking up at Clementine. "You weren't in your office. Were you having a meeting in here?"

Clementine kept a watch on Milton. "Everything's settled now."

His small grey eyes seemed to observe her with more interest than they had before. "Yes."

Bryce held out a written list accented with dates and checkmarks. "Mr. Menon kept strict notes on what plants have been processed."

Clementine took the page, giving it a brief glancing over. "Perfect. Would you mind fetching the notebook on my desk for Mr. Longshaw? It should be the one with our most recent findings in it."

Bryce inhaled deep into his chest. "You mean the formulas and the schedule you and I worked so hard on?"

Clementine maintained her dismissive air. "That's the one."

Bryce simmered but left.

Milton squinted after him, perplexed and haughty. "What's going on with him?"

Clementine raised her shoulders and released them. "Things have changed. We don't need to consult the reports together like we used to."

"Ah." Milton bucked his chin up. "That explains it."

Bryce dropped off the notebook before vanishing into the hallway.

Clementine squeezed the cover to keep her hands from shaking as she steeled herself. "I'll bring you up to date on the plans for the year."

Chapter Twenty-One

Samvidha sat on the foot of her bed. Clementine perched beside her, wrapping fresh bandages around the young woman's stiff, curled hands.

The length of the room spread out in front of them, clouded in shadows. The two windows on the left stood like tall sentries with parted curtains, letting in shreds of dwindling daylight. From the middle of the ceiling, a small chandelier gave off a dim glow.

Clementine reached the end of the bandage and tucked it into the firm wrapping already in place. "I wish you'd let me turn the lights up."

Samvidha eyed the floor. "I don't want you to see me like this."

"I do see you. You're beautiful. Your skin has gotten healthier since I first came here. I've treated much worse."

Samvidha launched herself off the bed and raced a few strides away. "I don't care what you've treated. This wasn't supposed to be my life. Do you understand?"

Hard truths and forced choices weighed on Clementine. "More than you know."

"Don't you ever get so angry you could scream?" Samvidha kicked at the rug under her bare feet and whirled to confront Clementine. "I'm supposed to be a wife. A mother. Not a burden on my family. Already, the arguments rage day and night. My mother despises my sister-in-law, Damini. She has no job and has given my brother no children. She contributes nothing but overcooked food and malicious gossip. Meanwhile, she blames my mother for keeping me here where I endanger the entire family."

Clementine slipped to her feet. "You're not a threat to them. They take care of you because they want to."

"I'm not their responsibility. I'm old enough to be married. Who would have me like this?" Samvidha thrust up her tight, twisted hands.

"Anyone smart enough to look past your illness at the wonderful person you are."

Samvidha twirled away, pacing across the room. "I can't cook. I can't clean. I can't even read on a day like today."

Clementine lunged after her. "It's not your fault. You have to stop talking like it is."

Samvidha spun on her heel. "I used to visit him. The little boy in the street. And the others like him. Every day. I brought them leftover food and fresh water. I didn't know they were sick. My mother caught me sitting with them one morning, and she made sure I never visited them again. I thought I was healthy. I thought I was safe." Tears glistened in her eyes. "I wasn't. The disease slept, waiting to take me over when I'd finally forgotten about it."

Clementine gripped Samvidha's arm. "It's not your fault. You didn't do this. It's just the way things work."

"You said you knew someone who was sick a long time like me."

"My mother."

"You left her to come to Delhi?"

"I had to. Now I have a chance to make something that might help her." Clementine backed off to give Samvidha some space. "I've seen her struggle in some of the same ways you do. Pain. Weakness. Problems breathing sometimes."

Samvidha flung herself into the nearest chair. "I might spend the rest of my life like this? I can't!"

Clementine moved to Samvidha's side. The seated woman grabbed hold of Clementine's dress and sobbed against her hip. "Samvidha, I'm here to help you. You've battled this disease for years. Give me time to reverse it."

Samvidha cried. Clementine ached for her and strengthened herself for the long fight ahead. Home felt further than twelve thousand miles. It loomed unreachable at the farthest corners of her mind. She refused to picture her mother, or she would join Samvidha in tears. Chester played across her mind, followed by the others from Livingston. Only then could she allow herself the luxury of acknowledging Elvira Briley and Gertie Sands, the Nashville neighbors nurturing her mother.

Bryce floated by in her thoughts. Milton lurked there, too, like someone chasing her rather than being pursued. A wet trail slicked down Clementine's cheek, and she wiped it away. "Do you know what I do when I think I can't go on?"

Samvidha dried her eyes with the back of one bandaged hand. "No."

"I sing. Do you know any songs?"

"Do you know Ganesha?"

"Is that a ballad?"

Samvidha stood up, shaking her head. "He's a god, the remover of obstacles. I pray to him often and sing his sacred songs. He has the head of an elephant. Mother hangs pictures of him around the house."

"I've seen them."

"I think I know the English words." Samvidha sniffled and raised her head. Her high, dancing notes wavered. "Glory to you, Lord Ganesha! Born of Parvati and the great Shiva."

Inspiration lightened Clementine's heart, and she reached deep for her own Indian song from another tradition and another continent. "The earth is our mother. We must take care of her." She chanted low, "Hay-on, hay-on, hay-on-ya."

The creases loosened from Samvidha's brows. She swayed her body and the skirt of her sari. "You are merciful. You have one tusk and four arms. You bear a red mark on your forehead and ride on a mouse. People offer you paan, flowers, fruits, and sweets. Saints worship you."

Conviction and determination filled Clementine as well. She met Samvidha's eyes. "The earth is our mother. She will take care of us. Hay-on, hay-on, hay-on-ya."

Samvidha held her palms as close together as she could, her fingers curling against each other. "You grant sight to the blind and heal the leper. You bestow children to the barren and wealth to the poor. We pray to you day and night. Please give success to us."

Clementine held her chin high. She reformed her natural tether to the earth and its boundless energy, even from the second story of Samvidha's house. "The sacred ground we walk upon with every step we take. Hay-yonna, hay-yonna, hay-on-ya."

Samvidha wrapped Clementine in a desperate hug. "Your herbs are of the earth."

"They are."

"Do you trust them to make the Fountain of Youth work?"

"I do." Doubt trickled up through Clementine's stomach, and she silenced it with knowing resolve. She held Samvidha against her. "I need it as much as you do. I won't rest until I have it."

"I wish I could believe as you do." Samvidha pulled away, leaning her bent arms on Clementine's. "I put my faith in you and Ganesha. In my parents for trusting you."

"I have a whole company behind me. A team dedicated to working on this project every week. We have plants and ingredients from all over the country. My father researched these plants for years. We're bound to create something powerful."

"I should believe it, because look." Samvidha curved her mouth into a subdued but grateful grin. "You've already used your power to change my tears into hope."

Clementine rubbed Samvidha's arms. "I know it's a lot to ask that you trust me. It's painstaking to have patience to wait for the serum."

Samvidha spoke gently. "You need it, too. So it will be done."

Clementine kissed Samvidha's cheek and walked over to her bag of supplies. A cough erupted in the hallway outside the bedroom door. Clementine regarded it with brows furrowed in concern. "Who's that?"

"My mother. She caught a small cold in the market."

Clementine collected her bag. She almost said the cough sounded more urgent than that, but she stopped herself. Samvidha had enough to worry about, too much gravity taxing her mind. The difference in seriousness was not big enough to alarm Samvidha over.

Timid knocks echoed through the door.

Samvidha called out in Hindi.

Padma swung the door open, a humble smile softening her deepened lines. She responded in the same language.

Samvidha answered before she translated for Clementine. "My mother asks that we excuse her. She doesn't mean to interrupt. She only wished to ask what I wanted for dinner."

Clementine cleared her throat. "Tell your mother I'm more than happy to bring some herbs for her cough."

Samvidha relayed this to Padma and supplied Clementine with the answer. "She insists she's fine."

"Would she like some elderberries to give her energy?"

Samvidha asked Padma, but her mother shook her head. "She's just tired from taking care of the house and worrying about me."

Clementine read Padma's peaceful but resolute eyes. "Okay. If it gets worse, she can borrow some of your herbs. I can bring you more."

Samvidha told this to Padma, who gave Clementine's arm a squeeze.

"I should be on my way."

Samvidha related this in Hindi. "Mother will see you to the door."

Clementine walked with Padma out of the room and down the stairs. They crossed the length of the foyer. Clementine wanted to follow up with Padma and find out if the woman was really all right. The language barrier between them kept both of them silent.

Padma let Clementine out, and the American began her walk north to Civil Lines. Snippets of the two songs she had heard in Samvidha's room intermingled in her head.

Children's laughter bubbled from an unseen courtyard.

You are merciful. You have one tusk and four arms. Hay-on, hay-on, hay-on-ya.

A fly buzzed past Clementine's ear, and she swatted at it.

We pray to you day and night. Please give success to us. Hay-yonna, hay-yonna, hay-on-ya.

Blossoms scented the wind before spiced cooking smells overtook the blooms.

The earth is our mother. She will take care of us.

Chapter Twenty-Two

Clementine walked the office hall of Fitzgerald and Longshaw. She skirted around the corner as grunts of frustration emanated from the doorway ahead. Her chest lifted, and she quickened her steps. She had found her target, and no other noises sounded from the extraction room. She slowed as a frown washed over her, seeping all the way into her bones, remembering what she needed to do.

Shaking off the chill seeping into her limbs, Clementine breezed into the large room. As expected, Milton was its only occupant. He sat at one of the stations set against the right-hand wall. He pulled an elastic band off his head, the front of it holding a contraption that had nestled against his forehead. Its metal body and circles of glass glinted. He deposited it on the desktop and ran his gloved hand over his greying hair.

His back remained to Clementine, and she spoke up to announce herself. "Are the plants refusing to cooperate?"

He glanced over his shoulder, then followed her approach with his eyes. "In a manner of speaking. What brings you into the factory? I'm surprised anyone wants to be here after the accidents."

Clementine arrived at his side. "The best mechanic we could find fixed the machines. You're in here. Why wouldn't I be?"

"Because you don't want to end up like me." Milton knocked his left hand against the metal housing of the banded metal instrument. "I'm barely able to function with my dominant hand in limbo. Do you know what it's like to have a good hand and a bad hand?"

Samvidha's stiff, arched fingers tormented Clementine. "Some people have two bad hands."

Milton harrumphed. "I suppose that's true. Did you want to see me about something, or are you stopping for a chat?"

Clementine avoided the easy bait of his second suggestion. "I thought you'd want to know the pomegranates will ship soon from south of us. I finally found the best supplier for shilajit, as well, from the Himalayas. Although I'm still not sure what it is."

"Nobody is. Some kind of natural material they collect from the rocks up there."

"I didn't think you were familiar with it."

"The locals swear by it. We're increasing our odds of success just by including it, with sales at the very least."

Clementine contemplated the items on the desk. Besides the unfamiliar contraption, several small glass dishes sat on the spotless metal surface. Each one held a different substance in color and thickness. "What are you doing?"

"Ensuring the quality of our ingredients."

Clementine pointed to the headgear and goaded him with more direct questions. "You never showed me this. What is it?"

Milton gazed up at her with a skeptical eye but pulled the mechanism closer. "They're microscoping goggles."

Clementine leaned one hand on the desk. "What do they do?"

"First, if you're wounded, you struggle to put them on." Milton picked them up. In stretching the inch-wide elastic, the instrument wobbled in wild jerks.

"Let me help you." Clementine accepted the goggles. With steady pressure, she elongated the band and fit it carefully around Milton's head.

He issued a brief, self-loathing, "Thank you." He adjusted the white rubber goggles over his eyes. He continued in a more conversational cadence. "You wear them like any glasses or goggles. Then you adjust the lenses here."

Milton toyed with several of the concave glass circles. Each lens moved on a thin metal arm attaching it to the goggles' nearest outer edge. Five layers sat independent of each other in front of each eye.

"The closer I need to see, the more lenses I employ." Milton settled all ten of the lenses before his eyes, each jointed arm reaching its destination with a click.

"What are you trying to see?"

Milton tapped the shallow glass dishes on the desk. "Here we have strawberry juice, turmeric powder, and rosemary pulp. By utilizing the goggles, I can see if the results are well mixed or too uneven to be used in the trials."

"They look good to me."

"That's why we have the goggles." Milton slid the green, wet paste toward him. "The rosemary and the turmeric hold up under magnification. But the strawberry juice." He moved the vermilion liquid closer. It sloshed towards the rim of the dish and receded in sloppy movements. "Some parts are thicker than others. We have to remix it."

Milton examined all three samples, and Clementine sensed he was ready to move on from his task. "Would you like some help?"

"Please."

Clementine's gentle fingers elevated the goggles and their elastic band from around Milton's head. She held onto them.

Milton remained silent, investigating the ingredients on the desk with his bare eyes.

Clementine piped up. "I've never used a microscope. I'm not sure I believe it works as well as you say it does."

Milton cocked an eyebrow but gestured to the samples. "Go ahead. Put it on and have a gander. I'll give you my chair." He stood up and made room for her.

Clementine settled onto the high seat and pulled the goggles down over her forehead. The world lurched at her, larger than life and slightly misshapen. She ducked backwards, and Milton's hand alighted on her shoulder blade. She blinked, but the room remained daunting. "It's disorienting, isn't it?"

Milton chuckled. "Try the lowest setting." With a few flicks of his fingers, he swung all but the closest lens up and away from Clementine's left eye.

She laughed, and her right hand fumbled to raise the other side's four most powerful lenses. She lifted each one away, and the world retreated almost to its normal distance. "This is much better."

"Now inspect the samples." Milton placed the golden-orange powder in front of her. "Can you see the precision? The consistency of the grind?"

Clementine pored over the grains in the dish. Seeing herbs and spices in such detail arrested her. In slow succession, she arranged each additional lens into place before her eyes. The powder grew from a collective mound into individual pebbles in an edible mountain. "Astonishing. I see it. It's beautiful."

Awe in nature and science gripped her, but Clementine forced herself to give up the microscoping goggles. Milton took them, tracing his fingertips along their rubber contours.

Clementine smoothed her hair where the band had ruffled it. "I hope my interruption hasn't set you too far back."

Milton crinkled his nose. His grin strained. "What's a few extra minutes? Besides, you agreed with me. That's a worthwhile second opinion."

Clementine glanced over the room, all eighteen extractors still and unmanned. She patted her hand in a restless rhythm against her leg. "Where are the workers?"

Milton tossed his head toward the far wall. "I sent them to the other half of the factory. The bottling equipment needs to be prepared and tested. They're cleaning it. That's why it's quiet." He returned the goggles to the desk.

Clementine laid her hand on Milton's elbow. "Thank you for showing me your goggles. I'll never forget it, Milton."

The old man snapped his attention to Clementine at the sound of his name.

Clementine's heart leapt into her throat. She propped her other hand over her mouth in fake astonishment. "Did I say *Milton*? I'm sorry. I guess *Mr. Longshaw* sounds so formal. We've worked together long enough to be casual, haven't we? Would it be all right if I called you Milton?"

He blinked and relaxed into a genteel warmth. "I think that'd be all right."

"I appreciate how much you've taught me while I've been in India."

"Think nothing of it."

Clementine expanded her smile and squeezed his elbow. "Let me know if you need any more help with your instruments."

Milton leered at the microscoping goggles. "I wouldn't have needed your rescue if Miss Datta had worked today."

Clementine did not understand why Indira approached her at the tail end of the previous shift and asked for the day off. Indira could have – and possibly should have – sought Milton's permission, but Clementine did not belabor the point. Indira's sincerity, not to mention her barely contained determination and hopefulness, had won Clementine's agreement at once. Indira's absence fit Clementine's needs as well, the same demands that preoccupied her from wondering what Indira required the time off for.

Clementine rubbed Milton's arm. "Don't worry about Miss Datta. She's always been comfortable talking to me. I'm sure that's why she came to me instead of you."

"I'm direct but fair."

"Of course. That's why you made me your partner during our first meeting."

Clementine held her smile and Milton's gaze. His discerning eyes took her in.

"I should check on your hand while I'm here." Clementine reached for Milton's right glove.

He jerked it out of reach. "The doctors told me to rest it. It doesn't need to be investigated."

Clementine clucked her tongue. "You haven't rested it. You used it to put on your goggles." She lifted his hand into one of hers. "Are you afraid I'll hurt you?"

Milton stood up straighter, and his cheeks sucked in. "I'm not scared. I don't care to be fussed over and prodded."

"I'll do neither. Just a peek to see how it's healing." Clementine peeled the glove back from Milton's wrist. "Always gloves with you."

"It's cold."

"Not indoors." Clementine slid the material an inch off Milton's hand.

He laid his other hand over hers. "I think you've examined enough."

Clementine plucked his interference away. "Did you hire me to show me gadgets or to benefit from my medicinal experience?"

Milton sighed and dropped his strong hand. "I hired you as a business decision. We can accomplish more working together than on our own."

Clementine smoothed the skin on the back of Milton's recovering hand. Several scars shimmered at her. "We certainly can."

Milton shifted in barely noticeable increments.

"I can heal these, you know." Clementine traced the short marks with her fingertips. "Plantain leaves would help."

Milton resounded with wry laughter. He took his hand and pulled the glove on over it. "For what? No one's interested in an old man's appearance because nobody cares."

Clementine rolled her eyes. "I don't know why you insist on it. You're not that old. We need participants in the Fountain of Youth trials, if you're that worried about it."

Milton chuckled with distraction. The sound deepened, and Clementine joined him in enjoying her joke. He touched the sleeve of her dress against her elbow.

He studied her clothing and her hair. "You might be the Fountain of Youth yourself, young lady."

She grinned and tried not to pull away. "You're younger than you think you are."

Clementine was ready to back off and head to her office when Milton jumped his scrutiny to the doorway behind her. Bryce lingered there, wide eyed and slack jawed.

Clementine patted Milton's arm. "Well, my work calls me, and yours calls you."

"Right." Milton sat down at the desk. "The pomegranates and the shilajit, was it?"

"Correct. Both should be here within a week."

"Thank the British for the most extensive railroad lines in the world, eh?"

"Indeed." Clementine adjusted the cuffs of her sleeves as she strode toward Bryce. Her tone darkened to strict business. "Were you looking for me?"

He closed his eyes in a long blink, his verbal response faltering. "Yes." He stepped out into the hallway to clear out of Clementine's way.

She charged past him toward her office and rounded the corner.

Mr. Mustafa's voice traded off with Aatmaj's in the lobby at the far end of the hall.

Bryce scrambled up to her side. "I just got in from the shop."

"And?"

"The man said he'd check the tube system, but he wouldn't make any promises."

"Why is everything always broken around here?" Clementine stormed into her office. Bryce followed her, and she shot another question at him. "Why won't he fix it?"

Bryce held his palms up in surrender. "He wasn't the one who installed it. That man retired."

"Didn't he train anyone in these systems?"

"Yeah, but they don't usually break down. They're not as experienced at repairing them. He doesn't want to make it worse."

Clementine returned to her earlier question. "How come ours is broken, then?"

"Ours was one of the first ones they installed. They might've made a mistake. Or we might've overused it."

Clementine shrugged. "We've gotten along for two months without it."

Bryce's fingers tensed and retracted. "Milton might've broken it."

"Maybe." Clementine shuffled through random papers and notebooks on her desk. If Bryce did not get the hint and leave, she was prepared to send him on his way.

The door slammed shut. She flinched and pivoted to confront him.

Bryce glared at her, hands balled into shaking fists at his sides. "Clementine. Milton?"

Her heart thundered, stealing her breath away. She maintained her calm demeanor. "I didn't mean to accuse him. It's his part of the tube system that doesn't work, isn't it?"

Bryce stomped a step closer to her. "You were flirting with Milton?"

Clementine tightened her jaws. "I need him on the project."

"No, you don't. You said it yourself. We can operate the factory without him. We have Mr. Menon and everyone else."

"He has fifteen years of expertise he gained with my father. We can't afford to throw that away if we can help it."

Bryce huffed. "What's going on?"

"I'm keeping the project moving and on time. That's all."

Bryce opened his mouth to interject.

"Did you let Mr. Menon know the schedule for the upcoming deliveries?" Clementine dug the paper out of the mess on her desk and held it out. "The pomegranates will be in soon. The shilajit will take longer because it's coming straight from the source."

Bryce snatched the page. "I'll tell him."

"He's in the bottling room, I think."

Bryce stared at her, but she offered him nothing new. He ripped the door open and fled. Clementine closed the door behind him. She would keep the factory running, but at what cost?

Chapter Twenty-Three

Bryce narrowed his eyes at Milton sidelong from the next station behind the extractors. Bryce's scrutiny bored into Milton, singling out every tiny detail he hated about the man.

Greying hair lay straight and meticulous on his head. Nevertheless, his eyebrows tended toward curving and unruly. Beady eyes with a washed-out color like dirty dishwater. Crags spread out from the corners. Other canyons competed for the longest and the deepest around his mouth and along his cheeks. Bryce recalled his mother's tender terms. *Smile lines. Laugh lines.* Bryce scoffed. When had Milton ever enjoyed himself? At someone else's expense, perhaps.

Milton switched the glass dish in front of him for another, squinting at its contents. Bryce inspected Milton's charcoal suit, as precise and stodgy as his hair. Always neutral colors with him. A lack of color. And everything about Milton was so thin. From his hair, face, and neck to his shoulders, torso, and shoes. But he refused to wither up and blow away. Bryce imagined Milton willowing into a barely visible strand and disappearing into the air. Never to be seen or heard from again. What a wonderful gift that would be!

Instead, Milton glanced toward Bryce. "Would you pass me the other magnifiers?"

Bryce scowled. Why did Milton not just go away? There were plenty of nations Milton had not disgraced with his presence. Surely he could move on to any of those? Or deliver a fatal shock to everyone by revisiting his duties in the States?

Milton sized Bryce up from top to bottom. "Did you hear me? The goggles."

Bryce sighed. Once more, Milton requested him to perform, and Bryce had no choice but to dance to whatever tune Milton played. He felt like more of a monkey or a cobra than a man. Bryce picked up the microscoping goggles from his station and dragged himself off his high seat. "Why can't Miss Datta get them for you? Where is she?"

"She sent word she was too ill to work. I would've liked her here, too."

Bryce trawled over to Milton and handed over the goggles. "Why do you need these, anyway?"

Milton grabbed them with gruff strength. "My pair's broken."

"Clementine was right. Everything's in disrepair around here."

Milton raised the goggles and stretched the band to rest around his head. "Half the lenses shattered when I fumbled them. My grip is still weak."

"From breaking your hand." Bryce leaned over the seated man. "Maybe your bones are too old for the strains of this job."

Milton jumped out of his chair and whipped the goggles off, tossing them on the desk. "What's your problem? You know damn well I smashed my hand in that stupid machine." Milton pointed to the nearby extractor glinting in the flames of the ceiling lights. He poked his finger at Bryce. "I'm your boss. I could fire you for criticizing me."

Bryce reared up to shout back, but Milton's threat stopped him. If Milton barred Bryce from entering the factory, Bryce might never get this close to Clementine again.

Milton's eyes blazed. "What?"

Bryce shook his head and moseyed back to his station.

"You obviously have something to say."

Bryce's words almost strangled him as he sat down. "Forget it. I'm sorry."

Milton remained standing by his desk. "Don't add lying to being a coward. Is it the equipment? Your salary?"

Bryce looked down at his shoes. "I should get to work."

Milton laughed and took a few steps closer. "Don't tell me this is about Clementine."

Bryce met him with rage burning in his face. The sound of her name on his dry, pale lips made Bryce want to fly at Milton and beat her memory out of his head.

Milton strolled toward him, the fingers of his obnoxious gloves picking at one another. "A liar, a coward, and a fool."

Bryce glowered at him.

"Did you think she'd fancy you because you're the same age? Or because you'd do anything for her? Poring over Clements' books with her day after day in the meeting room. You're quite the romantic, aren't you?"

Bryce's nostrils flared with every steamy breath.

Milton set his left hand on the back of Bryce's chair. "You're jealous as the dickens. I wish you could see what an idiot you're making of yourself. I always knew you made bad decisions, but this? It takes the bloody cake, as the British say."

Bryce's blood boiled. "I'm not a fool."

"Of course you aren't. You're only in love with somebody who doesn't love you." Milton murmured. "Take my advice. Move on. She's not the only English-speaking woman in Delhi. Goodness knows she's not the most beautiful."

Bryce sucked in a breath.

"Save it." Milton retrieved his hand from Bryce's chair. "There are plenty of British girls traipsing through Civil Lines. They're either bored in their accepted routines or bursting to escape the confines of their relegated lives." Milton snapped his fingers, his glove muffling the sound. "I've got it. Miss Higginbotham. She'd fall over dead if you talked to her for longer than five minutes. Then again, so might I."

Bryce choked out a response. "I have nothing against Miss Higginbotham."

"Like you had nothing against Clementine before she arrived on the premises?" Milton *tched* several times. "You forget I was there. We both picked on her."

Bryce fought to form coherent syllables. "Clementine deserves better than you."

Milton clapped him on the back. "Some women might fawn over your doe eyes and disheveled hair. But wisdom and sophistication won out this week. Better luck next time."

Milton ambled back to the chair at his station six feet away. "It's a mark of a gentleman to defend Clementine's character, though. I hope it serves you well." He picked up the magnifiers and paused with them halfway to his head. "Have you ever thought about this?"

Bryce pinpointed Milton with sullen eyes.

"How much do we really know about Clementine Fitzgerald?" Milton perched the magnifiers on the desk. "Two months toiling in the same building. We knew her father's every move and habit. She's flirting with me, and I haven't learned that much about her."

Milton adjusted the microscoping goggles on his head. Bryce's muscles and bones crawled. All he could do was itch his arms through his suit sleeves.

Bryce had stood stock still outside Clementine's house in Civil Lines, waiting for her to secure their notes in the car while the macaque used him for a tree branch. Clementine rescued him with one quick-thinking throw of her arm. They laughed at the cinema in the dark. They kissed in the street and made warm memories on the study's green settee.

Bryce longed to tell Milton exactly how much the old man had no clue about. But rolling over Bryce were other scenes, conversations and actions littered with holes. Each one stole a little hope from him. How long Clementine had taken to open up to him about Nashville and Livingston. Her withholding of her true resentment toward Lowell Dodd. The way she took her personal letters and postcards out of his hands as he perused them.

Bryce landed a frustrated fist on his desk. Glass dishes jumped and rattled.

Milton called over. "Don't let it get to you, Bryce. I'm sure it's a passing fling."

Bryce smoldered under his collar. He stuck a finger between the fabric and his sweaty neck, but it gave him little relief. Clementine had shut him out. Completely, entirely, irrefutably. No more shared meals or jokes about monkeys. No touches, no kisses. Bryce sank his hair into his hands.

On a loop, worse than the pictures in his head, loomed Milton's taunting. *How much do we really know about Clementine Fitzgerald?*

Bryce squeezed his eyes shut.

How much?

Her light brown hair gleamed in the sun, brighter than everything except the smiles she aimed at him.

Do we?

She reclined against the settee's pillows, vulnerable, unclothed, and waiting for him.

Know?

No. She pushed him away. His fingers circled her wrist in the bedroom, and she flung her arm away from him.

Bryce fought a sob. Milton had a point.

He could recite the number of miles between Nashville and Oklahoma City, but how much did he know about the woman he had invited to make that trip?

Chapter Twenty-Four

Bryce spent three nights in anguish. He rolled one way, then the other, then completely around to his original position. Hot and annoyed, he flipped the covers off. Chilled and exposed, he scrambled to pull them back on. He stared at the high ceiling above his bed, a wrist resting forlorn and careless across his forehead. The shadows moved in the hazy moonlight at such a slow pace, he could not see them shifting from moment to moment. Only after lying awake for hours or stirring anew without realizing he had plunged into sleep could he measure the distance the shapes had traveled.

Travel. A word he cared nothing for these days.

Sunlight dared to impose on the room, warming its beige walls into a golden glow. The alarm clock on the round bedside table let loose its high-pitched ring. Bryce detested it. He had drifted half alert for at least an hour. He smashed his hand down on it, but the vibrating chime buzzed on. He grabbed the wind-up mechanism with its spindly metal legs and whipped it across the room. It hit the front of the wooden dresser and collapsed to the floor. The tone altered but continued filling the room – the very center of Bryce's brain – with its message.

Bryce swung his legs off the bed and grabbed one of his shoes off the floor. He slung the sole at the clock, breaking its round glass façade. The thin hands bent at sharp angles and lost track of the time. He dented the bell on top, reducing the song to a clinking sound that slowed to a stop.

He tossed his shoe aside and went into the tiny bathroom. He washed up and revisited the mirror hung above the dresser. Every agitated night left more of an imprint on his complexion and posture, not to mention his mood. Groggy and dreading the day ahead, Bryce ignored the darkening wells under his once-bright eyes. His shoulders sloped as he picked up his comb. In a daze, only convinced he was awake because of his heart's perpetual ache, Bryce attempted to wrangle his chaotic hair.

For what? He let the comb fumble out of his hand and clatter onto the dresser. He put on his clothes and topped his head with his newsboy cap. He pulled a half-eaten loaf of bread out of the box on the counter and sawed off two slices for himself. He fit each piece into one metal slot of his countertop toaster and struck a match to light the wick in the center of the device. While he waited for it to heat the racks and singe brown designs into his bread, Bryce tied on his shoes. He struck random patterns against his hips, wandering through the room. The earthy baking smell reached his nose, and he blew out the toaster's flame. He used the wooden knobs to open the bread slots and snatched each piece out with his fingers. The hot surfaces seared his skin, and he dropped the toast on the counter to run each fingertip through his mouth in quick succession.

He snatched up his breakfast, his first bite dry and flavorless. He left the loaf out and grabbed his keys. Managing to pry the door open with both hands occupied, Bryce sidled into the hallway. He locked up his apartment and jogged down the stairs. He floated through the lobby and out into the foggy white morning. He devoured more of his toast as he walked toward the parking lot alongside the small, rectangular building. His appetite crashed by the time he finished chewing, but he made himself swallow.

Bryce finished off the piece of toast, tossing the other aside for whatever wildlife would have it. He jumped on his steambike and nestled the newsboy on tighter. He brought the engine to life and eased out of the lot into the quiet street.

The farther he rode from his adopted home, the noisier the roads became. Other vehicles crowded in around him, seeming to trade off on which ones escorted him along his route. He made the turn into Meena Bazaar, feeling like he had already forfeited for the day. Clementine had moved on. Milton had told him off. Yet he returned to serving as part of their team.

Bryce forced the bike through its final curves, a wide one into the parking lot and a sharp pivot into his usual space. He silenced it and readjusted his cap on his way to the door. He strolled in, matching Aatmaj's touching palms with his own.

"The repairman is here," Aatmaj said.

"Already?" Bryce wondered if he was late but had no way of knowing without asking or reaching a room with a clock.

"Miss Fitzgerald had me send for him early. She said she was tired of waiting for the system to be repaired."

Clementine. Of course. Bryce wandered into the hallway toward the offices. Since he approached her about her involvement with Milton, Bryce could swear Clementine went out of her way to keep from being alone with Bryce. This change of plans proved it was not his overactive imagination. Something they had left unattended for months could wait an extra half-hour.

Past the closed door of the meeting room, Milton's office stood open. A man's casual but professional cadence issued out of it. "No, ma'am. If the rest of the system works, it's likely a local problem. I'll check for cracks in this section of the tube."

Bryce stepped through the doorway.

Clementine met his gaze for a moment but addressed the repairman. "All it could take is a crack to stop working?"

"It's a pneumatic system. It moves the canisters with air. If it was mechanical, I'd suspect clogs in the gears or broken pistons. What we need in a system like this is to control the airflow without letting it slip out through added holes." The repairman patted the pockets of his neatly ironed jumpsuit. "I have a few extra tools in my truck I need to bring in."

Clementine wrung her hands. "Is it popular? This kind of system?"

"I'd say so. Air is all around us. Why not use it?" The repairman stepped toward the door.

"What else is it used for that I would've heard of? I want to understand it better."

"Oh." The repairman swung back into his previous stance.

Bryce groaned at the rug. How long were the unnecessary questions and avoidance going to drone on?

The repairman swept his hair off his short forehead. "Did you ever send a fax, ma'am?"

"Sure."

"The Blickensderfers run on air. It gets piped through all the tubes and cylinders. When those ladies at the post office type out your message, each key lets through a certain amount of air." The repairman brought one hand's blade down onto his opposite palm. "At the other end, the second machine translates those specific bursts of air into the original message. You didn't know that?"

"No, but I've used them several times."

"Handy invention. It's a lot more accurate than it used to be. You know why they call it a fax, don't you?"

"No."

Bryce scooted the sole of his shoe back and forth across the rug.

The repairman laughed. "It took a lot of tries to set the Blickensderfers right. If the key for a popular letter, like *e* or *t,* wasn't calibrated exactly, the message came out all garbled at the other end. They said the outcome was a bad facsimile of what was intended."

Clementine failed to erase all the tension from her voice. "Very funny, indeed. It must've been frustrating to create something so precise."

"I agree. But in the end, it beat out the telegraph. I guess it was worth all that. Let me get my tools from the truck. You probably don't want to be in here while I'm testing the system. I have to power up my compressor to locate the problem, and I might have to cut a hole in the wall. Mr. Longshaw said that was okay?"

"Yes. Do what you have to do."

The repairman exited the room, and Clementine attempted to sweep past Bryce out the door.

He lunged into her path. "Don't act like I'm not here."

"Don't do this now. Let me out."

Bryce moved out of her way but followed close behind her into the hall. "When would be a better time for you to explain yourself?"

"Explain what? I already told you–"

"You told me almost nothing."

Clementine darted into her office. Bryce chased her in and closed the door. She stayed on the other side of the room, her eyes barely meeting his.

Bryce tucked his hands inside his pockets to keep them from fidgeting. "This is how it is? Either I don't exist or I'm not to be too close."

Clementine stood straight and unmoving. "I'll talk business with you, but if you only want to talk about personal matters…"

Bryce bobbed his head. "I have some business questions. You're my new boss, and I never got the chance to make as many inquiries of you as Milton did."

Clementine squirmed. "What do you want to know?"

"Why do you want this serum to reverse aging?"

"I can't stand to watch people suffer."

"Really?" Bryce's throat tightened. "I've been going out of my mind for the last four days over this Milton thing."

Clementine eyed the door behind him.

"I'll keep to the topic. Clearly, you don't want to erase everyone's problems, so who is this for? Clements is dead. Is it your mother? The farmers? The basket weavers and whoever else you've barely mentioned to me?"

"Drop it."

Bryce inched closer. "It can't be about making money. You've given thousands away to get on this project. Do you think Milton would've paid the workers as much as you did while the factory was closed? Milton's not even convinced we'll make a bigger profit with the new Fountain of Youth compared to the old one."

Clementine trembled. "It's the right thing to do. A medical remedy is what the world needs."

Bryce advanced a full pace toward her. "Who are you?"

She recoiled from him. "You know that. I'm Clementine Fitzgerald."

"Where are you from?"

"North of Livingston. I told you that."

"Where did you go to school?"

"We had a schoolhouse in town."

"Why do you want to reverse aging?"

A muscle in her jaw twinged. "I want to help people."

"Who's your mother?"

"Adelaide. She's in Nashville."

"I know we're at work, and this isn't business." Bryce's words stuck in his throat as he approached her. "Have you..." He slid a clammy palm down his face. "Have you slept with him?"

"Bryce, don't do this."

"Why'd you push me away?"

"I didn't push you away." Clementine slipped past him and lingered by the door.

He gestured to her. "How can you say that from way over there? You take one glance at me or hear one step of my shoes, and you bolt."

"That's what I was trying to tell you." Clementine's features hardened. "I made myself clear I was willing to do anything to make this project succeed."

Bryce's eyes popped wide open. "You never said it included meddling with an ancient man. Did you–"

"No." She struggled to swallow.

"But you'd do it if you had to, wouldn't you?"

Clementine moved her mouth but failed to form words.

Bryce's chest caved in. "How many other lovers have you had? I mean, were you only with me to keep me on this assignment?" He gave Clementine time to answer, but she only looked at him. "Did you care for me at all? What happened to us? I thought we were happy. I blinked, and you were gone."

Clementine opened the door. "I asked you to keep your questions professional. As your boss, all you need to know is that I'm doing everything I can to make the project you work on succeed."

A whirring noise gained strength on the other side of the wall in Milton's office. Clementine rushed out the door, and Bryce stood on the rug of her office with his mouth ajar.

Her father's former office. Right next to his desk. Bryce took off his hat and ruffled a hand through his hair. His gaze roamed in listless circles over the desk.

He and Clementine had been happy, he was sure of it. They had stood in the study of her house – her father's house – and perused some of the things she had collected there.

No, Bryce corrected himself. He played the memory back through without idealistic edits.

He picked up the letter from Gertie Sands, and Clementine plucked it away. He sifted through Clements' postcards, and Clementine cleared them out of his hands.

She was hiding something.

No. Bryce fought to keep a lock of his hair parted how he wanted it.

He stopped, staring at the desk. With calm fingers, he raked his hair into a semblance of order. He put on his cap.

Clementine might be keeping something from him, but she had not come to India empty handed. The house she inherited from her father held evidence of who she was and where she came from. She spent long days at the factory ensuring the workers mixed the extracted ingredients at ratios palatable enough for product trials. If Bryce could slip into the Fitzgerald house...

He walked out of Clementine's office. The contained roar of the compressor reminded him of Oklahoma's frequent tornados. He reached the end of the hallway and let himself into the vacant employee area. Today, he needed to clear his head.

Soon, he would dive in up to his neck and dig up everything he could find on Clementine Fitzgerald.

Chapter Twenty-Five

Sharp knocks startled Clementine awake. She must have been lucky enough to escape into heavy sleep. Breaking out of it plunged her into a foggy mind as full and dense as the city. She groaned. The barrage sounded again, raucous and urgent.

Bryce. Was he really so upset he would wake her up at whatever unholy hour this was?

Clementine flung herself out of bed. She grabbed her dressing gown and threw it on as she strode out of the bedroom. She wrapped it around her body before giving it a snug tie at her waist. The knocks escalated to bangs as she flew down the stairs and unlocked the door. She swung it open.

Mr. Mustafa panted in front of her. His turban rested askew, and a blanket of mist hung in the cool air behind him. "Miss Fitzgerald–"

She squinted, unbelieving. "Mr. Mustafa? What are you doing here?" Adrenaline overran her confusion. "What's wrong? Is it something with the factory?"

"My daughter." His voice squeaked.

She waved him in. "Tell me what happened."

Mr. Mustafa stepped into the house, wiping his eyes. "She fell and scratched her arm. We thought it was nothing. Now it looks terrible, and she's burning with fever."

Clementine sped off on sure feet. She pointed to the study just around the corner. "Go into that room and gather up any herbs I have in there. I'll be right back."

She raced through the dining room with its small set of table and chairs she rarely used. Accessing the servants' hall, she rushed through it to the courtyard. Her bare feet padded across the dusty stones of the patio, and she let herself into the kitchen. Clementine grabbed a basket full of herbs in pouches and jars. She plucked up stray bags and envelopes from the counter.

Rushing back to the great room, Clementine found Mr. Mustafa waiting with a half-dozen packages in his hands. He dropped them into the basket and took it from her.

"You can come now?" he asked, his dark eyebrows knitted together.

"Right now. Let's go." She glanced out the open door at the empty driveway. "How did you get here?"

"I ran."

"It's several miles."

"I know."

"We'll take my father's autocarriage." Clementine grabbed the key from a peg by the door.

"Have you ever used it?"

"No."

"Does it run?"

"I hope so."

Clementine led him outside and locked up the house. She scurried across the front of the property to the garage and entered its side door. Edith Higginbotham's advice from two and a half months earlier surfaced to aid her.

The water tank will take a while to heat up from a cold start. Prime the engine before you raise the door. It'll save you time.

Clementine jumped into the driver's seat and engaged the key in the ignition. With a sputter and a twitch, the autocarriage responded to her request. She left the fresh flame to do its duty and hurried to the front of the garage. A wheel was affixed to the wall beside the main, articulated door. She grabbed its peg and rotated the mechanism as quickly as she could. Its attached ropes and pulleys drew the door up out of the way.

Edith's instructions continued. *Check the fuel and water levels.*

Clementine had inserted a cautious question. *Isn't that dangerous with the fire struck?*

Edith had shrugged. *It's what my father does. If the levels are serviceable, the vehicle should be ready to drive in no time.*

Clementine opened the autocarriage's front panel. Thanks to the high quality of its parts, plenty of water remained in the tank. Fuel pellets occupied the other chamber. She slammed the panel closed. "Get in, Mr. Mustafa. I think we can use it."

They climbed in, and as soon as the vehicle rumbled around Clementine, she made an audible gulp. "Here we go." She backed up with a lurch into the driveway. She thought about stepping out to close up the garage, but Mr. Mustafa's wild eyes prompted her to drive. There was little for intruders to steal if they happened upon the open door. Mr. Mustafa's family came first.

Clementine piloted the vehicle backwards into the street, then lunged it ahead toward the main road out of Civil Lines.

Mr. Mustafa kept one hand on the basket of herbs in his lap. His other hand wiped sweat off his forehead. "I'm sorry to come to you like this."

"It's okay."

"You're not even properly dressed. You have no shoes."

Clementine could arrive in front of his entire family in her nightgown and robe. She shook off her tingling concern. They would forgive her. "Your daughter has a fever. That's more important."

"We've barely spoken in weeks."

"That was because of work. We had different tasks to take care of."

"I also…"

Clementine urged the autocarriage faster down the almost-abandoned road deeper into the city. "We don't have to talk about it now. I know you're upset about your daughter."

"It's Mr. Milton." Mr. Mustafa rubbed his forehead and tugged his turban on straighter.

Clementine's heart boomed like a kettle drum. "What about him?"

"I've seen the way he treats Miss Datta. The way he ogles you. He shows disrespect."

Clementine hesitated, but she had always been honest with Mr. Mustafa. "I can't argue with you."

"He pretends to have manners and refinement. It's an act."

"Have you seen this from him before Miss Datta and me?"

"Once. Mr. Clements and Mr. Milton hired an Englishwoman to sit at the front desk when the factory opened. Mr. Milton often tried to hold her hand and offer her rides in his autocarriage. She quit, and Mr. Clements hired Mr. Aatmaj to handle the lobby."

Clementine shook her head. "I'll take care of it. Mr. Longshaw only plans to stay with us this year. He'll fly to the States, and he won't be our problem anymore."

"I don't want him to be anyone's problem."

Clementine's hope sank. "Me, neither. Are we getting close to your house?"

"Yes. Go around the mosque."

Clementine zipped past the Jama Masjid and followed the rest of Mr. Mustafa's directions. In a long row of close-standing houses, he told her to stop. She parked at the side of the road, and they clambered out of the vehicle.

Mr. Mustafa ushered her inside and joined her with the basket of herbs in hand. Clementine glanced around the room, furnished in scarlet cushions and dark wooden tables. Heavy curtains covered the windows. Small lamps lit the space, where three pairs of wide eyes took her in.

A woman in a sky-blue headscarf and long black dress sat on a cushion. Her hand swept through the hair of the restless child lying beside her. Mr. Mustafa spoke to the woman, but her eyes remained glassy with panic.

Two boys perched on other cushions around the room, alternating their curiosity between Clementine and the girl.

Clementine stayed by the door, not wanting to further disturb Mr. Mustafa's family. "What's your daughter's name?"

"Tayeba."

"I need to see her scratch and feel how hot her fever is."

Mr. Mustafa explained this to his wife, leading Clementine toward the figures on the cushions.

Clementine knelt down in front of the girl, assessing how little and young she was. Only a handful of years old, five or six, the exact count did not matter. Clementine murmured to her. "Hello, Tayeba. I'm Clementine. How are you doing?"

Mr. Mustafa uttered to his daughter with the same gentle approach.

Tayeba responded in a weak drawl.

"She's exhausted," Mr. Mustafa relayed. "It's not her stomach or her head that aches. She's just hot and very tired. She has no energy left."

Clementine stroked Tayeba's arm. "Can you show me the scratch?"

Mr. Mustafa addressed his wife, and she pulled up Tayeba's sleeve. She bent her daughter's arm, and Clementine saw the mark above the elbow. Sure enough, a three-inch split had festered into a red, swollen wound. Clementine held the back of her hand to Tayeba's forehead. Her skin blazed above the normal temperature but not as hot as Clementine had experienced before.

Clementine reached for the basket of herbs. "How long has she had the fever?"

Mr. Mustafa set the basket on the floor. "Since the morning."

"That's good. It means her body is fighting what's wrong. With these herbs, she should only have another day of fever. Maybe two." Clementine sorted through the basket's pouches and containers.

She felt the nearby presence of others and spotted Mr. Mustafa's sons peering over her shoulders.

Mr. Mustafa shouted, his flat hand aiming out of the room. The boys scampered out. Their hair and eyes reappeared, peeking through the doorway.

Clementine singled out thyme, turmeric, and clove. "I'll treat Tayeba with a tea and a poultice applied directly to the wound. It's the best way to make the scratch heal up and the infection go away."

"Whatever you need."

With Mr. Mustafa translating, Clementine worked with him and his wife to transform her basic materials into the healing tools she needed them to be. She taught them how to prepare the poultice and apply it with clean bandages. Mr. Mustafa's wife supported Tayeba in sitting up to sip the strong, cooling tea. She wrinkled her nose at the taste but accepted it with maturity.

Clementine maintained her post on the floor atop a patterned beige rug. Every so often, she removed the bandage and poultice to check on the wound's progress. Mr. Mustafa's wife brought her a dish of hummus and a piece of naan. Clementine kept her strength up through the long vigil as the swelling subsided, leaving wrinkled, pink skin.

The two boys snuck into the living room and fell asleep on cushions. Mr. Mustafa sat on the floor, observing everyone in turn. His slumbering sons, his desperate wife, and the herbalist tending to his ailing daughter.

Bells pealed from a few streets away. Wisps of sunlight eked in past the edges of the curtains. Clementine rubbed her dry, weary eyes.

Mr. Mustafa breached the subject first. "It's morning."

Clementine exposed Tayeba's wound one last time. "It'll take a few days to heal, but she should be fine."

Mr. Mustafa closed his eyes. He relayed this to his wife, who gushed out words in a rush. "We were very scared," he admitted. "I knew you would be our best choice."

"Why me?" Clementine wrapped Tayeba's arm and pushed herself up on wobbly legs. "Why not a hospital?"

"The doctors might not take her illness seriously. My sons, they would. I knew you'd help her."

Clementine examined the arrangement of bowls Mr. Mustafa's wife had supplied for her on the floor. Clementine had partly filled each one with the herbs she had administered to Tayeba. "Your wife should be able to take perfect care of Tayeba whether you're here or away."

Mr. Mustafa bowed to her, pressing one palm over his heart. "Thank you, Miss Fitzgerald."

Her eyes watered. "You're welcome, Mr. Mustafa." She picked up her basket and moved to the door. "It'll be all right if we're an hour late to the office. Or two."

"I owe you so much."

"I believe this was my way of repaying earlier debts to you."

His lips perked up. "That is the way it is."

Chapter Twenty-Six

Clementine drove north in the autocarriage, the basket of herbs occupying the passenger seat. She veered right at the Jama Masjid followed by a left to arrive at its front. She directed the vehicle to the side of the road and climbed out.

Through the archways in the outer wall, she noticed several men already in the courtyard. Clementine resolved to enter anyway and passed through one of the arches. The men gathered at the rim of a large, square pool in the center of the courtyard. They pulled off their shoes and washed their feet.

With nothing on her feet to remove, Clementine sat down in the nearest corner some distance away from everyone else. She folded her legs and let her eyelids fall closed.

Exhaustion quieted her mind, but threads of memory trailed through it.

Mr. Mustafa's family had fled Afghanistan when he was a boy in search of a better life. Mr. Magar had left Nepal, possibly for the same reason.

Clements, Milton, and Bryce had all trekked far from the United States. The Higginbothams and the Dodds had deserted their native England.

Tears dripped onto Clementine's bare feet.

In the small cabin north of Livingston, Clementine had spent more days and nights curled up in her mother's bed than she could count. The same scene replayed itself over and over through the years, no matter how many times Clementine had heard the stories or how tall she grew.

Adelaide stroked her daughter's golden-brown hair away from her forehead. "Your grandmother's maiden name was?"

Clementine had forgotten the days when this question tripped her up. She supplied the right answer in perfect rhythm, letting it roll off her tongue. "Inessa Schneider."

"And we have the name Heidel because?"

"Grandpa was part German."

"That's right." Adelaide's fingers swept across Clementine's forehead, cooling in the summer heat and comforting in the winter frost. "Her mother was?"

Clementine closed her eyes to sharpen her recall. "My great-grandmother's name was Maple Parish. She married Grandpa Schneider, and he tailored men's suits."

"Yes. And he was?"

"German and Russian."

"Her mother was?"

Clementine beamed because this was her favorite part of the drill. "They called her Flying Squirrel, and she was full-blooded Shawnee Indian."

"And her husband was?"

"British. At least, in part."

Adelaide gathered Clementine's long locks behind her, coaxing stray strands off her daughter's neck. "Flying Squirrel did what she was supposed to do. She was encouraged to make better relations between her tribe and the white people who came to Tennessee. She fell in love with a white man, and they got married. She was pregnant when the government changed its mind."

Clementine's heart saddened. "They sent the Indians away."

"Far away from the land where they'd lived for over one hundred years. Generations of Shawnee, who'd known nothing else, were forced to abandon their homes." Adelaide parted her daughter's hair into three sections and interwove them in a lazy braid.

"Flying Squirrel stayed."

"She said goodbye to her parents and her grandparents, her sisters and her brothers. Many of her cousins."

"Did they ever see each other again?"

"I don't know, but I hope so. It's not likely, but they were strong people. Smart and determined. They might have arranged it somehow."

The mattress shifted as Adelaide sat up behind her daughter. Clementine rolled onto her back to peer up into her mother's shaded face.

Adelaide's long, straight locks hung loose like a dark cape around her shoulders. She brushed Clementine's hair away from her cheeks and tucked it behind her ears. "This is why it's important to remember these names. To remember the story of our family. If I hadn't learned them, two generations is all it would've taken to erase their lives forever. Flying Squirrel's legacy would've disappeared like smoke on the eastern breeze. We would've belonged to all these other countries and traditions – and we do – but we would've cut off our roots."

The heartache and loss hiding between the sentences of the stories were not lost on Clementine. Her mother had seen to that. "Flying Squirrel sacrificed almost everything. Do you think we'll ever have to give up that much?"

Adelaide smoothed Clementine's cheek with the backs of her fingers. Pride and admiration shone in her brown-green eyes. "You are the only thing I couldn't live without. I said goodbye to my parents, my grandparents, and the rest of my family. I grieved, but I lived on. I left the home I knew, and I made a new one here."

Clementine balked with a mischievous pout. "You could get along without me. If I fell in the creek and got carried away in a flood, you'd be all right."

"I wouldn't. Don't you ever say that." Adelaide scooped Clementine up in her arms and left a definitive kiss on her temple. Only a hint of good spirits lightened her serious mood.

Clementine basked in her mother's warmth. "What would you do if that happened to me?"

"I'd jump in the flood, too, and let it carry us both away."

Clementine's limbs felt buoyant as she pictured the flow. Sooner or later, the swell of waters would deposit their bodies on dry land. "Then we'd build another cabin and start our new life."

"Life is an adventure, my darling." Coughs and wheezing shook Adelaide's final words. She unfurled herself from her daughter to shield her forceful exhales with her hand.

Clementine leapt off the bed, targeting the black iron stove. She kept a tea kettle filled with water warm on a burner at all times for instances like this. She poured a cup of steaming water and dunked a small cloth bundle of herbs into it. She handed it to her mother, setting a hand on Adelaide's shoulder to steady her.

Adelaide glugged down half the tea, pausing to test its effects. She cleared her throat, and her breathing returned to normal. She passed the cup to Clementine, who set it on the bedside trunk.

Adelaide held her daughter's face in her hands. "If I was fully cured tomorrow, I'd still die without you."

Clementine hooked her hands onto her mother's wrists. "Then you'll never die."

Sitting on the solid blocks of the mosque's courtyard, Clementine brushed tears out of her eyes. The fog thickened, haunting the wide expanse in the cool morning. The men from the water tank reached the entrance to the mosque, carrying their shoes as they went inside.

Clementine wrapped her arms around herself, rocking in gentle sways.

Chester's face had been hard to look into. Clementine's mind, even now, steered her toward their meetings between his injury and their parting. Whispering under the stars. Chancing casual banter in front of the others working on the Ledford farm. Balled tightly in each other's arms in the dark of the oak tree standing guard like a fortress.

The sun blazed into Chester's features, too low on the horizon for his hat brim to deflect it. He squinted at Clementine, the corners of his mouth lifting and twisted. She knew better than to believe his grimace was fully due to the blinding rays. She understood his pain because she shared it, too.

The tree, once their ally, stood beside them like a screen for their awkward exchange. What a shame if anyone should see them and feel awkward. What a shame if they were seen and the whole world changed for the better.

After she breached the suggestion and silence dragged them under their sorrows, Clementine took the reins of the situation. "One last time is all I can do. It's too dangerous, more so for you than for me."

"It'd ruin you." Chester's gaze burned. He barely controlled his insistence. "They'd treat you like a carnival sideshow. I won't have that."

"You wouldn't have any say in it if they killed you."

Chester shook his head. "Not in these parts, they wouldn't. The Ledfords know me."

But Chester's hushed words trembled enough to tell Clementine he had the same worry. He was just trying to be brave. "They'd..." Clementine stopped herself. *Spurn you.* She did not need to say it. It would only poison the good relationship he had with the owners of the land.

"One last time, then." The sun dipped behind tree-topped mountains, and Chester risked setting his hands on Clementine's waist. "You'll always be in my thoughts."

"I'll think about you, too." Clementine's mind jumped to the future. She had to move her mother to the city. The distances to ride in the country were too big if Adelaide's health continued to slide. "Wherever I go. Whatever I do. There'll be a part of me right back under this tree with you."

"Don't let 'em..." Chester cut himself off and guided Clementine to sit opposite him in the tall grass. He kept his hands on her arms. "Don't let 'em get to you. I know what that doctor thinks of you, the one Mr. Ledford sends for sometimes. Don't let 'em talk you down. You're not down. You're the most up person I ever met."

"You're up, too. You could have your own farm if you wanted or a shop in the city."

Chester stroked his chin. "I could sell tools, I guess. And seeds. But my place is here. I'm a country boy. Do you have thoughts about running away to the city?"

Clementine hesitated. She wanted to leave reality out of her private moments with Chester. But she liked being able to share the absolute truth with him. "I have to. For my mother's health. If I could, I'd stay."

Chester covered her hand with his. "It'd be harder to see you. Mr. Ledford would still ask you to tend injuries around the farm. I know I would if something else hurt me."

"But goodbye? Forever?" Clementine clutched at his arms. The hard sculpt of his biceps always surprised her. The necessity of such large, dependable muscles amazed her as much as their bulk.

Chester angled himself towards her. "I can write a little. If I get Ollie or someone to help me, I can try to send letters to you."

Clementine inched closer to him. "That'd be nice. I won't know anybody in Nashville when I get there, except my mother."

"Write to me, then, and tell me where to mail messages back to you." Chester reached behind Clementine and pulled a few pins from her hair. He arranged the fallen locks over her shoulder and caressed their waves. "I'd like to know you're doing okay out there in the world."

"It's just the city."

Their talk fell away, and Clementine met Chester in a kiss as the sun continued its darkening descent.

She clung to him afterward, held onto him with interlinked fingers like a stubborn child. She would not let herself cry the way she wanted to, though, and show him how hard their separation was for her.

His quiet tenor hummed in her ear. "I'm gonna squeeze you close. Then we gotta walk away. Okay?"

She nodded. He constricted and released his embrace around her. Clementine maintained her grip.

"You gotta go," Chester whispered, fearful tension driving him. "It's late. You can't be here no more."

Clementine pulled away and made a half-hearted effort to tidy her clothes. Chester did a more thorough job with his, and they jumped to their feet at the same time.

Chester plastered his hat on top of his head. "I gotta walk away, but not because I don't love you."

Clementine swallowed down as much of her grief as would obey her. "I love. You. Too."

They retreated from the tree, Chester toward his house and Clementine toward her horse.

A whisper nabbed her. "Hey."

She whirled toward Chester.

He grinned in the moonlight. "What's the brightest thing I ever did see?"

A riddle. Lighter times bubbled up inside Clementine, and she licked her lips. She tossed out a guess. "The sun."

He wandered a few steps toward her. "I see why you'd think that. But it's not. The answer's Clementine Heidel. You light me up more than anything."

She broke into a full sprint at him.

He caught her in his arms, lifting her and twirling with her in a circle. As he set her down, he rested his head on hers and sang. "Oh, my darling Clementine. I'll be lost back here without you. Hope to see you, Clementine." He left a kiss in her unkempt hair. "I don't care how the darn song goes. I won't move on so easy."

She grabbed his hand as she wandered away. "I'll write. I promise."

She dashed off into the night.

In the chilly Delhi mist, Clementine lowered herself onto the mosque stones. She lay there counting her grief, not in numbers but a mass of accumulated sadness and regret.

The United States government had pushed the tribes of Tennessee and its neighboring states westward. The rules and laws continued to change for territories and relations. Here in India, the British, like other rulers before them, let the natives keep their land in general. Both conquering parties set out to mesh radically different cultures or else give up to wade through the resulting mess.

The sandstone formed a rigid surface under Clementine's temple, but its direct nature reassured her.

She murmured to herself in the sunrise, or perhaps to people she used to know. "I walked away in Livingston, but I stayed in Delhi. I said goodbye to Chester, and Flying Squirrel said farewell to her family. Guns and fences and rules and biases." She pushed herself up, straightening her arms and keeping her palms flat on the ground. "But tonight, I, a white-and-Shawnee woman from America saved the life of a Muslim girl whose father came from Afghanistan. And we did it here, in India, under the gaze of the British where we had few ties before. So maybe it's possible."

Clementine hefted herself to her feet. Her eyes traced the mosque's roof and minarets. "In a world of chasms and walls, I did a good thing. I built a bridge. That will have to be enough for today. It's the only thing left to do."

She wrested her focus from the holy place and walked out of the courtyard through an archway. Vehicles puffing steam and horse-drawn carriages crowded the street. Thanks to the lackadaisical stance of a white-and-brown cow, Clementine fired up her autocarriage and drove away without waiting.

Chapter Twenty-Seven

For how often Bryce fixated on the clock, he might have assumed something unbelievable would happen to it. Time after time, the hands merely ticked along a little further. It neither leapt off the wall nor sprouted wings and flew away. After two hours of staring at it, struggling to concentrate on his work, the clock in Clementine's office remained as it should. The hour, growing increasingly late, proved correct. Bryce had left the room once to confirm this by inquiring if anyone had reset the clock as a prank. The workers gave him odd looks but cemented his problem. The morning was clicking away, and two of the people intrinsic to the company's success remained missing.

Bryce lifted himself out of the desk chair, paused, and collapsed back into it. He huffed. Going to Milton about this would be pointless. The old man would only say things to humiliate Bryce. To top it off, Milton would accuse Bryce of sabotaging his intricate labors with meaningless interruptions. Bryce preferred to avoid all that.

He almost stood up again. Indira, since her sick leave, had been learning English from Mr. Mustafa in their spare time and on the job. She might know something about a change in the translator's schedule not noted in the records. Indira had also stuck herself to Milton's side more than ever. Getting her alone might be harder than gaining a private audience with Clementine.

Bryce picked at something caught between two teeth. Conversation sounded in another room, and he perked up his ears, dental nuisance forgotten. The jovial chatter came from the lobby rather than deeper in the factory. Bryce shot out of the chair and waited just inside the door, listening.

The good humor shook him. Clementine's laugh. "I'm so glad."

Mr. Mustafa's unique inflections followed. "It's not perfect, but it's better."

"Yes. It'll get much better over the next few days."

Bryce peeked around the door frame. Sure enough, Clementine and Mr. Mustafa lingered in the lobby, barely visible down the hall.

"Yasaman insists you join the family for dinner. I do, too. She'll make manut and kabuli palaw for you. And the best korma you ever had."

"I can't accept."

"You must. I'd like it very much."

"Then I'll be there." Clementine's voice chirruped higher. "What do you have in your hand?"

The turbaned man held up a cylindrical box tied with a white ribbon. "It's nothing. When we first met, you bought yourself a present."

Clementine accepted the box with a quizzical tilt to her eyebrows. "The headscarf."

"Yes. To prove you accepted the cultures around you. I want to show you the same thing and thank you for what you did last night."

Bryce stared in disbelief. He made sure no one spied on him from the other end of the hall and kept watching the lobby.

Clementine touched the ribbon's bow, making it bounce. "I can't take this."

Mr. Mustafa ducked his head closer to her. "I'm giving it to you because you shouldn't try to change yourself too much for us. You've never tried to change us."

Clementine read his eyes for a moment. She unwrapped the ribbon and popped off the lid. She brightened with a gasp, and Mr. Mustafa took hold of the box.

Bryce could barely breathe.

Clementine lifted out a brilliant yellow cloche decorated with a large fabric flower.

Mr. Mustafa raised an eyebrow. "Do you like it?"

Clementine replaced the hat on her head with the new cloche. "I love it. Is it too bold to ask you how I look?"

Bryce's eyes bulged, and he nearly stormed over.

Mr. Mustafa beamed at her, professional but proud. "It suits you. Wear it in peace and good health."

"Thank you so much." She bit her lip.

They burst out laughing at the same time.

Bryce ripped away from the door frame and sauntered down the hall. "Here you are."

His announcement, meant to shame them into shreds of common decency, might not have happened at all. The room swallowed it, absorbing the intent and leaving no trace of it behind.

Clementine deflated with slight inconvenience. Her hand alighted on the side of the yellow cloche. "My new hat."

Bryce swung his view up to Mr. Mustafa. "It's very nice. What's the occasion?"

Clementine deposited her old hat in the box and took it from Mr. Mustafa. Her tone flattened. "It's back to work, I'm afraid."

"Yes," Bryce piped up. He slung his fists into his pockets. "You're two hours late. Both of you."

Mr. Mustafa fielded the remark. "We expected we might be. Miss Fitzgerald said it'd be all right. Technically, I'm not late, having clearance from a co-owner of the company."

Bryce rocked towards him on the balls of his feet. "How convenient. And you still call her Miss Fitzgerald. Interesting."

Clementine aimed a strained but gracious smile at Mr. Mustafa. "I'll…" A yawn cut her off, gaping her mouth wide open. She covered it with her hand. "Excuse me. I'll handle things with Mr. Bloom. You're free to start work, Mr. Mustafa."

Bryce bristled at the use of his formal name but kept his focus on the turbaned man. "Yes. We should all get to work now."

Mr. Mustafa walked around the empty front desk to a door beside the corridor. He opened it and went inside.

Clementine grabbed Bryce's arm and steered him up the hallway of offices. "What's wrong with you?"

Bryce sputtered. "Me?" He flung his other arm back toward the lobby desk. "Where's Mr. Kakkar?"

"How should I know? I just got here."

"That's exactly what's wrong." Bryce tore his captive arm free. "What are you doing with Mr. Mustafa?"

Clementine gave an exasperated grunt and bolted into her office. Bryce followed her and swung the door toward closure. Clementine slid her shoe against the jamb, blocking Bryce's attempt.

He threw his hands up. "Fine." He constrained himself to a harsh whisper. "Do you realize Mr. Mustafa has a family?" He counted off the members on his fingers. "A wife. Some children. Some brothers." He muddled the rest of his physical bookkeeping for lack of facts.

Clementine snorted. "I know that. We were just talking about them. Yasaman is his wife."

"I didn't know her name." Bryce struggled to maintain his dignity. "I guess that's something. Milton probably didn't mention his wife."

Clementine remained indifferent. "He did. You both mentioned he had one."

"No, he didn't *have* one, Clementine. He *has* one, right now. Lydia. She lives in Oklahoma City. Didn't you know that?"

Clementine blinked with cool self-assurance. "No. I thought maybe she was dead."

"She's not. But things are different with Mr. Mustafa, aren't they? Were you planning to become his second wife or just fool around? Is this to keep him on the project as well?"

Clementine fled across the room to the desk. "Not everything is about the project, Bryce."

"Since when?" He slammed the door.

"That's not what I meant." Clementine took her hat off and sat it on the desk.

Bryce gestured to her. "You show up ragged and exhausted – *late* – on a Monday morning with no explanation–"

Clementine leaned on the desk, sounding breathless. "There's no time."

"That's what I thought." Bryce popped the door open. "I'm sure you won't mind if I get straight to work. I won't be around the factory much today. I have outside duties that will keep me away for a bit. That should make you happy."

Clementine's torn and weary frown made Bryce cringe inside. He did not regret saying it as he threw on his coat and newsboy. As he barreled down the hallway into the lobby, Aatmaj emerged from the door around the corner. He acknowledged Bryce with a smooth bow, and Bryce supplied a curt jerk of his chin. He careened out into the parking lot, not just resolving to explain Clementine's obsession with the Fountain of Youth. He hoped to find irrefutable evidence, once and for all, as to whether she had ever loved him.

Chapter Twenty-Eight

Bryce squeezed the steambike's rubber horn more times in his ride to Civil Lines than he had in the previous years combined. Multiple blasts sounded each time, diverting steam from the exhaust valve to alert his fellow drivers with trumpet-like bursts.

"Come on, come on," he urged through gritted teeth. He cursed the fog enveloping the city like yogurt folded over fruit. Bryce swore at the carts, vehicles, and pedestrians blocking his path. He shook a fist at a pack of dogs fighting over scraps at the side of the road and lamented yet another cow slowing traffic to a trickle.

At last, most of the morning already spent, Bryce broke away from the stranglehold of crowded streets. He crossed over into the roomier neighborhoods and rode straight to Clementine's house.

For once, her preoccupation with the project worked in his favor. He parked the bike in the middle of the driveway. If a neighbor spotted him and bothered to mention it to Clementine, Bryce would explain it away. He used to come to Clements' house frequently for reports and paperwork. If he could not locate something at the office, why should he not come retrieve it himself? In the case of his visit proving to be a mistake, he would simply apologize.

Bryce made his way past the garage for the side of the property. In a sudden recollection of the macaque's daredevil attack, he hunkered down, but no monkey appeared. He hurried along, then calmed himself. Acting suspicious would not confirm his alibi of seeking out missing papers.

Past the two-story main house, Bryce reached the shorter barricade around the courtyard. He glanced at the surrounding yards and houses, but no one loitered close by. He shimmied up the branches of a young tree, just high enough to pull himself up and over the courtyard wall. He landed in a bare garden patch, not quite as spry as he used to be. His knees and ankles warned him against making too many jumps. But he moved forward, free of sprains and broken bones. Thank goodness he had spent his childhood preparing for this day, climbing anything in sight and sneaking tools with which to tinker with his bicycle. Those days had ended with a too-loose front tire that shot out from underneath him and tossed him headlong through the air. With the help of his siblings and more relief than anger on his mother's part, Bryce's day had ended in laughter instead of tears.

Maybe he would have the same luck today. He doubted it.

Bryce tiptoed past the double doors on his left that led to the great room. Close to them in the adjoining wall was the only door Bryce had rarely seen anyone use. It accessed the back hallway, meant to give servants the opportunity to slip in and out without disturbing the house's owners. Clementine employed none, and Clements had not required such strict formality from Edith Higginbotham.

Bryce snuck a screwdriver out of his coat pocket. He wedged its narrow tip between the door and its jamb, a trick Clements had taught him on several occasions.

The big man had winked at him. "If you misplace your key, this is the door to break in through. It's a little loose, like Milton's morals, but I won't replace it. I need it for my own devices as backup. Who's really going to hop that wall and try this one door out of all the ones available?"

Paranoid, Bryce glanced behind him. He could only see one of them from here, the entrance to the storage room right across from the great room. He hurried up, dislodging the locking mechanism and jiggling the door ajar. He rushed inside and closed the door.

He took a steadying breath and let out a shaky exhale. Okay, he was in. Where should he begin?

He crept ahead to the study's double doors. His quiet footfalls were the only sounds in the house.

As usual, a dizzying array of papers sprawled across Clementine's desk. It drew him to it like a bonfire calls to cold hands on a winter's night. He tucked the screwdriver into his pocket and shifted some of Clementine's memorabilia to see what lay under it.

Clementine's defeat echoed through his head. *I've left it such a mess already, I can't find anything.*

Bryce gave up being tactful. As long as he replaced the letters, postcards, and other pieces in roughly the same areas, Clementine might never know he disturbed them.

He picked up a familiar bundle. "Ah-ha! Miss Sands' letter." Spotting the chair beside him, Bryce hopped in and delved into the note.

January 26, 1917

Dearest Clementine,

Your mother caught a cold, but I assure you it's quite minor. We all agree it's nothing to worry about. You left us wonderful instructions on how to handle such things. Adelaide's in good spirits.

We hope you're enjoying your trip despite the terrible circumstances. We've all been through hardships and come out the other side. You're just as strong as we are. Maybe stronger. It hurts, but it'll be better if you forgive yourself.

Bryce bunched up his eyebrows and consulted the back of the page as if a direct answer would miraculously appear. The blank sheet sent him back to the end of the script.

You're meeting such enchanting people. Could this place really exist in the same world? Surely not! We send you so much love, especially from your mother. She really is all right.

Gertie Sands

Bryce tossed the letter onto the desk and scrounged up another one. The distinct change in handwriting threw him off. Instead of curling letters forming rows that slanted upwards, stark lines created perfect symmetry.

December 29, 1916

Dear Mr. Fitzgerald,

A great joke, indeed! Nothing will ever bring down the great Clements, as I'm sure you're well aware. If you were still stateside, you no doubt would've heard the entire office ringing out in laughter over this news.

I hope you'll forgive the slowness of sending my reply as a letter. I try to keep correspondence costs down by only using faxes for urgent matters. I trust you understand this as a respected businessman.

Bryce's stomach wrenched. The top of the page dated it two and a half weeks after Clements' death. Whom did the sender think they were responding to? Bryce took up the rest of the reading.

I'll honor your request not to pester Mr. Longshaw about his prank. He's not my client. I have enough of them to keep track of. I'm only glad I was offended by the ostentatiousness of his stunt rather than the true loss of your friendship.

In high spirits and good health, your humble servant,

Lyman Morris

Bryce scrambled to place the name in his thoughts while he recovered the envelope from the bottom of the pile. The sender's address quoted a lawyer's office in Oklahoma City, jogging memories of a cigar smoke-filled room and good-natured banter. Lyman Morris possessed a bark-like laugh constructed of hearty, clipped cries issuing from his barrel chest.

Did Clements' own lawyer not know he had died?

Bryce set the letter down, his blood sluggish with bad omens. In the desk's far left corner, the various colors of Clements' postcards peeked out at Bryce. He picked them up, rummaging up a few more he had not perused before. He laid them out in order, moving some aside when he found another one that filled in the sequence. The globe in the rosewood stand grabbed his attention, and he pulled it over to the desk. One by one, Bryce charted Clements' movements through the years and the countries.

The very first postcard displayed a red-roofed pavilion overlooking a placid lake marked *Overton Park, Memphis, Tennessee*. Clements' bold handwriting covered it. The year startled Bryce. 1899, the year he and Clementine turned six.

My darling Clementine,

I hope this finds you well. The new park shown here has many plants of significance. Notably, several kinds of ferns, four species of clover, and an exciting array of healing herbs. Perhaps you'll visit it someday.

Your father,

Clements Fitzgerald

Bryce blinked. A full signature? He had delivered this dissertation on flora to a child? And with no mention of Clementine's mother.

He flipped the card over to the address side. *Clementine Heidel.* Bryce's eyes popped. Who the heck were the Heidels?

The tension in his belly sprouted tendrils that snaked up into his stomach. He laid the card in place and picked up the next one. A dozen people in summer clothes lingered by the shore where two small rowboats floated. The caption placed the scene at Hot Springs Reservation in Arkansas. Clements' message dated it a few weeks later.

Clementine,

I find the hot springs very refreshing, but I still believe a cup of carefully chosen tea provides a better cure-all.

Bryce skipped to the end, where again her father had signed off with his whole name.

Exasperation made Bryce sling the card on the desk. He would have relished conversations like this with Clements, and he had for three full years. But this was Clements' daughter. Where was the warmth? The interest in her activities and schoolwork?

Bryce grabbed the next correspondence. A prickly cactus erupted in large, pink blooms against a clouded sky. *San Antonio, Texas,* spelled out black letters in the corner.

Bryce barely glimpsed Clements' message, finding the word *cactus* among the favorites he repeated. Bryce traded the card for another. Mountains flanked a steep valley where men rode on horseback and donkeys lapped water from a shallow stream. *Monterrey, Mexico.*

Clementine,

I crossed the border into Mexico. The city is old and beautiful. The mountains are all around it. But the plants intrigue me. What might be possible here? I may stay in Mexico awhile.

The next note proved this. A yellow sky oversaw a wide boulevard lined with leafy trees. Spring, 1900.

I still love Mexico City, even after several months. There are good opportunities for me to finally use my knowledge of plants to make a bit of money.

Bryce skimmed more and more as he went along, searching for changes in the pattern. A spectacular, rounded archway supplying the view to an erupting volcano in Guatemala. A native village of thatched-roof huts along the edge of jungle brush in Honduras. Sparse, long leaves decorated angular branches against a backdrop of azure lake and green rolling mountains in Nicaragua. Bryce followed Clements' trail through Central America on the globe, never missing a country.

In Costa Rica, benches sat empty in a park full of blossoms, towered over by a military statue. Lush vegetation bookended rippling blue water to represent Panama. Palm trees in a garden, backed by square buildings with arched windows, embodied Colombia. Another horse-mounted military statue stood in the center of multiple converging pathways, accompanied by thriving plant life. The printed words *Caracas, Venezuela* stopped Bryce. Summer, 1901.

Clementine,

For the first time since leaving home, I have a business partner. We need to decide where to begin making our fortunes, and time will tell where we end up.

Bryce tapped the card against his fingertips. *Milton.* Bryce continued his investigation, fueled by Clements' first foray into the lore he had shared with Bryce. Villagers unloaded sacks of goods from small boats along Ghana's Gold Coast. Tan buildings lined a river where larger vessels sailed through Nigeria. The mailings became less and less frequent, finally making the changeover to divided-back postcards where Clements' script no longer covered the images.

Bryce jumped to 1913, the year he met Clements in the elevator of the Lee-Huckins Hotel. There was no correspondence marking the occasion. Shuffling through the next few cards, Bryce discovered the trains, elephants, and blossoms of India.

My daughter,

With a new assistant in tow, my partner and I have arrived in India. What promise exists here! I can't quite explain it.

Bryce scanned the opening phrase again. *A new assistant in tow.* He threw the postcards down. No mention of his name! He mixed up the cards and tucked them away at the back of the desktop. No wonder Clementine did not pass these out for visitors to fawn over. Clements' obsession with his business and profits embittered Bryce's stomach.

Through all those years, at Clementine's same ages, Bryce had reveled in a completely different life. Racing his brothers on bicycles. Pushing his sisters on the rope-and-board swing his father tied to the branch of a spreading elm. Wriggling in his mother's grasp while she brushed a washcloth across his dirty cheeks. Laughing at his father's puns while they fished, holding long grasses between their teeth.

His parents had not passed a single day without talking to each other. On errands in the City, Bryce had often heard his father mention his absent spouse. The farmer would scratch his head under his hat. *What'd your ma ask me to get? I should've written it down the second she told me. She's going to be pretty mad if I show up without it, whatever it was.*

Bryce regarded the half-hidden postcards. In seventeen years, not a single question or word about Clementine's mother. He carted the globe stand to its corner with a huff. He almost gave up on the desk's contents, but the strange letters called him back. There had to be an answer here somewhere.

He grabbed a stack of opened letters and stationed himself in the chair. He flew through them, combing for information.

Our hole family wishes you nuthin but the best luck for ever! You'll be in our harts and prayers. The Ledfords

We won't never forgit you, Clementine. We're naybors forever. We'll drink a lil extra moonshine fer you every nite. Jeremiah, Sally, Walton, Judson, and Agnes Lloyd

Bryce skipped past similar well wishes from the Johnsons and the Colemans. The misspellings and rough grammar slapped him across the face. If his own writing had been so sloppy, his mother would have whipped him with a corn stalk. And how did Clementine emerge from these same parts of Tennessee almost as well spoken as her father?

Wobbly, deliberate handwriting piqued Bryce's curiosity.

Dear Clementine,

I got Ollie to help me with this letter like I sed I wood. I sure am sorry to see you go, but I beleev you're ment for grater things in life than we can give you. You are the bravest person I ever new. For leaving and for being my friend. Always think of me as I think of you.

You're in my hart, Clementine.

Always, Chester

Bryce pondered the letter, but it gave up no more of its secrets. Whether Clementine had ever been more than a friend to Chester, Bryce could not tell. Either way, she had never mentioned him.

Bryce switched to the next page. The change to a practiced, fluid hand confused Bryce anew.

Dear Miss Heidel,

Bryce thrust his hands up, crinkling the pages. Heidel again!

Remember everything I taught you. Keep your wits about you, and you'll do fine. I wish you nothing but the best on your trek to India. You have every justification for going, and I hope you'll meet with the generous reception you deserve. If fancy words or phrases fail you, speak from the heart. You've got a great one, and many of us in Nashville know it for certain. I'm eager to hear your stories of international travel.

Sincerely,

Miss Betty Crawford

Bryce read through the sentences again. Not a single error he could detect, and signed off with another name Clementine had never uttered. She knew a vastly varied assembly of people back home. That much Bryce was coming to understand. He flipped to the next piece of correspondence.

The letterhead for the Farmers National Bank in Oklahoma City greeted him.

Dear Clements,

After all these years of doing business with you, I'm sorry to see you take your money and go. Your countless stories of touring the world delighted me, no matter how few times we actually sat down together. I'm wiring the totality of your funds to you in US dollars through the Blickensderfer system – isn't it a marvelous invention? – straight to your address in Delhi.

Enjoy your magnificent future. I'm sure it's never shone brighter. If you're ever in the City, stop by for a visit. I'd be glad to reopen your accounts.

Most sincerely,

Royson Callaghan

Bryce hunted for the date. January 2, 1917. "But Clements was dead!" Bryce exploded. He checked the date on Miss Crawford's letter, November 27, before he tossed the stack of them on the desk.

A few weeks before Clements' death, Bryce realized.

No.

He blinked at the disarray of pages. His mind made connections that churned acid at the base of his throat, pathways he could not untravel or wish to follow.

He made a new arrangement, putting the letters in order of their dates and traced Clementine's progress through her personal history.

Bryce pointed at the letters as he passed over them, muttering. "Her uneducated friends from Livingston before her move to Nashville in 1914. Then Miss Crawford's advice on arriving in India. Followed by two letters to Clements around the time Clementine started at the factory."

He picked up Miss Crawford's guidance and Lyman Morris' message about a prank Milton might have played on him. Bryce could barely swallow, and his hands shook. "Clements died in between these letters."

The papers tumbled to the desk with a shiver. Bryce searched for a calendar Clements used to keep in the room and dug it out of a drawer. He slapped it down and peeled it open to the final months of the previous year. "Clementine would've had Miss Crawford's letter by Thanksgiving. Her father died a week and a half later, just enough time…"

Bryce's forehead pushed out pinpricks of sweat. He made himself finish his thought. "Enough time for Clementine by any name to board a steamship and arrive in Delhi before her father died."

Bryce strode out of the study and stopped at the corner of the dining room. He stared the length of the massive great room to the bottom of the steps. He recited what little Milton and Edith had told him about Clements' death. "He tripped down the stairs, preoccupied by getting ready to meet Milton for dinner. He landed at a terrible angle, breaking his neck. That's where Miss Higginbotham found him when she returned from shopping."

Bryce sprinted to the staircase. He tore up the steps to the high landing and the few upper stairs. He pulled on the railing without a budge and pried at the boards he was not standing on. Accidents happened. They occurred all the time, and for the last three months, he believed one had taken Clements' life. But the fact remained that nothing except human error would have caused his fall. No nail or spindle stuck out of place to cause his fatal tumble.

Bryce splayed his hands over his head. "Unless it wasn't an error!" He gazed down the final flight of stairs where Clements had crashed to the wooden floor.

A floor Clementine had decorated with new rugs, placed new furniture upon, and offset with different paint colors on the walls of every room.

"This is bigger than me." The air drained out of Bryce like gas from a balloon. "Clementine, did you murder your father?"

Chapter Twenty-Nine

Bryce sped away from Clementine's house, having picked up after himself as much as he could. The heavy air caressed his cheeks as he raced through Civil Lines.

Frantic thoughts whizzed through his brain even faster. Clements' postcards hardly provided the caring, supportive messages Bryce had assumed them to carry. Clementine lived in a country cabin surrounded by simple neighbors while Clements traversed the continents. Were any of these reasons for murder?

Bryce made a quick turn and a knee-jerk decision. He parked in the lot for the Civil Lines police station and strode inside the white building.

A cacophony of voices launched from all directions. Several people sat packed into an area on the left, jabbering with such thick British accents, Bryce did not bother to discern what they said.

Men in suits and constable uniforms went in and out of a hallway to Bryce's right. He envied them. That passage probably led to the information he coveted. Instead, he strode straight ahead to the long desk. A woman with her hair pulled back and a stern frown observed him with rapid blinks.

Bryce took command of the situation. "Yes, I'm a reporter who's interested in gaining more details about a death – a suspicious death – that happened last December."

The woman's tone came out flat while her accent flew high and sharp. "What's your name?"

"Bryce, er, Robinson."

"The name of the newspaper you're reporting for?"

"All of them, actually. Well, not all of them, you know. Just the big ones. They all want to print what I have to write about."

Her pale eyes remained dull. "Is that so? I'll have to see your identification. Then I can find out if anyone's available to answer your questions. But as you can see, we're quite busy."

She adopted a harsh whisper. "There have been arrests of people trying to form groups against the British government."

Bryce's bones caved in as he thought of cramming into the Hindu shop's supply room with Clementine and the others. "That's too bad," he muttered without specifying which side he sympathized with. He patted his pockets in search of identification he had no intention of offering. "I must've lost my driving license. Or forgotten it."

"How did you get here?"

Bryce sputtered at the stranglehold of his own lies. "That's not – I walked. I'd really like to speak with someone regarding Clements Fitzgerald. Does that name mean anything to you?"

She regarded him with the spaced-out focus of a cow chewing cud. "Should it?"

"Yes. The man was crucial to the economy of this city. I have reason to believe–"

Two constables approached the secretary from the other side of the desk. Bryce intended to make himself heard all the same, blurting out Clements had possibly been murdered. The constables' imposing stances and gruff orders made him reconsider. Should he really, neither a Robinson nor a reporter, throw the word *murder* around in a crowded police station?

"Good day." Bryce fled the building, returning to his steambike.

What a tragedy! His best chance at real evidence – policemen giving official statements, sketches of the scene – barred from him. In any timeframe that mattered, anyway.

Bryce steered the bike toward his apartment. He might as well stop off for a bite to eat and reorganize his thoughts. He should probably make another appearance at the factory by the end of the work day.

He pulled up to the intersection with the main road. A figure waved from his right. He squinted at the woman, topped off with a white hat above a faded purple dress. She towed a small cart behind her. When she parted her lips in a wide smile, he recognized the gap in her front teeth from where he sat twenty feet away.

Edith Higginbotham.

Bryce almost peeled away to avoid her, but she had discovered Clements' body. She cleaned and cooked for him at the house. She helped Clementine get situated in Delhi. Maybe she knew something the police never would.

He backed the bike up and rolled it forward to the side of the road in case other traffic came along. He doffed his cap. "Good afternoon. I haven't seen you in months."

"It's gotten colder, though." Edith pulled her coat collar more snuggly around her long neck. "I could do without it."

He jerked his head at the two-wheeled cart. "What do you have there?"

"Groceries. Mum and Dad want a nice thick stew on a day like today. So I bought some potatoes and carrots and onions and the like. What're you doing? Are you on a break from work?"

"Something like that. Tell me, uh, I know it's a bit of a morbid subject. But there's been a reporter I heard about asking questions about Clements' death."

Edith's thick, angular eyebrows rose. "Oh?"

"Yeah, nothing too serious. I just wondered if there was any truth to what he was saying. That it seemed suspicious in some way. Like maybe it wasn't an accident. Do you remember the police saying anything like that when it happened?"

"It was a terrible day." Edith's eyes glassed over under their thick, sleepy lids. "I went to buy groceries in the market like I did just now. He was excited about his dinner with Mr. Longshaw. I got back to the house, and I opened the door, and he was lying there. Blood was making a puddle on the floorboards from the crack he took to his head." Edith touched the right side of her tall forehead. "He wasn't moving. He didn't answer when I called out to him. He was dead."

Bryce hummed. Edith had repeated this several times in a daze to anyone around her following the incident. He made every attempt to sound sympathetic. "I know. What did the police say? You must've overheard something." His eyes flicked to her big ears, but he held his tongue.

"Nothing I can recall right now."

Bryce sagged against the steambike's handles. "That's all right. How are your parents?"

Edith crinkled her nose up. "Eh. Mum's still with it, but Dad's ailing."

"I'm sorry to hear that."

"It's what I've got to deal with now that I'm back home with them. Dad used to be in the royal army, you know. We finally got him to sell his gun. It was no use having it around when he's the only one who knows how to use it, and he really shouldn't. You know."

Bryce almost let the words slip over him instead of interacting in the conversation, but Edith's personal admittance stayed with him. "You don't like it at home. Not as much as you liked working for Clements, did you?"

"Nah." Edith shot upright in fear and looked around for passersby. She let her shoulders droop again. "Mr. Fitzgerald was the best. He let me come and go as I wanted so long as I didn't bring a bad reputation on his house. He complimented my cooking. I had a quiet space to myself in the servants' quarters. I don't get any of that with Mum and Dad. They expect me to do it all without complaining. Like they can keep their mouths shut."

Bryce saw a way out of his dark theories about Clementine and relaxed. Edith despised moving back in with her parents. Maybe enough to set Clementine up to take the blame for a simple accident. "Do you hold a grudge against Miss Fitzgerald for firing you?"

Edith pulled her head back, puckering her visage. "No. Whatever for?"

"You could've worked for her. You got on well, didn't you? Instead, she sent you to your parents' house."

Edith swatted her mitt of a hand through the air. "Go on, Mr. Bloom. It's true, I would've worked for her if she asked me to. But she didn't need me, so home I went. It's all fair enough. I'm needed where I am anyway. She did what she had to do. My opinion isn't the only thing that matters around here. Clearly." She eyed the back of Bryce's bike. "Too bad you don't have a way to hitch this cart up to your vehicle. It'd sure beat pulling it all the way on my own two feet."

"I'm sorry. Maybe another time." Bryce moved to shift the steambike into gear.

"Oh, wait!" Edith trotted up to his side, eliciting a squeak from a cart wheel. "I remember something the police said while I was there. It was kind of gruesome, and I don't like to recall it."

Bryce's heart thumped. "What?"

"His wounds." She rubbed her head and her hand. "The policeman said he'd encountered many people who took terrible tumbles. Mr. Fitzgerald's wounds were deeper than he was used to seeing, like there was greater force behind his fall than usual. But Mr. Fitzgerald was a large man, so they didn't spend much time talking about it."

Bryce's imagination leapt ahead, far past Edith's explanation. "Did they find any evidence of someone breaking into the house or being at the house with him around the time he died?"

Edith shrugged. "I don't think so, sir."

Betty Crawford's letter jumped to the forefront of Bryce's mind. If Clements had failed to tell Clementine the names of his two closest associates or any details about them, who else would Clementine have planned to receive her in India? Of course no break-in would be necessary because Clements would have opened the door to let in his own daughter!

Edith pointed to her forearm. "Mr. Fitzgerald broke his arm in the fall. The policeman said it was from trying to brace himself."

"Thank you." Bryce changed the bike's gear to forward momentum. "You've been very helpful."

He cruised away, leaving Edith in a burst of dissipating steam, coughing as she clutched the handle of the grocery cart.

Chapter Thirty

In the factory's hard, beige halls, reality loomed larger than in the streets of Delhi and Bryce's apartment. If Clementine killed her father, possibly plotting it before her trip overseas, it could only have been to take over his place in the business. Money was no object. Neither were her safety, her reputation, nor her personal relationships.

But what evidence did Bryce have? Only a gap in the correspondence gathered on Clementine's desk that morning. No receipts for Blickensderfer faxes placed her in India before Clements' death. No telling letter explicitly shouted, *Ah-ha, Clementine! What a brilliant plot to overthrow your absent father and seize hold of his manufacturing company!*

Bryce scratched his head. He had spent so much time concentrating on motive and timing, he had ignored other important questions. Was the tall but willowy Clementine physically able to murder her father? Or emotionally capable? She had nearly broken down in tears the first morning she had met Bryce and Milton. Just because people addressed her by two different last names and he could not pinpoint her whereabouts the week Clements died did not make her the cause of it.

Or did it?

Bryce wandered into the extraction room. Milton sat at the closest workstation. Indira rested beside him on a stool borrowed from the next desk over. From down the hall, grunts and thumps resounded as workers unloaded the latest delivery truck. Any workmen not needed for that task would be in the adjacent room preparing to rinse and dry the materials.

Milton glanced at Bryce without pausing his duties. Indira flashed a welcoming smile that made Bryce feel like less of an imposition.

Bryce strolled closer to them. Clementine had insisted on multiple occasions she would do anything to ensure the project's success. But to sacrifice her own father? Clementine traveled halfway around the globe to see him for the first time in seventeen years. She had spoken quite plainly and professionally to Bryce and Milton at the factory on the first of the year. Surely, she could have convinced her father, through emotion or logic, to bring her onto the project, no blood spill needed?

Milton barked at him. "Where have you been?"

"Out on errands." For once, Milton's marginalizing of Bryce paid off. He tucked his hands in his pockets as he arrived at Milton's side. "You don't need me. You have Miss Datta."

The light of recognition and appreciation in Indira's eyes arrived slowly and wavered.

"I'm just relieved to have the room to myself." Milton slid a sample dish in front of Indira. "And my assistant, obviously. Miss Datta, do you mind placing this in cold storage? We need to make sure our mixtures will hold up under temperature fluctuations."

Indira carried the dish across the room.

Bryce watched her go. "I'm glad Miss Datta has worked out so well."

She swung around at the sound of her name and smacked into one of the extractors.

The clash of glass made Milton's shoulders hunch up around his neck. He could barely articulate his words through his tense jaws. "What's the damage?"

Indira's wide eyes landed on Bryce. "Pardon?"

Bryce walked over to investigate. The collision had chipped the dish's rim, but there was little harm done. "We'll replace the container. It's all right, Miss Datta."

Milton hissed. "It's not all right. Put the contents in something else." He whipped a pair of work gloves at the station beside his.

Indira jumped and continued on her way to cold storage. Milton threw a small metal tool, and it pinged off the wall. He launched a notebook at the floor, pages fluttering in a wild mass. He sank his head into his hands.

Bryce's heart galloped. Years had passed since he saw Milton this angry. Mad enough to kill?

Bryce examined Milton, a greying man in a charcoal suit. Milton had always despised Bryce and Clements' decision to hire the young man. The two older men had shared many dinners together without Bryce, as Milton happily explained to Clementine. Bryce did not have proof of Milton's whereabouts on the evening of Clements' death, either. Who was he to say Milton had not stopped by Clements' house early, tangled with him, and left his business partner dead at the foot of the stairs?

Clements would have let Milton in for sure, in keeping with no evidence of a break-in. And Milton's gloves.

White and spotless. Why was the old man so obsessed with them? Was he covering up his hands to keep from leaving fingerprints around?

Bryce backed up a step.

Milton sighed as he left his stool and collected the notebook. He crossed to the other side of the workstation and grabbed the metal tool.

On top of this evidence, really no more than Bryce had against Clementine, an old story Clements had once touched on chilled Bryce's blood.

Clements had shaken his head at Milton's relentless pursuit of Miss Constance Peabody, their original receptionist. "He's going to end up with another Brazil on his hands."

The two of them had been alone, entering Clements' house through the back door to retrieve some notes he wrote the night before.

Clements' remark confused Bryce. His face scrunched up. "Whose hands?"

"Milton."

"What's Brazil?"

"The country. And what happened there."

Bryce followed Clements into the back hallway. "You never talked about Brazil before."

Clements clapped Bryce on the back and led him into the study. "It was a brutal business. Milton fell in love with a girl who already had a man in love with her. We were only in Brazil for three weeks, and by the end of it, they found her dead."

Bryce gulped.

"Jealous rage, I assume. Bashed her – well, here we are." Clements picked up a loose sheaf of handwritten pages.

They left the house, and Clements never verged on the subject again.

In the extraction room, Bryce forced down another hard swallow. Did Clements think Milton attacked the young woman? Bryce had always figured Clements did not want to dwell on such a tragic story. Replaying Clements' testimony in his head, Bryce detected more than a wish to move on to brighter subjects. There was a wobbling of confidence, as if entertaining the idea Milton might have played the jilted assailant.

Milton stood in front of Bryce, clearing his throat. "Have you forgotten your duties?"

Bryce eased back another step. "No."

Milton's condescension hung in the air, accented by his judging, beady eyes. "I can't have both of the assistants here making mistakes."

Indira approached from cold storage. "Do you have too many people? I do not need the job as much as Mr. Bloom does."

Milton grunted. "That's not my point."

Bryce leapt at the chance to test the waters with him. "I'd like to speak to you about something in private."

"I'm busy, unlike you." Milton took the cracked dish from Indira, running a gloved finger over the jagged edge. "This will have to go into a report for Mr. Menon. We're recording every little expense these days."

Bryce bounced with impatience on his heels. He tried again above conversational volume. "Clements' death might not have been an accident."

Milton gaped at him. He pushed the damaged dish into Indira's hands. "Take this to Miss Fitzgerald. She'll help you write the report."

Worry filled Indira's eyes, but she swept out of the room.

For a moment, Bryce wondered if Milton would slap him.

Adrenaline shot vile through Milton's voice. "Where did you hear that?"

"Some policemen." Bryce cut out Edith Higginbotham as the go-between. Milton would only strive to discredit her. "Clements' injuries were too bad for a mere fall."

Milton snorted. "That again."

"It's real this time." Bryce inched closer. "The police might open an investigation. They have enough evidence of foul play."

Milton balked. "Like what? There was no tampering with the locks. No signs of a struggle."

Bryce played up the one card he had left. "That's the point. It could've been someone Clements trusted, someone he gave access to."

Milton's eyes grew two sizes. "A friend or investor or worker?"

Bryce balanced back on his heels. "It narrows the suspect list a bit, eh?"

Milton closed his eyes, deflated. By the time he opened them, rage flared in his irises. "Clements was a great man, the closest friend I ever had. If that were true – if somebody killed him – I wouldn't wait for the police to snare their justice. I'd kill the bastard myself."

Bryce's arms recoiled against his chest. He backed away in horrified increments. "I wouldn't blame you." He spun and hurried toward the door. "Sorry to interrupt your work and distract Miss Datta."

He darted off down the hall and around the corner. He almost smacked into Indira and hopped aside to avoid her. "I don't want to cause two accidents in one day."

She grinned, holding a piece of paper and the broken dish. "If I don't see you again today, I'm saying goodbye to you now."

"Okay." Bryce's lungs faltered, but he forced a pleasant expression. "Good night."

She walked over to Nithya's office door.

Bryce signaled to her. "Is Miss Fitzgerald in her office?" He stopped himself from adding, *If you can call her by that name.*

"She is. She's writing new…" Indira's eyes rolled up to the ceiling. "…*recipes*. For the plants."

"I won't disturb her."

Bryce passed Clementine's closed door and let himself into Milton's office. The shelf above Milton's desktop had accumulated several new pieces of mail in the last few months. Bryce began his search at the bottom, where Clementine's first fax lingered.

He skimmed it for any pieces that would complete the Fitzgerald family puzzle.

Received at Chandni Chowk Road Post Office, Delhi, India. December 12, 1916.

Mr. Milton Longshaw

I'm shocked and heartbroken to hear about my father's death. I have many arrangements to make before I leave the US. May I ask you to see to the funeral? You have my eternal gratitude. I'll let you know when I will arrive in India.

Clementine Fitzgerald

The message disappointed Bryce. Then its holes revealed themselves.

Like the letters apparently sent to Clements' lawyer and banker, this fax could have come from anyone. If Clementine was already in India, she could have instructed her friends back home to send this on her behalf. Why a Blickensderfer fax, not a letter? The greater speed would prove a huge help, but the clerk could – and would – also be smart enough to correct the grammar and spelling.

Bryce tapped the page against his hand. The fire in Milton's eyes and the threat he growled were not for show. They were not cover-ups of his own involvement in Clements' death. They were real, and so was Milton's temper.

The clues stayed so scattered and few, only someone as close to Clementine or obsessed with her as Bryce was might ever connect them. The perfect plan, the perfect crime.

But had Bryce pushed Milton closer to forging those notions for himself?

The air thinned in the room, or at least in Bryce's lungs.

A friend or investor or worker?

It narrows the suspect list a bit, eh?

Bryce tore the fax up without thinking and sprinkled the scraps into Milton's garbage can.

If Clements' demise had truly pushed Milton into a murderous mood, Bryce might have pointed him straight at Clementine.

He knew what he had to do.

Win Clementine back. Save her project, her reputation, her future, and her freedom.

If Milton would kill her as soon as he knew, Bryce would beat him to it.

Bryce was going to kill Milton.

Chapter Thirty-One

Bryce left his steambike in the company parking lot. Milton would recognize its rare, purring motor if he heard it, and the whole attempt would collapse. Bryce had worked too hard to give it all up now.

First, Bryce had excused himself from the premises for the second time that shift. He had wandered an unfamiliar neighborhood, posing as a lost tourist until a dozen locals crowded around him, eager to help. An Indian guide-for-hire knew enough English to spread Bryce's question to the others.

"Where can I buy a gun?"

They tugged and pointed him in every direction. The guide suggested a shop south of Civil Lines, where retired British officers and military widows sometimes pawned unneeded weaponry. Bryce finally succeeded in disconnecting himself from the well-meaning group and drove on his way.

Edith's story of her father serving the British army calmed Bryce's nerves about owning such a powerful weapon. The Webley pistol, now tucked in his pocket, could easily belong to one of India's thousands of Englishmen rather than one of its few, straggling Americans. If Bryce had to use it, he reminded himself to sprint directly to the Jumna River and toss it in.

Up ahead in the thick fog, Milton's dark figure coughed into his hand. Bryce set his mouth in a determined grimace. He had gone through too much trouble to let Milton disappear in the dense, low clouds. The fuel pellets from Milton's autocarriage resided in one of Bryce's other pockets. Two of the tires had leaked air through the holes Bryce had stabbed into them with his second purchase of the day, a folding knife.

A length of thin, sharp-fibered rope rested in another pocket.

Milton took a few quick steps, no doubt impatient to arrive at home. Bryce followed suit with several strides, not even blinking to keep Milton in his sights through the blinding white cover.

Bryce wondered what he would do or say if a constable stopped him and found all this violent contraband. He almost smirked. The explanation was simple but grisly.

Bryce had never tried to kill anyone before. He had no way of knowing what opportunities Milton would give him or what methods he would be capable of employing.

On the other hand, Bryce might already be working with two accomplished murderers. How difficult could the task be?

Milton reached the edge of Civil Lines, and Bryce held himself back with all of his will. Why not take Milton down here at the side of the street? Why not lure him into a courtyard or a garden in this accursed cold and bring all this madness to an end?

With a single step, Milton was gone.

"No," Bryce exhaled.

He scrambled forward, almost losing his balance and his mind. The curtain of white clung to the air around him, moving with him, always preventing him from seeing more than thirty feet ahead. He burst forward, and Milton's charcoal suit reappeared. Bryce slowed to keep from exposing himself but tried to err on the side of keeping Milton within his view.

Sorry, old man, Bryce taunted. He clutched the gun handle in one pocket and the folded knife in another. *You can't find out Clementine killed her father. I won't let you ruin anything more than you already have.*

Milton curved off along a side road, and Bryce picked up his pace to reach the same fork.

The mist all but absorbed Milton's cursing. "Dratted vehicle. Stupid shoes. Darn this long walk, and blast this country to the dickens."

Milton let himself through a short gate and latched it closed. He strode up the path to the porch and shut himself inside the house.

Bryce hopped over the gate and crouched low, crossing the yard in a dozen steps. He hid behind a bush by the big front window, barely able to see anything inside. A glow rose up from another room, casting a haze into the one Bryce peered into.

A fire smoldered in the hearth at the back of the room. A huge portrait filled the space above the mantel, wrapped in a wide gold frame. A woman posed there, captured in splotchy but realistic strokes. Pins fixed her wavy blonde locks, greying lightly at the temples, back into a flat bun. Under thin, arched brows, her lavender eyes shone with triumph. Diamonds glinted in her long platinum earrings from the studs and the drops, where they looped around oval sapphires. Indigo stones decorated her extravagant necklace. Three silver chains adorned each side of it, accented with pearls. Her gown, no less ornate, featured a sheer hunter-green floral over golden silk.

Except for the increased formality, Mrs. Lydia Longshaw appeared much the same as when Bryce had briefly met her three years before.

Milton's muffled shout erupted inside. "Yes, I'm hungry!"

Bryce ducked down, afraid to peek up over the bush in case someone saw him.

Milton lashed out again. "Give me that letter. Where are my pills? I'll be right in."

Bryce took a breath and eked up over the top of the bush's branches.

"I said, I'll be in!"

Bryce shuddered but maintained his vantage point. Milton flew into the room and flicked the chandelier flames up to full burn. He kicked the door closed, several bottles fumbling from his hands. He cursed as he stooped and gathered them up. He secured the envelope between his lips and struggled to twist a bottle's lid. The container slipped to the rug, and he issued it a firm kick. It sailed into one of the floor-to-ceiling bookshelves lining the left-hand wall. Milton tossed the envelope onto a chair and shook as he coaxed another bottle open. He emptied several pills out into his mouth.

He wheeled toward the door, and it opened in slow inches. A maid in a white cap and uniform handed him a glass of clear liquid. Milton swatted it to the floor. She slammed the portal closed between them.

Milton stormed over to a waist-high cabinet against the right-hand wall, fetching a caramel-colored liquor bottle. He poured himself a glass and drank his pills down with it. He topped his glass off and set the bottle down. He snatched up the envelope from the chair and rested his glass aside to pull the letter out. Finally situated, Milton reclaimed his drink and pored over the pages.

Bryce's thoughts roamed the property. Did Milton hire more than one servant? Was she the only other person in the house? Where were additional entrances besides the front door? Were any of them close to this room where Bryce could sneak in and creep out? Or should he prompt Milton to let him in peaceably the way Clementine had with her father?

Milton cried out, arresting Bryce's attention. The man stared at the letter, eyes wounded and brows raised high. Milton swiveled his head for what seemed like half a minute, his chest caving forward.

Milton screwed his cheeks up and launched his half-full glass at the humongous painting. He flinched at the splintering glass. The fire reared up beneath Lydia, devouring its offerings.

Bryce stumbled away from the bush and the window. Milton flung himself into the chair, the letter tumbling to the floor. Milton covered his face with his hands, and Bryce's anger ebbed out of him. What news could Milton possibly have received?

Bryce backed up across the lawn, brows hunched in confusion at Milton's quivering arms. Could he kill an old fellow while he was down? Could he take advantage of a withered, wrinkled man and live with himself? Did he really want to risk imprisonment and discover his own murderous potential over this trembling, pathetic soul?

Bryce bolted through the rest of the yard. He vaulted over the gate and hustled on.

Even if someone saw him through the unrelenting fog, it did not matter. He had planned to return to the factory and retrieve his steambike following his business with Milton. Bryce formed another plan as he raced through the streets.

Milton would have to figure out his own messes for now.

Clementine was still in danger of having her darkest secrets found out, and Bryce had to warn her.

Chapter Thirty-Two

His fist beat furious knocks onto the door. Bryce's heart thundered at a reckless speed. He banged again, the door opening before he heard anything but his own raucous raps.

Clementine slumped against the edge of the door. Her voice fell flat, almost edgy. "What can I do for you, Bryce?"

"He knows." Bryce could scarcely catch his breath. "I need to come in. He knows it might've been you."

Clementine huffed but stepped aside. Bryce flew in and helped her close the door more quickly than she seemed inclined.

"Milton." Bryce gestured with nervous hands. "I'm sorry. I'm the one who gave him the idea it might've been someone close to him."

She held a blink closed. "Who?"

Bryce focused his addled brain. "I know you killed your father."

Clementine shrieked, her agitated façade puckering into tormented folds. She leaned back against the door and choked out a sob into her hands.

"I'm sorry," Bryce insisted, shifting his weight from one foot to the other. "I figured it out, then I put Milton onto the idea on accident, trying to find out if he did it. I walked all the way to Civil Lines to kill Milton to protect you, but I couldn't."

Clementine sank to the wooden floor, wiping her eyes with her sleeves.

Bryce balanced himself on his haunches. "It's all right. I see why you'd want to do it. I didn't know what Clements was like to you. He treated me more like a son than he treated you like his flesh-and-blood daughter. And your mother's still sick, isn't she?"

Clementine sputtered anew.

"I know everything." Bryce took his hat off and wrought it in his hands. "I invited myself in this morning. I was worried about you. I read your letters and Clements' postcards. I understand why you didn't want me studying them before. You had a different life back there than you've had here. Those things were private, and the letters from Mr. Morris and Mr. Callaghan were sent after Clements died. You wrote to them, didn't you?"

Clementine plastered her hand over her eyes, the sounds of her crying evaporating several feet into the enormous room.

"Clementine, say something. Please." Bryce nudged her knee with his hat. "I loved Clements like my own father. I've never gotten over his death. But you don't have to worry. I won't turn you in. I just want you to talk to me. I barged in here."

The scents of crispy-skinned chicken and curry reached Bryce's nose. "Did you finish your dinner?"

Clementine sniffled and raised her hand from her eyes, resting it on her frazzled hair. "I killed my father."

"I know. That's what I'm saying. I don't know how or when exactly you got to Delhi–"

"It was an accident."

Bryce stopped, his mind whirling. "An accident?" He had never given any consideration to that scenario.

"What do I do, Bryce? I killed my father." Clementine's focus slipped away from him to the base of the staircase.

Bryce lowered himself to the floor, level with Clementine. "Why don't you tell me what happened? From the beginning."

Clementine sucked in a deep breath. In a flash, she stood on her father's doorstep three months earlier. The only person besides her father she had seen coming and going from the house in the last two days had traipsed away with a shopping basket. Nervousness clenched every muscle to its bones. She knocked and waited.

A boisterous greeting sang to her as the door swung in, its Irish-Virginia accent born thousands of miles from where it resounded. "Edith, did you leave something..." His watery blue eyes, graced with a touch of green, landed on her.

They both stopped breathing.

Clementine adjusted her shoulders. He had aged since the last time she saw him, but there was no mistaking him. Same towering height, wide body, and wild, blondish-red hair. "Good afternoon, Da."

His crimson cheeks blanched pale. "Clementine."

The hint of a question bent his tone, and she wondered who else he thought would address him as her father.

Dazed, he waved her inside. "Won't you come in?"

Clementine walked into the house. Only months of preparation made her slightly more confident than her father at this moment. Her heart lunged against her rib cage, thundering in her ears. She tried to keep her cool. "It's good to see you."

"How did you get to India?" He closed the door.

Clementine bristled. He might as well have inquired, *What are you doing here?* She concentrated on the facts. "The same way you did. By boat."

His fingers twitched. "Is your mother with you?"

Again, Clementine heard a revised speech. *Do I have to deal with your mother, too?* But she had planned this reunion for too long to react in bitterness already. "I came alone."

"That's good. I mean, traveling by yourself. It's an interesting way to see the world."

"You've had a partner for years. And an assistant."

Clements managed a smile. "You got my postcards. Good."

In an uncertain silence, Clementine glanced around the huge room. From its periphery, her eyes flitted over the expensive, precise furniture. The exotic rugs, the ornate knickknacks, and the columns flanking the doorway into the room ahead on the left. Even her father dressed in a fancy, well-fitting suit. It suffered no rips or stains Clementine observed. She thanked providence she had saved up extra money to spend on her own clothes for the trip. She wanted to present her best, and a worn dress would have put her out of place in this pristine palace. Even the ceiling fan revolving the air was more of a luxury than she had ever known. Her gaze lingered on it.

Her father broke the trance. "Would you like to sit down?"

"No. What I have to say is very important, but I hope it won't take long."

His dense, scraggly eyebrows rose. "Oh? What sort of business is that?"

It struck Clementine like a blow to the chest. He was going to make this difficult for her, guessing nothing and forcing her to say every word she had ever rehearsed. She replanted her feet in a firm stance. "I've grown up in your shadow, Da. I went into plants and remedies just like you did. I set up shop in Nashville, like I told you in my letters."

Clements stood watching her for an ageless moment. "Good for you."

Clementine fought the urge to cave and crumble. She tossed her head, trying to keep her bearings without her chin quivering. "*Nikya* is sick."

Clements spun away on the heels of his polished, black leather shoes. "There's your mother's influence. Shawnee words. It's been generations since there was an actual, full-blooded native in her family."

Clementine advanced a quick step toward him. "Only three. Nikya's great-grandmother was Flying Squirrel, and she married a Parish."

Her father gestured for her to settle down. "I never approved of her filling your head with her ancestors. There are two sides to your family. Hers may be muddled, but half of you is good Irish stock, and they were Scottish before that."

Clementine's eyes swam with anger. "You didn't care what Nikya's family was when you met her and took her away from them."

Clements snarled. "You mean when I shared what little I had with her and she chose – of her own free will – to come with me."

Clementine choked on her ire. "You want to talk about family? What about yours? The one you made outside of Livingston. You had a responsibility to care for us. To support us. Do right by us. I don't know." Her eyes flitted around the foreign room. "Maybe even stay in the same country as us."

Her father's eyes crinkled askew.

"You're bothered by me, aren't you?" Clementine jerked her chin up to seal it. "Nikya said you would be. I look too much like you for you to brush me off. I'm not a bumpkin like you thought I'd be. I grew up ambitious like you, and I'm not afraid to stand up for what I believe in."

Clements crossed to the fireplace with a hitch of annoyance in his step. He agitated the hearth's modest glow with a metal poker. "Is this what was so crucial for us to talk about?"

"You know it's not." Clementine stayed where she was, but she longed to follow her father to the mantel and talk to him directly. "I sailed halfway around the world to see you. My life and Nikya's are on the line. I've had most of my life away from you, not really knowing you. I quit school so I could provide for us so we wouldn't starve. *You* cost me more education."

Clements snorted. "I saved you from that dingy, stuffy place. Teachers aren't so grand. The kind ones are too placid, and the stern ones unreasonable."

Clementine jabbed a finger against her chest. "I wanted to be there, Da. To learn things. I wanted to know what there was in the world from knowledge inside my head, not all this complicated traveling."

Clements walked halfway across the rug through the loose grouping of living room furniture. "How much schooling do you think I got? Eh? I turned out plenty all right by my own hard labor."

He stalked toward her. "What kind of a family – what sort of origin – do you suppose I came from? It was nothing like this." He cast his arm out, indicating the room. "I had what you had, maybe less because there were more of us to feed. And house. And put clothing on. Let me tell you something. *Humble* is a rich man's word for *poor*. When you made a mistake…" Clements pointed to Clementine. "Your mother coddled you…"

"She hugged me." Clementine hung back, unsure what he would do.

"She told you everything would be all right. Isn't that nice? Drop a potato on the filthy floor." Clements raised his palms. "It'll be okay. Track muddy feet in across a clean floor? Fine. You know what my mother would've done?" He grimaced. "She would've whipped me herself before my da got home and doubled the job."

"I didn't know." Clementine raised her voice. "I didn't know because you weren't there to tell me!"

"How was your voyage to India? Hmm?" Clements arrived in front of her and tucked his thumbs into his pockets. "Everybody sweet to you? Helpful? Did they offer to carry your bags and ask what part of the world you were off to explore?"

He scoffed. "You and I sound smart now. But I got doors slammed on me – physically and otherwise – when I traveled out of Virginia. It never got any easier until I educated myself. Men wouldn't hire me. Women wouldn't acknowledge me unless I could reach something, fix something, or haul something for them."

Clementine nodded. "There are doctors in Nashville who treat me like that."

He leaked a tense sigh as he sized her up. "I regret naming you after me. I've never done much in my life out of pride, but that was the high point of it."

"Why?" she demanded.

"It'll never let you forget who your father is. And you've caught me at a bad time. I have plans for dinner, and I'm not ready."

Clementine reeled and almost toppled to the floor. "Dinner's more important than me, and I came all this way."

"I'm sorry about that." Clements touched her arm. "Maybe if you'd told me you wanted to visit me…"

Clementine shrugged away. "It wouldn't have helped. You clearly have no room for me in your life and don't want to make any."

"I'm managing a company. I have a lot to do, and it keeps me busy."

She gawked at him. "You had a daughter and an ill woman to take care of. It didn't stop you from taking a break."

He took gentle hold of her arm. "Go back to the States, and I'll try to visit you next time I'm in Nashville."

She jerked her arm free and tottered back a few steps. "Don't send me away. Nashville's not the kind of place you can get to from India without going there on purpose."

Clements deflated with a breathy exhale. "You have more to say."

Clementine's spine shot upright. "How little did you think there would be after seventeen years? Or didn't you think I could count? Especially after the way you left us."

Clements strode off to the stairwell. "I don't believe this. There's no such thing as a good farewell."

Clementine marched after him. "I'm well aware."

"I did what I could for you, and I kept my promise to your ma." Clements stomped up the steps.

Clementine climbed up behind him. "What was that?"

"To write to you. To keep in touch so I wouldn't be completely gone from your life. In not one of those years did I fumble my duties."

Clementine balked. "A chore and a burden, that's how you saw me."

"My childhood wasn't exactly picking daisies and floating on my back in the creek, either." Clements mounted the top of the stairs. "And I had my da around. You think you're the only child pressured to work?"

He spun on Clementine as she reached the second floor. "Don't you know some kids work their fingers to the bone in factories – some of them *lose* their fingers – and there are worse places than that?"

Clements darted off up the hall, and Clementine trailed after him. He railed on. "I never asked for a family. I never wanted one. I left Virginia on my lonesome for a reason. Your ma came with me to northern Tennessee for the same motivation: I'm a wanderer and a free man. I put down roots when she got pregnant with you, and I stayed as long as I could stand it."

Clements burst through a wide doorway into a sitting room. "Your ma wasn't in perfect health when I met her, but we got by. She got sicker every year, and I couldn't tell what was wrong with her. I tried to help, but I saw my independence getting further and further away."

Clementine followed him in, surprised the sitting area expanded into another part of the room twice as large. A double bed and dark, wooden furniture occupied that side. "It wasn't Nikya's fault. She loved you with all her heart. It nearly broke her when you left. We needed you."

Clements wheeled toward her, stationed in front of a narrow chest of drawers. "I only made one pledge to your ma, and I kept it. I never married her, Clementine, and I did more than right by you both." He jerked the top drawer open. "Neither one of you shared my name. If I hadn't called you Clementine, you'd have no idea you were tied to me."

She marveled at him, crestfallen. "I loved you. I was proud of you, and I tried to feel close to you in spite of everything. Aren't you proud of what I've made of myself?"

Clements dug through the drawer's contents. "What am I even searching for?"

Clementine swallowed a lump of grief. "Probably something you don't need for several more hours."

Clements picked out two silver, jeweled cufflinks and inserted them into his shirtsleeves. "I told you I didn't have time for this discussion." He propped his elbows on the armoire. "How accomplished of an herbalist can you be when your principal patient is still ailing after all these years?"

Clementine cried out. "I know every bit as much as you do, I guarantee you. I'd tell you everything if you gave me time. And you owe Nikya."

"According to what?"

"You profited from what she taught you. The Shawnee and the other tribes used plants as medicine long before you got there."

"They don't have a monopoly on it."

Clementine erupted in a growling squeal. "I've spent most of my life doing your job, taking care of her. I'm getting closer to figuring it out and making her comfortable. But I'd appreciate your help. It'd be most timely if you returned to Tennessee."

Clements slammed the drawer closed. "How am I supposed to do that? Leave my company and my business partner and traipse off to see a woman I haven't spoken to in almost two decades? Abandon the team I put together with my sweat and big decisions and the research we've slaved over for three years?"

Clementine patted her chest. "Once again, my life and sacrifices aren't as important as something you built for fun and profit? How can you say you don't act out of pride? It's all I've seen from you today."

Clements whisked past her into the hallway. "I can't help you. And might I add, I assume *help* means you want money."

She flew after him. "I came here for my father. Don't talk like I didn't earn the right to come and ask you to do right by us. Like sailing around the world isn't something I worked hard for."

Clements stopped at the top of the stairs to peer at her. "I think you read my notes of how well my company was doing, and you came into my house, and you realized I was your ticket to keeping your mother alive." He descended the first leg of the stairs.

Clementine seethed. "How could I not want more? The most I ever got from you was a string of postcards." She charged down at him.

Clements tilted an eyebrow. "And life."

Clementine reached the landing behind him and shoved him. Without a sound, he soared through the air. Clementine caught her breath and covered her open mouth in horror. "I'm so sorry, Da."

With a jarring thud, he crashed to the floor, his legs sliding down the last few steps.

"Da?" Clementine's whisper disappeared as quickly as warm breath on a cold, black night.

A soft rasping came from the bottom of the stairs, but Clementine stood frozen on the landing. A pool of blood spread out from beneath his head, and the life drained from his eyes.

Clementine's screams echoed in her ears, sitting with Bryce not far from where it happened. She shook her head to free herself of the horror. "I came asking for help he wasn't willing to give. Hoping for an explanation, an apology. Something. My own father back in my life. And my mother's. But he was mean, and we argued, and I pushed him from the landing." She pointed at the staircase. "He fell, and I watched him die."

Bryce scooted closer to Clementine. "Why'd you tell me your mother was better?"

"She is, but only compared to how sick she got years ago." Clementine blinked tears out of her eyes. "Her health is impossible to predict. She's out in the fresh air on her feet one afternoon. The next morning, or by dinnertime, she might be fighting to breathe and wincing in pain."

"Is that why you wanted to change the Fountain of Youth into a medicine? To make her better?"

Clementine's reasoning made her feel silly and ineffectual now. "My father left when I was six. My mother tried to be brave and stay happy for me. Months later, I heard her crying in the middle of the night. For all of us. She'd left her family to be with my father. She was too sick to travel back to them and scared of how they'd react to her." Clementine wiped her cheeks with the cuffs of her dress sleeves. "I wanted the real Fountain of Youth to give my mother everything she missed because he abandoned us. Her health, youth, and happiness."

Bryce leaned over as if to hug her.

Clementine shied away, her wet lashes clumped together around desperate eyes. "I'm a fraud, Bryce. I lied to you and Milton from the moment we met. I didn't let you go through my letters because they'd expose me for who I really am."

"Clementine Heidel?"

She nodded. "My parents never married."

"You never claimed they did."

"But I wanted you to believe it. I needed you to recognize me as his daughter in blood and name. I never called myself a Fitzgerald until after his death. It's still strange to me."

"What about the letters from Clements' lawyer and banker? Did you pose as your father and write to them?"

She averted her gaze. "After my father died, I panicked. I fled. I holed up in a little town north of here and tried to figure out what to do. I wrote to my friends in Nashville and told them what happened. I asked them to hide any correspondence about his death and keep it from my mother until I could break the news myself. Police contacted our family, and I timed my second arrival in Delhi according to the steamship schedule. I found my father's will stating he wanted his whole estate contributed to the company. I used the postcards he'd sent me to learn his words and phrases. I practiced forging his signature and convinced them both he was still alive. I didn't know how else to keep control of his house and his money. I've never had so much money to use." Clementine dotted perspiration off her forehead.

"Milton's going to get suspicious."

"Maybe not. He seems to agree that paperwork takes time. Soon enough, we'll be scattered apart in the States. Would Mr. Longshaw really track me down in Tennessee? He doesn't even have my real name."

Bryce ruffled his hair. "I can't believe I planned to kill him." He pulled a pistol from his pocket and sat it on the floor. He drew Clementine's stare as he dug out a knife and a rope, discarding them alongside the gun. "You should've seen him. It was like spying on somebody's grandfather. Agitated and weak. Crying over some letter."

Clementine could hardly picture it. "Crying?"

"Weeping. He threw his glass and shattered it." Bryce slid the weapons away. "I should've talked to you first. I'm embarrassed now. I was drastic and brash."

Clementine drew her knees up in front of her, playing with the ends of her sleeves. "I appreciate what you tried to do for me. I'm sorry it was to protect someone who doesn't exist."

"You're real." Bryce cupped his hand over her knee.

She gave him a sad wisp of a smile. "I'm Clementine Heidel. Nikya raised me by herself after Da left. Because back home, that's what I call them. Da and *Nikya*. It's a Shawnee word for *my mother* that's been passed down through her family. I brought the feathers you saw to remind me of her and give me strength. I didn't always have an official business. I used to roam the fields, picking wild plants I healed my neighbors with. They rarely paid me in money. They'd pay me in trade. Clothes, food, baskets, and moonshine."

"What was the letter from a woman in Nashville? Something about preparing you for your reception in India."

"Da was a world traveler. I couldn't show up and ask him to come home without sounding more educated than I am. That was a trade, too. Betty Crawford's a school teacher. I cured her indigestion, and she taught me how to sound smart. She said she couldn't double my vocabulary in a handful of weeks, but if I took her advice on how to string my words together, I'd do all right. I needed to be Clementine Fitzgerald, one of only two nonmedical healers in Nashville. It seemed to do the trick during my first meeting with y'all."

Bryce perked up in a brief grin. "Where is Clements now?"

"I sent his body home. Nikya and our friends buried him there. It was quiet and dignified."

Bryce slid his hand away from her. "I guess I only have one more question. Did you really care about me–"

"Yes." Clementine watched him, her fingertips outlining the floorboards around her.

"What about Milton?" He could barely push out the words.

Clementine rubbed her temple. "Nikya's life is at stake. He wanted to leave the project, and I didn't know what to do. Haven't you noticed I'm bad at making plans?"

"Mr. Mustafa was the same way?"

She shook her head. "There's nothing going on between us. We're friends. I was up all night tending his daughter's infection. He gave me that hat out of pure relief."

Bryce released a puff of air. "He's not the only one who's relieved."

Clementine unhooked her earrings and tossed them on the floor. "All of this was an act to earn your trust. I was jealous when Mr. Longshaw said the factory uniforms were Da's idea. I grew up wearing other people's clothes. Da practically adopted you and gave you that steambike."

Bryce's eyes took on a murkier hue. "I'm sorry."

"You said Da never mentioned much about me."

Bryce closed his eyes. "That's what upset you. I was careless. I didn't understand how things were between you and your father."

Clementine cleared her throat. "You reminded me I had important reasons for sailing to India. I wasn't here for fun. I came to work, to redeem Nikya's life." She wrapped her arms around her knees, securing a hand over each elbow. "I heard you, you know."

"What?"

"Singing the song with my name in it. The day we met at the factory."

Crimson spread across Bryce's cheeks like brushfire. "I didn't think you did. You never said anything. You were so professional."

"I needed a favor. What good would it have done to react to it? A song people at home used to make up lyrics for to honor me or cheer me up. Like Chester."

Bryce dropped his chin. "I found one of his letters, too."

"We're just friends. I haven't seen him in two years." Clementine used the wall behind her to push herself to standing.

Bryce scrambled to his feet, leaving his newsboy and assorted weaponry on the floor. "What do we do? The fact remains you had a hand in Clements' death. Your mother's life is in danger along with your freedom. Milton threatened to harm anyone connected to Clements' fall. He can destroy you if he finds out."

"I have to consider my moves carefully and make sure that doesn't happen. I only planned on being in India for a few days or weeks. It's drawing out into an entire year." She tugged on a drooping section of her hair. "If Nikya dies while we're developing this formula..."

Bryce cradled her jaw in the tenderest contact. "She won't. It's only a cold, and your friends are tending to her. If they need your advice, you can fax back and forth in minutes."

Clementine squeezed her eyes shut, sending fresh tears down her cheeks. "I missed you, Bryce. When I think about the things I said to you–"

He kissed her high cheekbones and rubbed her tears away. "I deserved it. Just don't meddle with Milton anymore. I couldn't take it."

Her words came out barely audible. "All right. But what do we do?"

Bryce swept his thumbs along her jaw. "We keep our wits about us. Milton doesn't know anything that went on. If we can keep him from finding out, we really get to keep our heads."

Chapter Thirty-Three

Clementine walked the factory's back hall with Mr. Mustafa. Despite hitches in cultivating and shipping the shilajit, its delivery proved uneventful. For the first time that week, Clementine relaxed.

Mr. Mustafa, however, retained stiff shoulders as they strolled along.

"Is something wrong?" she asked.

He glanced back at the unpacking room. "I dislike being referred to as a Mohammedan. It suggests we worship the prophet, which is false."

Clementine sighed. "I know how you feel. People from a certain area in Ireland are called Scotch-Irish in my country. For most of them, it's not true. For my father, it was."

They turned the corner near the offices as the front door banged open. They exchanged a loaded glance of adrenaline and déjà vu.

Aatmaj spoke up. "Sir, we want no trouble." He continued in another language.

Clementine and Mr. Mustafa jogged to the end of the corridor. Ravi Lal loomed in the center of the lobby, hunched over and heaving with anger. Mr. Mustafa greeted him with pressed palms in front of his chest, but Ravi scowled at him.

"Indira Datta," Ravi seethed. The rest of his words simmered in a second language.

Mr. Mustafa replied to him, then conferred with Clementine. "Mr. Lal wants to see Miss Datta. He insists she must be here."

Clementine shook her head, bunching her brows over the bridge of her nose. "Miss Datta sent word this morning she wouldn't be in. She apologized profusely for the inconvenience."

Mr. Mustafa relayed this in firm but gentle tones. Ravi pulled a crumpled page from his pocket and thrust it toward Mr. Mustafa. The turbaned man took it and unfurled its creases. Clementine peered at it, not expecting to be able to read it. Complex, flowing script accented the flyer, which held pictures of a shaven-headed, mustachioed man talking with tool-wielding workers in a farm field. Shaky curves formed handwritten English at the bottom. *Train east to Motihari. Mr. Gandhi will be there by end of March.*

Indira had hung on every word from the confident man in the green kurta in the Hindu shop's supply room. Clementine understood Indira had not been there to appreciate his looks. At least, it was far from her focus. Clementine's mouth dried up.

Ravi questioned them in musical syllables.

Mr. Mustafa addressed Clementine. "What should I tell him? He can't read English, and the Hindi details Mohandas Gandhi's peaceful resolutions to workers' problems. It calls on India's native people to rise up and take their country back from the British."

I knew she was involved in this. Clementine kept it to herself. Even Milton, in his casual answers to Indira's questions, had encouraged her to seek independence for her nation. She swallowed with a catch in her throat. "Tell Mr. Lal I'm sorry. I assumed Miss Datta stayed home because she took ill again. Although it's likely she never did. I believe Miss Datta's gone."

Mr. Mustafa flipped the paper over. The handwriting appeared on the back in four humble words. *For all of us.*

Clementine's hands trembled. "I'm not sure how much Mr. Lal wants to know or how much he should know. But Miss Datta's left Delhi. I can't say if she'll come back."

Mr. Mustafa folded the paper in half and once again, pinching his fingertips along each bend. He spoke with Ravi until the young man tore at his hair. Ravi droned on, Mr. Mustafa translating.

"He bemoans the years he worked for Miss Datta's father, as they were a waste. He's ashamed and betrayed."

Sympathy tugged at Clementine's chest. "He's heartbroken."

"Miss Datta was supposed to marry him and obey her parents. Put her family first."

"She may have done a selfish thing where Mr. Lal's concerned, but she did it for selfless reasons. She's helping her whole country."

"I doubt that would comfort Mr. Lal at this point."

With a few blurted phrases, Ravi tore out of the building.

Mr. Mustafa handed the flyer to Clementine. "I told him nothing he didn't already read."

Aatmaj resumed his paperwork at the desk, and Clementine moseyed away with Mr. Mustafa.

Curiosity lightened his mood. "What do you think about India seeking independence from the British?"

"I'm American. We live for it."

Chapter Thirty-Four

A familiar slam made Clementine fumble the glass communication tube she was holding. It tumbled halfway to her office rug before Bryce helped her catch it.

Exasperation furrowed her features. Whether Ravi had come to beleaguer his situation or someone else had stormed in, Clementine could hardly believe less than a week could pass without such an interruption.

She spared a glance for the tube's intended recess in the wall. "I'll never learn how to use this with all these distractions." She clattered the tube onto her desk, and Bryce followed her toward the lobby.

The rapid Hindi came too hushed and uncertain to be Ravi's.

Aatmaj responded as Clementine arrived to see the man for herself.

She stared. In a white turban and clothes, the main servant from the Varmas' house wrung his hands just inside the door.

"What is it?" Clementine begged Aatmaj.

"There's been a death at the house."

"In the family?" Fear gripped Clementine's stomach. No servant would come to report the passing of a fellow servant. Her mind grasped at other explanations. *Maybe an important visitor or family friend?*

"Yes, miss."

"Samvidha." Clementine fumbled with Bryce's sleeve. "I have to go." She ran past Aatmaj's desk and ripped the door open to the largest room in the factory. Cavernous, it stretched the same size as the mixing room, extraction area, and cold storage added together. Conveyor belts and chutes would soon carry the finished elixir from the bottling stations at the far end through packaging and labeling to the boxing area around her. Metal gleamed and workmen nodded while Nithya Menon instructed them, patting the boxy machinery.

Clementine's voice boomed through the space to the blue-turbaned man near the foreman. "Mr. Mustafa, please come with me. I need you."

He swiveled on his heel with words of excusal. He jogged toward her from the jungle of metal posts and eight-foot-tall machines. "What's happened?"

"There's a death at the Varmas'. Their servant came. I want to get there as quickly as possible."

They whisked from the room, and Clementine doubled her pace. She skirted around Bryce to her office and snatched up her coat with her keys in the pocket. She met Mr. Mustafa in the lobby, and the servant ushered them out the front door.

Mr. Mustafa spoke up. "Do you need me to drive? Should we borrow Mr. Milton's keys?"

Clementine rattled her set. "I'll drive. I have my father's autocarriage."

She took the wheel, and the two men piled in around her. She ignited the engine fire and waited for the steam pressure to rise. Throwing the autocarriage in reverse, she shot off toward the road.

The man in white murmured from the seat behind her.

Mr. Mustafa translated. "He's sorry for bringing you bad news and interrupting your day."

"That's all right."

Mr. Mustafa relayed this to the servant, but Clementine scarcely heard him. She concentrated as much as she could on speeding along the roads. More often than racing along, other vehicles and pedestrians clogged her path. She pulled into the Varmas' long driveway with relief sanding the edge off her dread.

Clementine parked and shut the autocarriage off before jumping out and hastening for the house. Mr. Mustafa and the servant hurried to catch up. The servant ran up ahead and held the door open. The two visitors rushed into the entry hall.

Sobs and raw whines swelled through the rooms. A man's deep, unfamiliar intonations thrummed somewhere out of sight.

A more recognizable timbre spilled out of the stairwell at the back of the foyer. Congested wails sent out a continuous stream of drawn-out, anguished, *"Ma, Ma, Ma."*

A cold trickle danced up Clementine's spine. "Mr. Mustafa, who died?"

He exchanged words with the servant.

Clementine crept toward the back of the room. Sitting on the second-lowest step, Samvidha lifted her head from her hands. Her magenta sari and periwinkle head wrap dazzled with color. She peered at Clementine with dazed, swollen eyes. Her bandages hung loose from her wrists.

"Samvidha," Clementine breathed in disbelief.

Mr. Mustafa approached her. "Miss Fitzgerald, I regret to inform you Mrs. Padma Varma passed away this afternoon. Miss Varma has been crying for her mother."

Clementine fell to her haunches and wrapped her arms around Samvidha. "Please tell her how sorry I am." Her throat clenched, and she waited for it to release before she spoke again. "How is this possible? I don't understand."

Mr. Mustafa conferred with Samvidha and the servant. "It seems there were things Mrs. Varma neglected to share with us. It was Mr. Varma who sent for you, and he'll explain the situation."

"I've never even met him." Clementine pulled back from Samvidha, leaving her with a kiss on the cheek. She smoothed wrinkles from her coat as she joined Mr. Mustafa. "What do you think he wants to say?"

"I'm not sure. He's waiting in the private sitting room. The servant will take us. If you're ready to see him."

"His wife died. I can't say no." Clementine glided her palms across the fabric of her coat. "I'd like to go to him now."

With a few words from Mr. Mustafa, the servant led the visitors past the kitchen through a door Clementine had not entered before. They walked across a formal living room to a pair of carved wooden doors left an inch ajar. The servant knocked, and one of the doors flew open.

Nishil regarded the trio with an ugly glare. He strode off, leaving Clementine unsteady and trembling. What sort of mood would they find the young man's father in?

The servant spoke with the deep-voiced man and waved the visitors in. Clementine and Mr. Mustafa stepped into an ample sitting room. Only one man remained inside, and he stood up from a plush sofa to greet them.

He stood shorter than Clementine, his suit in finer condition than Clementine would have anticipated after the day's tragedy. His brown-black hair lay straight and neat except for a few places brushed awry. Damp lashes and red veining around his mahogany irises provided the only other signs his life had suffered such a blow.

Clementine and Mr. Mustafa offered him the ceremonial touching palms. Mr. Mustafa repeated his Hindi words of condolences from earlier in their arrival.

"I know some English," Udit Varma admitted. "Samvidha insisted on it. So did the British presence in our country. Please, sit down." He gestured to several chairs across from him as he regained his seat on the couch.

Clementine and Mr. Mustafa eased into armchairs.

She cleared her stiff throat. "Mr. Varma, I'm speechless to meet you under such awful circumstances."

Udit bobbed his head. "My wife and daughter told me about you. My son, too, but he's less reliable in certain matters."

"We didn't come here to disrespect him. Why did you send a servant to fetch me?"

Udit licked his thick lips. "Padma was very fond of you. She was grateful for the way you care for Samvidha, not only her illness but her soul. Your friendship has made a huge difference in our house. We could never repay you for that."

Clementine shook her head. "It's not a debt. Samvidha and Mrs. Varma have been wonderful. I'm far from home, and they welcomed me. I'm so grateful Mrs. Varma, acting on your behalf, maintained your investment in the Fountain of Youth."

Udit got up and closed the doors. He resettled into his seat. "That's what I want to talk to you about. You see, my wife had cancer, and she hid it from all of us until recently."

"Why?" Clementine set her forehead on her bunched fist. "I should've known something was wrong. She said it was nothing."

"When Padma wanted to keep a secret, she did. None of us had any idea for a long time." Udit wiped his forehead with a white handkerchief. "Family is everything. It's the most important resource we have. Once it's gone, you can't get it back. You can't harvest or manufacture more. You can make more, but it's not the same as what you lost."

Clementine nodded. "I know. It's why I changed the serum's recipe."

"It's also why Padma kept her silence. Samvidha's been afflicted for years. It was hard on Padma to see that, and when you came, you brought the sun. You brought us hope, and you gave reprieve to Samvidha for her misery." Udit's eyes sparkled with pride amidst the pain. "Padma put her family first. She knew that speaking up about her discomfort would take money away from Samvidha's care. It would remove the attention and the herbs Samvidha needed."

"There was enough to go around."

Udit's mouth curved in a bittersweet revelation. "Padma wouldn't take that chance. She couldn't steal doctoring from her own daughter. Would you?"

Clementine had no daughter, but Adelaide had sacrificed plenty over the years to secure Clementine's comfort. "I understand. I'm sorry the medicinal product came too late. In another year's time, we could've helped Mrs. Varma. I'm sure of it."

Udit uncovered an envelope from the end of the sofa beside him. "In Padma's eyes, your timing is not to blame. She died knowing she supported the formula that will restore our daughter to the loving, outgoing girl she once was."

Clementine widened her eyes. "It's not guaranteed. We're just doing our best."

Udit stood up and extended the envelope towards her. "It will help Samvidha," he said with conviction. "This will help you."

Clementine took the envelope, too humbled to open it.

"In my wife's name, I'm making an extra investment in your company."

"I can't take this." Clementine's forehead itched with sweat.

"Your change in project and nurturing of Samvidha meant everything to Padma. It made her heart sing again. My family is my world, and so there is a debt I owe you. I can think of no better act within my power than to enable you to forge ahead with the Fountain of Youth with my money and my blessing."

Clementine leapt to her feet. She stopped herself from hugging Udit in case it would be inappropriate, but she could not stop a smile from bursting out beneath her teary eyes. "I thank you, Mr. Varma, from the bottom of my heart. I'll do everything possible to make sure we manufacture the most successful cure we can."

Udit placed his palms together in front of his chest. "Then I would be back in your debt. I anticipate that day."

Chapter Thirty-Five

Clementine sat at her desk, Bryce lingering close by. The office door yawned open to suggest she made herself available to inquiries, but she certainly did not want to entertain any. Only the few small favors of those around her mitigated the burdens of her heavy heart. She had cleared the air with Bryce and rewon his trust. Udit had gifted additional funds, and the production of several serum trials ran on schedule.

Still, their bad luck haunted Clementine. "Miss Datta's gone."

Bryce propped himself against the corner of the desk. "She did what she wanted, at least. Milton will find a new assistant. I'm surprised he hasn't asked for one yet."

"He feels abandoned. She left without saying goodbye."

Bryce hesitated. "I think she tried, but... never mind."

"Has Milton told you anything new about his recovery?"

"Something he didn't tell you? I don't think so. It's gradual, but he seems to get along all right."

Clementine sat up straighter. "The one good part about Miss Datta leaving is that Mr. Lal has no more reason to burst through the door and yell for her."

Bryce moaned. "Thank goodness. I hate meeting people under strange circumstances. I bet we would've liked him if we encountered him in the street."

Clementine dropped her volume. "The best thing is no one suspects anything about me."

Bryce patted her hand. "I told you. There's too much work to do. No one has access to your letters. It's airtight."

"I guess I expected some suspicious glances or something once I'd told you the story."

"I roamed half the city to gather that information. Who else is going to do that?"

Clementine shrugged.

Bryce tapped her arm. "Milton's ecstatic about that check from Mr. Varma. He's not going to suspect you of any wrongdoings now."

Clementine's throat ached from grieving. "I miss Padma."

"I'm sorry. We really will do everything possible to make the best medicine we can. Our research is solid. Our factory crew is thoroughly trained on the machinery."

"Thanks to Mr. Menon. If he'd have left us, we'd be done."

"We'd find a way to get by without him. We got the tube system fixed, didn't we?"

Clementine relaxed her solemn mouth. "We did." She swept a stray fuzz off her sleeve. "I promised the Varmas I'd continue to visit Samvidha."

Bryce bunched his nose up. "That's kind, but be careful. I can't have you getting sick. The factory would really be in trouble then."

She flashed him a smile. "What happened to finding the second solution to every problem? I have a hard time believing–"

A metallic slam reverberated through the building, accompanied by a horrific scream of pain.

Bryce sprinted to the door, and Clementine pushed herself up from her chair. They raced down the hall.

He glanced at her. "Maybe you shouldn't see this."

"It's my factory. I didn't think anyone was still–"

They reached the extraction room and thundered in. At the nearest machine on the right, Milton draped through its jaws. Blood spilled out around his dangling arms and legs. Clementine spun away. She plastered her hands over her mouth, where rising nausea threatened to spurt out her breakfast.

Bryce gulped. He sounded as pale as his complexion drained. "Milton?"

Clementine laid a hand on Bryce's arm as she forced her muscles to turn her back around. "We have to go to him."

They crept toward the silver-and-crimson scene. Milton sputtered and inhaled with a ghastly sucking squeal.

Clementine kept her hand on Bryce, its tether steadying her and making her capable of approaching the accident.

From the side, Clementine could see the arrangement more clearly. The machine's metal extractor squeezed down on Milton's back, trapping his torso against the base. He lifted his head mere inches before it hung down again.

Clementine crouched beside him. "Milton?" Words failed her. What question could she possibly ask? He had to be in pain, in shock, or both. He obviously could not extricate himself. Should she try to reassure him? She could call for help and send for a doctor. But did he know an injury like this might be irreversible?

Milton gasped.

"Don't try to talk." The same strength of purpose that had fueled Clementine to close the factory in light of Milton's first accident flooded her veins. "Bryce, what's the schedule? Where is everyone?"

"There was a shipment." Bryce closed his eyes as if to think better by shutting out the sight of Milton's body dripping scarlet drops. "The others are probably testing the bottling equipment." He met Clementine's eyes. "There's a lot of insulation in these walls. If it weren't for the open doors, we wouldn't have heard him, either."

"All right." Clementine stood up and laid a hand on Milton's shoulder. "We're going to get you out."

The softest sound answered her. "No."

"No?" Clementine ducked down and worked to find Milton's eyes. "You've had an accident. We're here to help you."

"I had to reach in," he explained in exhausted wind. "They rolled away before I could…"

Clementine glanced at the cement floor. Several green grapes littered the area. "It's okay. It doesn't matter. We've got to get you out. It's the only way to get you to the hospital."

She thought she saw Milton's hair swing in disagreement. He picked his head up, grunting with the effort, and struggled to hold her gaze. Tears wet his eyes. "End it. Finish my life."

Clementine peddled backwards to her feet. "I can't."

He forced angry air through his throat. "This is more than a broken hand." His breath faltered and ran out.

Clementine splayed a hand on her head. "It's probably cracked ribs. A punctured lung. Broken back. Maybe you'd never walk again, but–"

Milton's head collapsed, banging his chin against the side of the machine. "Can't fix me. No time. No reason to."

"No reason?" Clementine lurched a step towards him. "This is much more than asking me to decide whether to close the factory or not. This isn't choosing between meeting with investors or reading profiles on plants. I've never – purposefully – taken a life."

Blood dribbled from Milton's mouth. He strained his neck to raise his head in jerks and spasms. "You can do anything. Isn't that the point?"

Bryce ran his fingers through his hair, leaving it in disarray. "I wish I'd brought the Webley. I could've done it in one shot."

Clementine shook her head. "You had no way to know." She crouched down by Milton to hear him better. "The machine's broken. How am I supposed to…?"

Milton pushed each word through by itself. His eyelids fluttered. "Not broken. Finger slipped. Please."

Clementine stood up, her arms shaking as she sized up the towering machine.

"What'd he say?" Bryce asked.

"It operates. It just doesn't have a safety measure for when you push the wrong button." She walked around to the other end of the base. She wracked her brain for the few times she had seen the extractors used. The gaping panel exposed the controls. Clementine skipped over the dial that regulated the steam valve and the switch in charge of the glass housing. Her fingertip hovered in front of a button. "This might hurt, Milton." She tapped it, and the motor pried the hefty metal block off his body.

He cried out. Wet blood matted his suit to the misshapen mush of his torso. Clementine and Bryce convulsed, cringing.

Fresh tears sprang into Clementine's eyes, and she wiped them dry. "We've got to move him."

Bryce's eyes widened. "Where?"

"Not far." Clementine could not bring herself to verbalize her plan. "Help me slide him a little."

Clementine sidled around the machine and folded herself onto her haunches beside Milton. Her focus trailed down his limp arms to his bare hands. Swollen joints dotted his bent fingers. She touched his knotted hands and kissed his temple. "It was a pleasure working with you. Thank you for the opportunity."

He took several moments to pick his head up halfway. "An honor, Clementine."

"Let's get you out of this misery." She rose and returned to where Bryce waited for her. "Grab his other foot. We have to be careful he doesn't slip to the floor."

Clementine and Bryce took hold of Milton. Bryce mirrored her every move. They pulled in sure, deliberate motions. Milton's body threaded out through the machine. His grey hair appeared above the machine's base.

"More," Clementine directed.

They tugged on Milton's ankles until his head and shoulders emerged onto the screened platform.

"Stop." Clementine lowered Milton's leg to the floor. In truth, she wanted the word's utterance to finish it all. The impossible situation's cruel conclusion. The stream of bad news unraveling through the last few months. The madness that had plagued most of her life.

The only thing she retained control over was how much Milton suffered before he died. Her chin quivered, but she dredged up more inner fortitude. She reached past Milton's midsection to the control panel. "I'm sorry, Milton."

A raspy response rattled. "Don't be."

Clementine pushed the button and bolted away from the machine. The metal press bore down, meeting the obstacle in its path with a crack that flipped Clementine's stomach. "Milton?"

Silence greeted her. Beyond the room's walls, vibrations from conversations, motors, and movement carried on as if nothing had changed.

Bryce spoke up, his throat dry. "Milton?"

Nothing.

Bryce glanced at her. "Clementine?"

She could hardly breathe or wrap her mind around what they had done. "Yes?"

"Are you okay?" He peeked over his shoulder at Milton and the machine. He cringed. "I wouldn't look if I were you."

"I don't know what I am." Clementine avoided the carnage as she bent over to access the machine's controls.

"What are you doing?" Bryce closed his fingers around her wrist.

"I want to switch the motor off. He deserves a few moments of peace." She glanced up at Bryce, his cheeks white as snowflakes. "You don't think I should?"

"Do what you think is best."

Clementine hesitated and found the main switch. She disengaged the machine, the flat plane of something inside Milton's suit coat brushing against her arm. She unfastened the buttons and retrieved a collection of folded pages from his inner pocket. She stood up and wandered several paces from his body.

Bryce meandered over to her. "What have you got?"

"Letters, I think." The pages were folded into two groupings. Clementine opened the thicker one.

The stationery's design popped at her, white lilies on a green border. The handwriting was the prettiest Clementine had ever seen.

March 1, 1917

Dear Milton,

I believe I've only ever done two brave things in my life. I took the dare that sent me down the street where we met, and I later married you. It's time to do another brave thing and divorce you while I'm still young enough to love and be truly loved by a man who appreciates me.

I think more and more of Philadelphia, where you were the richest of the poor, and I was the poorest of the rich. I had no business being in your neighborhood, but that's why it took a friend's prodding to put me there, isn't it? You stood around bored with a group of friends, but for the moment, I walked alone. I must've presented the part of the perfect, spoiled lady. You broke away from your compatriots and offered to escort me to safer places.

I won't deny you your praises due. You charmed me in your way, fawning over me and playing the good knight to a bold but errant damsel. Your continued pursuits flattered me although my father raged about your lack of money. My mother wept for me. It wasn't your light coin purse that bothered me. Even then, your desires wandered to so many others. When that snooty doctor's son found me captivating, I hated it, but I admit I used it to my advantage. I made sure you knew everything he said to me and the presents he gave me, but I only wanted you. I wanted to marry you, and your jealousy flared up as I hoped it would. You asked, and I said yes.

Now I can't help wondering if you really cherished me or if you only prevented him from having me.

The honeymoon glow faded so quickly. My family's fortune made life easier than you had ever experienced, but I know you resented benefitting from it. You were a hard worker, and you had big aspirations. Philadelphia kept you down – it held us both under. The only jobs you could get were the ones you wanted to break away from. Fixing bicycles. Moving boxes around warehouses. Driving a cart for the laundry service catering to the penny-pinching elite.

Then you heard about the Oklahoma land rush and decided we should move west as well. The City started small, but we helped it grow. It blossomed into the state capital, for goodness' sake. We were proud of it. Staying in the city kept you from being a farmer. But what jobs did you get? I could do nothing as Philadelphia played out all over again. You worked for the meat packing plants and painted trolley cars. We gave up our Philly accents just to fit in.

But you got your big idea, didn't you? The one that trumped all your other ambitions. You built it first-class all the way. You demanded high rates for the workers you supplied to the companies you'd once sweated for, and you paid those workers a premium wage. Men acquired new skills in order to be good enough to be championed by your business! You didn't just improve your reputation, Milton – you made your small fortune in your own way. I was thrilled to see you soar, and I basked in the knowledge our lives would soon be perfect.

But they weren't, were they? Your plots to squash similar businesses interrupted quiet dinners at home. You tolerated zero competition. I considered you a leader, a visionary. Now you warped into a wheeler and dealer, a cut-throat negotiator, and a ruthless money maker. On top of it all, you renounced me, who'd supported you through every decision you made. You swooned over your secretary, even in front of me. She was too young for you, and you knew it. Or you should've known. You liked the illusion of power gained by her attention. You wanted to know that other women besides your wife found you attractive as you greyed and earned lines around your mouth.

You never seemed to care – or notice – you didn't entice her! She needed the job. She wanted to afford a life, not be ogled by her boss!

After years of this, the new century came, and still everything remained the same. I had what I thought was superb inspiration. Let's take a vacation, Milton, to anywhere in the world, just you and me. You put a manager in charge of the business, and we went from dusty, landlocked Oklahoma all those miles to the Venezuelan coast. I was ecstatic. Finally, instead of a surplus of money and no husband to enjoy it with, we'd spend some of the cash to explore the tropics together.

No such luck exists! My exuberance and calm were squelched by your wandering eyes and that fateful evening at the restaurant. It might have been better for me if you met a woman at dinner instead of Clements Fitzgerald! Did you even talk to me for the rest of the night? Except to mention him? He fascinated you with tales of the life you craved – roaming, unattached and uninhibited, through Mexico and Central America. He wasn't forming a business so much as an empire, and your eyes glazed over with wonder. This could be your story, too. Isn't that what you imagined?

You hit it off from word one, and he had room to expand his company into a partnership. You leapt at the chance – did you physically jump from your chair? I can't remember. Suddenly, the trip I envisioned as uniting us ripped us apart. You cast me aside, crushed and forsaken. You kept the manager in charge at home to make money for me as I returned to the City and you deserted me to chase your dreams. Your real aspirations of doing whatever you wanted every single day of your life.

I stuck by you although I didn't see you for months or years at a time. I supported you through your fragile state after your infatuation led to that young woman's murder in Brazil. You were so distraught, I hoped it would dissuade you from your wanton ways, but I was foolish. Even when you visited me between continents and enterprises, we could scarcely leave the house without you surveying the landscape. Did you fancy yourself a lion or a tiger in search of radiant prey?

The only time you changed was the end of that last trip home. You sulked, but you showed me more interest than you had in a decade. You commissioned that grand portrait of me and had me send it to you once you settled in Delhi. Call me naïve, but I swore your affections were genuine. Perhaps I'm wrong, and it was only your jealousy over Clements hiring that young man to help out. I believed there was still a fraction of hope for us. Isn't that sad?

Because I'm fifty-nine and you remain on the opposite side of the globe, this letter has grown into everything I've never been able to say to you in person. I want this divorce to separate me from your lies and grant my freedom. Both of ours, actually. I understand what a blow Clements' death is to you, and I'm truly sorry he's left you behind. But you've stranded me for fifteen years, and I can't wait any longer for you. I've given you four decades – isn't that enough?

I'm prepared to fight if you won't grant it freely. I've secured an aggressive lawyer, and I plan to leave with everything I believe you owe me.

I hope this news makes you happy.

Your wife, quite sincerely,

Lydia

Clementine realized she had been holding her breath and drew a long inhale.

Bryce took the pages. His voice came out hushed. "Clements mentioned Brazil to me. I assumed Milton committed the murder. This must be what Milton read the night I spied on him at his house."

"But why did it make him so upset?" Clementine unfolded the single page remaining in her hand.

March 22, 1917

My lovely Lydia,

Please, don't do this! I love you more than I ever have. I must've transformed from a man you adored into a monster overnight. I'm coming home to you – really – at the outset of next year.

It's insane to ask you to believe this and give me one more chance when your patient mind is clearly made up.

I wanted to leave the company when Clements died. I stayed because of the money I was promised. It will make life in the City lavish for us! It's all arranged for me to fly home. The project will be completed. If it's not, I'm abandoning the team and joining you anyway. I only kept it a secret from you as a surprise. I didn't realize you had grown so lonesome and angry with me.

I don't even know how to word this. I don't know how to ask you – beg you! – to wait another nine months on top of forty years, but I must. I need you, and I ache for you. I'll apologize in front of the entire City on bended knee if that's what you want. Don't make me come home to an empty house or no home at all. I can build businesses, but that's all. I'm no good without you. Please, be there for me when I come back.

Lydia, I love

Chapter Thirty-Six

A shaky breath whistled through Clementine's throat. She released her fingers, and the letter fluttered to the floor. Her whole body spasmed, and she wobbled on her feet. A damp heat rolled across her skin. "He wanted to leave."

Bryce tossed the sheaf of Lydia's pages on the floor and grabbed hold of Clementine's arms. "Don't think about it. You'll faint."

"I kept him here. Twice." She stared without seeing. "I ruined his marriage. I destroyed his life. I killed him."

"He asked you to."

"He would've been in Oklahoma City if it wasn't for me." Clementine's knees collapsed from under her.

Bryce kept her from crashing to the floor. He struggled with her weight and eased her down to sitting. He settled on the cement with her. "You don't know that. He might've died going home or something. You're not responsible for the man's mortality."

Clementine brushed a hand across her cheek. "I should be crying."

"You're freaked out. I'm sure tears will come later."

Her shoulders slumped. "I killed my father and Milton." Hysteria tinged her dry laughter. "Two men are dead because of me and my mission to save Nikya."

"They were accidents." Bryce scooted close to her and braced her collar bone against his.

"There's a slim chance we'll even be able to do it."

"It's not small. We have the best materials in India." Bryce tried for humor, wiping a clammy palm against his pant leg. "I hear the woman running the show is an expert."

Clementine pulled back from him, a grim grin parting her lips. "You don't have to be brave. I know you don't want to be here any more than I do. Milton's dead, and we have tons of new problems. I have a lot of blood on my conscience."

Bryce took her face in his hands. "Clements was an accident. You weren't even in the room when the machine crushed Milton."

"I saw his hands. He was hiding arthritis from us, probably for a long time." The irony twisted in her chest. "He was trying to avoid being seen as old while working on a product called the Fountain of Youth." A tear rolled out of the corner of Clementine's eye.

Bryce wiped it away and kissed her cheek.

"I gave up so much to be here, Bryce. I left Nikya and my friends. I lost Da, and Milton sacrificed himself. Lydia will never be the same. There's a world of difference between choosing divorce and grieving as a widow."

Bryce rubbed her arm.

Clementine grabbed hold of him. "What if someone finds out I was visiting Da when he died? They could imprison me for two deaths. They point at each other."

Bryce shook his head, steeling his jaw. "We blame Milton's arthritis. We switch the extractor on before anyone comes in. It'll look like he squished his back, tried to save himself, and the machine killed him. We'll pretend we found him like this. Okay?"

Clementine gasped in agreement from her constricted chest. Her floating head reattached itself, albeit loosely.

Bryce hugged Clementine. "I'll have Mr. Mustafa tell the crew to go home. We can pay them for the full day if you want. We'll send for the police and an ambulance. They'll handle it from there."

He kept his voice quiet but serious in her ear. "Because of your letters to Clements' lawyer and banker, we're the only ones who know Clements is dead and his estate should pay out to the company. You can keep the money, the house, even the autocarriage without trouble."

Clementine inhaled a ratty breath. Did this truth comfort her? Her locked muscles gave only the tiniest release.

"No matter what Milton's will says, you were his partner. You're in charge. You can do whatever you like. No more consulting. No more games."

Clementine played with the extra fabric of Bryce's suit jacket sleeve. "You'll be here with me, won't you?"

"Always. As long as you want me." Bryce traced a gentle fingertip under Clementine's eye before the next wet bead could fall.

Welling tears warped her vision. "I miss Nikya so much. It hurts to think of her so far away. Another nine months, like Milton said."

"We'll bring her here. We'll send for her."

Clementine lifted her hand in a useless gesture. "Put a sick woman on a boat? Expose her to the Indian heat that lasts most of the year?"

"We'll splurge for an airship. She could be here in days." Bryce tucked a wayward lock of Clementine's hair behind her ear.

Relief soothed Clementine even as she clung white-knuckled to pessimistic logic. "The train rides would be tough on her."

"We could pay for a nurse or some of your friends to accompany her." Bryce forced a smile. "We can reverse time, but we can't install extra fans to keep your mother cool?"

Clementine caught easier breaths and blinked away droplets of gratitude. "She could stay in the extra bedroom."

"Exactly. We won't have to budget for Milton's salary anymore, so we can hire more workers to speed up production. We'll save your mother. I know it."

Hope ballooned to a place where Clementine believed it, too. She admired Bryce with all the love she had come to accept in herself for him. "Mr. Bryce Bloom, would you be my new co-owner of Fitzgerald and Longshaw? We'd have to draw up the papers."

Bryce's jaw dropped. "I don't have half Milton's knowledge or experience."

Clementine tutted. "Don't you know by now how to make a good case for yourself and win an argument?"

He kissed her. "I'd be honored."

"We might have to change the name, though."

Doors opened and closed, echoing in the hallway.

Clementine and Bryce stood up. He went to the extractor while Clementine avoided looking at Milton's trapped body. With the flick of a switch, the motor chugged to life.

Bryce squeezed Clementine's hand. "It'll be all right." He stooped to pick up the fallen letters. He tucked them into a pocket inside his suit jacket. "I'll take care of everything."

Shoes squeaked, drawing closer to the doorway.

"Not everything." Clementine's mind whirred toward fresh, exciting possibilities amidst the torment and guilt threatening to drag her down. "I have some ideas, too."

Chapter Thirty-Seven

Clementine used the door's gleaming metal knocker. She folded her hands in front of her, but she did not wait long. The door parted, revealing a short, clean-shaven young man in white.

She greeted him with a broad smile. "I'm Clementine Fitzgerald. I have an appointment with Mr. Dodd."

The servant bowed, and she passed by him into the foyer. Murmurs bubbled from other rooms, Daisy's feminine undertones mixing with energetic younger chatter. The servant secured the door and led Clementine on bare feet into the living room. They accessed the passageway beyond it, and the servant motioned her into the study.

In the nearest desk chair, Lowell swiveled to greet her.

She grinned. "What a pleasant surprise. You're already waiting for me."

Lowell mirrored her enthusiasm. "How could I pass up the opportunity to chat with you in the middle of my morning?"

The servant closed the door, and Clementine walked over to the chair across from Lowell.

She settled in, focusing on him instead of the knickknacks decorating the room. "How's construction this week?"

"Flawless except for those arguing architects." Lowell knotted his hands together on the desk. One eyebrow ticked. "I'm quite curious to learn why you've arranged this talk."

He held up his index finger. "Would you like some tea?" He rose from his chair.

"No, thank you."

Lowell adjusted the fit of his suit coat and returned to his seat. "It's just as well. Since Sandeep left our services, we've had trouble finding someone to integrate into our staff."

Clementine's mouth twitched, and she fought it.

Lowell gestured to her. "So, what's this all about?"

Clementine folded her hands in her lap. "I'm not sure if you know. Mr. Longshaw suffered a fatal accident one week ago."

Lowell sighed with a deep nod of his head. "I heard. I'm sorry. He was a great man. I didn't think it warranted you meeting with me. Unless you've made other changes you think I should know about."

"I've acquired a new business partner, but our goal for the Fountain of Youth remains the same." Clementine shook her head. "This isn't about the serum, Mr. Dodd. It's about you."

"Me?" His head jerked in surprise. He huffed a breath of amusement or confusion.

"You hate India."

"Preposterous." Lowell leaned back in his chair. "I love it. Two of my children were born here. Why would I choose to live in a land I detest? Whatever gave you that idea?"

"You did. You show no respect for this country or its people as they actually exist. What you see is something to be conquered. Resources to be moved about as you wish. You love India as something to play with and experiment on."

"I thought you'd be on my side."

Clementine raised her eyebrows. "Because you assume all my ancestors had pale skin?"

Lowell averted his attention.

Clementine waited until he met her eyes again to continue. "You wrongfully guessed I had no earthly idea what it was like to suffer at invaders' hands. That I had no compassion for others who find themselves in the same boat and don't know how to get out of it."

One side of her lips curved up. "They're figuring it out, aren't they? They want freedom the same way my country won its independence from yours."

Lowell bunched his eyes up. "Don't make this personal."

"It's personal for every citizen giving up the normal life they could lead to join the cause for liberty and human rights. For every person who needs a job and ends up working for disrespectful people like you."

Lowell tossed a hand up. "I wondered what Sandeep would do after he left this job. You took him from me, naturally."

"I offered him a better rate and showed him more understanding in ten minutes than you had in years." Clementine opened her handbag and withdrew a white envelope. "It was an easy decision Sandeep made on his own. But we can tell the story your way. I stole Sandeep, and my foreman trained him in our facilities. But I won't take your money." Clementine slid the envelope across the desk.

Lowell picked it up and peeked inside. "A check?"

"For your full investment in the Fountain of Youth."

Lowell cast the envelope down on the desk. "You'll fold in months. You'll lose everything."

"Without your money? I doubt it. You see, you're not the only person in the world – or the city, for that matter – who can invest in our company. Mr. Longshaw's will devoted a generous portion of his assets to us. The rest goes, deservingly, to his widow. I also made friends with a certain family during my time in Delhi. A friend is someone you care about and aid in times of need–"

Lowell grunted. "I know what a friend is."

"I'm sorry. I assumed you didn't. They're quite affluent, and they eagerly invested an additional sum in our efforts. Your contribution was well placed but is no longer needed. Or wanted."

"Do you think you've won something, Miss Fitzgerald?"

Clementine's haughty humor dissolved from her mood. "That's the problem, isn't it? People like you see everything as a war, a competition, a race. You want to separate the victors from the losers like a child sorting out a marble collection. You're playing a game, and the rest of us are simply trying to live."

She stood up and gathered her handbag. "Do you know what today is?"

He gave a slow, sarcastic blink.

"It's the twelve-week anniversary of our only other meeting. I sat here, and I held my tongue while you cut down your household staff. Even your family. I was timid. Scared.

Overwhelmed. Here I stand, leading my father's company, refunding your money, and speaking my mind."

"I wish you hadn't."

"Of course you do. Then you wouldn't have to admit you've done something wrong." She took in Lowell's immaculate, tidy desk and the put-out purse of his lips. "If we're keeping score, I think I won."

Clementine walked to the door and let herself out. She followed the hallway to the living room and reached the foyer. The young servant hurried towards her from the kitchen. She opened the front door herself.

She did not know what languages he understood, but she said, "If you ever get tired of working for the Dodds, stop by Fitzgerald and Longshaw. We'll take care of you."

She stepped out into the warm, late-morning sun. Mr. Mustafa stood outside the autocarriage in the driveway, one hand wrapped around his other wrist. He loosened his stance as she approached him.

He opened the front passenger door. "Did they treat you with respect?"

"About as much as I was due, considering the lashing I dealt the master of the house." Clementine climbed up into the seat.

Mr. Mustafa shut the door and jogged around to the wheel. He settled his pince-nez glasses into place and directed the vehicle toward the street. "I wish I could've heard it."

Clementine gazed out the window at the passing trees and houses, each placed with care and well maintained. "There was so much I didn't say."

"What did you leave out?"

"I'm grateful for your friendship. I'm glad I got to know Miss Datta, even though it brought her disapproving fiancé into our building. The Varmas have touched me deeply. Everyone at the factory. Our investors have humbled me with their acceptance of me and their belief in the Fountain of Youth."

Mr. Mustafa's voice smoothed with the hint of a smile. "A healthier, happier world is a better world. How could we not believe in it?"

Chapter Thirty-Eight

Clementine and Bryce stood in the study, collecting the disheveled array of papers from the desktop.

"Anything addressed to my father after his death has to go." Clementine sorted out her father's postcards, slipping them into a drawer to keep them safe.

Bryce held up the pages signed by Lyman Morris and Royson Callaghan. "Like these?"

"Especially those."

He scattered them into the waste basket at their feet. "What about letters that just sound suspicious?" Bryce tapped the neat handwriting of Betty Crawford's instructions.

Clementine squinted at it. "It could mean anything, but we'd better be careful. I'll mail it home and store it there."

Bryce added it to the growing pile on a shelf beside the desk. "What about your well wishes? The Lloyds, the Johnsons, Mr. Alred?"

Clementine answered softly. "I'll keep them here."

Bryce designated the letters in his hand to the bookshelf beneath the other pile. He perked up with a wry grin. "I see how it is. I signed the papers to become your partner in the company. But I'm more your assistant now, shuffling paperwork, than I was before. Except…"

Clementine frowned. The few weeks she had treated Bryce as a stranger and a workhorse weighed on her chest. "I had to. I was so guilty over my father. I didn't know what would happen to me if anyone found out I contributed to his death. I couldn't risk Nikya's life by being removed from the project. It'd kill her if I was imprisoned in India and she didn't know when she'd see me again."

Bryce kissed her cheek. "Her airship flies out Monday."

"Three days sounds like forever. She still has to cross the ocean and ride the train from Bombay."

"Then she'll be here. The spare room's all set. She can stay with you as long as you're in Delhi and travel back to the States with you. You never have to be apart again."

Clementine threw her arms around Bryce, clutching him close. "It's been a long four months without her. I'm glad I've had you to lean on."

He pressed his palms against her back. "We're all rooting for you. You don't have to feel alone anymore."

She pulled back and smiled at him. "You root the loudest."

"And the longest." Bryce stole another kiss from her. "Is that everything for the basket?"

"I think so."

They had stripped the desk's sloppy collection away to its surface. Numerous pages and Blickensderfer fax receipts rested in the bottom of the waste basket. Bryce hefted it off the floor, and Clementine led him out of the room. They streamed out the servant's door into the courtyard.

Bryce positioned the metal can on the paving stones and pulled a brass lighter from his pocket. Clementine folded her arms, the sun setting far away on the other side of the house. Bryce fluffed some of the larger papers up near the top of the pile. He set fire to the upper corner and stepped back.

He sidled around the flames to stand closer to Clementine. "Here it goes. The last evidence you were ever in India before the end of December." He tucked the lighter into his pocket.

"I can't say I'll miss those papers."

"No?" Bryce lifted his eyebrows and extended an arm around her shoulders. "You pulled one over on two of the best professionals in Oklahoma City. Clements' banker and lawyer were no fools."

Clementine shifted her shoulders, enjoying the tether of Bryce's arm. "I guess I knew Da well after all. Maybe he should've sent them postcards for so many years."

Bryce gave a short chuckle. "I know you're still not comfortable using his name."

Clementine traced the flames' movements in the trash can, leaping up for air and sinking again to devour the pages below.

"It seems like it's in memoriam now. I'm not sure it's appropriate. Fitzgerald isn't my given name, and with Nikya coming, I don't want to offend her by continuing to use it."

Bryce kicked the can's base, stirring up a shower of sparks and soot. "I know what you mean. Whatever you decide to do, we can always rename the company. New management, fresh beginning. We haven't had new labels printed up for the Fountain of Youth yet. We can be Heidel and Bloom if you want."

A bright smile painted itself on Clementine's lips. "I'd like that."

"Maybe, in a couple of years..." Bryce peered down into the can's embers. "It'll be Bloom and Bloom." He cleared his throat, sneaking a glance at her.

Clementine blushed and rubbed the back of her neck. "We really can do this, can't we? Develop what we set out to? If we do it right and work hard enough."

Bryce regained his full height at her side. "All the machinery works. The workmen are fully trained, and we're on schedule."

Clementine's twinkling eyes danced over the sparse leaves and tree branches around the courtyard. "We can do way more than I ever intended. We can save Nikya, maybe thousands more. We can give people their lives back, and in the process, we'll prove women can accomplish bigger things than getting married. We're showing the British that Indians and their compatriots are more than burdens and servants."

She faced Bryce. "I want the Fountain of Youth to succeed so much." She set her hands on his chest. "This time I'll have you and Nikya by my side."

"Is it better than going it alone?"

Clementine nodded, focusing on the positives. "She has no idea how far I'm going to give her some of what she's lost."

"Rather than tell her, you can show her. Very soon. There are worse places in the world to bring her."

Clementine ringed her arms around Bryce's neck. "Let's rename the company. I can sign the paperwork with my real name, and everything will be out in the open that can be."

Bryce rested his hands in the shallow curves of her waist. "You deserve every success you get."

Clementine leapt up on her tiptoes, embracing Bryce and laying her chin on his shoulder. From his arms looping around her, Clementine watched the fire blacken the white pages and the inside of the metal can. The flames petered out to a red-orange glow highlighting the edges of burnt scraps in the chamber's bottom. Smoke twirled up in ribbons as the embers dimmed to carbon. Clementine closed her eyes and hummed a sigh of relief.

She might never agree the cost of her father's and Milton's lives were worth the company's achievements. They could never reassure her they accepted their sacrifices or congratulate her.

Clementine would always miss her father and wonder if they could have reached an understanding. But her mother would be here, and Bryce, and all the wonderful friends whose help she needed and could never repay.

She had lived through many dark days, but for now, they hovered behind her. She opened her eyes to the tan threads of Bryce's jacket, her arms encircling his neck, the dwindling daylight, and the courtyard around them.

On her first day working at the factory, Mr. Mustafa had wished her peace. It had taken three months of dedicated, heartbreaking work, but she had finally earned that calm.

About the Author

Cassandra Leuthold's hilarious fantasy adventure, *The Corundum Conundrum*, won recognition as a New Apple Book Awards official selection. Writing hooked her at age seven, and she never really stopped.

She loves playing with ideas most people think of as opposites: the magical and the everyday, the modern and the vintage, the darkest nights and brightest lights. Even while delving into fictional worlds, she remains a tea aficionado, DIY crafter, and unapologetic music junkie.

Cassandra stretches out in front of the TV with her writer husband and their cats. She wields a Bachelor's in Liberal Studies and a Master's in English.

Find freebies and more book fun at her website, cassandraleuthold.com.

www.ingramcontent.com/pod-product-compliance
Lightning Source LLC
Chambersburg PA
CBHW030638260626
47157CB00007B/2386